PRAISE FOR
MARYA
A Life

"Evocative . . . rich . . . fierce imagination."
—*Boston Globe*

"Oates is superb, convincing . . . a novelist of the first rank."
—*Newsday*

"Compelling . . . Oates's seductively intelligent prose
kept me turning the pages."
—*Glamour*

"Oates's most personal statement . . . her most compelling
heroine . . . her most intensely moving novel."
—*Ms.*

"A major work by an important writer."
—*Library Journal*

Joyce Carol Oates is the author of numerous novels—including
most recently *My Heart Laid Bare*, *Man Crazy*, *We Were the
Mulvaneys*, and *What I Lived For* (all available in Plume editions), a
finalist for the 1995 PEN/Faulkner Award and a Pulitzer Prize—
and collections of short stories, poetry, and plays. The recipient of
the 1996 PEN/Malamud Award for Achievement in the Short
Story, she is the Roger S. Berlind Distinguished Professor of
Humanities at Princeton University.

Joyce Carol Oates

MARYA
A Life

A WILLIAM ABRAHAMS BOOK

PLUME

PLUME
Published by the Penguin Group
Penguin Putnam Inc., 375 Hudson Street, New York, New York 10014, U.S.A.
Penguin Books Ltd, 27 Wrights Lane, London W8 5TZ, England
Penguin Books Australia Ltd, Ringwood, Victoria, Australia
Penguin Books Canada Ltd, 10 Alcorn Avenue, Toronto, Ontario, Canada M4V 3B2
Penguin Books (N.Z.) Ltd, 182–190 Wairau Road, Auckland 10, New Zealand

Penguin Books Ltd, Registered Offices: Harmondsworth, Middlesex, England

Published by Plume, an imprint of Dutton NAL, a member of Penguin Putnam Inc.
Previously published in a Dutton edition.

First Plume Printing, November, 1998
10 9 8 7 6 5 4 3 2 1

Portions of this book, in earlier versions, have appeared in the following magazines:
*Antaeus, California Quarterly, New England Review, New Letters, Northwest Review,
Mademoiselle, Shenandoah, Southern Review, TriQuarterly,* and *Western Humanities Review.*

 REGISTERED TRADEMARK—MARCA REGISTRADA

The Library of Congress has catalogued the Dutton edition as follows:

Oates, Joyce Carol.
Marya: a life.
"A William Abrahams book."
I. Title.
PS3565.A8M38   1986   813'.54   85–16283
ISBN 0-525-24374-7 (hc.)
ISBN 0-452-28020-6 (pbk.)

Original hardcover design by Earl Tidwell
Printed in the United States of America

PUBLISHER'S NOTE

This is a work of fiction. Names, characters, places, and incidents either are the products
of the author's imagination or are used fictitiously, and any resemblance to actual
persons, living or dead, events, or locales is entirely coincidental.

FOR LEIGH AND HENRY BIENEN

My first act of freedom will be to believe in freedom.
—WILLIAM JAMES

I

It was a night of patchy dreams, strangers' voices, rain hammering on the tarpaper roof close overhead. Before Marya was awake she could see through her trembling eyelids her mother's swaying figure in the doorway; she could hear a hoarse level murmuring—not words, not recognizable words, only sounds. Her mother's angry breath catching in her throat. Half sobbing. Coughing. Earlier, through much of the long night, Marya had been hearing voices and footsteps outside the house, the noise of car motors, car doors slamming shut, the churning of tires in gravel. She waited for her father's raised voice—he often shouted if somebody was backing out of their driveway crooked, headed for the deep ditch by the road—but she hadn't heard him. She had heard her mother instead.

Several times during the past summer Marya had wakened frightened from sleep—there were often men in the house, her father's friends, co-workers, union organizers— and she'd run out of the house to hide in the cab of a derelict pickup truck in the field next door. She was safe there in the truck: she could sleep on the seat until morning, nobody would know she was gone. Once, when she'd been particularly frightened at the loud drunken talk and laughter, she had taken her brother Davy with her—but he cried too much, he wet his pajamas like a baby, she hated him sucking his thumb the way he did and nudging his head up against her. She wasn't sure if she cared what happened to him: him or the new baby either.

"You! You and you and *you*! I don't give a shit about you, I wish you were all dead," Marya's mother once screamed at them, but right away afterward she said she was sorry. She hugged them, kissed them all over like crazy; "You know I didn't mean it," she said, and Marya believed her.

Once when Marya slept out in the truck her father had found her. It was freezing cold: her teeth chattered and her fingers and toes were turning blue. Her father hadn't been angry, in fact he had laughed, poking his head and shoulders through the rust-rimmed window of the truck to peer at her upside down. "Hey, what's this? What the hell kind of hiding place is this?" Marya was his favorite, he liked to run his fingers through her curly hair, playing a little rough, teasing: but he never meant to make her cry when he was teasing. Another time, though, Marya's mother was the one to find her in the truck and she hadn't thought it was funny at all. It was a new trick of Marya's. Something Marya did to spite her, to shame her. Another thing that required punishment—a succession of hard quick slaps, a blow to the buttocks with her fist. "We're not animals," Marya's mother said, her face flushed dark with blood, "we don't sleep out in the fields like animals!"

In Shaheen Falls they stared, they talked, and Marya's mother knew though she couldn't always hear. Such people, they said, hill people, whispering, staring. Marya was lost in Woolworth's, separated from her mother and Davy, so she ran up and down the aisles, wild, panting, half sobbing, bumping into people, pushing her way through a knot of women shoppers, using her fists, even butting with her head. "Isn't she a little savage," someone said in disgust, "just *look* at her, those *eyes. . . .*"

Marya clapped her hands over her eyes and disappeared: she couldn't see anybody then and they couldn't see her. She just disappeared—the way dreams do when a light is switched on.

"Wake up," Marya's mother was saying.

"Wake up," she said, her voice rising impatiently, "we're going out."

Marya heard the rain still hammering on the roof, dripping from the eaves. At the corner of the house the rain barrel would be overflowing. The smells were of tarpaper, asbestos siding, kerosene, rain-rotted wood. . . .

Marya was watching her father back out of the driveway, one arm on the back of the seat, the other snaked around the steering wheel. He gunned the motor so hard that the Chevy's chassis rocked and the rear bumper struck the gravel. She and Davy were playing in the rain, trying to jump over the longest puddle without getting their feet wet; but they were already wet. When the mud dried on Marya's legs she picked it off like scabs, which was maybe why her mother was so angry. "Stop touching yourself, stop picking at yourself, you kids are driving me crazy—"

Marya's mother was hunched over the bed, shaking her by the shoulders. The overhead light that Marya hated had been switched on, a single naked bulb that made her eyes ache.

"Marya, God damn it," her mother said, panting, "get up, I know you been awake all along and I know you been listening, get up and get Davy dressed."

Marya's mother was wearing the black cotton slacks that were too tight at the waist, and one of Marya's father's flannel shirts, only half buttoned. Marya could see her heavy breasts swinging loose inside the shirt. Her hair was matted and wild, her eyes looked wild too, you could see that most of her lipstick had been worn off, or caked in queer little cracks on her lower lip.

Davy was already awake, whimpering, frightened. When Marya tried to haul him out of bed he kicked at her: so she pummeled him and said, "God damn it, don't you try none of those tricks on *me.*" Her mother had already gone back into the kitchen.

Davy was three years old, small for his age, always whining, crying, wiping his nose on his sleeve. When he groped at Marya, blinking like a kitten only a few days old, saying, "Mamma, Mamma," she slapped his hands away. "Damn baby," Marya whispered, "you hadn't better of wet the bed."

"Where are we going?" Marya asked, trying not to cry. The kitchen smelled of kerosene, wood smoke, spilled scorched food from the night before. "Are we going to town?"

"Never mind," her mother said. She wasn't looking at Marya: she was stooped over the baby in his high chair, spooning cold baby food into his mouth.

"Where's Daddy?" Marya asked. She knew the driveway was empty but she looked out the window anyway. "Where's the car?"

"Make sure Davy eats something," her mother said. Her voice was low, flat, quick. It was a voice Marya hadn't heard very often. "And don't you spit that stuff out when I'm not looking—that's all the breakfast you're going to get."

Marya was supposed to be feeding Davy while her mother fed the baby in his wobbly high chair. But it was too early to eat. The clock on the windowsill had stopped at three twenty-five. The sun wasn't up, the rain still pounded hard on the roof and against the windows, Marya could hear a drip, a rapid dripping, in one of the corners; her eyelids closed and when she opened them she became confused and couldn't think what to do. The yellow plastic cereal bowls, the spoons, the box of Wheat Chex with the monkey on the side, the milk she'd brought from the refrigerator that had gone slightly sour. . . . Davy gagged, or pretended to; and Marya didn't want any cereal herself, her stomach was too excited. . . .

Marya's mother must have scrubbed her face hard with

a washrag, her skin shone like dull metal; like the spoons. Her eyes were threaded with blood and moved about the kitchen without coming to rest on anything, like fish darting.

"Is Daddy in town?" Marya asked. Her voice always came out louder than she meant. She was afraid her mother would suddenly turn to her and see something she was doing wrong, but at the same time she wanted her mother to look: she hated it when adults didn't take notice of her: when they looked right through her.

But her mother was wiping the baby's messy face with a paper napkin and didn't seem to hear.

Marya didn't think she was in any danger of falling asleep at the table if she was aware of herself sitting there, the bowl of cereal in front of her. But people were talking nearby—people she didn't know. In another room. Inside the rain. Men's voices, a woman's raised voice, the slamming of car doors, car motors running.

She woke and her heart fluttered because her mother hadn't seen her: because now there was a stink in the kitchen and her mother had to change the baby's diaper.

There was sugar on Davy's cereal but he wanted more, so Marya let him have more, then she poked her finger in the sugar bowl herself and sucked it. She had on two sweaters but she couldn't stop shivering. It was too early, it was still night, where was her father, why wasn't the car in the driveway if they were going out . . . ? They would have to get a ride with old Kurelik, or maybe his son. Marya's father got very angry when her mother asked the Kureliks for a ride, or if she could use their telephone. . . . "I don't want anybody knowing my business," Marya's father said, and Marya's mother said, fast and mocking, "Nobody gives a damn about knowing your business, don't flatter yourself."

But it wasn't true. Even Marya knew that people talked.

"Don't you start crying," Marya's mother warned her. "Once you get started you won't be able to stop."

She wasn't drunk because she didn't smell of drinking but

she swayed and lurched on her feet, and when she zipped up her jacket a strand of hair caught in the zipper and she didn't notice—just left the zipper partway up. When she lifted the baby she grunted and staggered backward, as if his weight surprised her, and Marya thought, She's going to drop him and I will be blamed.

They left the house without locking anything up and hiked over to the Kureliks' farm through the rain, Marya and Davy running ahead, pushing at each other, squealing, as if nothing were wrong. Even out here the air seemed to smell of kerosene and rotting tarpaper. The sky was lightening minute by minute from all sides, a cold glowering look to it, not exactly morning. Marya couldn't remember what time it was. She splashed through a mud puddle, flailing her arms: but she was thinking of the secret tunnel she sometimes made in her bed, in the bedclothes, burrowing down to the foot of the bed like a mole and lying there without moving. She could hide there forever, she thought, not even breathing.

They followed the old sawmill lane, which was partly grown over with scrub willow and cottonwood. The roof of the mill had nearly rotted through, there were open spaces in the shingles, and patches of green moss: bright green patches that leaped at the eye. Marya thought it was funny that trees —small trees, baby willows a few feet high—had begun to grow in the drainpipes. How tall could they get, she wondered, before their weight broke everything down? Then the building would collapse.

Marya's father had worked in the mill until the mill shut down, and then he started work with the Shaheen Mining Company until there was trouble *there*—but Marya didn't know what kind of trouble except he was "dropped from the payroll," that was how he phrased it, but he was expecting to go back, he was waiting to go back any day. Marya didn't even know where the Shaheen mine was except somewhere in the foothills north of where they lived, six or seven miles away.

Marya's father told them not to play around the sawmill because it could fall in at any time and kill them. And not to run barefoot in the grass because of nails—there were rusty nails and spikes dumped everywhere, and pieces of broken glass. His youngest brother had died of blood poisoning, he said, from a rusty nail that went halfway through his foot when he was nine years old; he didn't want his kids ending up like that. Marya pretended to listen because her father would have been angry if she hadn't, but really she was thinking her own thoughts: she wasn't going to die of anything so silly.

(Then it happened, not long afterward, Marya, running around barefoot in the weedy grass behind their house, stepped down hard on something sharp and cut her foot; but she hadn't told anybody about it. And though her foot bled for five or ten minutes, and throbbed with pain, she didn't cry —just sat hunched in the drainage ditch, where no one could find her, waiting for the bleeding to stop.)

Marya's mother, carrying the baby on her hip, managed to catch up with Marya and give her a cuff, a light blow on the shoulder. "Come on," she said, "get going, the two of you— I don't have any time for smart-assing around." So Marya and Davy followed along behind her, where the path was wide enough for only one person, a fisherman's path along the creek. Marya's head felt strange, her eyes too—she kept blinking to get her vision clear. Her throat tightened up—the muscles of her face tightened too—as if she were about to cry: but there was no reason for crying.

"Once you get started," Marya's mother always said, "you can't stop. So you kids don't start—hear me?"

Sometimes, when Marya's father was away for a few days, her mother would lie in bed all morning, even into the afternoon, not bothering to dress. Maybe she'd have Marya bring her a sweater. She wasn't drunk, she said—just didn't feel like getting up—she had a touch of the flu, maybe—her head ached like hell—she had to take medicine straight out of the bottle —had to get back her strength. If the baby cried and cried it was up to Marya to take care of him, she just wasn't strong enough to climb out of bed. "Get out of here and let me alone," she told Marya and Davy, and they obeyed.

Other times, sprawled lazy and smiling in the bedclothes, propped up on pillows twisted any which way, she wanted Marya to nap with her, just the two of them; she hugged Marya close and held her tight as if she thought someone might snatch her away; her breath was hot and smelly in Marya's ear—"*You* know what's going on, you're just the same as me, you and me, we know it ahead of time, don't we?" Marya had to hold herself very still or her mother would get angry, and hug her harder, or push her away with a slap. "Don't you love me? Why don't you love me?" her mother would ask, staring her direct in the eye, shaking her. "You *do* love me—you're just the same as me—*I* know you!"

Marya was embarrassed that her mother refused to come inside the Kureliks' house when Mrs. Kurelik invited her. Wouldn't they like to dry off a little, wouldn't they like to get warm? Mrs. Kurelik asked nervously, staring all the while at Marya's mother, who never seemed to exactly hear what was being said and wouldn't look her in the face—just stood at the edge of the veranda with her shoulders hunched in the soiled wool jacket, the baby sleeping and twitching in the crook of her arm, her gaze sullen and hooded, looking over toward one of the barns where Mrs. Kurelik's son was loading up. Mrs. Kurelik was saying that she'd made sweet rolls the day before, maybe the children would like some, but Marya's mother didn't reply and Marya and Davy knew better than to answer on their own. Away from home, when people talked to Marya's mother or asked her questions, she never replied right away, always a minute or two later, when you thought she wasn't going to reply at all.

Suddenly she said in a flat hard angry voice, "They already had their breakfast. They do their eating at home."

Marya remembered, a long time ago, her and her mother walking along the road toward town. There'd been a quarrel at home and Marya's mother dragged her out, she hadn't brought Davy, the baby wasn't born yet, just the two of them, Marya and her mother, walking toward town. Marya's mother was saying things but not for Marya to hear. She had broken a willow branch off a tree and was slashing at weeds alongside the road, at the Queen Anne's lace in particular because it was growing all over and it had a tiny black dot at the center, she told Marya never to look because it was nasty, the tiny black dot at the center, you'd think it was an insect or something, a surprise, not a nice surprise—this pretty flower that looks all white but has a tiny black thing in it, hidden unless you got close. She told Marya not to look but of course Marya did, when her mother wasn't around.

They'd been walking perhaps half an hour when a car braked to a stop, raising dust. A man asked out the window would they like a ride, were they going to town?—a man Marya hadn't ever seen before, not one of her father's friends who came by the house. But Marya's mother kept on walking as if she didn't hear, as if she hadn't noticed the car. She was still switching the willow branch about; her long black hair was all windblown and snarled down her back. Marya wouldn't look at the man but she knew he was staring at them both.

"I asked you, you two want a ride?—you going to town?"

Marya's mother ignored him and kept walking, and he drove on alongside them for a while, watching out the window, saying things Marya knew she wasn't supposed to hear, saying them over and over again in a mocking, low voice, certain words, certain combinations of words, Marya knew she wasn't supposed to hear but sometimes repeated to herself when no one was around. Only when he asked Marya's mother if she had Indian blood, was she part Mohawk maybe, did she turn to him and say, "I'm Joe Knauer's wife and he'll kill you, he lays hands on you, you bastard fucker, you better get out of here."

The drive to Shaheen Falls took about twenty minutes; once they turned off the highway Jerry Kurelik drove fifty, fifty-five, sixty miles an hour, as fast as his father's old truck could go.

In the rear the tall milk cans rattled and vibrated against one another, a noise that lulled Marya into sleep, then startled her awake again. It was confusing—the raw glaring sky, all massive clouds that looked like outcroppings of rock, had something to do with the fragment of a dream, or with the sore insides of her eyelids: but when she blinked hard and stared, it drew away again and was nothing that could touch her.

Even in the cab of the truck, where they were jammed together—the baby on Marya's lap, Davy on her mother's, Kurelik big and fleshy behind the wheel—Marya could see her breath steam. She hated the smells: exhaust and gasoline and Kurelik's manure-splattered overalls and the sweetish mixture of milk and urine that shook loose from the baby's blanket; and the strong rank smell of Marya's mother's hair, which hadn't been washed for a while. Marya told herself she wouldn't have to breathe until it was safe, but she always gave in and sucked at the air like a fish.

The rain lightened. Kurelik turned on the windshield wipers, then turned them off again, then turned them on again, until the windshield was smeared and Marya hated to look through it. There were parts of insects mashed against the glass; near-invisible rainbows shone from all sides. For a while, headed down the curving Yew Road, Kurelik didn't say anything except to Marya and Davy; then on the highway, when he was driving faster and maybe his words didn't count for as much, he asked Marya's mother a few questions in a low guarded voice as if he thought Marya and Davy might not hear: Was anybody going to do anything about it, where had the sheriff been, did she need any money? But Marya's mother was staring out the window at the cars they were passing and didn't seem to listen. Marya could feel the muscles of her mother's body stiffen as they did sometimes when she was holding Marya close and Marya wanted to squirm away; she knew her face was tight and closed as a fist.

Kurelik shifted behind the wheel, embarrassed, or maybe angry—you couldn't tell with men like him or Marya's father. Finally he said in a different voice, "I got some leftover cherry cough drops in the glove compartment there, you kids want to reach in and help yourself''—and Marya didn't wait for her mother to say anything, she scrambled around and got the box out and shook three of the candies into the palm of her hand, her mouth already watering. Davy took two: he loved anything sweet. Marya let the candies melt on her tongue, sucking slowly at them. The faint medicinal fumes made her eyes water.

"Keep the box, take it with you," Kurelik said, and Marya murmured, "Okay," without thanking him. She shoved it into her jacket pocket.

As soon as they came to town Marya's mother told Kurelik to let them out. He stopped the truck and said irritably, "You're going to need a ride back, aren't you? When are you going back?" Marya's mother swung the truck door open and climbed down with Davy in her arms, then leaned back to take the baby from Marya. Marya saw that her face was hard and tight and closed but her eyes were red-rimmed, the whites tinged with yellow, still threaded with blood. When she spoke her voice was hoarse as if she hadn't used it for a long time. "I got my own plans," she said.

"You're not going to take those children in there," a woman was saying. She was as tall and as big-boned as Marya's mother: but her face was neatly caked with powder, her eyebrows had been penciled in, her wide fleshy mouth was bright with red lipstick. "You're not going to take those children in there," she said, her voice rising in a way Marya would remember thirty years later, "you can leave them out here with me."

Marya's mother wiped her nose roughly with the side of her hand. She was facing the woman, standing with one shoulder slightly higher than the other, smiling a queer gloating smile Marya hadn't seen before. "It's my fucking business what I do," she said.

In the end they talked her into leaving the baby behind; and Davy too—he started crying and couldn't be quieted.

"What about the girl?" a man was asking Marya's mother. He worked a burnt-out cigar around in his mouth, shifting it nervously from side to side. He wore soiled clothes, a kind of uniform—a short-sleeved white smock over dark trousers. "You could maybe leave your little girl outside, Mrs. Knauer," he said.

"She goes with me," Marya's mother said in her flat hard satisfied voice.

Marya was sucking on another of the cherry cough drops. Her mouth flooded hungrily with saliva. She knew better than to try to twist away—her mother's fingers were closed tight on her wrist.

The man with the cigar hesitated; he ran a hand through his thinning hair. He began to speak but Marya's mother cut him off. "She goes with me," she said. "Her name is Marya but she's the same as me—she knows everything I know."

"Mrs. Knauer—"

"Fuck Mrs. Knauer," Marya's mother said.

She wasn't angry; she didn't even raise her voice. Her words were short, flat, calm, hard with satisfaction.

"They really worked him over, didn't they?" Marya's mother said afterward, to anyone who would listen: the woman with the bright lipstick, clerks in the sheriff's office, people outside on the street who had never seen her before and didn't know what she was talking about. "They really worked him over, didn't they?" Marya's mother said, marveling. "Shit, I wouldn't even know who it was."

She wiped at her nose, her eyes. When her big-knuckled hand came away from her face you could see she was smiling —one side of her mouth twisted up.

While she was in the sheriff's office Marya and Davy ate chocolate peanut sticks from a vending machine in the foyer. A woman came over to Marya and gave her two dimes— Marya hadn't glanced up to see who it was, her fist had simply closed on the coins—and now she and Davy had a treat, and it was still morning, not even ten o'clock. Marya was so hungry her hand trembled holding the peanut stick; she felt a tiny trickle of saliva run down the side of her chin.

Davy didn't ask about anything and Marya didn't tell him: there was nothing to tell. She'd seen a man lying stretched out on a table—a table that was also a kind of sink, but tilted, and badly stained—she'd seen a man who must have been naked, covered with a coarse white cloth that hung down unevenly—but she hadn't had time to see his face because her eyes had filmed over: or maybe because he hadn't had any face that you could recognize. The skin was swollen and discolored, the left eye wasn't right, something had sliced and sheared into the cheek, the jaw must have been out of line because the mouth couldn't close. . . . Marya thought of a skinned rabbit her father had dropped into the sink at home, she thought of squirming rock bass the boys caught in the creek and tossed onto the hard-packed ground, stunning them with the heels of their boots. Once, her cousin Lee Knauer, who was maybe four, five, years older than Marya, slammed a carp—a garbage fish—against a rock, again and again, until most of its head was gone: Lee was madder than hell, he'd wasted a worm on a fish he didn't want.

Why hadn't there been any blood on that table, Marya wondered, licking chocolate off her fingers. And there hadn't been any smell except a faint trace of lye soap—maybe because the room was so cold, like the inside of a refrigerator.

"So *that's* it," Marya's mother had said, her hands on her hips, rocking slightly from side to side, "so *that's* it."

She didn't say anything else. There wasn't anything to say. Her voice was hard, jeering, but not very loud.

"So *that's* it. . . ."

Marya had slipped her wrist free of her mother's fingers but she hadn't run away. And her mother hadn't noticed in any case.

Now Davy stretched out sideways on the orange plastic chairs and fell asleep, sucking his thumb. His pale-blue watery eyes weren't quite closed. His mouth was smeared with chocolate and the front of his canvas jacket was dribbled with snot but Marya didn't give a damn: if anybody asked she'd say she didn't know who that kid was.

She got restless waiting. She tore little strips of a magazine cover, one after another, as narrow as she could get them, then she put the magazine back; nobody was watching. She went across the foyer and asked one of the clerks for a dime —just stood there until a woman noticed her, a woman with fluted pink glasses and tiny creases beside her mouth—maybe the same woman who had given her the dimes before. Marya didn't smile, she didn't wheedle or even complain that she was hungry, she just asked for a dime, and she was given it, as easy as that, so she treated herself this time to an ice-cream bar from the vending machine. Though the chocolate wafers were stale, the bar tasted even better than the peanut stick: she devoured it in five or six bites.

She left the building when nobody was watching and stood on the steps, not minding the rain. Traffic circling the square, a Greyhound bus with its headlights on, a farmer's pickup truck that looked like the one her father had junked in the field. . . . She stood watching, staring, seeing no one she knew, expecting nothing. Gusts of wind blew the rain slant-wise across the pavement. Then it lifted and the rain seemed to disappear. Then it came back again, stronger. Marya shivered in the cold but she didn't think it was because of the cold, she was really trembling with hunger.

The secret thing was, she still had Kurelik's box of cherry cough drops. There must have been four or five candies left, wadded up in the waxed paper, and all for Marya, only for Marya.

2

He instructed her to hold still. Not to move. *Not* to move. And not to look at him either. Or say a word.

Marya froze at once. "Went into stone," as she called it. And stared at the grimy, partly broken windshield of the old car. And said nothing.

It was only Lee, her cousin Lee, who liked her. Who liked her most of the time. Who meant her no harm. "Stop teasing Marya," her aunt used to shout at him, "stop teasing Davy: you're going to *hurt* him." But that was in the first months, back when they'd just come to live on the Canal Road and Lee really hadn't liked them; when he'd whispered one morning to Marya that her mother "better ought" to drown her and her brothers than leave them with people who hated them. Afterward, though, Lee didn't mind them so much. It was a way of getting on his father's good side, to pretend to like his young cousins.

He was twelve years old, Marya was eight. He didn't

mean to hurt her and he never *really* hurt her unless by accident.

In the old wrecked car, in the smelly old Buick at the back of the lot, Marya knew how to go into stone; how to shut her mind off, to see nothing without closing her eyes. She was afraid only that her neck might snap: she knew how chickens' necks were wrung, how a garter snake might be whipped against the side of a barn and its secret bones broken. Lee was strong—it was a joke around the house how strong he was—shoulder and arm muscles, fingers that could twist off jar tops for his mother when *her* fingers (which Marya judged strong enough) were inadequate. "Lee's going to be big as his daddy," people said; and Marya's aunt Wilma pretended not to be pleased, shaking her head, frowning, remarking that one of them around the house was enough for her. But all the Knauer men were big. Big and handsome. It ran in the family, Wilma would say, along with other traits that weren't always so nice. (And here, if Marya or Davy or Joey was present, she shifted her gaze meaningfully and said nothing more.)

These were the years of secret glances exchanged over Marya's head. Of mysterious allusions and hints. "The trouble," it was sometimes called, "the bad luck." Embarrassed words trailing off into silence. What were they saying, Marya wondered, pretending never to listen, pretending to be intensely absorbed in one of her schoolbooks, or in drying the dishes, or in minding her baby brother. Something about her mother, was it: her mother who was known simply as "Vera": or from time to time (but this Marya only overheard) as "the bitch" or "the Sanjek bitch"—Sanjek being her maiden name. Had anyone heard from her, or of her?—and the answer was invariably the same.

Though sometimes Marya's uncle Everard would add, "She'd be better off dead, *I* get my hands on her."

Marya was eight years old for a very long time. And nine years old. And ten. A very long time: the years stretched and buckled, the days were always the same day, only the weather differed. The inside of the old Buick was stifling hot and so dry you couldn't get your breath, or the windshield was splattered with rain that soon began to leak inside, or it was cold, too cold, and Marya couldn't stop shivering and whimpering. "Be quiet," Lee would say, grunting. "Or I'll wring your skinny little neck."

He didn't mean to hurt because, really, he liked her; she knew that. She could tell. "Lee's just teasing, Marya," her aunt Wilma would say, half chiding Marya for being upset. "Stay out of his way and you'll be better off."

She was afraid only that her neck might snap because of the pressure. He gripped her so tight—his forearm jammed beneath her chin—his clenched fist straining hard, hard into her back, just above her buttocks.

She never closed her eyes because—how did she know this?—the gesture might anger him, might make him rough. There was something about being weak or showing weakness that all the boys were roused by: a dog slinking and cringing, inviting a kick; a cat shying away instead of arching its back when it was stroked. And other children, of course. Smaller children. Of course.

She stared at, she must have memorized, the windshield of the old wreck. It was cracked in cobweb-like patterns that overlapped with one another, doubly, trebly, dense and intricate and fascinating as a puzzle in a picture book. A maze, such things were called. A labyrinth. Can you get to the center *without raising your pencil point and without crossing any line?* Sometimes Marya could do it at the first try, sometimes she couldn't. If she got angry she cheated: but then getting to the center didn't count.

When it rained the raindrops fell in unanticipated patterns on the windshield, rushing in little channels, slanted rivulets Marya could not have predicted. The cracked glass, Marya thought, was like the underside of ice on the canal. Seeing it from beneath. If you were trapped there, lying there . . . seeing it from beneath. The surface was cracked but not broken through the way some of the other windshields in the lot were broken. (How many people had died in these cars, Marya wondered, the first time she explored the lot, poking into the wrecks, frightened of seeing bloodstains. But of course she *wanted* to see bloodstains. And Lee and his friends said there was worse than that if you knew where to look—in that green Studebaker, for instance—and what to look for.)

When it was over Lee wouldn't wait to catch his breath but drew away from her at once, flush-faced, panting, his wet lips slack. He never looked at her—they never looked at each other, at such times. He rarely spoke except to mutter, *"Don't you tell anybody, you."*

Hold still. Don't move. Don't tell.
As if Marya Knauer required such warnings.

Marya remembers the Canal Road stretching between Innisfail and Shaheen Falls: nine miles of unpaved dirt and gravel, all but impassable in winter, so dusty by mid-June it had to be oiled. She remembers the lush-growing scrub willow and oak and beech; the roadside wildflowers, chicory and Queen Anne's lace; patches of milkweed; poison ivy; pink sweetpeas. Along the desolate stretches there were apt to be sudden surprises: strangers' debris dumped by night, an old sofa overturned in a ditch, a junked refrigerator with its door swung open, one day a Formica-topped dinette table which Marya's uncle Everard shamelessly hauled back home—he could use it, he said, in his "office." (By which he meant a corner of his garage, where he kept records of a sort. He was a licensed mechanic, after all; he thought of himself as a businessman.)

Along the Innisfail Pike the countryside changed: now it was farmland, acre upon acre of farmland, sloping hills, woods, fields of wheat, rye, corn, soybeans, acres of apple trees, pear trees, the wide mud-colored Shaheen Creek. The big farms along the pike belonged to the Erdrichs and the Maccabees. There was the Jelinski cider mill on a hill above the creek, the Baptist church, the white clapboard Methodist church, the granaries, the tavern owned by the Dubnov broth-

ers, the old Lerner farmhouse and the "new" Lerner house—
white brick with black shutters, a tall chimney, an evergreen
hedge, a curved blacktop driveway. Then a sprinkling of
smaller farms and houses. Fields, pastureland, barbed-wire
fencing. Then the old bridge above the Shaheen Creek that so
frightened Marya she frequently dreamed of it: the planks
rattling beneath the car's wheels, the rust-streaked girders
trembling. (The bridge had been built in 1922—not that long
ago, as Wilma said. But it was cheaply constructed with a
dangerously steep ascent, so narrow only one car could cross
it at a time.) Then they came abruptly to the outlying area of
Innisfail, the railroad yards, the warehouses along the canal,
houses that were hardly more than wood-frame shacks in
which entire families lived, then the slow cobbled climb to
Main Street and the central business district that never failed
to excite the children.

The first thing that caught their eye was the marquee of
the Royalton Theatre: what was playing this week?

On Saturday mornings Marya's aunt Wilma did her gro-
cery shopping at the Loblaw's store on Ash Street. Sometimes
Marya was welcome to ride along to town with the others,
sometimes not. (Wilma's own children, Lee and Alice, were
always welcome, of course.) If Marya asked timidly the night
before whether she could come along to town, Wilma would
say, "That depends," in a mysterious voice, not meeting
Marya's eye. She was boss of the household, after all—second
in power only to Everard, who rarely troubled himself with
household matters—which meant she could give out favors or
withhold them according to whim. Or she could offer a favor,
then abruptly withdraw it. Then abruptly offer it again. Marya
was to learn: her aunt Wilma couldn't be manipulated into
anything, Oh no she couldn't, just try her! Then you'd get on
her bad side and she'd give you sidelong nasty looks or no
looks at all, which was worse. That was Wilma. Hotheaded
one minute but the next minute you'd hear her singing, a
husky throaty voice like somebody over the radio—Harry
Belafonte was her favorite singer these days—still that didn't

mean Wilma was really truly in a good mood because she could change back in an instant if she caught Marya staring at her. "What are you looking at, for God's sake?" Wilma might say, coloring in exasperation. "Go on away! Go back in your room! Can't you read a comic book or something? Where's Alice? Go play with Alice."

I hate you, thought Marya, her face caught in a frozen little half smile. I wish you were dead.

But no: Marya wished Alice was dead. So that she could be Wilma's daughter and wear Alice's clothes, sleep in Alice's bed, sharing it with no one. Maybe it would be that Alice hadn't ever been born so that nobody would remember her, Wilma wouldn't miss her, all along it had been Marya who was Wilma's real daughter, then they'd sit in the kitchen having cola the way Wilma liked it in a glass, not out of the bottle the way the men drank, Wilma liked the "sizzle" she called it, that funny sensation going up your nose like tiny bubbles popping. And so did Marya.

And if Alice was gone then maybe Lee was gone too?

But Marya never thought about Lee when there was no reason to think of him, her mind backed away, broke, and scattered like milkweed fluff being blown in the wind. It was easier to think of Alice gone, then Wilma and Marya shopping at Loblaw's together, Marya pushing the rickety shopping cart and Wilma reading off from her list, sending Marya off to get things to drop in the cart: a big heavy box of laundry soap called Tide, Campbell's soups in the white-and-red-labeled cans, Wonder Bread, canned peas canned beets canned applesauce, those big salty dill pickles Everard loved.

Wilma was boss, Wilma was in charge. You had to please her or watch out! Her changes of mood made Everard laugh 'cause as he said he knew how to handle her. But her changes of mood frightened Marya. It all meant so much! And it was confused in Marya's imagination with the wild crackling bushy frizz of Wilma's hair—a mixture of browns, blond, even silver —so pretty!

While Marya's hair was dark and heavy and inclined to be oily. And always snarled.

Like her own mother's hair, wasn't it. That was the shame.

But Wilma was pretty, Wilma liked to look in mirrors tilting her head pursing her lips letting her hair fall over one eye like somebody in a movie poster, these were the times she didn't want Marya spying on her.

"For Christ's sake don't you have anything to *do*? Go play with your brothers, go on right *now.*"

And one terrible Saturday morning in town, in Woolworth's, Marya had been invited to come along with Wilma and Alice shopping for a new lampshade for the floor lamp in the living room and there was some woman friend of Wilma's and the two of them got to talking, laughing, the woman asked about Marya and Wilma said sharply, not lowering her voice so that the girls couldn't hear, "Her? I told you she's not my kin, she's my husband's niece." Marya edged away pretending she hadn't heard but she thought about what Wilma had said for a long time afterward, that day and days following. She knew that what Wilma had said was true but what did it mean?

She's not my kin, she's my husband's niece.

Far back from the road, at the rear of the lot, was the old scrapped Buick that had once belonged to Ron Coons (drunk, he'd sideswiped it on the Shaheen Falls bridge, almost killed himself), stripped gradually of all its valuable parts, now a tireless abandoned hulk, listing to one side in the high grass. Marya sees it clearly, has almost no need to remember: the glamorous Buick "coup" with the crazy blue paint, peacock-blue, and the red zigzag lightning bolts on its fenders, the chrome long ago gone to rust. . . . One summer hornets had tried to build a nest in the rear window, until the children had driven them away. Occasionally there were mice, garter snakes, unknown scampering creatures beneath its ripped seats. Depending upon the degree of dampness in the air its smells were varied, complex: oil, gasoline, cigarettes, stale urine, perhaps even blood. (Coons had lost a lot of blood in the crash, it was said. But the stains inside appeared to be oil. They smelled mainly of oil.)

Inside it could be cozy, on days when the air was slightly chilly but not cold. When it rained only lightly. When the sun didn't beat down too fiercely on the metal roof. The children played at driving the car, played at racing, pressing down the clutch, the gas pedal, the brake, screaming as they pounded at the dead mute horn. They turned the steering wheel violently to one side and then to the other, they half shut their eyes and saw the road fly beneath them. . . . (The steering wheel was still covered by an elasticized strip of fuzzy blue cloth, faded, filthy, unraveling: like a caterpillar's fuzz to the touch, Marya thought.) The dials and gauges on the dashboard were badly rusted but their mysterious numerals remained; the glove compartment was still locked, and so twisted it couldn't be pried open. The blue Buick was the children's favorite because it had the most style and because it had belonged to Ron Coons. Also, it was at the very rear of the lot, a considerable hike from the house.

Each of the cars had a story to explain it, to fix it in place. Marya's uncle knew them all. Who had owned what and approximately how much he'd paid for it; who had done what to whom, and where, and when; what the consequences were; how many deaths, cripplings, hospitalizations; how much money had changed hands in the final transaction. (Everard Knauer would pay as much as $100 for an old car if he really wanted it; but sometimes the wrecks were so bad he was paid to haul them away.) The black Dodge with the broken radio antenna; the skeletal old Studebaker; the dump truck that had belonged to a local contractor named Dietz; the wrecked Franklin with the wide rusted grill; the Ford sedan; the hulks so battered and corroded they no longer had names or former owners. . . . Old tractors and wagons (the kind once drawn by horses), old motorcycles, an oddly shaped jagged implement the children called a snowplow, on which they loved to climb in tireless, pointless games. . . . It was a child's paradise, a wonderland, filled with surprises. It covered only an acre off the Canal Road, behind Everard Knauer's house and garage, but it seemed immense; it might have been an entire world.

Things that happened in the lot—things done to the younger children by the older children—related only to the lot itself and were rarely spoken of elsewhere. There was a logic of secrets that pertained to the lot as it pertained to the schoolyard and to the towpath along the canal, where adults were almost never seen. These were no-man's-lands, limbos of a sort, places where language did not prevail and the only protection was flight, if you could run fast enough; or submission, if you couldn't.

"Don't you tell anybody, you know what's good for you," Lee whispered. He buttoned himself up, crawled from the wreck, never looked back. Marya lay without moving, her head against the armrest, her fingers still gripping the torn seat. She could hear flies buzzing, she could hear the whine of a solitary mosquito. She wasn't really hurt; he didn't *really* do anything to her, only rubbed himself fast and hard against her, chafing the soft skin on the inside of her thighs, poking against the crotch of her white cotton underpants. She was eight years old when it began, then she was nine, ten. . . . If he hurt her she couldn't stop herself from crying but he rarely hurt her badly, the sensation was more likely to be numbness, pins and needles darting through her legs or the small of her back. She was meek, docile, shrewd, not really there. She stared at the cracked and splintered windshield, marveling at its intricate patterns, seeing ice, cobwebs caught in ice, something stony-hard and frozen and unbreakable.

Off the pike, along the unpaved Canal Road, there lived three families—the Pitmans, the Michalaks, and the Knauers. They weren't really close enough to be neighbors and they tended to hold one another in mutual distrust. The Pitmans lived in a trailer permanently set on concrete blocks that looked, Wilma said contemptuously, like a big sardine can dented and scraped. The Michalaks were the poorest—all nine of them squeezed into a tarpaper shanty that caught fire one winter from a wood-burning stove, then was rebuilt in a crude jigsaw-puzzle way. The Knauers owned a one-story wood-frame house Everard had built himself with the help of his younger brother Joe. It was a good-sized house for the Canal Road area, a real house with a cellar, three bedrooms, a bathroom with modern fixtures including a shower stall. Everard and Joe had nailed up asphalt siding so clever in its design and grainy texture it looked from the road like genuine red brick.

Marya loved her aunt Wilma and most of the time her uncle Everard (she was his *niece,* after all) but she could hide from them even while she was in their presence. She slipped away, she was there but not there, *not-there* became a place familiar to her. It was lightless, shadowless, but not dark. Sometimes it had actual space like a hollow space she could curve into. There, she had nothing to do but breathe and feel her heart beat quietly. She couldn't be surprised and she couldn't be hurt, there wasn't even the danger of overhearing words she wasn't supposed to hear.

She could be *not-there* yet fully present to the others, even listening to what they told her. Eating supper, dressing herself in the chilly bedroom, her back to Alice, helping Wilma with the dishes, helping Wilma with the wash, minding her little brothers—she could do anything in safety being *not-there.* At school sometimes things were more difficult but she learned to manage. She soon discovered that, at school, she wasn't picked on because she was Marya but because she was one of the younger children and a girl.

If he wanted to, Lee protected her from the bigger boys. Told them to leave her alone. Told them she was his cousin —Davy and Joey were his cousins too—it angered him to see them tormented unless he himself was doing the tormenting.

Then at other times, unpredictably, Lee abandoned her to her fate. Marya would have to fend for herself. She was pummeled, her hair pulled, her arms pinched and bruised. She was chased for a mile along the muddy canal patch, told she'd be drowned, made to retrieve her underpants from the muck near shore. How they all laughed and jeered!—she *was* a comical sad sight. All the younger girls were teased and poked and pinched, Marya was the only one who didn't scream for help. It did no good to fight but Marya fought, striking out with her fists and elbows, butting with her head, kicking, using her knees, though her tormentors were twelve, thirteen, fourteen years old and could hurt her if they wished. Lee had to laugh, watching. "You really go crazy, don't you," he said, "like a little monkey or a bobcat or something." She understood that he approved of her though he didn't make a move to help.

Still, Marya and the other girls were more fortunate than poor Ethel Meunzer, whose plump nervous body and wet-eyed stare provoked the boys to remarkable feats of cruelty. Ethel was "slow"—Ethel "wasn't right" in the head—Ethel had no older brothers or cousins to protect her, and her thirteen-year-old sister held her in contempt. So the big boys chased her out into the fields for the hell of it, barricaded her in the boys' outhouse, they bloodied her nose, ripped her blouse, pinched her arms and legs, pulled her hair. It was part of their amusement that Ethel absorbed it all in silence—she was too terrified to shout for help. Even her sobs were choked and swallowed. Marya thought, She can't cry at home, they've taught her not to.

One chilly November day after school the boys "baptized" Ethel Meunzer in the canal—they dragged her to the bank, forced her down, actually held her head underwater for a few frenzied seconds until she fought free, sobbing and gasping for air. Marya ran back to the schoolhouse where the teacher, Mrs. O'Hagan, was just preparing to leave. She was a tall thick-bodied woman of no precise age, vague, nervous, ruddy-faced, a miner's widow who lived in town and whose manner in the classroom was abrupt and passionless. She liked Marya well enough—in the classroom; Marya was one of her two or three good students. But when Marya told her about Ethel, Mrs. O'Hagan said curtly that the boys were only teasing; they meant no harm, it was just play. Rough play. In any case, as she said, nearly pushing Marya out the door so that she could lock it, what the children did on the way to and from school was outside her "jurisdiction."

Marya told her aunt Wilma about the teasing, the relentless tireless tormenting, the Hughey boy and the Pitman boy and the Bannermans—brother and sister—and that gang on the other side of the canal on the Hobbs Road; but Wilma shifted her gaze impatiently, or in embarrassment, and cut Marya off in mid-sentence, saying that as long as they didn't do anything "bad" to Marya and Davy and Joey. . . . "You got Lee to protect you," Wilma said. "Those other kids, they've got to take care of themselves." She was smoking a cigarette, holding it between her thumb and forefinger as if it were a delicacy, her smallest finger curled. Marya loved to watch her—she loved *her*—she didn't want to provoke Wilma into scolding. "Anyway they didn't drown her, did they?" Wilma asked, amused. "The poor little mutt. She'd be better off. As for the Meunzers. . . ."

Eventually Ethel Meunzer *was* drowned: not in the canal but at Lake Shaheen, in what was said to have been a swimming accident. But this was years later. Marya heard the news third- or fourth-hand from Wilma, who wasn't always reliable. "I *think* it was Ethel—she was the young one, wasn't she?— sort of heavy-hearted, moping," Wilma said carelessly. "Though maybe it was the other one. What was her name— June?—Janey? She was sort of pretty, I remember. Didn't have the Meunzer face. And only a few months married when it happened." Wilma stubbed her cigarette out roughly in an ashtray held on her lap; she gave herself up to a spasm of coughing that sounded to Marya's ear oddly luxuriant, like laughter.

These were years, interminable seasons, of overhearing-by-accident, poking about in Wilma's things when Wilma wasn't in the house, crouching in the darkened kitchen while her uncle and his friends were drinking beer out in the yard, in the midsummer heat, their talk punctuated by angry laughter. Marya shut her eyes and listened hard and could hear her father's voice with theirs. Occasionally she could hear her mother interrupt—cajoling, teasing, laughing in her high shrill full-throated way.

Everard Knauer had worked at the Shaheen mines until the trouble started; in fact he had begun there two or three years before Marya's father. But after he was laid off he never made any effort to get mine work again—he was too lazy, he said, and too smart. He intended to go underground just one more time; and for that he wouldn't need a contract.

His daytime manner was loud, good-natured, unreflective. He was a big man—six feet three or four—wide-shouldered, thick-necked, broad handsome face, very pale blue eyes, a heavy hurrying tread, unmistakable. He sweated like a pig, Wilma complained. He tracked mud and dirt into the house as bad as any of the boys. No matter how she fussed with recipes out of *Woman's Day* and *Family Circle* and the *Innisfail Gazette* he preferred meat loaf—meat loaf with onions and green peppers, lavishly doused with ketchup. He loved french fries, potato chips, fried onion rings, anything salty and greasy, eaten by hand. He hadn't, he said, a sweet tooth, but he sometimes ate as much of one of Wilma's berry pies as Lee himself: Lee, whose appetite was that of a horse's.

He could drink a case of ale in a single day, beginning at, say, ten o'clock in the morning; but only if he had company. He never drank alone. He never got really drunk. There were always men hanging out at the garage, friends of Everard's— he had many friends—who needed work done on their cars; and naturally they drank. Lee and his friends hung out there as well, doing odd jobs for a few hours' pay, putting nickels in the vending machine for candy bars and Planters' peanuts, joining in the anecdotes, the ribald laughter, the snorting derision, the complaints about high taxes, high prices, county officials who were crooks, men in Washington who were no better. Everard always voted the straight Democratic ticket, he said, though he hadn't much faith in anyone after Roosevelt. He believed in electing wealthy men to high public office, he said, because they were the only ones who couldn't be bribed.

He was fond of Marya for the very reasons that Wilma, maybe, wasn't always so fond of her. She was stubborn, strong-willed, "sneaky" around the house; given to fits of loud silly giggling if provoked (or tickled); and rarely, like his own daughter Alice, susceptible to tears. She didn't whine; she might have been moody but she kept her moods to herself. Everard teased her for what he called her "bulldog" look—squatting in front of her and making a comical long face, his lower lip slack and pouting. He could always make her laugh, which made *him* laugh: they got along companionably: Wilma was (maybe) a little jealous.

He might have favored Marya because of all the children she most resembled his dead brother, but this was a thought he wouldn't have allowed himself to think. In fact he didn't exactly favor Marya. He could be rough with her as well. His tone with all the children was jocular and bantering; but if provoked, or spurred by Wilma's complaints, he moved swiftly from being "himself" to being extremely angry. It wasn't his style to give any warning before he reached out to slap, cuff, shake, even punch. Once, in Marya's hearing, Wilma told him he didn't know his own strength, he might break someone's bones or something: Joey was sobbing and burrowing into her lap, acting very much the baby of the household, and fully deserving (so Marya thought) of whatever had happened. "These are just kids," Wilma said; and Everard replied at once, with a logic that had sounded, at the moment, unassailable, "But they won't be kids forever."

When Marya and her brothers were first taken in by the "Canal Road Knauers" (this was their local designation), Marya went through a phase of saying virtually nothing; of being there but not-there simultaneously; of listening for the warning crunch of gravel when a car turned into the drive-way. . . . She didn't sleep: she lay awake, cautious and shrewd, beside her cousin Alice: she listened for voices, footsteps, the slamming of car doors, that strange little radio voice that meant one of the sheriff's cars was close by. Because Davy whined for his mother, continually asked when she was coming back, cried himself to sleep in pointless anguish, Marya reasoned there was no need for her to behave like that. She had been the "big girl" of the other household; she didn't care to relinquish her position.

Everard Knauer was called back again and again to give testimony. He knew what his opinion was—all the men knew what their opinions were, who had done the killing and who paid for it and why—but as for what he *knew,* what he'd actually *witnessed,* that was something else entirely. In town, they tended to brush aside opinions; they wanted to know what he had seen; what had been told to him—exactly, "in the exact same words," without paraphrase or speculation. When he lost his temper he found himself in the presence of men very much like himself. It got him nowhere, it got his dead brother nowhere, if he shouted, cursed, banged his fist on a table, said that everyone knew who'd killed Joe, they could ask the first person they met on the street, people who hadn't known Joe Knauer personally at all. . . .

The months passed. Seasons passed. There was a grand jury investigation (so Marya learned later, much later—as a young woman in her early twenties) but no indictments were handed down. A death in a tavern brawl, a man savagely beaten, a certain alcoholic content in his blood, a certain reputation in the area for making trouble. . . . And of course any number of wild unfounded charges were being made against the mine owners in those years, "unfounded" because they had never been proven. "Everyone knows," Everard said, "*everyone* knows," he said in a low mean slurred voice, slumped on the old sofa on the back porch, a bottle of ale in his hand, Wilma sitting beside him, late at night, very late, when Marya was meant to be asleep and not to hear. The adults' voices were dim; then suddenly loud enough so that their words could be overheard. Marya knew this was always the way if you listened closely and didn't give up.

The months, the seasons, a year, a second year. During the daytime Everard never spoke of the situation but sometimes at night, when he and Wilma were drinking together in the kitchen or on the back porch, or a few of his friends were over, drinking, his voice rose in that special tone of anguish and incredulity—a young voice—almost a boy's voice: *They're going to get away with it. Aren't they. They're going to get away with it.*

Now that the union was organized, now that a fairly good contract was signed, people tended to forget. Because it was pointless to remember. Because it confused things, to remember. And in any case Joe Knauer had quite a reputation in the Shaheen area—much more hot-blooded and unpredictable than Everard—he'd been in a number of fights over the years —the Sandusky Inn, the Tip Top Inn, that place out on the pike owned by the Dubnov brothers—look how he'd slapped Vera Sanjek around before they were married, always so jealous, always so bossy—but then she'd married him anyway: must have been crazy in love.

It was how things happened, Wilma tried to console Everard. She was tense, cautious, pragmatic, shrewd. She knew enough not to baby him—he flew into a rage if she "came on to him" like that—but she also knew how to console him, at least for the remainder of a night.

Why do you hate me, Alice might have asked Marya, is it because I try so hard to like you and can't? Or would you hate me anyway?

She was plump-faced, slow-moving, almost pretty, with her mother's fair skin and wide-spaced gray eyes and honey-colored hair—hair that Marya coveted—but she hadn't Wilma's special air, that razorish edge that Marya feared and admired. She was three years older than Marya but oddly intimidated by her. It must have seemed to her an amazing stroke of ill luck, that she and her sallow-skinned little cousin were suddenly *sisters.*

"I didn't ask to come here," Marya whispered more than once. "I didn't ask to be born."

They were to share a bedroom for many years—nine, nearly ten—but were never to take warmly to each other. "Marya doesn't like *me,*" Alice complained to Wilma. "She isn't my type," Marya would think when she learned the helpful word "type" some years later; the explanation made as much sense as any.

Still, they were close as many sisters; they rarely fought; they played Parcheesi together, gin rummy, checkers; they read comic books and Wilma's cast-off magazines, sometimes in the house, sometimes in the old blue Buick, cozy and companionable in the front seat on a drizzly afternoon. When it came to games—"games" being anything done on two legs, rough, rowdy, shading into actual violence—Alice was no good at all: silly, helpless, contemptible: spurned even by Marya, her "sister."

The bedspread that covered their slightly sagging mattress was a bright orange chenille, fuzzy and rigid, that Wilma had won at bingo at the Shaheen Falls Volunteer Firemen's picnic one August. They had a wall lamp—"brass"—with a sharply fluted shade; and another lamp ingeniously fashioned out of a white ceramic lamb with enormous blank eyes. The carpet that inadequately covered the floorboards of their room had once been in Wilma and Everard's room, and retained still a certain slapdash glamour—it was a deep-piled russet splashed with black streaks, with long russet tassels, wonderfully soft beneath Marya's bare feet. There was only a single window in the room, an absolute square, framed by filmy white "draw-back" curtains from Woolworth's; its view, unfortunately, was the messy rear of Everard's garage, an area in which old tires were heaped, rusted hubcaps, odds and ends of lumber left over from building the house, nameless things no longer useful but not precisely useless, not outright junk. There, hidden from most eyes, men patronizing the garage sometimes went to urinate, quickly and stealthily: it was Marya's habit to turn away from the window as soon as she saw a man approaching, but Alice sometimes watched, hidden behind the curtains. . . . "Oh isn't he a pig, isn't he *nasty,*" Alice might say, genuinely disgusted. "Do you recognize him? Is it Kyle Roemischer's father? Is it what's-his-name Dietz?"

Marya made no attempt to distinguish the men from one another. It was enough to think of her uncle Everard and remember that he wasn't her father; that someone else had been her father.

As for Lee, about whom Marya was condemned to think for most of her life, long after he'd married a girl from Sha-heen Falls and fathered three or four children . . . Lee was perhaps a brother, after all: closer to Marya temperamentally than either Davy or Joey, her "real" brothers. She hated him, she was terrified of him, in her long passionate daydreams (forgotten for years, recalled suddenly at a later crisis in her life) she plotted against him; but she never forgot him, or looked through him, as she did with other members of Eve-rard Knauer's household.

Sometimes Lee liked Marya well enough—liked her bet-ter, in fact, than he did Alice. (Alice was slow-speaking and slow-moving, burdened by the age of eleven with a precocious womanly flesh; Marya, angular and boyish, was at least capable of holding her own around the house. She didn't *cry.*) Some-times, however, Lee recoiled from her as if he saw something ugly where she stood: Joe Knauer's bad luck, perhaps.

The Bulldog, Lee sometimes called her. Snot-nose. Fuck-face. Shithead. And sometimes, with a killing simplicity that commingled pity and contempt and a mild threat, *you.* ("Hey, I'm talking to you, *you.*" "What kind of a face is that you're making, *you*—?")

He grew taller, bigger, heavier; hard little pimples blos-somed on his forehead and chin; his dark hair fell into his eyes in quills; his manner was abrupt, never entirely predictable. He did odd jobs for his father and was said to do them well, when he made the effort. He worked for a while at Cappy's, a general store that also sold coal, on the other side of the canal; he surprised everyone in the family by buying them

Christmas presents with money he'd saved—everything from Grant's, in Innisfail, only perfunctorily wrapped, but very nice things indeed. (A pink lamb's-wool sweater for Marya, a little too big for her, with mother-of-pearl buttons. . . .)

After his fourteenth birthday Lee gradually lost interest in forcing Marya to accompany him out into the lot, and in going through the motions of something neither of them would have known what to call. But this was mainly because he lost interest in the family in general—he got around more on his bicycle, acquired a friend with a car, had better things to do than hang out at home. Wilma complained angrily that he didn't give a damn for her, missing meals, coming in late at night; next thing she knew, he'd sign up for the navy. (This turned out to be true, but not for several years.)

Sometimes when he was a little drunk, on Sunday afternoons in particular, Everard got onto the old subject of Joe, his dead brother Joe: there were scores to be settled, Everard wasn't going to forget, he didn't want fresh trouble but he wasn't going to forget. . . . And that Sanjek bitch, that cunt, where had *she* gone and why hadn't she ever sent any word? . . . Lee was intensely interested in all this though he kept his voice low and guarded. Why couldn't they do something?—even now?—he remembered his uncle Joe pretty well, was it too late? They discussed the possibilities, the dangers, drinking bottle after bottle of ale together, their words lurching and heated and curiously abstract. Once, cleaning up after supper, Marya happened to overhear Lee say passionately that what *he'd* have done, back then, he'd take a shotgun and stick it up somebody's rear and pull both triggers, he'd do it even now: all Everard had to tell him was *who*.

An old subject, familiar, discussed tirelessly over the years, yet still capable of arousing pain and exhilaration. Marya learned not to get upset when she overheard. Eventually she learned not even to hear.

Twenty years later, crossing a street in a distant city, Marya happens to see a teenaged boy straddling a bicycle at the curb nearby, talking and laughing loudly with two of his friends: thick-necked, long-limbed, sinewy, brutish and childish at once: the very image of her cousin Lee.

Her cousin Lee as he'd been, of course—long ago on the Canal Road.

That age. That physique. Braying with laughter, showing his big white teeth, poking one of his friends in the shoulder. Marya stares; freezes at the curb; feels her heart beating rapidly; wonders what the boys are talking about. . . . The slang, the hearty smut, the companionable gestures and mannerisms, the camaraderie of adolescent boys. . . .

Marya who knows herself tough and resilient and supremely capable of blocking unwelcome incursions from the past nevertheless feels a powerful welling-up of dread, excitement, vertigo. She finds herself staring helplessly at the boy as if she were waiting to recognize him. Waiting for him to recognize her.

Then someone says: "Marya? Is anything wrong?"

"No. Nothing. I'm fine," Marya says.

The moment passes swiftly, the faint roaring and buzzing in her head has already lifted. She is supremely in control, it is twenty years later, she is in Cambridge, Massachusetts, a very long way from the Canal Road, and the boy straddling the bicycle looks nothing at all like her cousin Lee Knauer. It must have been a trick, Marya thinks, of the hazy May sunshine.

Vera wasn't well, she slept through much of the day, sprawled on top of her dirty rumpled bed, breathing so hoarsely and erratically that Marya thought she might be dying.

Then she was up, swaying on her feet; sliding a dress over her head, wriggling her shoulders and hips, humming loudly to herself. It was dangerous for Marya or Davy to approach her from the rear, she might turn on them, strike out blindly with the flat of her hand.

In the night, she said, *he* came to get her. Rapped on the window, tugged at her covers, wanted to slide in with her. *He* wasn't going to be left behind.

The telephone often rang late at night, there were frequently cars, strangers' cars, in the driveway. One or two of the sheriff's deputies dropped by "just to check." Some of the men hauled in cases of beer, bottles of whiskey, even soda pop; even bags of groceries. Vera left the baby with a woman friend in the Falls because his crying got on her nerves: she might lose her temper, she explained, and do something she'd regret.

Marya and Davy learned not to snivel either, or get in her way.

On her bad days, sick groggy headachey vomiting days, the bedroom stank and Marya wouldn't go near. Men knocked on the front door and called Vera's name. Sometimes they came around to the rear, sometimes they even threaded their way through the shrubs and thistles to peer into the windows. They were drunk, or angry, or simply in high spirits—it wasn't possible to tell which.

Marya and Davy hid behind the winter coats in the clothes closet, waiting for them to go away.

Sheer good luck, but Vera was up and dressed and cold sober when a woman from the county services dropped by. There were complaints, she said uneasily. What kind of complaints, said Vera. About the children, the woman said. What children, said Vera. Marya and David and I believe there's a baby, the woman said. "Marya and David and I believe there's a baby," Vera mimicked. Her own wit vastly amused her; she surrendered to peals of laughter. She wasn't drunk, she'd even taken a bath and shampooed her hair that morning, except for her puffy swollen eyes she looked pretty good. She looked like Vera Sanjek had always looked.

The next day she promised Marya and Davy that things would be better, quieter. She had a friend who respected her, thought the world of her. . . . She wouldn't have to take any more shit from anybody if their plans worked out.

Ft. Hanna was mentioned for a while, then Kincardine. Kincardine was on a river, she told Marya. There'd be sailboats, motorboats, yachts. Did Marya know what a yacht was? —a big white boat that could take you anywhere you wanted to go.

Marya was ashamed that her mother's old blue sweater was missing so many buttons you could see her white drooping flesh just inside. And her hair hung down in greasy strands. And she was nasty to Uncle Everard when he came by. ("So where's hot-shit Wilma," Vera asked, "sitting out in the car? —afraid to come inside?—afraid it might be catching or something?")

Marya had been absent from school for twelve days running when the man from the school district office drove out: and by then Vera had been gone for three or four days. Marya wasn't sure how many, Davy of course didn't know, they'd cried themselves sick and dry-eyed, they'd eaten all the food in the refrigerator except what was spoiled. Why didn't you go down the road to tell somebody, Marya was asked.

Marya, chewing her fingers, didn't answer. For a while it was thought she might be mute.

Davy, on the other hand, chattered and babbled like a parrot. He had all sorts of things to say. But he couldn't explain why there was so much talcum powder spilled around the house, especially in Vera's bedroom. (He and Marya had had a talcum powder war, a crazy giggling frenzy, shortly after Vera had left. Marya had started it by trying to dust him with their mother's big white powder puff. . . .)

What were the games of your childhood, lovers sometimes inquire of one another.

Checkers, Parcheesi, Old Maid, gin rummy. . . . (Wilma taught Marya how to play gin rummy; it surprised her that Marya caught on so quickly.) Outside, in Uncle Everard's lot, the games were rougher, crazier, without rules—you shouted

Go! and scrambled from car to car, crouching behind the snowplow, crawling frantically beneath the old dump truck, lying flat in the dirt. Marya's breath came in ragged gasps. She felt the boys' footsteps thudding past, then she was safe, for a while she was safe, her face splotched with dust. In the distance voices lifted. Where's Marya? Didn't you find Marya?

She was credited with discovering the most ingenious hiding places.

On slow lazy winter days, afternoons following school, Wilma could sometimes be talked into joining the children at the kitchen table. She shook the dice hard, shut one eye in a shrewd comical wink, snapped her fingers, and cried "I knew it!" if the shake was good. When the cards went against her she said it was the story of her life. She played seriously, strangely seriously, for an adult; the games seemed to matter; it infuriated her when (for instance) Lee was discovered to have been cheating. "Aren't you ashamed of yourself," she said, giving him a slap, and Lee, shrugging his shoulders, laughed and said, "Oh, who gives a damn? It's only a game."

"Damn" was swearing by the standards of the household but if Everard wasn't present it seemed not to matter.

Smoke curled from Wilma's cigarette and made Marya's eyes water but she never complained, never shrank away. The odor was mixed in with the sweet familiar scent of her perfume, which Marya would always remember as the most mysterious and wonderful scent on earth. (What precisely was Wilma's perfume? White Shoulders Lily-of-the-Valley, in a sturdy cut-glass blue bottle from Woolworth's in Innisfail. Marya would have stolen a few drops for herself except she reasoned that her thievery would be detected; Wilma would punish her, or, what would be worse, she'd ridicule her in front of the others.)

Hundreds, perhaps thousands, of games over the years; each building to a virtual fever of anticipation and excitement; each intensely real . . . and not one to be recalled. Only the slapdash way Wilma dealt out cards or shook dice, her wrists suddenly graceful, elastic, a cigarette slanted between her lips.

Only the way she grinned when things went well, as if she were genuinely surprised. And, when luck went against her, that sigh, that shrug of the shoulders, which Marya was still imitating twenty years later: "The story of my life."

When the games took place somewhere else—at a neighbor's house, in one of the junked cars in the lot, over by the canal—they lacked a certain spark, a certain momentum. No one seemed to be observing from above; no one knew enough to make wise statements. Only children played. Outcomes didn't matter. There were winners and losers, sometimes rather nasty losers (Marya herself could turn nasty in an instant), that was all.

The first time Lee approached Marya she thought it was just a game, the things he did to her. One of the boys' games.

It left no mark, in any case. She couldn't claim that she was hurt.

Only afterward—years afterward—did she realize that Lee must have been as surprised as she. Because it happened so swiftly in such choking half-sobbing confusion, a matter of seconds, scrambling and twisting—wrestling? tickling? was it one of the rough tickling games?—in the front seat of the blue Buick—and that was all.

"Now don't you tell, you," Lee whispered, panting, frightened, giving her a little shove as if he wanted her *away* from him at once.

Marya's greatest astonishment arose from the fact that he had allowed her, a girl, to see the most secret part of his body. And it frightened her that he was frightened; she'd never seen a boy his age in such a state. Face flushed, hands trembling— he might, if he wanted, actually hurt her quite a bit.

Years, days, seasons. Marya recalls the cracked windshield of the old car, the fuzzy blue covering on the steering wheel, the rusted gauge . . . but couldn't begin to estimate how many times Lee had taken her there. It was like the games played with cards or dice, one game shading into another, always the same game, really, indistinguishable from any other. And was it finally important, Marya demands of herself; was it finally significant, giving a certain *tone,* a certain poetic *flavor* to that distant period of her history called childhood . . . ?

She doesn't want to exaggerate. She isn't sentimental, she wants no excuses, she is likely in fact to be rather pitiless with herself.

One day soon she will tell her lover about Lee Knauer, but the opportunity must present itself gratuitously, like fate. For Eric Nichols isn't in the fullest and richest and most magnanimous sense her lover. (He claims to love her, to be devoted to her, but Marya knows better: it's just his notion of her, a kind of capsule-sized female in his brain, "Marya" in this pose, "Marya" in that, "Marya" imagined, of all things, as deserving of love.)

However, she will tell Eric Nichols about her boy cousin; she is conventional enough to believe that he has a right to know.

For if this man loves her, even if he is deluded in his love, he must have a sense of her history, of who it is he believes he loves.

And telling him about Lee will serve the purpose of explaining certain hesitancies and doubts in Marya's nature, that stoniness of soul he has surely noticed. (Not that Eric Nichols has said anything to Marya. He is kind, patient, gentle, supremely civilized. Not at all what Marya Knauer deserves.)

When I was eight years old. . . .

There was a cousin of mine, a boy, a few years older than. . . .

My parents died when I was eight and my two brothers and I were taken in by. . . . And I had two cousins, a boy and a girl. And the boy, he didn't really mean any harm, he didn't really know what he was doing. . . .

This sort of thing happens all the time, it isn't uncommon though I once thought it was. In recent years . . . the statistics. . . .

One day Lee was working in the garage, doing repairs on the Jelinskis' Pontiac, lying flat on his back on one of those wheeled contraptions that roll under a car, when the jack somehow slipped and the car came crashing down and his left leg snapped—the bone called the "femur" (as the Knauers would later learn). It broke in two places, causing such pain that Lee fainted. He'd had time to cry out—a single strangulated cry Marya would hear many times in the course of her life.

And Marya, who happened to be in the garage at the time, ran terrified to the house, shouting that Lee had been killed.

Lee was supposed to have finished with the Jelinski car by noon but he'd wasted time that morning, friends of his had been hanging around the garage; and now he was in a hurry. Everard, in town on business, was due back soon. Lee might have been a little careless with the jack, he didn't remember. But he didn't think so. He didn't really think so. He hadn't after all wanted to kill himself.

By this time his friends had gone home. The younger children were playing back in the lot, Alice was away somewhere, only Marya happened to be within earshot . . . so Lee shouted for her to bring him a Coke from the house. He was dying of thirst, he said. He was having a fucking hard time with the car.

Marya said that Wilma wouldn't let her take a Coke from the refrigerator, and Lee knew it. (It was the wrong time of the day, too many Cokes disappeared from the house, they didn't, as Wilma said, "grow on trees.") But Lee said for her to get her ass in the house and bring him a Coke. "Just don't let Ma know," he said.

So Marya ran across the sunny tarry patch of pavement to the house. And let herself into the kitchen as stealthily as possible. And went to the refrigerator, and opened it, and took out a Coke—all without Wilma knowing. (Wilma wasn't in fact inside the house at that time, she was out in the back yard hoeing in the tomato patch. And though her ear was so attuned to the sounds of the household that she might ordinarily have heard the refrigerator door open and close, even at that distance, she didn't hear Marya that day; Marya must have been unusually cautious.)

She had the presence of mind to open the bottle in the kitchen—if she'd gone back to the garage without opening it, and without the opener, Lee would give her hell—and even to dispose of the cap in the garbage bag beneath the sink. So that, until she counted the remaining Cokes in the refrigerator, if she troubled to count them at all, Wilma wouldn't know that one was missing.

She also took a small swallow of the drink on the way back to the garage, reasoning that Lee wouldn't notice. Which of course he didn't.

Though he was rude enough to take the bottle from her fingers without a word, Marya lingered close by as if she hadn't yet been dismissed. She watched with intense interest as he drank down the Coke, sitting up awkwardly on the wheeled seat. Lee and his friends could guzzle soft drinks in virtually one long swallow, it was amazing, a phenomenon less of thirst than of piggishness and stamina. . . . A series of small rapid swallows, forehead creased in concentration and eyes half closed in a kind of ecstasy. . . .

Marya watched; said half sullenly that it didn't look like he was going to leave anything for *her*. Lee didn't hear, or pointedly ignored her. He finished the bottle, wiped his mouth with his arm, belched, set the bottle down, and rolled it in the general direction of one of the corners, where bottles were collected for deposit.

The bottle began to roll in a crooked trajectory, so Marya stooped to pick it up.

Lee said, "Okay now, get the hell out, I don't want any distractions or fooling around."

Marya said, ". . . I wasn't fooling around."

She saw that the jack was pumped up as high as it would go; this was to save Lee from working in the pit, which was filthy—it hadn't been cleaned out in months. She might have felt a tinge of danger—because of course the jack *could* slip.

(Everard was always warning the children against playing with his tools. Never were they to poke around in the garage when he wasn't there!—he'd burn their asses if they did. His own forefinger and middle finger were misshapen from an accident he'd had putting chains on a neighbor's truck stalled out in the snow and once he'd narrowly avoided getting killed when a tractor he was repairing overturned, he'd started the motor got the damn thing going suddenly it bucked forward knocking him down. . . . "What you think afterward is how fast it all happened," Everard said. "You think if you had it to do over again you wouldn't make the same mistake and that's true, but you don't get to do it over again, right?")

Marya stood studying the jack. Wondering how it would feel to the touch: how greasy, how nasty. But there was a smell about the garage and the repair pit she liked too. A smell of oil, rubber, old rags. She wouldn't have minded learning some of the things Everard had taught Lee just for the fun of it. Or just for the hell of it. Why not? She was as smart as Lee, wasn't she. "How does this thing work?" she asked. But she knew enough not to touch it not even lightly, experimentally, with her thumb.

"Lee?" she said. "How does this thing work?"

He didn't hear, or he didn't feel like answering.

Is she going to tell her lover about the accident too?

For of course it was an accident. It was sheerly an accident.

No one was responsible, she hadn't touched the jack or she'd touched it so gently it couldn't possibly have slipped, but suddenly everything buckled and gave way—the car crashed down, Lee screamed in shock and pain, Marya stood there frozen, mute, staring. She was too frightened to think except for the crazed thought that car tires are made of rubber so Lee couldn't be killed could he?—his leg couldn't be severed from his body could it?

She saw that he had lost consciousness. Still, the upper part of his body writhed, convulsed. She backed away in terror. Was he dead? Who was to blame? How could there be blood if the tire was made of rubber, wasn't rubber soft, wouldn't rubber bend?—blood on the filthy cement floor, blood mixing with oil lifting tiny flecks of dust and dirt, snaking its way in her direction.

How do you like it now pig pig pig pig pig.

Marya backed away slowly. She didn't want Lee to open his eyes and see her. Her jaws were clenched hard against crying, then she turned and ran for the house, ran for help. *Pig pig pig pig pig.* But nobody had touched the jack, nobody was to blame except Lee himself, Lee must have kicked it himself with his foot not knowing what he did.

She called for Wilma. Began shouting now, screaming. Now it was all right to scream. And once Wilma heard her cries then everything was out of Marya's hands—it had nothing to do with her.

The ambulance arrived in ten minutes from Innisfail: a feat nobody along the Canal Road would have believed.

Lee didn't die. Of course Lee didn't die. Afterward everybody joked—you couldn't kill a Knauer that easily.

Even Wilma, who'd been hysterical at the time waiting for the ambulance to arrive, even Wilma joked about it. Goddamned fool so clumsy he almost killed himself and what if he'd been crippled for life, *then* what?—his mother'd have to wait on him, right, help him dress and undress, right?—take care of him the rest of her life?

He was in the Innisfail hospital for nearly three weeks, his leg in a heavy white cast. Then for the rest of the summer he made his way around on crutches, swinging noisily through the rooms of their house, forcing the younger children out of the way. He took no special notice of Marya but he was bossy, vain, irritable, self-important, swallowed down codeine tablets when the pain was bad but also drank a good deal of beer: almost as much as Everard, Wilma complained. Wilma prepared Lee's special foods for him while he was on crutches, his special desserts, he'd tease her for acting so crazy when she found him in the garage, not having sense enough to try to jack the car off him, thinking right away he was dying, or dead —it'd take a lot more than that, Lee said, to kill *him*. (Though in fact Lee had gone into shock by the time the ambulance arrived and might well have died if the emergency crew hadn't known what to do. Nobody knew exactly what "shock" was except it had to do with your blood pressure suddenly dropping.) "I wasn't going to jack up that car," Wilma said frowning, not liking to be teased yet liking her son's attention, "Jesus, what if I'd only made things worse! This kind of thing happens so awful *fast*."

Lee turned sixteen in August, which meant he could have his driver's license as soon as he got off crutches and he and Everard had already picked out the car for him: a four-door Plymouth with extra horsepower, only a few years old. In the hospital his hair had grown long, curling past his collar, and he insisted upon keeping it that way. With sideburns razoring into his cheeks, slicked-back quills of oiled wavy har. He was shaving now too. He looked older than sixteen, he looked good.

By the time the cast was removed it had turned filthy and was covered over in Lee's friends' signatures. The colored inks —blue, green, bright red—gave the cast a cheery air, and many of the signatures were those of girls: *To Lee K., love Sue Ellen. To Lee, love Ginny. To Lee—Get Well Soon! love Fran.* Alice signed it *Love Always Your Sister Alice* but Marya signed it only *M.K.* in ordinary blue ballpoint ink.

3

By the age of thirteen Marya was one of the tallest girls in the eighth grade: not precisely big-boned, not stocky, but solidly muscular, with long legs and narrow hips and alert nervous mannerisms. Like a young horse, one of her teachers said to another in an aside surely not meant for her to hear, that hasn't been expertly broken.

Marya was pitiless with herself, thought obsessively about herself. She wasn't going to mind being ugly, she thought, if she could look *distinctive.* Her facial bones were too prominent, her eyes shadowed. "Didn't you sleep last night, Marya?" Wilma often asked, looking at her critically, suspiciously. Marya's eyebrows had begun to grow in thick and dark, nearly meeting across the bridge of her nose; her brown hair, so dark and lustrous as to appear black in certain lights, had to be tightly plaited to keep from frizzing in humid weather, and hung in a single heavy braid between her shoulder blades. It was her ill luck to seem older, near-adult: sometimes men stared at her in the street, mistaking her maybe for a high school girl, and she'd stare back coldly, unsmiling. Glimpsed by accident in mirrors and reflecting windows, her image struck her as simply unacceptable—she didn't want *that,* she wouldn't accept *that.*

Still, Marya was Marya. She sent her mind off daydreaming, telling strange little stories in her head, but there she was in her body, so often graceless, so tall, and when her first menstruation came in the middle of a school day she went white-faced and trembling to the girls' gym teacher to say there was something wrong with her—she was bleeding, she didn't know why—and the woman stared at her puzzled as if temporarily confusing her with one of the older girls. "Why are you so upset? Aren't you used to this by now?" she asked, not unkindly.

Embarrassed, speaking in an uncharacteristically low voice, Wilma had tried to tell Marya something of what she might expect one day soon when "it" happened. Had Marya any questions, she'd asked afterward, but Marya hadn't had any: too stubborn, too shocked. Her gym teacher, Miss Heinke, had asked her too had she any questions, and Marya said coldly, No. She didn't want to know anything more.

That was the year, the memorable year, of Mr. Schwilk. In fact it had been Mr. Schwilk's English class Marya fled that November morning, to go to Miss Heinke for help: and she'd required a special pink slip afterward, from her, to be admitted fifteen minutes late into class. When Marya wanted to torment herself she thought of what Miss Heinke had scrawled in pencil at the bottom of the slip—*personal health instruction*—and wondered what Mr. Schwilk had made of it. If he'd thought about it, or her, at all.

Why did you hate him so much? the students were asked after Schwilk's collapse, when rumors of his death circulated in the Innisfail school. And the question bewildered them—they hadn't hated him, so far as they knew, at all.

Marya was questioned in particular: not because she'd been among the worst of his persecutors—those were boys, naturally—but because she was said to be his favorite student, the one for whom Schwilk had had the most hope. ("The most hope"—this was an expression, oddly sobering when Marya first heard it, Schwilk had used in speaking of her to his fellow teachers.) But Marya had no answer. She said evasively, almost sullenly, "Things happened to Schwilk because—he couldn't stop them from happening."

Mr. Schwilk, the newly hired English teacher at the Innisfail Consolidated School, was observed, back in September, walking slowly along the canal towpath, his head bowed, his chin creased against his chest. His gait was irregular, there was a slight drag to his left foot as if he knew of his doom—but it was only the third week of classes and everything lay ahead.

Schwilk, his observers whispered, crouched some twenty feet above him. There's Schwilk, why's he walking home so far out of his way?

They were hiding behind the enormous scarred boulders marked, over the years, with initials and names and "forbidden" words; it was an accident, or almost an accident, that they had sighted their English teacher along this stretch of the canal. But now, suddenly, they were seized with an unaccountable hilarity that threatened to burst into jeering laughter. Even Marya felt the need to clap her hand over her mouth.

It was a mystery, that Schwilk nearly always provoked these responses. Except in the classroom—he taught seventh, eighth, and ninth grades—where he communicated a certain capricious authority, Schwilk, observed on Innisfail's Main Street, or glimpsed walking alone in the hilly residential neighborhood—the "good" northwestern edge of Innisfail now "going to seed"—in which he'd recently come to live, often struck an odd clownish note. Marya couldn't have said why, exactly: it might have had something to do with the way he held his shoulders, or with his purse-lipped brooding manner, or his clothes—or with the erratic pace at which he moved (sometimes self-consciously brisk, sometimes inordinately slow)—or with the prim set of his head, the way his silky chestnut hair flared out from his forehead, the way light struck his glasses with an element of surprise. (When Marya envisioned Schwilk she saw him in the act of turning—his head, his narrow shoulders—and light striking the lenses of his glasses as if, in that instant, he was blinded by a sudden thought: Ah yes! I see! But, no, I *don't* see—I seem to have gone blind!)

It was said that Schwilk sometimes walked to the house on Bayberry Avenue where he rented a small apartment by way of the old canal—cutting through the weedy fields behind the school property, carrying his heavy briefcase, a solitary figure, rather comical when he wasn't dominating a classroom. He worked late at his desk and rarely left school before four, four-thirty: long after most of the other teachers had gone home and the faculty parking lot was nearly empty.

What, precisely, was so amusing about Mr. Schwilk?—or so disturbing?

"Jesus," Lester Hughey said, peering at him from behind one of the rocks, "you think there's something wrong with him?"

"He's thinking about something," Kyle Roemischer said, poking Lester in the shoulder, "he can't shut his brain off like *you.*"

"He's talking to himself," Erma Dietz said.

"Just don't let him hear you, for God's sake," Marya whispered.

"*He* wouldn't hear anything outside his own fucking head," Lester said. " 'Mr. Schwilk!' 'Mr. Schwilk, *sir!*' "

They watched him, swallowing their laughter. Of course he was totally oblivious of them—they could probably have spoken in their normal voices and he wouldn't have heard.

Only two or three hours before, they had been intimidated by him in room 110: Schwilk pacing dramatically about, telling his anecdotes—which were always designed to "prove" something they should have known all along—covering the milky-gray blackboard with his eager sloping scrawl, quick to call on students who were inattentive or frankly daydreaming or who gave nervous signs of being unprepared. He had his allies, of course—even two or three clear favorites—but there were days when he seemed impatient with correct answers, strangely greedy for mistakes, for students who might make fools of themselves and provide an occasion for raucous laughter. Hence he frequently called upon louts like Bob Bannerman, who was taking eighth grade English for the second time, or Ron Jelinski, who rarely spoke above a frightened whisper. *No, no! And again—no!* Mr. Schwilk cried in a high perturbed voice, as if he were deeply insulted: and half turning on his heel, whipping about so that his silky hair flashed, he gazed expectantly out over the thirty-odd faces to call on someone who knew the right answer. *Ah yes!—yes.* And he would smile a sudden happy smile as if nothing on earth could delight him more.

His teeth were small, childlike, perfectly white, and perfectly even; his cheeks dimpled when they were exposed.

From the first, Mr. Schwilk's eighth-grade students were uneasy in his presence, awed by something indefinable and *urban* in his manner. Even if they had not known that he was from out of state, that he was said to have "traveled widely" in Europe, they would have understood that he did not quite belong in Innisfail. He was impetuous, he was bullying even when he meant well: for his high-toned praise was so profuse, so vehement, it was as intimidating as his outright scorn. None of their other teachers addressed them with such emotion, with such gravity. Marya thought, perplexed, He thinks we matter: doesn't he know us?

(In his boyish enthusiasm Mr. Schwilk had several times tossed down an eraser or a piece of chalk on his desk and strode forward into the classroom to shake hands—to *shake hands!*—with a student who had, by design or the wildest happenstance, managed to say something intelligent. He had shaken poor blushing Marya's hand not once but twice; he had shaken the limp hand of the Ducharme boy, whose mother taught in the Innisfail high school. It did not unsettle him, in fact it probably escaped his notice entirely, that his sudden smiling attention frightened certain of his students, particularly the girls; or that, behind his back, other students were stifling their laughter or making rude gestures at him. "I congratulate you," he once said to Marya, making a little mock bow, "for having said something intelligent—truly intelligent! —in this remarkable 'local accent' with which you've all been contaminated.")

Now Kyle was saying, "Suppose we loosened this big rock and rolled it down—y'think we could start a little avalanche?"

The girls laughed in a pretense of horror and slapped at his hands.

"He *is* talking to himself," Erma whispered. "Or is he singing?"

"Maybe he's going to walk in the canal and try to drown himself," Marya said. She meant it as a joke—the thought of anyone in that filthy water was disgusting—but as soon as she said it aloud she knew it might be true. So she went on, stifling her laughter, "He won't know how to do it right—he'll get stuck in the mud near shore—we'll have to go down and pull him out!"

"Shit, I ain't going to pull that cocksucker out," Lester Hughey said.

All boys spoke this way—bluntly, brutally, without much thought of what they said, or why they said it: or so Marya believed. But girls weren't supposed to talk that way or even to pay close attention. Unless, like Erma Dietz, they pretended shock and disapproval—maybe gave a boy a light slap: "You wouldn't talk like that if he could hear you!"

They followed Mr. Schwilk along the canal, running crouched, ducking behind rocks, nearly overcome with fits of giggling. Marya struck her bare ankle against something that protruded but didn't allow herself to cry out or even to feel pain. There wasn't time, the mood was too exhilarated, wild.

Suppose Mr. Schwilk *was* intending to drown himself?

—commit suicide? For some reason the subject of suicide had come up in one of their class discussions and Mr. Schwilk had spoken at length, and rather passionately, about ancient attitudes toward the taking of one's own life. He had launched into one of his inspired monologues, speaking of nobility, and courage, and honor, and something he called "chastity of spirit." Eventually the class lost interest because the subject had nothing to do with the day's lesson and couldn't be the basis for a homework assignment, it was just Mr. Schwilk talking, showing off his superior knowledge, using big words, making references to places—Rome? Athens? the Orient?— nobody in Innisfail knew anything about, or cared. Only Marya listened, staring at the gawky loose-jointed youngish man who was her teacher, and whose words tumbled over one another as he spoke, by now oblivious of his restless audience. She thought, That was how my father died, it was honor, it was —something of *spirit*: but nobody wants to talk about it.

Afterward, when she tried to remember what Mr. Schwilk had been saying, and what her own sudden idea was, it had all evaporated. Bullshit, Marya thought. She even said the word aloud, lightly, experimentally: "Bullshit." It was one of her uncle Everard's favorite words.

Why Mr. Schwilk didn't become aware of them, spying on him from behind the rocks, whispering to one another and fooling around, was a mystery; it made him all the more comical. But he continued to walk along at his slow dragging pace, staring at the ground in front of him, not even taking much notice of the canal. Marya had a flash of panic that he could somehow see them reflected in the rust-streaked water —somehow, at an angle—she knew it was impossible but she worried just the same. If Mr. Schwilk knew that Marya Knauer was behaving like this, hanging out with Kyle Roemischer and Lester Hughey, even with silly Erma Dietz, who, as Schwilk once said, was pretty as a porcelain doll and had as empty a head. . . . If he knew what Marya Knauer was like outside school. . . .

"Maybe he's going to meet somebody out here, some

woman," Lester said in a low sniggering voice. "This is the place for it."

"How the hell do *you* know," Kyle said at once. "*You* don't know shit."

"I know a hell of a lot more than you know," Lester said.

They were arguing with each other for the girls' sake, especially for Erma's: so she said, to distract them, in one of her sly hoarse asides: "Maybe it's Mrs. Bannerman."

"Schwilk and Mrs. Bannerman!" Lester said, snorting with laughter.

"Schwilk and Mrs. Bannerman!" Kyle said. "He wouldn't know which end was up, with *her.*"

(Ella Bannerman was fat, slovenly, defiant, an alcoholic —a "disgrace"—one of the town jokes. She had six children ranging in age from seventeen to less than a year, and no husband at the present time; it was even said of her—despite the fact that her hair was dirty blond, and her skin fair—that she had a drop or two of Indian blood. Which was why she was such a bad drunk. Which was why, in the idiom of the town, she "fucked anything in sight" for a few dollars.)

Marya didn't think it was funny, Marya gave Kyle a good hard poke in the ribs to quiet him down. "He's going to hear us," she said. "You guys and your loud mouths."

"Marya's jealous," Lester said, grinning, swaying over her, "she's Schwilk's real girlfriend. Schwilk fucks anybody, she wants it to be *her.*"

They all laughed, even Erma: Erma, her cheeks blazing, pressing both hands against her mouth.

Unsmiling, pretending she hadn't exactly heard, Marya said, "Shut up, he's going to hear you, you guys are crazy."

At this point one of the boys accidentally dislodged a rock about the size of a basketball that rolled noisily down the hill behind Schwilk, bringing with it a small cascade of pebbles; and the odd way Schwilk glanced over his shoulder, alert, concerned, frowning, yet vague and blinking as someone roused from a deep sleep, struck them as helplessly funny.

They nearly choked with laughter, doubled over, tears starting from their eyes—even Marya.

But Schwilk suspected nothing. He saw no one, heard nothing, merely glanced up the hill with a quizzical expression. As Marya watched—she couldn't *not* watch—she saw him draw one of his white handkerchiefs out of his vest pocket and wipe his face carefully: forehead, upper lip, chin: then he removed his glasses and dabbed at his eyes. (As he sometimes did in class, to Marya's extreme discomfort, for without his heavy tortoiseshell glasses and the lenses that gave his eyes so cunning a cast, Schwilk wasn't—Schwilk.)

Then he continued walking, carrying his briefcase, his left shoulder a few inches higher than his right, as if nothing was wrong. Poor Schwilk! Later it would be common knowledge that he was only thirty-one years old but that age didn't seem right for him: he was either a kid, not much older than the high school students, or already middle-aged. During the first week of classes he had boasted—it was a joke but *maybe* serious—that he heard and saw and "intuited" everything in his classroom, he picked up every whisper, every wink, could even read minds. "Where, needless to say, there are minds to be read," he added. But it seemed clear now that his powers vanished outside the classroom.

They trotted along after him, Lester and Kyle in front, hunched over like Indian guides in a western movie, and the girls a few yards behind, whispering and giggling together as if they were close friends. (Marya envied Erma, maybe even adored her, but she didn't really like her: she didn't really like anyone.) None of this was funny, Marya thought, yet she had to stuff her knuckles in her mouth to keep from laughing; and she didn't want to turn back though they'd been fooling around now for over an hour. She had told her aunt Wilma that she might have to stay after school—Marya was co-captain of the girls' basketball team—but now it was getting late, it must be going on five o'clock.

Schwilk, Marya's favorite teacher. Schwilk, who praised her, shook her hand, stared at her as if—what?—he couldn't quite believe in her, in what she'd written for a homework assignment, or murmured in class. "Speak up! Speak up, Marya!" he was always saying, his thin lips twisting in a smiling sort of pout, as if something about her irritated him. She felt her face go hard, willed every muscle to turn to stone, and her eyes too, glassy and invulnerable; *she* could never be provoked into crying in class like certain of her weaker classmates, boys and girls both.

None of the students at the Innisfail school had ever encountered a teacher like Schwilk. He wore tweed coats even in warm weather—gray, brown, green flecked with russet— he wore old-fashioned vests, shirts with cuff links, a black fedora hat set smartly on his boy's head, red neckties, even bow ties. His briefcase was said to be of *crocodile skin*, and "probably very expensive—fifty dollars at least." (According to Eulalie Steadman, whose father owned Steadman's Shoes.) His hair receded sharply at his temples but curved down over his shirt collar, worn a little too long by Innisfail standards— but very attractive, a few of the older girls thought. Like someone, maybe, in a movie or in a magazine photo; someone from Europe; a poet, an artist, an actor—?

He hadn't been hired by the school board until midsummer—to replace poor Mrs. Siegel who was dying of cancer, after all, and would never be strong enough to teach at the school again.

Opinion was divided as to whether Brandon P. Schwilk was good-looking, in a sallow, rather undernourished way, or whether he was homely; even ugly. And was he bright and clever and all-knowing as he seemed or, as his harshest critics (among them a number of adults) said, frankly, crazy? It was true that he had too much energy, he seemed to take up too much space. He was in the habit of roaming the classroom, firing out questions and answering them himself, not trusting his students to get things right. By the end of a typical class period he would have covered most of the blackboard with his looping scrawl. Names of famous persons, fragments of poems, grammatical problems, "memorable phrases": he told the class to memorize as much as they could, "someday it might save your life."

Both Robbie Ducharme and Warren Maccabee, whose grades were as high as Marya's, frequently stumbled over their answers when Mr. Schwilk called on them abruptly; they were simply intimidated by his manner, his smile, his distended pale-blue gaze. "He talks too fast, I can't understand him," Robbie complained. "He talks too *crazy,*" Warren said. Marya rarely had any trouble understanding Schwilk but it was her strategy to give no sign—she had learned to be cautious, even stony-faced, in school—but sometimes his jokes were so bizarre, so shocking, they took her by surprise and she heard herself laugh even when nothing was funny.

(Once or twice Schwilk used the expression "brown brain," as an insult. He strongly suspected, he said, that certain of his students suffered from "brown brain." No one quite understood what he meant and even Marya found it hard to believe that he would be alluding in his glib scornful way to a condition many of the local miners suffered from— "brown lung." Was he crazy, Marya wondered, to say such things in Innisfail?—or didn't he know where he was?—or what he was really saying? Marya's own grandfather had died, she knew, of "lung trouble," he was said to have coughed himself to death after twenty years in the mines; the majority of the students in Schwilk's classes had relatives who worked in the mines and whose health, surely, had been affected. Did Schwilk precisely *know* these things?—so Marya marveled. And who was going to tell him?)

If he was embarrassingly lavish with his praise he could be as abrupt and unreasonable with his contempt. An answer was wrong—"grotesquely wrong"—or mumbled and not properly enunciated: "That's the way idiots talk," Schwilk might rage, "behind their hands!" Someone yawned, someone poked a neighbor with a pencil, one of the "overgrown louts" at the rear of the room shifted restlessly in his seat, cracked his knuckles, rolled his eyes in boredom. And suddenly Mr. Schwilk was enraged. Despite his tweed coat, his starched white shirt, his cuff links—despite his air of superiority—he lost his temper as savagely as anyone they knew. "How dare you! How *dare* you! *You!* See me after class! And the rest of you—be quiet! Face the front of the room! Sit *still!* You pack of—" And his voice trailed off, stymied, frustrated, for the word he sought was perhaps too strong a word to be uttered: even in his rage he understood that some insults, given specific form, might never be retracted.

"You pack of—Innisfail boys and girls."

And he drew out his handkerchief and wiped his face with care, smiling and pouting at them, elated, triumphant, but so upset they could see his hands trembling.

"Go on down, Marya, and keep him company," Lester Hughey said, giving Marya a poke. "Go on."

"Yeah, you're his pet, you're the secret girlfriend, you get all the A's," Kyle Roemischer said, grinning meanly, taunting. "Go down and give Schwilk a kiss."

"Go *on,* Marya, what're you waiting for? Go down and give Schwilk a kiss," Lester said.

"Wouldn't he shit his pants!"

"Wouldn't they both!"

"Hey, leave Marya alone, you guys," Erma whispered. "Don't talk so loud."

They were only joking but Marya seemed to take it so seriously—why not carry the joke a little further? Tickle her a little under the arms, in the ribs—push her out into the open where Schwilk might see her if he glanced up—give her a good hard push and send her stumbling down the slope? Poor Marya, hot-faced, panting, Marya with that stubborn bulldog look of hers, what a wild idea, to drag her out of hiding and expose her to Schwilk—!

Marya pleaded with them to stop, she'd tell her cousin Lee on them both, but they only laughed at her distress and said they'd tell Lee themselves: how she'd been hanging around the towpath with old Schwilk, screwing behind the rocks. They wrenched Marya's fingers off a misshapen boulder she'd been clinging to, and, calling out, yodeling, "Here's Marya! Here's Marya Knauer! Oh, wait for me—it's Marya!" they sent her running and stumbling down the incline amid a small avalanche of stones and pebbles and loose dirt.

Shame! Would she ever outlive it!

And Schwilk whirling about to see her—that flash of light in his eyes.

She was terrified of examining her face too closely in the mirror for fear of seeing something forbidden: her mother's face, that slack-lidded wink, the glassy stare, the smile rimmed with lipstick and saliva.

And that low jeering murmur—*Marya you know who you are, Marya you can't lie to* me.

Though her mother had been dead for a long time; nearly as long as her father.

(Was she really dead? Marya sometimes wondered. Wasn't it just a story they had made up, agreed upon, to tell her and Davy and little Joey when he was old enough to understand? A story like any other story, lies braided together with some kind of truth too painful to be told outright.)

Marya had a fantasy in which she told Mr. Schwilk about her father who had disappeared but who was buried out in Shaheen Falls, and her mother who had disappeared but wasn't buried anywhere.

And what would Schwilk say? Adjusting his glasses, pursing his lips, frowning, smiling, blinking at her as if she were some sort of remarkable local insect—"Why, Marya, what is that to *me*? And what is it, really, truly, to *you*?"

Mr. Schwilk wrote carefully on the blackboard:

We are led to Believe a Lie
When we see not Thro the Eye.
                              —*William Blake*

At the start of the school year he spent most of the class period on grammar and spelling exercises and going laboriously over homework assignments: "Are there questions? Yes? No? Who's perplexed? Who's lost? Speak up now or it will be too late!" By November he managed to complete the exercises and hand back compositions within twenty flurried minutes, so that he could turn his attention to what he called the "great issues" of literature—life, death, and what lies in between.

Marya sought out "William Blake" in the school library (the library was really just a wall of bookshelves at the rear of the study hall) but found in the B's only Eloise Brent and L. H. Burns, the authors, respectively, of *Priscilla Jones, Student Nurse* and *A Boy's History of the Yukon.* When she told Mr. Schwilk that she couldn't find Blake, his initial retort was: "My dear, I'd be astonished if you *had,* in these surroundings." Then he said, more soberly, that he'd be happy to lend Marya his copy of Blake's poems—"provided you be very, very careful about returning it."

"Yes," Marya said, flushed with pleasure. "Thank you."

But—oddly—Schwilk must have forgotten the exchange because he never brought the book, nor did he take Marya aside to explain.

There's too much on his mind, Marya thought, trying not to be resentful.

(He disliked her, she suspected, because of that episode on the towpath. He would never forgive her: he knew her for white trash: and of course she *was* white trash, why deny it?

Poor stricken Marya—she'd been running with such helpless momentum down the incline that she might have charged into the canal if Schwilk hadn't reached out instinctively to stop her. "Why—is it Marya? Marya Knauer?" he said in a faint incredulous voice. *"Is* it you?—*here?"*)

In early December for a composition assignment Marya attempted a short story about a man who was beaten to death by "unseen enemies" and his body dumped into a swamp, his "whereabouts unknown forever"; and Mr. Schwilk, handing it back to her, troubled, quizzical, smiling his boyish pouting smile, said, "This is strange, strange, *strange,* Marya—but do write more."

Though Schwilk's practice was to mark most compositions up heavily with red ink, in exclamatory asides or questions, he had written virtually nothing on the five or six pages of Marya's story; at the end he'd noted only *? ? ? ? ?*

Marya's second story, written a few weeks later, was about a girl named Annie who was threatened with strangling by a male cousin if she "told" on him—the exact reasons for "telling" being obscure—and at the end of this composition Schwilk noted *See me after class!* in his bold flowing hand. But, though Marya waited patiently for as long as she could, Schwilk seemed to take no notice of her in his rapt absorption —authentic? mocking?—with some school gossip several of the other girls were relaying to him.

Marya retreated, hurt and annoyed; and avoided Schwilk for a week; then approached him with the story in hand, and asked him why he wanted to see her. Schwilk took the story from her, frowning, as if he'd never seen it before, paged through it, murmured vaguely, "I really don't *know,*" and seemed at a loss for words: actually rather embarrassed.

So Marya stood there, feeling her cheeks pulse with blood, and Mr. Schwilk stood there, not looking at each other, for what seemed to be a very long time but was probably no more than ten or fifteen seconds.

Finally Schwilk said airily, "You have a most *feverish* imagination," and handed the story back; and that was that.

Don't give in, Marya counseled herself. Once you start crying you won't be able to stop.

Still, Schwilk needed allies in the classroom; he needed them, as the year progressed, badly. And Marya Knauer was after all his principal ally.

He could rely upon her to answer questions when even Robbie Ducharme and Warren Maccabee failed—he could rely upon her to diagram sentences correctly on the blackboard—and most of all to understand, and to register with a smirk or a surprised little laugh, his allusions and his fanciful asides. "Dear Marya!" he said once, after class, blinking at her. "It would be so lonely here without you!"

One midwinter day, as if relenting, he inquired after her "knotty little stories" and asked why she hadn't shown him any more; and Marya said, deeply embarrassed, that she thought he hadn't liked them—they weren't very good, were they?—"just stupid stuff."

He said, licking his lips, that they were, well—"imaginative."

He added, after a pause, that Marya had an "unusual gift for words."

While Marya stood tongue-tied, with no idea what to say, he went on, clumsily, rather miserably, praising her for her ability to organize her compositions; and to write; simply to *write*. "And to spell—not the least of the virtues!" He laughed.

Marya raised her eyes to his and saw how keenly, and with what apprehension, he was watching her. Why was he afraid, she wondered; had people been talking about her to him?—talking about the Knauers? Was he afraid she might say something he didn't want to hear?

She knew he was waiting for her to leave. She could see the perspiration beading on his short upper lip—the faint feverish blush to his cheeks. Something turned coldly in her heart, a key in a lock, knowing, smirking, bitter. Marya heard herself say scornfully, "Yeah, thanks, I can *spell*."

One afternoon when the old radiators were knocking and the room was overheated and nothing seemed to be going right —when even the butts of Schwilk's humor sat dumb and unmoved as lumps of cotton batting—he suddenly lost his temper and began raging at them. They were hopeless, he said.

They were matter—inanimate matter—and he should have known better than to try to "inspire" them.

The outburst lasted five minutes or more. Schwilk paced from one end of the room to the other, his hair rippling, his pale gaze flashing, so *disgusted,* so *furious,* why had he tried to fashion silk purses out of sows' ears!—until finally the tantrum ran down and the classroom was unnaturally silent and Marya saw that Mr. Schwilk was a ridiculous figure in a brown tweed coat too big for him across the shoulders. Breathless, nearly panting, he looked out at them and said suddenly, "Well—I didn't mean to say all *that*—please forgive my outburst."

And long afterward it was a joke, whispered, or said daringly aloud in Schwilk's very presence: "Please forgive my outburst!"

(The joke acquired arcane meanings, developed in unpredictable and always hilarious directions: Marya overheard boys who weren't in the class, ninth-grade boys who probably didn't know the origin of the remark, poking at one another in the hall and sniggering over "liverwurst"—as in, "Please forgive my liverwurst!" And again her heart tightened against Schwilk, that fool Schwilk, who deserved all that would happen to him.)

Late winter and rain was being blown against the windows, and the high-ceilinged room was still overheated, drugged and slow, impervious to Schwilk's excited patter. He paced about, gesturing with a stubby piece of chalk, speaking of action—the consequences of action—the way truth isn't absolute but fluid and mutable and willed—yes, *willed.*

Marya watched him coldly, her head slightly lowered, her forehead creased. What the hell is he talking about, she wondered; does he really imagine anyone understands, or is even listening? Schwilk, *Schwilk*: that idiotic name. She inked it out, blotted and tore at the cardboard cover of her notebook. Schwilk: let him throw himself into the canal, let him drown: *she* wouldn't raise a hand to save him.

Since he had pleaded with them to forgive his "outburst"

he'd surrendered something of his authority. Or, perhaps, he was simply wearing out, wearing down—his energy wasn't limitless after all. Poor high-flying Schwilk, Marya thought, discovering that Innisfail isn't so contemptible after all: that it will very likely survive his scorn.

She frequently sighed; she saw no reason to disguise her boredom; why not, when everyone else was bored?—and openly, sometimes blatantly. There was little Jerry Starer half-consciously pressing the flaps of his ears against the ear canal, as if to discover whether the high monotonous drone of Mr. Schwilk's voice might not mix with the tedious sound of the rain against the windows, to comprise a single sound. And Lester Hughey, his snoutish face flaccid with indifference, his eyes heavy-lidded; Lester whom Marya had once thought she "liked"—and who, in turn, was said to have "liked" her, for a few weeks—now slouching in his seat at the very rear of the room, mud-stained boots in the aisle. And Agnes Roemischer leaning forward to draw her long sharp nails lightly up and down Stan Fitzsimmons's back: and Stan, good-looking Stan, adrift in an erotic doze in which poor Schwilk, preening and smirking and posing his rhetorical questions, must have played a curious role indeed.

Now Schwilk was speaking of freedom, and necessity, and determinism, and the "transcendence of fate," and the radiators clanged and thumped, and Marya, drowsy herself, felt her eyelids close . . . and saw at once the battered face rise as if it had been waiting for her all along, snug beneath her eyelids. That hideous face, utterly familiar: the jaw broken, the skin discolored, something "not quite right" about one of the eyes: the nostrils wide and black as if flaring out in a final impassioned attempt to draw breath—to live. Life, only life! —what mattered but life!

Where had the body been laid?—upon a kind of table? —a table made of metal—cold to the touch—so high Marya had to stand on tiptoe. The air was cold, too, and tasted of metal. And the smell—the stink—faint but unmistakable—of beer, vomit, intestinal gas: Marya drew it in with every helpless breath.

Marya jerked awake. Her heart kicked once in her breast, then resumed its normal rhythm.

She was suffused with a sudden rage toward Schwilk, who was speaking now of faith—faith in free will—a faith that "creates its own future." He presented the example of the mountain climber caught somewhere in his climb, unable to descend, forced to leap across an abyss to save himself. Marya gathered that it was a philosophical proposition of some kind. Schwilk quoting William James, whoever William James was, Schwilk speaking rapidly and haughtily, tapping a piece of chalk against the blackboard. He seemed to know beforehand that his words weren't diverting enough, weren't *provoking* enough, to rouse the class from its torpor, but he continued nonetheless: ". . . it's impossible to retreat and it's dangerous, very dangerous, to go forward . . . the distance he has to leap is such that he might fall to his death. . . . Do you see? Are you following? Though we don't climb mountains . . . most of us . . . it's a situation that strikes a deep chord . . . doesn't it? . . . for the mountain climber is faced with a *choice* of beliefs that determine action. He can believe he'll make the leap safely; or he can believe that he will fail, and fall to his death. Well—do you see? Do you understand the point?" Mr. Schwilk said brightly, looking about the room.

When no one answered he added, "The situation is such that if he believes he can make the leap, if he has sufficient faith, he *will* make it. Because, as I've said . . . haven't I said? . . . the distance isn't beyond his powers. But on the other hand, if he lacks faith. . . ." Mr. Schwilk's gaze darted up and down the rows of impassive students: Marya steeled herself as it settled upon her. "Marya understands, I'm sure," Schwilk said reproachfully, "even if the rest of you don't. Marya understands the very *American-ness* of James's proposition: the melancholy of spirit must triumph over their own nature, for otherwise they will perish. And simply not to perish—why, isn't it heroic!"

Someone snickered at the rear of the room; a number of persons coughed. Marya, her cheeks burning with a dull sullen heat, maintained her neutral expression.

But Schwilk, being Schwilk, would not let the matter rest. Perhaps because only five minutes remained in the class period and he couldn't dismiss them before the bell rang, or very reasonably introduce a fresh topic, he stood with his hands on his hips, cocky, censorious, scornful. "Well! There are *no* questions? You really presume to think you've understood it all? The subject of your next composition is the *will to believe* —the *faith that creates faith*—"

Marya suddenly raised her hand and asked, "How many mountain climbers made the jump? How many *made* it, and how many fell?"

Schwilk blinked at her as if he'd never heard anything so idiotic.

"I just wondered—is it in a book or something—is any of this real," Marya said, "or just made up to talk about?"

No one, including Marya, could have said why her remarks—childish, defiant, obstreperous—should have struck the class as irresistibly funny: but everyone began to laugh: and as the exchange continued the laughter mounted. Shorn of its overwrought and claustrophobic setting, it was a puzzling or mildly amusing incident at best, but in room 110 of the Innisfail Consolidated School, that rain-locked March afternoon, it provoked such peals of adolescent laughter that Marya was to remember her triumph—for surely it *was* a triumph, in all its silliness—all her life.

Schwilk stammered a reply. Of course the mountain climber wasn't "real," the proposition was a philosophical proposition, and Marya asked, "What happens to the brave mountain climber who has faith, and jumps, and falls just the same—didn't *that* happen all the time?" Schwilk, hurt, rattled, told her she misunderstood, she *willfully* misunderstood, the distance wasn't supposed to be beyond the mountain climber's powers—"for of course that would make the situation tragic —hopeless—meaningless"—the proposition had only to do with *spiritual faith*. Marya, pretending to be unaware of her classmates' laughter, asked how the mountain climber could know that the distance was, or wasn't, beyond his powers: "Wouldn't he need a long yardstick or something to measure it with?" Schwilk said angrily that an expert mountain climber could gauge distances with the eye, very likely: and Marya shot back, with a glance over her shoulder at her grinning companions, "Some expert! Stuck up in the mountains! Anybody that stupid, he deserves to die!"

Schwilk tried without success to quiet the class. He told Marya that she was being ridiculous, she must *know* she was being ridiculous; and Marya said, drawling, that the mountain climber was the ridiculous one: *she'd* never gotten stuck up in the mountains, and never would.

Schwilk told her to shut her mouth and keep it shut.

Marya said, "You asked if we had questions and I asked a question and I still want to know—how many mountain climbers made the jump?—how many made it, and how many fell?—seeing as how they had *faith*—"

One of the boys in the back of the room called out, inspired, "Helicopter! Send out a helicopter!"

Now the class roared with laughter—wave upon wave of wild adolescent laughter—imbecilic, uncontrollable, splendid in its volume: and there was Schwilk, poor hapless Schwilk, the butt of it all, trapped at the front of the room.

When the bell finally rang Marya threw her books together and made her way out of the room with the pack, not troubling to glance back at Schwilk, or to hear his feeble protest, "You haven't understood!—you've distorted everything!—you're no better than savages—savage *beasts*—"

Why did it happen, the eighth-graders were asked, afterward. Why did you hate Mr. Schwilk so much . . . ?

They tried to explain that they hadn't *hated* him. He was all right, really. He was strict, and a hard grader, and he made fun of some kids, but he *was* funny, and probably he made them learn things . . . and he hadn't ever hit anyone. . . . (It wasn't uncommon in Innisfail for teachers to strike offensive students in class, or to send them to the principal's office for punishment.) But Schwilk was just—Schwilk: and things got out of control.

After the pandemonium in March, after the spectacle of Schwilk, perspiring and red-faced at the front of the classroom, a kind of collective harassment began, not only in eighth grade but in all the grades: until, near the end, not even the worst troublemakers seemed to be in control of what was happening. Why do you hate Schwilk, why do you give him such a hard time? students from the high school asked, but there never was a coherent explanation. Lester Hughey said, without pity: "That fairy bastard cocksucker—ask *him.*"

A few days later Mr. Schwilk made the strategic error of punishing his eighth-graders for their general "rowdiness" by springing a surprise grammar test on them: but, as if by agreement, only about a quarter of the class handed it in. (Marya, newly emboldened, ripped her paper in two—and was gratified to see a few other students, seated near her, following suit. Poor Schwilk, hunched over his desk and pretending to be deeply absorbed in a book, never so much as glanced up.) Outside class they were exhilarated, fired with a delicious sort of energy. After all, what could Schwilk *do*?—could he really fail them all?—the very best students along with the worst?

Another time, Schwilk wanted them to memorize a poem by Emily Dickinson, which he had printed carefully on the blackboard before the start of class. But when he recited it, in his high, quavering, absurdly *passionate* voice—

> I like a look of Agony,
> Because I know it's true—
> Men do not sham a Convulsion,
> Nor simulate, a Throe—
>
> The Eyes glaze once—and that is Death—
> Impossible to feign

naturally everyone, including Marya, burst into laughter.

Was anything ever so hilarious as Mr. Schwilk and his "poetry"?—so irresistibly, wildly funny?

Day followed day of grammar school silliness, Schwilk imitations throughout the school, boldly defiant answers to Schwilk's questions, hidden chalk and hidden erasers in room 110, a general carnival atmosphere in his classes, intoxicating, cruel, contagious. Suddenly everyone was saying "I like a look of Agony!" and making references to "homely Anguish!"— and dissolving into helpless fits of giggling. The more pathetic Schwilk became, the more they loathed him: the more Marya loathed him. She wondered why his opinion had ever mattered—how he'd ever had the power to so deeply wound *her*.

Schwilk grew visibly more haggard; his classroom performance was less and less controlled; his instructions were frequently incoherent. One afternoon in April his briefcase was stolen from his desk, and though he raged and nearly wept, and threatened to call the police, it wasn't returned; nor did anyone inform on the thief. (Who was Kyle Roemischer, as everyone knew. Kyle had walked off with the briefcase— hidden it in his locker—smuggled it out of the building— eventually tossed it into the canal. He had so little interest in Schwilk's things he didn't even bother to force the lock. "What do I want with *his* shit?" Kyle asked.)

Another afternoon—when the pranks were, perhaps, not *quite* so funny as they'd once been—a number of the boys held the door of room 110 closed against Schwilk so that he couldn't get *in* the room, though the second bell had rung and classes had begun. He rapped on the door, tried futilely to push it in, finally begged, *begged* them to have mercy, to relent. . . .

In more confident moods Schwilk threatened to fail them all; he threatened to fill out "detailed reports" on their behavior. He even, to Marya's especial amusement, threatened to "jeopardize" their high school and college "careers"! A hopeless fool, Marya thought. She stared at him as if she had no idea who he was.

Schwilk's sudden end came on a balmy May afternoon when the scent of lilac was heavy in the air and only five weeks of classes—only five weeks!—remained in the semester. In the midst of a conventional grammar lesson someone, for some inexplicable reason, began to hum loudly; and almost at once another student joined in; then another; and another. Even as Schwilk stared and blinked at his young tormentors the humming spread, grew bolder, more resonant, coming at him from all corners of the room. Who had thought of it, and why did the others so readily join in? The prank was totally unpremeditated but all the participants knew enough to hold their jaws rigid, purse their lips, maintain innocent neutral expressions *as if nothing were wrong.* "What is this? Why—?" Schwilk whispered. The eerie vibrating noise came at him from everywhere, it seemed, and nowhere; it was as anonymous as Nature itself. Though Marya felt uneasily that the persecution of Schwilk had gone far enough, she couldn't resist joining in with the humming—its very ferocity, its pretense of innocence, seemed to draw her in. So she hummed along with the others, watching Schwilk covertly, feeling her jaws and teeth vibrate with the cruel melodic sensation.

I cross you off my list, she thought.

Within a few minutes the man retreated—simply retreated—went to sit quietly at his desk—hid his perspiring face in his hands. He'd dressed too warmly for this spring day in one of his well-worn tweed coats with leather elbow patches; his checked necktie was askew; his trousers looked as if they had been slept in. When the bell rang they all trooped out, somewhat more soberly than usual, but no one cared to pause at Schwilk's desk and ask if he was all right; and by the time the next class arrived the man had slumped forward, unconscious.

Schwilk was taken by ambulance to the Innisfail General Hospital where, according to immediate rumor, he died—or *almost* died—of a heart attack; or a stroke; or something called "cerebral hemorrhage."

In fact he didn't die; he had merely collapsed. Innisfail's eighth-graders, after all, hadn't *that* much power.

Eventually Marya and her classmates learned that Mr. Schwilk had collapsed of strain, overwork, and exhaustion—total physical exhaustion. That he suffered from a particularly severe case of diabetes might have been related to his breakdown as well; and he'd been taking a variety of drugs for many months—some by prescription, others over the counter, unwisely mixed. (It was even thought that Schwilk's nervous excitability—his curious attitude that classroom teaching *mattered so much*—was a consequence of drugs.)

Well, the eighth-graders said uneasily, guiltily, half resentfully, how could we have known? How is it our fault?

As soon as Schwilk was discharged from the hospital he disappeared from Innisfail forever; his classes were taken over by a substitute. But in June it was announced that he had done a curious thing—he'd turned over his salary for the remainder of the school year so that a poetry prize could be instituted in his name. Isn't that just like Schwilk, they said, recalling now, with exasperated fondness, how *odd* the man had always been about poetry.

So it came about that Marya Knauer was to win the first of the annual Brandon P. Schwilk Poetry Awards for a poem she had written in his memory—though the fifteen-line poem, rigorously rhymed, stiff with an archaic and faintly outlandish diction, wasn't "about" any individual at all: it seemed to be about the defilement of the Shaheen Creek by the paper pulp and chemical factories to the north.

It quite pleased her that her poem had been chosen; she didn't want to consider what sort of competition, in that school, it might have had. Enough to know that she'd won, and been praised, and flattered; that her prize (prizes, really: a small scroll stamped in black ink and pseudo-gilt, *A Treasury of English and American Poetry,* a check for $35) would make her a figure of some importance in her aunt's and uncle's eyes, at least for a while. She leafed through the poetry anthology, five hundred tissue-thin closely printed pages, and felt a sensation of excitement mixed with cold sick dread: had her silly little well-intentioned poem announced, as if by accident, her wish to compete *here* . . . ?

She thought about Schwilk. She wondered what he had had in mind, repaying evil with good; defiantly repaying evil with good; and so very publicly, so consciously. What was the motive? To make everyone at the school feel guilty? To pronounce his own superiority, in the face of their ignorance? Or was it, Marya wondered, simply because he loved poetry and couldn't help himself; because he wanted, insisted, that others love it too. . . .

After the awards ceremony in June, Marya walked home alone along the towpath, carrying her trophies. She tried unsuccessfully to envision Schwilk across the canal, walking parallel with her—carrying his briefcase, head bowed, his chestnut-red hair stirring in the breeze. She tried to envision his tweed coat, his gray trousers that fit so poorly. "Mr. Schwilk!—Mr. *Schwilk!*" she called. But her voice was faltering, shamed. She couldn't see him there; she seemed, oddly, to be forgetting him.

A story unfolded in her head about a man who had drowned—or had he drowned himself?—here in the canal; his body found drifting and bobbing one morning in the scum along the bank. No one knew his name or where he'd come from, his pockets were empty, his face ravaged. . . . Marya's heart began to beat rapidly. She knew the story already, it seemed: it was about Schwilk: it had to do with his death, here in the canal, back in September.

She had been a witness. She'd seen.

The old canal was fairly wide but it looked deceptively shallow; it didn't give an impression of depth, or danger. Difficult to believe that anyone could drown in it, Marya thought, shivering, even on purpose.

4

The winter, fierce and prolonged, when Marya was fifteen, she went twice weekly—usually on Mondays and Thursdays, directly following school—to visit Father Clifford Shearing at St. Joseph's Hospital in the hilly Riverside section of Innisfail. She was a sophomore in high school; she had no friends and told herself that she needed none; she was *not* in love with Father Shearing (that would have been a sin) but she had lavish fantasies in which the proposition was put to her that she might exchange her life for his, she might die in his place: Yes, Marya whispered, desperate and elated. Oh yes.

As it turned out, not even a blood donation was required of her.

Marya's week centered around the visits, which had an air of the half illicit, the subversive, about them. She didn't keep them secret from her family but she didn't exactly tell them either. (None of the Knauers in this generation was a practicing Catholic though all of them—Marya included—had been baptized Catholic. Wilma had been baptized Methodist and said it was all a lot of bull, churches, priests and ministers, nuns stuck away in convents, low-minded people boasting that Jesus was their friend when, in Wilma's words, He wouldn't give them the time of day. If you needed Him He'd come to you directly or not at all. The same held true for God—didn't it? Because He spoke out of whirlwinds and tongues of flame in the Bible, after all. When Marya informed her—tremulously, defiantly—that she had decided to become Catholic, to become Catholic *really,* Wilma had stared at her as if she'd been personally betrayed. "Now what do you want to do *that* for . . . ?" Wilma asked faintly.)

So Marya rarely spoke of the visits to Father Shearing. She would not have wanted to be quizzed about his health, his condition—whether he was "making progress" after his operation or not. It was hateful enough if, in the corridor outside his room, or in the elevator, she found herself trapped in a conversation with one or another of Father's parishioners: had he lost more weight?—was that new medication affecting his eyesight?—*would* there be a second operation, did anyone know?—but wasn't the man a model for all to look up to: wasn't he a *saint?*

Marya repeated certain exchanges to Father Shearing, offering up little nuggets, gems, for his amusement. "They're saying now that you are a saint," she told him daringly, and he laughed harshly, and began to cough, and said, "Will I be offered any *choice?*"

It was always a mild shock to see him in bed; in white; graying frizzy curls at the V of his hospital gown, forearms bare, flesh pale and bruised and needle-pricked, the elegant white collar gone; a certain haggard look about his face. He was only in his late thirties and too young for any of this: too vigorous, too well-liked, too good-humored. Wasn't a sense of humor a protection against such bad luck . . . ? And what if it began to shade into bitterness, resentment . . . ?

One rain-darkened afternoon when Marya was his only visitor, he said suddenly, "What we're going to have to do,

Marya, is arrange some sort of abduction. 'Roman Catholic Priest Spirited Away From Hospital.' A secret plot. A conspiracy. And someone else can take my place in this damned bed.'' The remark was meant to be jocular, half teasing, but something was wrong: the tone was flat, the words slurred. It must have been the effect of the drugs they were giving him, Marya thought. It wasn't *him*. But she laughed just the same.

This was the long arduous winter when Marya, who knew herself generally disliked below (she *was* rude, she *was* haughty and impatient, why couldn't she help herself?), reasoned that she might have a chance with God. With Jesus Christ. With Mary most of all: Mary was a comfort, a human woman elevated to sainthood but still human, and not (so Marya supposed) inordinately bright. *She* loved the virtuous and the sinful alike, it was not her business to measure, to judge, to monitor thoughts and actions on earth. . . . Such intellectual vigilance belonged to men; to the male God and His Only Begotten Son.

Though Marya usually managed to impress and to please men—men of a certain type; and not often women.

Who made the world? the simple catechism began—God made the world, the catechism answered itself; and why did God make man?—to know, love, and serve Him in this world, and to dwell with Him in the next. It was all very clear. It was all very straightforward, uncontaminated by irony. (Irony, being sarcastic, being in Wilma's words "sour-mouthed"—these were Marya's most conspicuous defects. But she was struggling to overcome them. She *had* overcome them, generally.) Marya liked it that God had promised to be fair and just and merciful, punishing sin and rewarding virtue in keeping with the tenets of the Roman Catholic Church.

She liked it too that God cared not at all for outward appearances. He saw directly into the heart, the soul. He *was* the heart, the soul, even the body of man. . . . He dwelt within as sheer spirit and yet body. . . . (So Father Shearing had tried to explain to his catechism class at St. Anne's Cathedral. Spirit and body were one; Christ was man; the Eucharist—which they would one day soon be privileged to take, at Holy Communion—*was* both a wafer and the very body of Christ. *This is my body and this is my blood.* Did they understand? No? Yes? Then why did they look so puzzled? There were nine young people in the class—six girls and three boys—and apart from Marya they were subdued, slow to respond, vaguely anxious. They were in fact so docile that they sometimes forgot even to nod in agreement with what they were being told. And it struck them as faintly scandalous that Marya should laugh so loudly at Father Shearing's remarks when he gave every indication of speaking seriously, even solemnly. . . . It pleased Marya to shine even in that lusterless context; and if belief in the Catholic cosmology was a challenge to her natural sense of doubt, wasn't Marya the very person to meet such a challenge?)

In any case God saw the inner person, the real Marya Knauer, and would not judge her crudely, as her classmates did. That she was a "Knauer" first of all—that she lived in the backcountry, off the Innisfail Pike, on the unpaved Canal Road—that something mysterious had happened not only to one of her parents but to both: all these factors, disreputable enough in the human world, and, in the febrile little world of the Innisfail Senior High School, drawing frank pity and scorn, must serve to elevate her in God's judgment, if He was a just God. To be born a second time, to have the sins of one's parents washed away, to be free of personal history, at least for a space of time. . . . To contemplate the possibility (wild, terrifying) of declaring an actual *vocation* in the Church. . . .

God concerned Himself with souls, not bodies; certainly not faces. In the high school everything female depended upon being *pretty* or *not-pretty,* the universe divided along those blunt Manichean lines, but God, being pure spirit, scorned to take notice of such trivial things. It could not matter to Him that Marya Knauer was too tall for her age, too long-waisted and angular; that her chest was flat; that her mouth reflected discontent when she believed herself in a neutral mood; that her cheekbones were too prominent, and her brows thick and dark and straight—indeed, they grew across the bridge of her nose and might almost have formed one single censorious brow if, in rage and self-loathing, she didn't pluck them every few weeks. (Marya vowed not to be the kind of idiotic girl who worries constantly over her appearance— slipping into the lavatory between classes, for instance, to peer anxiously at her mirrored reflection. Nor would she turn into the kind of woman, like her aunt Wilma, who visibly warmed when paid a compliment; or, again like Wilma, who complained aloud about getting older.)

In other respects, however, the fact that God saw, or actually dwelled, within might bring with it certain complications. For when Marya successfully curbed her natural instinct to be impatient, or sarcastic, or frankly vicious—there *was* this side to her, she couldn't help it, being confirmed in the Catholic faith hadn't worked a miracle—did that mean that God read her instinct as *her,* and wasn't deceived by her behavior? Did that mean that God could not be deceived in any way, that one stood naked before Him, abject and trembling? *I have sinned in thought, word, and deed,* Marya whispered in the confessional, hiding her burning face in her hands; *deeds* and *words* being difficult enough to monitor, *thoughts* all but impossible. (She couldn't control her thoughts, Marya told Father Shearing not long after her confirmation at St. Anne's. She was half sobbing, squirming in shame and misery. "I try but I can't. I can't. Sometimes I think I might be going crazy," she said. To her relief Father Shearing did not make one of his condescending witticisms—he was often condescending about what constitutes "sin" for most Catholics—but said instead in a grave voice that she must try harder. And yet harder. "Such discipline is a matter of will," he told her. "And the will itself can be strengthened through exercise. *Don't despair.*")

Marya prayed not to think impure thoughts or to wish improper wishes; if, when saying the rosary, she began to pray mechanically, her imagination running wild, she forced herself to go back to the beginning and start again. Saying the rosary was the penance for most of the sins to which she had learned to confess, and saying the rosary again, and yet again, and again, was the penance for not saying it carefully enough, for skipping along the Mysteries when she ought to have been making her way on her knees. A flame of panic touched her, at such times, that she might be condemned to saying the rosary forever; to saying a few beads, losing the thread of her thought, going back to the beginning, and starting again; and again; never advancing more than a few wretched beads, a few murmured words, *Hail Mary full of grace, the Lord is with Thee, blessed art Thou amongst women and . . . Forever and ever, Amen*: Marya Knauer imprisoned in the circle of hell *that was the rosary itself.*

She didn't speak to Father Shearing of this particular terror, which she recognized as mad. Since the early days of her catechism class she had learned to suppress certain aspects of her personality in his presence: above all, any hint of weakness. She might be sinful in thought, word, and deed, but she was not going to be weak.

"Hello? Father Shearing?" Marya says in a low uncertain voice. "Are you awake?"

It is a cloudy afternoon in late January and Marya, breathing quickly and shallowly (because of the exertion of hurrying up the steep icy hill to St. Joseph's, because of the hospital smell which she hates), stands in the corridor just outside room 411, staring inside at the figure in the cranked-up hospital bed; telling herself as she invariably does at this moment —Marya is such a child, such a coward—that it isn't too late, she can always slip away, he hasn't seen her.

If he had another visitor, or if the room was crowded as it sometimes is in the late afternoon, Marya would be justified in slipping away. She seems to have nothing much to say to Father Shearing in the company of others, nor has he anything of substance to say to her: Marya's manner is silent, vaguely embarrassed and resentful; his is abstract, jocose, strained. But this afternoon there are no visitors and he is sitting propped up awkwardly with pillows, the crooked-neck reading lamp burning beside him, a book opened on his lap. Perhaps he is waiting for Marya, perhaps he has forgotten. Mondays and Thursdays are her days to visit, without fail. She has become a creature of fierce fidelity. Immediately after school, before she goes to her job at Cappy's Groceries (her hours are from six to nine-thirty, five days a week), she takes a crosstown bus, transfers to the Riverside Boulevard bus, hikes a quarter mile to St. Joseph's . . . which is in the "good" section of Innisfail, where the Knauers have no friends. It is a neighborhood of enormous houses, spacious lawns, steep leg-wrenching hills not perhaps meant to be covered on foot, and in such rotten weather.

Marya hesitates in the doorway, fumbling with her woolen scarf. She is still short of breath; her cheeks are probably flaming, her eyes too bright. She is a ferocious sort of angel, beetle-browed, glaring, when she wants only to be an angel of glad tidings.

"Father Shearing? It's Marya—"

As always, it is something of a shock and an embarrassment to see Clifford Shearing in bed, in a white gown. And pale, ravaged, thin, not altogether himself. . . . When he looks around at Marya his bruised eyes narrow at first as if he's blinded by light: there is a terrible moment (so Marya thinks, steeling herself) when he won't know who she is. Then of course he recognizes her, he smiles and welcomes her in, even lifts his good arm in an ebullient gesture—"Marya, how nice! —what a lovely surprise!—come in, come in, take a seat—are you alone?"

Are you alone! Marya thinks, subtly offended. As if she has ever *not* been alone in his presence.

She comes shyly forward, carrying her bookbag, shaking her long hair free of the collar of her coat. She knows herself ungainly and without charm, her feet enormous in salt-stained boots, her nose running. At least she has brought Father

Shearing a few of the books he'd requested last week; at least she has some excuse for being here.

He shakes her hand, formally, rather hard, as he always does; she feels her face redden even more deeply; is grateful for the distraction of taking off her coat, laying it awkwardly over a chair, murmuring replies to his barrage of bright falsely cheery questions ("And how is the weather today, *is* it as terrible as it looks?" —"Did you have a very hard time getting here?"—"Dear Marya, *did* you bring the books? you're amazing").

The first several minutes of a visit are always, to Marya, wonderfully giddy and confused, disorienting, as if she has blundered into a sheerly adult and codified situation. There are questions to be asked, remarks to be made, observations, small oblique witticisms. Father Shearing is in resolutely high spirits, it isn't one of his weak groggy days, though his voice is hoarser than Marya recalls, and the pupils of his eyes are dilated, and is that sickly sweet smell *his,* the smell of his smile, his wide bared teeth, his breath?

She sits, self-conscious and exhilarated; hands the books over to him; pretends not to notice the trembling of his fingers, the papery-thin texture of his skin; pretends not to mind how fully absorbed he is in leafing through the books, as if he has forgotten her. Shortly he will turn back to her, she knows: she has a purpose, after all, for being there (she is "assisting" him in certain professional tasks, even the stern-browed nuns who oversee St. Joseph's will grant her that), she isn't an idiotic besotted high school girl, one of a number of adoring parish females, who simply wants . . . who yearns. . . .

It is a pretense too, a strategy of hospital *politesse,* that one does not precisely see certain alarming medical accouterments: the clear plastic tube, for instance, that is attached to a trolley beside the bed, feeding into a vein in Father Shearing's left forearm.

Not long ago Father Shearing was awakened in the night by a severe coughing spell, so violent and prolonged that two of his ribs were cracked. Learning of it Marya responded in a childlike way: "Is that *possible?*" she asked. She was baffled, vaguely scandalized. Were such things possible? . . . a coughing spell, broken ribs. . . . She hasn't dared ask if the ribs are mending, or if anything like the coughing spell has recurred.

He is leafing hurriedly through *The Religious Dimension in Hegel's Thought* by Henrik Van Dorne, S.J.—published by the Fordham University Press, unavailable locally. (It had to be ordered from the university library at Port Oriskany, along with two of the other books.) He pauses, squints, reads a paragraph or two, holding his head at a new odd angle as if his vision is slightly askew. Marya is immediately jealous of the book. She is jealous of Van Dorne, a Jesuit of some reputation, one of Clifford Shearing's former teachers. Riding on the bus, Marya looked into the book, tried to get a sense of its voice, its general tone, though its larger pretensions, she knew, would elude her. *Determinism, destiny, the World-Spirit, Christ*: Marya was impressed, disturbed, finally rather restless: for had "Van Dorne" any voice at all?—weren't these simply pages of words, close-printed pages numbering more than five hundred? Granted, such words exert a curious sort of authority.

Clifford Shearing thinks well of himself, someone observed neutrally.

Clifford Shearing certainly thinks *well* of . . .

But this was before last September's trouble: the tests, the first exploratory surgery, the operation itself.

It was painful to see him now, Marya thought, carefully ridding her expression of anything resembling pain, and to remember him playing softball last summer. At the St. Anne's picnic in July. At Riverside Park. Lithe and fast and audacious and slightly bullying with the boys, but funny, quick-tongued as always, an exceptionally good pitcher. Gracious when he performed well; yet more gracious when he erred. Remarkable man! Watching him then, Marya had felt her gaze go hot and greedy, felt her blood beat in slow helpless adoration. Celebrating Christ. In motion, in the flesh. Celebrating God, that most elusive of spirits.

The thought eases into Marya's consciousness, cruel and quick as a sliver of glass, that if Father Shearing can die then anyone can die. Those whom he has blessed, those to whom he has fed the Holy Eucharist, those who adored and believed in him. . . .

Which is not an intelligent reason, after all, to hate him. Or even to be angry with him.

Marya must resist the impulse (it is too womanly, too solicitous) to help him with the books, to haul up into his arms that heavy grim-bound theological volume that has shifted to the foot of the bed. Father Shearing's left arm seems to be nearly useless now and his right less reliable than Marya remembers. (His pitching arm?—*that?*—but the thought is unworthy of her, the thought is immediately banished.) If Marya gives him aid with small things he can manage, or even with things he can't quite manage any longer, his genial expression will suddenly shift, he'll be wounded, angry with her. She knows, she has made that blunder; she has been present when others have made it. (One of the nuns, for instance. A youngish woman, plain, with colorless eyelashes and eyebrows, a nurse's air of sunny confidence awkwardly and not altogether convincingly overlaid upon a far more basic shyness; a fear, perhaps, of touching and of being touched; an awe of masculine flesh. And Clifford Shearing is a priest, after all: one never really is allowed to forget.)

So she lets him paw at the books, arrange them on his lap, panting slightly, muttering to himself. They are treasures of some mysterious sort though it is pointless of Marya to feel jealous of them. Her turn, surely, will come; he'll want to dictate a few letters to her, work on his essay ("Teilhard and the 'Mystery of Being' "), allow her to be of service, *use* her. . . .

And if it isn't too late by then, and no other visitors have dropped by, and Father Shearing seems to invite it, Marya will confide in him as she has now and then in the past. "What seems to be troubling you, Marya?" he has asked; the gentleness of his voice, the smiling solicitude of his manner, made her want to kneel before him, and press her warm face against his hands, and surrender everything in her of pride, rage, deep unhappiness . . . everything that was *Marya,* and consequently damned.

She is desperately lonely but she detests other people: she hates to be touched: recoils sometimes from a mere word, a smile, a smirk: vows to forget nothing and to one day exact her revenge.

She doesn't detest other people, that's a falsehood. (She is always telling lies. One lie propagates another, helplessly, luxuriantly.) In fact she is sick with envy of other people, lovesick, craven, in awe. . . . She would like to humble herself (humiliate herself?) before them. . . . The person she truly detests is herself: Marya in her silly spiritual pride, and Marya in her unspeakably disgusting body.

(She will glide rapidly past details. Father Shearing, as fierce and chaste as she, would be repelled by anything so low as physical details of this sort. How can an angel of glad tidings inhabit a body!)

And she is obliged to speak frankly of certain doubts that have begun to trouble her . . . that had in fact troubled her before her confirmation. (But let that pass, Marya doesn't want her confessor to suspect her of intellectual deceit.) In the beginning was the Word, and the Word was God. . . . And God is pure essence, containing no potentiality; and Christ is the Godhead made Flesh; and Mary, sweet Mary, Mary the Mother of God, was *bodily assumed* into Heaven. . . . Marya is fearful of succumbing to an attack of laughter; it can rack her like any physical spasm; she isn't herself at such times. But of course none of this is amusing. Only an imbecile would find it amusing. *I can understand,* Marya will say, frightened, pleading, *but I can't believe.*

It has crossed Marya's mind that her "doubts" constitute a kind of virginity. A more valuable sort of virginity than the merely physical sort. The struggle for Marya's soul, for her absolute conviction, is like a struggle for her virginity: she will surrender but without resistance, defiance. Perhaps she will even require being hurt.

(Once, in this room, in this spare white-walled cell adorned with a crucifix on one wall, she and Father Shearing had come very close to arguing. He was dictating notes to her on some abstruse theological point, Marya grimaced and shifted uneasily in her seat, he asked her what was wrong, she told him it all sounded improbable, he answered at once that it might sound *improbable* . . . but wasn't the nature of the atom improbable, the existence of the peacock improbable, man's pride and stupidity at this point in human evolution improbable? Marya made a faltering reply; Father Shearing answered; and Marya, knowing that she'd lost, groped for one further point—reached out literally, in fact, and picked up Father Shearing's wristwatch from his bedside table, saying *this* was real, *this* she could understand because she felt its weight in her hand and heard its ticking, but that other dimension, that other world of which he spoke so readily . . . *where was it*? He simply smiled; allowed her to finish; then took the watch from her fingers and turned it over and pried the back open, saying, Could you guess at the precision of the mechanism inside, judging simply from the outside? could you invent for yourself the extraordinary fineness of these wheels and cogs and springs? And, set beside this watch, what was the human brain? what must the creator of that brain be? "Wonders yielding wonders," he said, his voice nearly shaking. Marya stared in astonishment at him. She had never seen him so moved. *This* was faith, the real thing: wonders yielding wonders yielding wonders.)

But today's visit is different. Marya sees with a sinking heart that he is distracted by the new books, leafing through them, squinting, moving his lips. He is certainly aware of her presence, he isn't precisely rude, but she can't imagine that she is very real to him: she's only Marya Knauer, after all, a high school girl, an assistant of sorts, one of the minor figures in his life. The drugs, the radiation treatment, the mysterious incalculable procedures of the hospital . . . *is* this Clifford Shearing, after all? She should leave. He wants her to leave. But if she leaves in anger she'll cry herself sick in the women's rest room on the first floor as she has done, oh God how many times in the past, and no one will ever know or give a damn; certainly *he'll* never know.

She's restless, overwarm. She notes with a benign sort of contempt the expanding display of get-well cards on the windowsill, all but a few cast in a lugubrious religious tone, deathly white. And the rarely touched gifts—flowering plants (mums, gloxinia), jams, chocolates, best-selling novels of the lighter kind, innumerable boxes of homemade cookies and candies, even a needlepoint cushion. So many female parishioners, so much grief and concern! But who would die for him, Marya thinks resentfully, who would exchange her life for his . . . ?

Farther along the windowsill, and ranged in orderly piles on the floor, are some of the books and journals Father Shearing brought with him to the hospital, suspecting he wouldn't be back in the rectory for some time. Several volumes of Teilhard de Chardin, with *This I Believe* on top; Marcel's *The Mystery of Being*; Rahner's *The Christian Commitment*; commentaries on St. Thomas, Aristotle, Hegel. Here and there are paperback books, some of them Penguin books, of another sort—Tolstoy's *Master and Man,* the plays of Chekhov, poems by St. John Perse, novels by writers of whom Marya has never heard—Lagerkvist, Kawabata, Kafka, France. Early on, Father Shearing lent her two novels by Graham Greene which she devoured in a day and has wanted to talk about with him ever since, if only she knew how to introduce the subject of guilt and sin and adultery and grace so passionately commingled. . . .

Minutes pass. "You are so sweet, Marya, to have brought. . . ." Father Shearing murmurs, his voice trailing off. "So patient. . . ." He is looking through his disorderly portfolio of notes; his breath is audible; his face slightly flushed.

Marya wonders if he is suddenly running a fever—if she should call a nurse.

His handsome white-gold wristwatch is lying on the bedside table, propped up carefully to show the time. Swiss-made, and probably very expensive. It was a gift from his stepfather, Father Shearing once wryly remarked, a going-away present. Where is his family, Marya wonders, hasn't he any family? She has heard that the mother died years ago but surely there are brothers, sisters. . . . Though perhaps he is as alone as she. . . . Alone in Christ: joined in a kind of sacred matrimony to Christ. (Marya has been making inquiries lately about religious vocations, particularly those of the cloistered life. She would wear a plain gold wedding band inscribed with the word "Jesus"; she would spend her days in silent adoration of Him, and of the Father, and of Mary; she would intervene for others before God. Perhaps she would become a Carmelite sister and wear the long heavy brown robes, the strong severe bones of her face emphasized by white, stiff starched white. . . . Yet more rigorous, she believes, are the Benedictines. And the Poor Clare nuns, who discipline themselves routinely by whipping their backs with scourges of knotted cord. . . .)

Marya sees by Father's watch that it is twenty to five. The minutes are passing helplessly, inexorably. He isn't altogether himself this afternoon and it is childish of her to be disappointed or hurt. "Dear Marya, sweet Marya . . ." he murmurs, glancing toward her, raising a corner of his mouth in a semblance of a smile, "you are infinitely patient and I don't deserve. . . ." Marya sees herself as a blurred figure in the corner of his eye, too eager, too expectant, doomed to despair. ". . . A message to Monsignor about the vulgarity of my displacement . . . I mean my *replacement*. . . ."

It is a slip of the tongue that adroitly becomes an amusing remark. But Marya is slow to laugh.

She tells him she'll be happy to take down a letter for him; she has her notebook here. She screws off the top of her pen and waits but Father hasn't exactly located his notes and he isn't ready to begin and Marya's eyes fill with tears of anger and dismay, watching.

Are you going to die? I will never forgive you.

She must eat her supper between five-thirty and six. A hamburger and french fries, probably, or a toasted tuna fish salad sandwich, at the diner near Cappy's; or, if it isn't too freezing on Main Street, at the Royalton Café next to the Royalton Theatre. (This is Innisfail's single movie house, a place that never ceases to arouse Marya's uncritical interest. Outside there are posters of Robert Taylor, Ava Gardner, Lana Turner, Alan Ladd . . . Elizabeth Taylor in *Elephant Walk* . . . Gary Cooper in *High Noon*. . . . Inside, the lobby is hung in crimson velvet draperies, gilt-edged mirrors, cupid-angels frolicking amid huge golden grapes and vine leaves; it smells richly and warmly of stale popcorn, heavily salted, which Marya loves. A place of refuge on windy Main Street, a familiar stopping-ground, associated with a running nose and tear-dimmed eyes. Beautiful cosmetic faces behind smudged glass, men's bare torsos thick with muscle, hands wielding in triumph spears, rifles, tomahawks, smoking revolvers, submachine guns. . . .)

Father Shearing has begun his dictation but he speaks so slowly, repeats himself so frequently, that Marya is free to daydream. A man or a woman—no, a man, it must be a man —is lying paralyzed in a space he can't recognize; trapped in that terrifying state (which Marya has experienced for as long as she can remember, even before her parents went away) when dream images and dream voices mingle with those of the real world. Yet the "real" world begins to dissolve too, revealed as simply an extension of the dream. The sleeper, panicked, tries to wake—tries to move his head, his legs, an arm—but he's paralyzed, every muscle useless. The dream is seen as no longer *his*. And all this unfolds against a blurred background: that rather large mahogany and silver crucifix on the wall above Father's bed, Christ's bowed head crowned with dainty little thorns, every finger and toe of His agony represented, a work of art so frightening that it can only be interpreted as art. . . . And then, mysteriously, the sickish-warm odors of the Royalton lobby intrude, the ornamental mirrors reflecting one another reflecting shadowy faces, faces without bodies, mere gestures, anguished appeals. . . .

By a quarter past five Father Shearing is exhausted, clearly in pain; though when Marya rises to call in a nurse he makes a show of protesting. "But you just arrived! . . . and we have so much to cover . . ." he says, reaching out to restrain her with his good arm. "Marya, we have so *much*. . . ."

She calls in a nurse, however, and prepares hurriedly to leave.

The nurse is young, in her early thirties perhaps, Marya's height, Marya's weight. It's amazing how deftly she moves about the bed in her long white woolen habit, her headpiece starched, fixed rigidly in place. She wears white rubber-soled shoes; her rosary beads click softly, consolingly; her manner is forceful, efficient, unalarmed. But Father Shearing is given over to being a patient again, a very sick man.

"So awkward—no coherence," he tells Marya. He tries to smile one of his old savage mocking smiles. "Don't judge me by—*this*."

For days afterward her eyes well with sudden tears, her heart beats in angry despair. As if he doubted her! as if he felt required to say such things!

A tumor, thought at first to be benign. And then another. And another.

Marya has learned the terrible word *metastasis* and is sur-prised when Everard knows what it means. "It's how my father—your grandfather—died, I mean it was what they said he died of, finally. Started in his chest and spread. *Me-tas-ta-sis. Carcinoma.* You don't have to be in school, Marya," he says with the barest edge of contempt, "to know certain words."

Marya, comes the voice, gently, urgently, *Marya* . . . and she wakes at once because her heart has stopped.

But it hasn't stopped, it has only kicked in her chest, once, twice, and now it is beating normally. But she is terrified of hearing the voice again; she doesn't want to go back to sleep.

She has been dreaming about something dark and liquid and faintly phosphorescent that has nonetheless a human quality, a human essence. Flowing away, slipping away, running like quicksilver across the surface of a table or a counter or a bed. . . . *Marya, Marya,* comes the pleading whisper. The surface is hard as porcelain, grooved. Tilted. It cannot be a bed after all.

Marya lies rigid, steeled against the voice. She feels her spirit fly across the miles to St. Joseph's Hospital to that corner room on the fourth floor where Clifford Shearing is, or is not, sleeping. Is, or is not, still alive.

Hail Mary, full of grace. . . .

. . . If I could exchange my life for his. Amen.

But such bargaining is childish. Superstition. She doesn't believe, can't believe. When Father Shearing raises the Eucharist high above his head, when the delicate bell is rung, then, for an instant, Marya believes. When she kneels at the communion rail with her fingers tightly clasped together and takes the Eucharist in her mouth, flat on her tongue, pressed there by Father himself . . . then, for that space of a few seconds, she believes. Her heart swells in gratitude, her very spirit sings. *I love you God, thank you God, thank you for giving me life, I will never sin again.*

When Monsignor says Mass and not his young assistant, Shearing, Marya tells herself that she believes just the same: it's the same thrill of certitude, of ecstasy, when the wafer is pressed onto her tongue. No difference. How could there be any difference? . . . all are united in Christ Our Lord. Amen.

Marya keeps her rosary of clear blue plastic beads beneath her pillow, has affixed an ivory crucifix to her wall, wears a small St. Christopher's medal (which leaves tarnish marks on her skin) on a silver chain around her neck. She has a prayer book with a mother-of-pearl cover and pale crimson endpapers; she even has a pair of white cotton gloves with an eyelet design at the knuckles. Each Sunday while the Knauer household sleeps Marya prides herself in waking early—it's pitch-black these winter days—and trudging down the road to the pike, where she catches a ride to town, to eight o'clock Mass at St. Anne's, with the Dietzes. (Marya no longer takes Erma very seriously but doesn't mind her chattering; she likes Erma's parents when they don't nag at her about Everard and Wilma and why the entire Knauer family isn't going to Mass. . . . "Doesn't your uncle realize how serious it is?" Mr. Dietz asks Marya, looking at her by way of the rearview mirror, "not only his own soul but the souls of his family? He's an intelligent man, can't he be made to realize, to *realize* . . . ?")

Marya has been instructed by Father Shearing to pray for the rest of the family, which she does, though without a great deal of enthusiasm. There is very little likelihood of converting Everard, after all ("What kind of horseshit is this?" he'd once inquired, frowning over the Sunday bulletin Marya had brought home from church); Wilma thinks Catholics are "back numbers" and Catholic women in particular idiots— "Just like brood sows, having 'all the kids God sends' "; Lee thinks no more of the condition of his soul than he might think, for instance, of the condition of his intellect; Davy and Joey are just little boys who cannot possibly matter (so Marya tells herself idly) to God. As for Alice—Marya has observed her eyeing the rosary, the gloves, the navy blue straw hat Marya wears in warm months and the navy blue woolen hat she wears in cold months, and is halfway worried that Alice will one day want to convert too. Much of the value of Marya's being Catholic, after all, has to do with the fact that the rest of the Knauers are not.

Marya wonders if her mother, if she is still living, is a practicing Catholic. If she goes to confession, takes Communion, prays to be forgiven. Vera Sanjek. Vera who cuddled her in a drunken embrace, pretended to love her, told so many lies. Vera who gave Joey away. Falling-down-drunk and staggering-drunk. Stinking of vomit. "That bitch"—as her brother-in-law Everard called her—of whom no one has heard in seven years. Or, if they've heard, Marya hasn't been told. Marya hasn't been told a thing.

(She has brought the subject up to Wilma from time to time; she would never dare mention it to Everard. Once Wilma said, angry, laughing, that it wouldn't surprise her if Vera had been up in Powhatassie all these years—by which she meant the Women's State Correctional Facility some three hundred miles to the north. Why do you say that? Marya asked, and Wilma backed down at once. No reason: just said it. Another time when Marya brought the subject of her mother up Wilma responded even more angrily. "Who the hell do you think has been your mother all this time, you ungrateful little shit.")

Marya believes, Marya wills herself to believe, the challenge is to force herself to believe that which her very reason rejects. That which Clifford Shearing has explained so succinctly and so beautifully. Faith is surrendering oneself to God, after all; surrendering one's *self*. A matter of will and discipline. A matter of following certain time-honored techniques for overcoming the rebelliousness of the mind. (*I, I, I*, says the ego in its pride: but the soul remains silent, in infinite patience. Marya is reminded suddenly of poor Mr. Schwilk speaking of the faith that creates faith: so very *American* a proposition.)

Father Shearing has confided in her that it was difficult for him too at her age. "But gradually I realized that faith comes and goes—it can't be a constant. So even when I doubt God I am still honoring Him; even when I fall into despair over His existence and His plan for the world I am still contained within His love. Do you understand, Marya? *You* of all persons should understand."

She flushed in gratitude. She stammered yes. She did, oh yes she did, certainly she understood, there was nothing Marya Knauer couldn't grasp.

There is talk of transferring Clifford Shearing to another hospital, in another city; there is talk—promiscuous, unfounded

—that he is rapidly recovering and will soon be back at St. Anne's. (He will never return to St. Anne's, to his position as Monsignor's second assistant. It turns out that even before his hospitalization he had applied for a two-year leave, to study Thomist philosophy in France. He and Monsignor had never gotten along well: they were too much alike temperamentally.)

Marya returns to St. Joseph's, Marya is relieved that Father Shearing is no worse, that he "holds his own," he's stubborn, grim, funny, intermittently his old self. But his humor is slightly askew. When Marya visits him one Thursday afternoon in February another visitor drops by, and still another—and Father Shearing, flushed, animated, cries out wittily: "No one visits me for days and here you are all at once—a case of a single bird being killed by three stones."

Marya grasps the sour subtle logic behind the remark but doesn't laugh; the others, though they don't quite comprehend, laugh uneasily. Is Father mocking them? What is he mocking? Marya, embarrassed, excuses herself and slips away early.

This is the afternoon she decides to skip supper, goes to the Royalton to see a movie. Her senses are so aroused, her mood so jangled—what else can she do? She wants something extreme. Glamorous, garish. Fated. Cruel. Her head is ringing with words she cannot say aloud, her blood pumps hot and steady, simply walking along Main Street at this time of day —early dusk, the stores closing, the streetlights and cars' headlights just coming on—excites her powerfully. To be alone; to be alone as she is, in downtown Innisfail; not trapped in that overheated ill-smelling room at St. Joseph's, or at the kitchen table at home; not fixed, not *seen,* in anyone's mind except her own: what unexpected joy, verging upon ecstasy!

She doesn't even mind the freezing wind. The uphill climb. The crowds milling past her, store clerks and office workers on their way home, shoppers, older schoolchildren like herself. No one knows her and she knows no one; by chance she doesn't even glimpse a familiar face; she might be in a distant city and not Innisfail after all—a place of infinite possibility, of unguessed-at riches. It is so simple, Marya thinks, her heart swelling with certitude, she *is* happy; she *is* blessed. But she will be required to leave Innisfail to realize it.

That afternoon she makes herself slightly sick on popcorn, a box of mints, a stale chemical-tasting ice cream sandwich devoured greedily in the dark. Each time she visits Father Shearing he urges her to take home something—anything—of the untouched candies and cookies and fruit on the windowsill; but Marya has always declined, worrying that a terrible greed, an incalculable hunger, might overcome her even in his presence. The very concept of *appetite,* he's said, has become puzzling to him; he has been on a hospital diet of liquids and soft foods for so long, he can't precisely remember . . . what it is he is trying to remember.

Marya sits in the dark, in her coat, staring mesmerized at the screen, waiting to feel something extraordinary. But the exhilaration of the day is winding down. Her nose is running; there is a faint persistent ache in her throat; she is anxious now that she'll be recognized, or has already been recognized going in the theater—it's slightly shameful, eccentric, going to a movie alone, especially at such a time. There are so few patrons in the house, Marya is acutely aware of them. A youngish man a few seats to her right (he looks familiar, does she know him? is he perhaps one of Lee's friends?) has been eyeing her covertly. . . .

She stares mesmerized at the gigantic images flashing before her but in truth she's seeing nothing, absorbing nothing. And in any case she is obliged to leave the film before its conclusion—she has to be at work by six o'clock. As she is leaving, however, the young man leans toward her with an air of urgency and says, "Hey—how come you're leaving? don't you like the movie?" He is sly, grinning, a little nervous. Marya sees that he's a stranger. "Go to hell," she says, without troubling to lower her voice.

She stalks out of the Royalton as if she is being observed but of course she is not. Who would be observing her, except God?

Afterward Marya will try to estimate how many conversations she had with Clifford Shearing during the eighteen-month period of their acquaintance. Probably no more than a dozen. Perhaps even less. It was an accident that he led the class in instruction at St. Anne's—she couldn't have known, making her blind request for help ("I'm Catholic—I was born Catholic —but I've never known what it means") that Father Shearing would be the person to answer her questions; she had had the confused notion that it would be a nun.

After the first session he took her aside, smiling, curious. He stood tall and lean in his priest's costume: black, sheerly black, with the stark white turned-around collar. Marya was abashed, slightly dazed, but took note of his amused expression, his air of friendly condescension, even the white-gold wristwatch on his left arm. "What is your motive for coming into the Church?" he asked. The question was so frank, so blunt, Marya answered as directly: "I don't know." "You've been talking with Catholics, I assume? reading about Catholicism?" he asked. "But no one in your family is a practicing Catholic at this time?" Marya resisted the impulse to stammer. She wasn't going to flinch beneath the gaze of this extraordinary man—she'd known at once that he *was* extraordinary, that there was no one like him in Innisfail—but it was difficult to sort out his questions, to guess what it was he might be most impressed to hear. So she told the truth, raising one shoulder in that half shrug that was so awkward a habit, speaking rather sullenly: "I told you I don't *know.* It just seemed to me time." She paused, flushing slightly; feeling the sharpness of his interest, his surprised approval. She said, "Maybe I was afraid I would die or something. I will die, I mean. Before I knew...." But here her brave voice faltered, she knew she was an idiot, she had better retreat. "Before I knew . . . what it was all about."

This must have been the perfect answer, since Father Shearing did nothing but nod, staring at her. She had not known that priests were so young. She may even have been somewhat disappointed in his very youth, his friendliness, at that time.

Marya daydreams in school, filling the margins of her notebooks with angular heraldic figures, sketching out stories and miniature plays, heated exchanges of dialogue (bodiless, characterless) pages long. For weeks it is so difficult to think of Father Shearing as the man in the hospital—*that* man, *that* particular hospital room—that she doesn't think of him at all in that situation: she thinks of him, sees him in her mind's eye, as the priest who welcomed her into the rectory office that afternoon, disconcerting her with his handshake . . . as if it were a commonplace in Innisfail, or out along the Canal Road, for adult men to shake hands with someone Marya's age. (In fact adult men in Marya's world rarely shook hands with one another. They would have been puzzled, embarrassed. Handshaking, like certain other gestures of camaraderie—equality? —belonged to another class entirely.) She draws priest figures in her notebook; tries, and fails, to reproduce Father Shearing's face; sits slouched and discontent, her mind drifting free, circling about an image of a man paralyzed in a state between sleep and waking, a spirit trapped in a body, yearning for its freedom. So lost is she in her reverie, so evidently distressed, one of her teachers calls upon her suddenly, half annoyed, joking, "Marya, wake *up*. The bell is going to ring in another minute and you won't want to be left behind."

Marya is in her glory through much of February, transcribing Father Shearing's thoughts. He has abandoned his essay on Teilhard in the interests of something more ambitious, a far longer work, unsystematic, wayward, springing from Van Dorne's study of Hegel but ultimately larger, more spacious; a meditation that will reveal its significance only at the end. The treatments, the intense medical attention, must be doing him some good: he speaks in inspired rushes, sometimes for minutes at a time, leaving Marya quite astonished. *Maréchal's challenge to Thomistic metaphysics. . . . Barth on Hegel: that great question mark, that great disappointment, yet also a great promise. . . . Künstler's vision of the ontic perspective and the God-world-happening, a phenomenon of God's free grace. . . .* Marya sits hunched over her notebook, her hair in her eyes, writing as quickly as she can. These are unique sessions, she is fairly glowing with excitement, she sees now that many of her worries were unfounded. Father has told the nurses to keep everyone else out, he's working and doesn't want to be disturbed.

As a seminarian, even in his early twenties, Clifford Shearing began to publish theological and philosophical essays. He has lent Marya several journals—*Thomist Quarterly, Thought, Renascence, American Metaphysics*—and she has carefully read his pieces, not with full comprehension, perhaps, but with unqualified awe. To be able to write so well, to wield such a vocabulary; to *argue* so powerfully; to ferret out miscalculations in a rival's thesis to a mere hair's-breadth of a degree . . . she wonders if it is an entirely masculine skill, an art of combat by way of language, forever beyond *her.*

Lately, however, Father has expressed impatience with his earlier writings. He has boasted that his new position will make certain fossilized priest-scholars sit up and take notice. "If only I can find the precise words, the perfect words. . . . If only I can duplicate my vision in this absurd fallen world. . . ."

Marya appears at St. Joseph's three afternoons in succession. The floor nurses have begun to regard her with a certain bewildered respect, or is it resentment? Surely in all the diocese a man of Father Shearing's distinction might find someone more appropriate to assist him. This graceless high school girl, shy, unsmiling, secretive, always hurrying as if she feared being challenged and sent away: where, they wonder, did Father come upon *her*? And isn't she in any case rather young?

If man tries to reach God through the discipline of the intellect the only God accessible is Aristotle's . . . the unmoved mover, the

*self-thinking thought . . . pure act . . . a God to whom creation can
have no meaning and the individual no existence. It is the God-
beyond-measurement we seek, wholly God and yet not specifically
God-as-man: for God-as-man is Christ, and Christ supremely, in the
mystery of the Incarnation. Consequently our perspective must be
violently altered if. . . .*

As Marya prepares to leave, Father Shearing takes hold
of her arm and says, "You won't abandon me, will you? Suddenly? Overnight? There's no one else," he continues, faltering, vague, confused, "this seems to be a corner position—
uncharted—*terra incognita*—"

Marya dreams of cool chaste white walls, a cloistered cell with
a grilled window, a small altar on which have been placed a
representation of Christ, a Bible, and a single votive candle.
She sees herself as a swift shadowy presence, clad in white, a
rosary clicking at her side. . . . But when she asks Father
Shearing his opinion of cloistered nuns his attitude is
bemused, doubtful. He objects first of all, he says, to the fact
that they are cloistered; which obliges others to take care of
them. And—as if he can't resist—"Each of the nuns prides
herself on being the bride of Christ! making of poor hapless
Jesus a sort of randy harem sheik, a manic polygamist. Really,
Marya," he continues, wriggling the fingers of his good hand,
"*you* must have more sense than that, *you* aren't going to hide
your talents behind a grilled window."

Wilma says with a chuckle that it's one way of solving the
problem Catholic women have.

Marya asks, "What is the problem Catholic women
have?"

"Wait until you're married," Wilma says. "Then you'll
know."

Talents? Marya wonders, hearing that rough hoarse lightly
jeering voice. Is he sincere, or simply trying to be kind? As

a Knauer, as a Canal Road girl, Marya is as accustomed to people being kind as she is to their being nasty. But it never rings quite as true.

"What exactly do you do there?" Wilma inquires, meaning St. Joseph's, meaning room 411. Marya tells her, quietly, with pride, that she is assisting Father Shearing with his literary work. She is in fact his "assistant"—he speaks of her to others in those terms.

Wilma asks if the work is hard. How many hours a week, approximately.

Is he paying her? or the diocese? Is the diocese paying her?

Marya, offended, says she is doing it because she wants to. Father Shearing can hold a pen (more or less) but he can't write at the present time; his handwriting is indecipherable. So she's helping him out. In any case she already has a job, hasn't she, at Cappy's.

"Yes, but they pay you for that job, don't they," Wilma says, sucking at her cigarette with a certain unmistakable zest, edging toward a fight.

But Marya, the new Marya, Marya who has converted to Catholicism and is even now wearing a dime-sized St. Christopher's medal around her neck, hidden beneath her clothes, Marya can't be drawn in that direction. She says in her new calm sweet maddening voice, "You wouldn't understand."

But she is beginning to feel exhaustion beforehand, running up the stairs to the fourth floor of St. Joseph's, settling herself into that hard-backed chair beside Father's bed. Her head rings at virtually any time with his droning insistent words; the rosy underside of her eyelids seems to be imprinted with his gaunt face, his thin-lipped smile. "Are you ready, Marya? Shall we begin? I've been waiting. . . ."

Even as she transcribes the flood of his words she notes his bruised arms, the prominence of his facial bones, the small glistening sores about his mouth. His curly hair has long since turned lank; each time it is shampooed by one of the orderlies it grows thinner, it seems to lose color. A new medication is being spoken of—a "radical" new form of chemotherapy. Or will he be transferred to another hospital after all? The Roswell Clinic in Buffalo, perhaps; Sloan-Kettering in New York City. Marya resists the impulse to flinch at the sight of the needle marks on his forearms—that papery-thin discolored flesh, so often violated. Always, the nurses are drawing out specimens of his blood; always they are monitoring his urine; he jokes that nothing is *his* any longer, it is simply being produced for the sake of the laboratory and its "inconclusive prognosis."

Sometimes he loses the thread of his thought and requires Marya to read what she has written. On that afternoon of her final visit Marya reads, stumbling: " 'The tragic error of all previous commentaries has been to substitute mere word-concepts for. . . . The tragic error of all . . .' "

Father Shearing tells her to stop; she must be exhausted.

"You *sound* exhausted," he says half accusingly.

Marya begins to protest but he silences her. For a long awkward moment—a very long moment—no one speaks.

Only the wristwatch's ticking is conspicuous, and Father Shearing's shallow erratic breath. He is angry with her; she has disappointed him; she shifts uneasily in her seat. Someone passes by the opened door but it is a stranger with another destination: Marya feels a sharp tinge of regret.

You don't seem to understand—I will die in your place.

If there is a just God, if there is any mercy in Him, something more than wrath . . . accident . . . stupidity. . . .

"I suppose you resent this drain on your time and I can't blame you," Father Shearing says. His head is resting lightly on a pillow; his reddened eyelids are half closed. But he eyes her narrowly, suspiciously. "There must be an infinity of things you'd rather do with your time . . . you're how old, after all? . . . seventeen? Or younger? Boyfriends, school activities. . . ."

"No," says Marya uncertainly.

"A girl your age. . . . And I'm a foregone conclusion, after all. A poor investment. Not really worth abducting, spiriting away."

They are both subtly shocked by what Father Shearing has said and for another long uneasy moment neither speaks. Then he says with a sigh, as if he has already blundered too far, he cannot retreat, ". . . Did you ever come close to drowning? . . . no? That's fortunate. Or maybe it isn't: you learn certain things, you're baptized. I was about eleven years old, diving off a dock, and somehow it happened that I struck the water at the wrong angle, stunned myself, couldn't surface, kept sinking . . . and everything was very green, very dark. . . . What struck me at the time was the perpendicular nature of . . . of the experience. The surface of the water was high up, far over my head, farther than any ceiling I had ever seen; the bottom was muddy, black. . . . I remember being pulled down. It was as if a force was pulling me down. And then . . ."

"What happened?" Marya asks. "Did someone save you?"

"I don't remember."

"You don't *remember*!" Marya says. The tension between them makes her nervously giddy, chiding. "How can you not remember?"

"I assume I was saved," Father Shearing says dryly. "Or maybe I saved myself. But afterward I was violently sick to my stomach and passed out and really didn't remember. Yes, someone hauled me out of the water, I was told that had happened, but I didn't really remember and I don't remember now." He pauses, breathing hard. "I've forgotten why I'm telling you this. Something about the green, the dark . . . being sucked down. . . . Baptized in that way. . . ."

"It must have been a terrifying experience," Marya says, licking her lips.

"Don't be stupid, Marya," Father Shearing says at once. "All experience is terrifying."

Marya blinks in surprise as if he has slapped her.

Then he says, reaching over suddenly to take hold of her hand, to grip her fingers tight in his, "But don't be afraid, *I can show you the way.*"

Marya is too shocked to resist. Her immediate concern is simply for the opened door—what if someone enters, what if they are seen? Her heart is beating so powerfully she is close to fainting. She has been thrown off balance and obliged to lean far forward, clumsily, precariously—

Father Shearing's words now tumble from his lips, not quite coherently, but with feeling, animation. He is trying to explain to Marya about something he always wanted: not Aristotle's God, not Thomas's. Not God at all, perhaps.

". . . everything," he whispers, staring at her.

Marya is suspended, undefined. She tells herself this is sin, sinful, but she isn't frightened, she can wrench her hand from his if she wishes, she can stammer an excuse and escape if she wishes.

He continues to grip her hand. Tight, tighter. He clears his throat and says dryly, self-mockingly, "I only wanted everything, Marya, was that too much to ask . . . ?"

Father Shearing is transferred in early March to a clinic in New York City; he disappears from Innisfail and from Marya's life overnight.

He lives on for months, months. The death doesn't occur until autumn, the funeral services are in a distant part of the state, a number of parishioners from St. Anne's makes the trip but Marya Knauer does not. She has been thinking of him as dead for some time, evidently. She has hardened her heart.

It excites a great deal of comment in the parish that Father Shearing has willed a Swiss watch to Marya Knauer—a watch like that must be expensive, after all, worth hundreds of dollars (so people speculate, complain); and in any case what can *she* do with it?—it's a man's watch.

The summer after Marya's high school graduation, the summer of the going-away party, Emmett Schroeder began suddenly to say, "We love each other, we should get married, shouldn't we get married?"—in his low rapid faintly embarrassed voice that made Marya think uneasily that he was angry with her. "We love each other, don't we? we should get married, then."

It had the air of an argument, an old quarrel. We love each other, *we should get married.*

The surprise of Emmett's interest, the prevailing miracle of it, did not fail to astonish Marya. That Emmett Schroeder should want to get married. That Emmett Schroeder should want to marry *her.* (For Marya was a Knauer, after all. No matter how she prided herself on being different, superior. And she'd made a spectacle of herself—so it was generally thought—giving that spirited valedictory address at the high school, reciting a memorized speech in a quavering voice that, emblazoned with quotations from Thoreau and Emily Dickinson and Dostoyevsky and Teilhard de Chardin, left nearly everyone in the audience baffled and resentful. Marya Knauer! so people murmured, disapproving, annoyed. Who does she think she is, putting on airs? *talking like that in public?*)

Emmett Schroeder must have been as offended by that valedictory speech as anyone. For days afterward he didn't call and Marya thought wildly that she'd lost him—as she was always losing friends, this past year in particular. Everyone is proud of you, Marya, her teachers said, because she was the only senior in Innisfail to win a state merit scholarship (and a matching "need" scholarship from the State University at Port Oriskany), and she'd won four of the nine awards presented to graduating seniors at commencement; but Marya knew that wasn't true. Aloud she said, Thank you. Secretly she said, Like hell. They hate me, they're *jealous* of me.

(It was even suspected that one or two of the other academic awards really should have gone to Marya Knauer: there was no one in the class who came close to her academically, not even Robbie Ducharme, who had been admitted to Cornell, not even Warren Maccabee, who was so dull, so slow, so plodding, so unfailingly thorough, Marya's classmates naturally believed him superior to them all.)

A few days after the commencement speech—in fact it was five, Marya counted them—Emmett came by to see her. Without an explanation for having failed to call, without even a word of praise for her performance. If Marya's defiant speech on the "repellent" nature of American conformity had stirred him, or if it had angered him, or disappointed, he never said; but then he was a fairly reticent person and his long silences often made Marya uneasy. What are you thinking about so hard, Marya sometimes asked, jabbing him playfully in the ribs, turning her nervousness into a joke (this had become such a habit with her, done with such high spirits and bravado, Marya never questioned what lay behind it), are you angry with me? She would lean against him, make a show of feeling slighted, left out, hurt; if the circumstances were right she'd even kiss him, burrow her face against him as if they were lovers. And Emmett would laugh in exasperation and say, Marya, other people aren't like *you*—just because we're not talking it doesn't mean we're thinking secret thoughts.

So it astonished her that Emmett Schroeder should want to marry her. That he should say, with that air of subtle reproach that greatly flattered her, We love each other, we should get married, it's time to get married—isn't it?

Marya wondered if he could be serious. If he would really marry her. (What about his parents? Mrs. Schroeder had never said an unkind word against Marya, so far as Marya knew, but she could judge by the woman's manner of greeting her—that prim little twisted smile—that she didn't like her at all.) Wilma said she didn't trust the Schroeders, and just the look of Emmett—taller than Marya by a good five inches, wide in the shoulders, with thick dark hair and broad Slavic cheekbones and a spare measured smile that cut through you like a knife (so Wilma complained) announcing, I am better than you, my family has more money than you—just the look of him offended her. He'd been in the marines and he was twenty-six years old (and Marya was only seventeen) and his father had built his construction business up out of nothing so naturally he was tightfisted and suspicious and wouldn't want a Knauer marrying into the family. . . . So Wilma fussed, speculated aloud. "And he isn't Catholic, Marya," she said (meanly, teasingly), "doesn't that make a difference?"

But Marya refused to discuss Emmett with Wilma; she shrank from discussing certain volatile subjects with her in any case. "You can't possibly have an opinion about him," she told Wilma. "Not an *informed* opinion."

To Emmett she said nervously, "But I'm starting college in September."

He was bemused, skeptical. "But are you really?" he said, smiling, as if he knew a secret Marya didn't know: she would never leave Innisfail any more than he would.

Faltering, vague, Marya protested that she *had* to go, didn't she? she'd been awarded that scholarship, in fact two scholarships, she couldn't disappoint people. There had even been such a flattering piece in the newspaper. . . .

Emmett told her she'd been saying that all summer. She really wanted to get married, she really wanted to stay in Innisfail, but she was afraid of making people angry with her —"disappointing" them was how she phrased it. And he went on to name, contemptuously, the names of various Innisfail teachers—a familiar litany he had long outgrown.

"You could turn those scholarships down and nobody would give a damn," he said. "They can't make you go anywhere if you don't want to."

"Emmett, I have to go, I can't back out," Marya whispered.

He closed his thumb and forefinger about her wrist, as he often did, in play. And then gave a little twist. Also in play: though it did hurt.

He said, "You don't have to go anywhere you don't *want* to, Marya."

Still, he wanted to drive her to Port Oriskany in early July, just after the holiday weekend, so that she could find a room for the fall, and a job of some kind. Marya didn't want to live in university housing if she could avoid it; she couldn't bear the thought of having a roommate—a stranger; some nights this past year her nerves were so raw, her pulses leaped with a startled urgency she couldn't define, she had to leave the bedroom she shared with Alice to sleep on the couch in the front room, or even on the porch. Her thoughts unusually sharp, her blood pulsing hot and sullen, she had a fantasy of wandering off into the scrub forest behind the car lot . . . losing herself in the foothills of the Chautauquas, or in the mountains themselves. She'd be alone then. Unobserved, unmonitored. With nobody picking at her or judging her or wanting to marry her.

"As soon as I leave home," Marya had been telling everyone during her senior year, "I intend to begin a private life. I've had enough of crowds!"

She was boastful, vain, not entirely serious perhaps; she often said things simply to hear how the words struck the air, what sort of spin they had. How they affected others—forcing them to laugh, or to arch their eyebrows quizzically, even to ask her to repeat herself, they hadn't quite *understood*. (Marya had long ago seen that to be *liked* demanded a sort of maidenly passivity, a hopefulness, she had very little talent for; but to be *disliked*—it was not only easier in many ways, but yielded a queer sort of pleasure.)

She *didn't* hate her family, *didn't* feel superior to them, but . . .

It was true that she and Wilma no longer got along, but . . .

She liked her uncle, and she liked Alice, and her brothers were all right (though in truth Davy was becoming a problem), but, still, she wanted to get away; she wanted a room that so much belonged to her she could shut the door and lock it and no one would even know it was locked.

All this didn't mean, she protested, that she didn't love Emmett. She half lay in his arms, her mouth pressed against his, for what seemed to be hours. His greedy clutching hands and his impatience with her were immensely flattering. If you love me, why don't you want to marry me? Emmett asked. As he had been asking, If you love me why don't you want to sleep with me . . . ?

Marya tried to tell him, I don't want to sleep with anyone.

She tried to tell him, I love you but I don't want to sleep with anyone. I don't *want* to.

But he didn't understand; he was hurt; and then again he was angry—one night, a week before he drove her to Port Oriskany (he insisted upon driving her, he didn't want her to take a Greyhound bus), he took her head in both hands and began to shake it up and down, and from side to side, as if he wanted to snap her neck. She'd been so frightened her knees had buckled; she couldn't even scream. She thought, My God, he's going to kill me and it will be my fault.

Afterward Emmett said, flushed, ashamed, "You don't

want to lie to me, Marya. About loving me or not. Because I can't stand to be *lied* to. Do you understand?"

On the drive to Port Oriskany, two-hundred-odd miles to the west, Emmett was good-natured, even husbandly. He was proud of his car, a new Buick, and he clearly enjoyed driving —the simple act of driving, pressing down hard on the accelerator, gripping the wheel tight, easing in and out of traffic, passing everyone he could manage, even trucks careening along at ten miles beyond the speed limit. Marya noted his air of authority, his satisfaction, his well-being. She was grateful for the fact that much of the time he wasn't aware of her at all (she could read a paperback book, she could scribble in her journal): except to ask her now and then to get him a beer from the back seat (if he couldn't have it chilled he'd drink it warm—he wasn't, as he said, fussy), or to tune the radio better, or to sit closer to him: so he didn't get to feeling he was alone. When rain drummed on the roof and windshield and the headlights of oncoming cars rushed at them out of the mist Emmett said, with a tenderness in his voice Marya hadn't heard often before, "Isn't it nice in here . . . isn't it *safe?*"

Marya lay against him, drowsily watching the highway. She hadn't been able to sleep very well the night before; there had been a number of nights that summer that she'd lain awake, her mind racing, thinking of the university, of Port Oriskany (which she had never visited), of the fact that she would be only one of 15,000 students. . . . It was one thing to impress teachers in Innisfail, or to have struck the eye of, say, Clifford Shearing; it would be quite another thing to excel in so competitive a setting. If her grade-point average fell below a B for more than two semesters she would lose the merit scholarship. She hadn't any idea how difficult college would be, Port Oriskany in particular, though the lawyer for whom she worked this summer, a man named Fowler, had gone to Port Oriskany before law school in Buffalo, and she thought *him* unexceptional: but he must have done fairly well as a student.

If I fail, Marya thought, if I have to come back home—
I'll kill myself.

(But why, why such thoughts? lying sleepless night after
night. She had fixed upon college, upon the possibility of
failure there; but if that subject—so vaporous, so speculative
—ceased to hold her interest, she simply worried about other
things. Her increasingly strained relations with Wilma, her
odd lack of feeling, or, at any rate, much feeling, for either of
her brothers; the fact that her mother *might* be living, *might*
be actually accessible. . . . On really bad nights she found
herself thinking of that November morning so many years ago
when she'd been awakened by her mother and taken over to
the Kureliks' and then to town and then to. . . . She drifted
off to sleep frequently, thinking of that trip to town, the airless
cab of the truck, the baby's smell, Kurelik's voice and her
mother's silence and something rattling in the rear of the
truck, bottles? milk cans? She drifted off to sleep still safe in
the truck, she never got as far as Shaheen Falls and the court-
house square.)

In any case she had Emmett. She loved him and she
would probably marry him after a year or two at Port Oriskany. Her cousin Alice was going to be married in a few
months and several of her classmates were already married
and a number were engaged and . . . and so, why should Marya
behave differently? It was a *coup* to have attracted Emmett
Schroeder's attention, let alone his love; she would be an idiot
to throw it away.

But she did want to leave Innisfail, at least for a year. She
wanted to see what it was like, living away from home. At
college. Where no one knew she was Marya Knauer, and no
one could feel pity for her, or jealousy. Where she could begin
again, give birth to herself (so Marya's lyricism soared, at such
times) at the age of eighteen.

Three hours to Port Oriskany, in the rain; steady driving. And
then three hours back that night. (Because Wilma wouldn't
allow her to stay away overnight, and where could they have

stayed but a motel? "That's all we need next," Wilma said sourly, "to have people talking about you and him, and that bitch of a mother of his on the phone with *me.*") Marya loved Emmett as she lay close against him, her arm slipped through his, her fingers lazily squeezing his wrist; she loved him when they stopped at roadside cafés like any young married couple, sitting close together in booths, reading menus aloud, nudging each other, whispering private jokes, kissing. Marya's hair fell to her waist in glossy waves, a thick dark mane that looked black in some lights, chestnut-brown in others, and though she privately knew herself ugly, her hair *was* beautiful. She allowed herself a measure of pride in it, reasoning that though it was hers it wasn't *her.* When Emmett buried his face in it and inhaled deeply, clowning, snorting like a horse, yet genuinely moved to admiration, Marya thought that he was right, he was justified in loving her and in wanting to be her husband; and his desire for her (of which she was much aware) had the power to make her desire him. *We love each other, we should get married.*

But sometimes the country-and-western songs Emmett liked to play on the radio grated against her nerves, and the places he stopped at, and the food he ordered. . . . Marya particularly found fault with the food, cole slaw doused in sugar, french fries dripping in grease: as Emmett said, you'd think from the way she criticized restaurants she ate in them all the time.

"I'm not criticizing anything," Marya protested in surprise, "I'm just pointing out what's wrong. . . ."

The city of Port Oriskany was so large, the university campus so sprawled and confusing, Emmett himself became intimidated. He was forced to stop at gas stations and ask directions: Marya saw that he was badly discomfited, having to ask directions. But he managed to make his way along the hilly one-way streets, stopping at houses that advertised rooms, boarding, rates-for-students, until Marya found something that was suitable (her first question was invariably, How much?); he managed to cheer her up when she became, by early afternoon, inexplicably depressed ("Come *on,* this isn't anything, you should have seen what they did to me in the marines"). When Marya stood at a long dirt-encrusted counter in the university's employment office filling out a job application, she stopped midway and looked back at Emmett, slouched against the wall, smoking a cigarette, his hands in the pockets of his jeans—handsome Emmett Schroeder, the most remarkable of her prizes—and she had two thoughts simultaneously: the first, that she really should rip the application in two, and return to Innisfail, and marry Emmett (who, tired and sullen and faintly contemptuous, would brighten into a smile if he saw her watching him); the second, that she was through with Emmett, and when she signed her name at the bottom of the form she was signing herself away from him. There, she thought, signing *Marya Knauer* with unusual clarity, that's done.

And then the ride back home. In the dark, in the slow drizzling rain. Stopping again for supper—spaghetti and meatballs, beer, black coffee; and, in the car, in the dim-lit parking lot, easing into their familiar embrace, not minding that Emmett's hard mouth hurt hers, or that his fingers clutched impatiently, almost angrily, at her, working beneath her clothing as his breathing grew hoarse and tight. She told herself, All right. And tried not to resist. Except to stiffen involuntarily as she always did, when his breath was nearly a sob, and she felt he might break her neck or her backbone in his passion—it was so blunt, so direct, so desperate. All right, she whispered, her teeth nearly chattering with fear, I love you, Emmett I love you, though a part of her mind wanted to rear away and laugh contemptuously: Why are you doing this? Who do you think you're deceiving?

Emmett sensed her apprehension, he might even have sensed that hard mocking voice. He moved away from her; though his face was slick with perspiration and there were grim lines running from his nostrils to the edges of his mouth, he looked down at her nevertheless with an expression of impenetrable dignity, and said, "All right then, *you*—go to hell."

He drove the rest of the way to Innisfail without speaking. Marya began to cry. "I love you, you know I love you," she whispered guiltily, but Emmett didn't trouble to reply, perhaps didn't even hear. He had worked the Buick up to seventy-five, seventy-eight, eighty miles an hour along a curving highway, slowing only when walls of fog drifted across the road. "Emmett please, I'm sorry, I can't help it," Marya said almost inaudibly, "I get so nervous, you know how I am . . . but you know I love you," while a part of her thought calmly: There, that's done.

By midsummer Marya's insomnia kept her awake through much of the night, night following night; she swayed and staggered through the days, her eyes bruised, her head aching. Everyone thought it was because she and Emmett had broken up (" 'Broken up'?" Wilma asked, pretending to take it casually, "was it your doing finally, or his?") but in fact it seemed to be because of Port Oriskany and what was coming in the fall: the steep narrow streets, the unfamiliar buildings; whether, with no one from home to observe, she would finally stop attending Mass; whether she would do as well there as everyone expected. If I fail I'm not coming home, she told herself; then again, a moment later, If I fail I could telephone Emmett and he'd come and get me, I know he'd come and get me.

But she wouldn't call him. And, in any case, he wouldn't have come.

He had loved her; but now, it seemed, he hated her. He really did hate her.

Bonnie Michalak dropped by at Fowler's office to ask Marya, with a cruel little half smile of bewilderment, "What on earth happened to you and Emmett?" And Erma Dietz, now Erma Jelinski, married six weeks and at least three months pregnant, caught at Marya's sleeve in Woolworth's and said in a soft pitying voice that made Marya want to jerk angrily away, "I think it's such a shame about you and Emmett. Ron was telling me he's going out now with someone from Mt. Horne. It's such a *shame*, Marya, God damn it, why did you let it happen?"

Marya muttered an inaudible reply.

Erma stared at her, blinking. Since the pregnancy, since the marriage, she was prettier than ever: shorter than Marya by three or four inches, with a doll's porcelain-perfect face and a small snubbed nose and eyes so beautifully lashed they looked almost unreal. They had never exactly been friends but now they were certainly not friends and Marya couldn't even bring herself to smile, to behave nicely.

"What? I didn't hear," Erma said.

"I said it isn't your problem," Marya told her, swallowing. "You don't have to concern yourself with it."

Erma stared a moment longer, then said, "You don't have to be so sarcastic, Marya."

"You don't have to be so *concerned*," Marya said at once.

"—Though maybe you can't help yourself. Maybe that's the problem," Erma said, turning away.

After the drive to Port Oriskany, Marya went out with Emmett only once, on a Sunday afternoon. They were headed for Wolf's Head Lake but never got there. Marya wept tears of a kind she'd vowed as a young girl she would never weep, and apologized, and tried again to explain that she *did* love him. . . . "You can say that I wanted to get married and you didn't," she said wildly, "you can say it's your choice if we don't see each other," and Emmett braked the car to a stop, furious, trembling, and said, "Do you think I care about *that*, is that how you think of me? I'd care about something like *that*?"

She saw how she had misjudged him, how stupid she was, how finally unworthy of his agitation. But how could she extricate herself from this, how could she escape? September was so far off.

"Anyway, nobody's going to ask me anything," Emmett said. "They know better."

Marya knew that her primary weakness, her primary sin, was being sarcastic: that penchant for irony (for being a "smart aleck," others would have said) that lost her so many friends. ("Your mouth is going to get you into real trouble someday," Wilma was always warning, and her very grimness made Marya want to laugh. She said airily, provocatively, "Oh hell, it already *has,* but here I am—see?—still breathing.")

Still, she was cautious around boys; she'd always been cautious around boys. Her cousin Lee, after all. . . .

And certain things that had taken place at the country school, down by the canal, along the towpath. . . .

Over the years, when she knew herself safe (in Innisfail, in the presence of adults, in the company of *men* rather than *boys*), Marya had developed a rather defiant and stylized flirtatiousness. It was nothing at all like her old manner with Father Shearing—she had never been so crude as to "flirt" with him; she would have been appalled at the very thought. Instead it was arch, vaguely theatrical—cinematic? She performed and others watched. She was on stage, so to speak, illuminated by their attention; they were *forced* to watch. At first, at the age of twelve or thirteen, she couldn't have known exactly what she was risking (trading witticisms with strangers, exchanging "knowing" looks with sailors, parading about with her girl-friends in tight-fitting jeans and sweaters, her thick hair swinging loose and wild about her shoulders); afterward it all became conscious, subtly nuanced, as if she were on film, protected by the very barrier of film, seen and admired by men but in no way obliged to see and admire them in turn. It was intensely exciting, exhilarating. It made her a little drunk, displaying herself like this. The entire adventure, even its incalculable risk, could be summed up crudely enough: it was all marvelous *fun.*

A few years later, when she began to go out occasionally with boys from school, she found herself painfully stiff and self-conscious in their presence. They knew her, after all; they knew who she was and where she'd come from. . . . How idiotic they are, how stupid and predictable, Marya complained to her friends, the things they do, the things they *try* to do. Marya was capable of imitating several boys in her class so cruelly and so hilariously that her little audience broke into peals of helpless gasping laughter. Oh Marya stop! they cried, mildly scandalized. Oh Marya aren't you *awful*!

(*Isn't* Marya Knauer awful, they said, shaking their heads. She said things they would never have dared say; she phrased her jokes in ways they would never have invented for themselves. Just as, years before, she'd learned to fling back into the faces of the cruder boys those words—those "dirty words" —they would never have uttered in such company, because they hoped to be thought good, and not "dirty" themselves.)

Being *good,* Marya thought, wasn't a problem she had to worry about.

Of course she hadn't ever mocked Emmett Schroeder.

In the beginning she had pursued him. She'd been cunning, plotting, even a little desperate. Falling in love—"romance" of one kind or another—behaving like all the other girls: these were things Marya hadn't much wished to experience, being proud and, in any case, uncertain of her skills. It was easier to be disliked than to be liked, after all—she'd known that all her life.

Her "feeling" for boys, for men, was largely a matter of daydreaming. If she fastened upon a boy in school he was never so interesting in person as he seemed in her head, in her wild, floundering imagination. If she tried to write a story or a sketch about love (but what, she wondered, is "love"?) it was invariably flat and dull and could not sustain her interest. Though she was no longer a really conscientious Catholic— she couldn't imagine, for instance, that God greatly cared whether her thoughts were "impure" or that she ate meat on Fridays—she felt nonetheless a vague sense of shame, even of anger, when her thoughts moved on to sexual subjects; when she couldn't control the impulses of her body. (You're getting like a bitch in heat, she told herself in disgust, a monkey in estrus: "estrus" being a word newly acquired in biology class.) While she assuredly didn't want to be good, or nice, or sweet, or ladylike, her repugnance for any display of weakness was equally strong. And falling in love, whether with film actors or "real" men, struck her as supremely weak.

Still, there were boys who excited her beyond her capacity to control. There were boys—"men," really—who made all her solemn admonitions seem beside the point.

She fell in love with Emmett Schroeder one hot September day, and pursued him, and plotted to get him, with an anguished stubbornness that was new to her. Emmett was the older brother of a girl at school named Lori, a pretty, popular, but not especially bright girl who'd never liked Marya. (After she began seeing Emmett, however, and asked him cautiously about his sister—"Why does she always avoid me, why doesn't she *smile* at me the way she does at everyone else?"—Emmett said it was only because she didn't think Marya liked *her*; she didn't think Marya liked anyone.)

In the company of a boisterous half-drunken group at a Labor Day picnic at Wolf's Head Lake, Marya, slightly high, was bold enough to make her way over to Emmett Schroeder (who was in another party, who'd come to the lake with friends of his own) because someone had talked her into drinking several cans of beer, and because the narrow spotted mirror in the women's bathhouse had given back to her, unanticipated, an image of Marya that had struck her as . . . beautiful? . . . miraculous? She had stood for several long minutes in a shaft of sunlight, staring hungrily at her reflection, brushing her hair in slow hard measured strokes. It was amazing, it was hypnotic: those eyes: that mouth: was she to be, after all, *beautiful*? and not *ugly*? Or was it only a trick of the sunshine, or of the dingy mirror? (Ordinarily she was shy of mirrors, as she was of being photographed. The person others evidently saw as "Marya" wasn't a person she recognized. She wasn't sour, sullen, frightened, suspicious; she didn't care to identify with a girl whose eyes were so frequently ringed in shadow, and whose mouth looked so narrow and ungiving. She *knew* she was lighthearted, cheerful, funny; after all, wasn't she always making jokes? weren't people always laughing?)

In the bathhouse she felt suffused with power, elation, a sense of certainty. Yes. Today. This afternoon. Emmett Schroeder. She wasn't drunk—she told herself she hadn't had half as much to drink as Bonnie Michalak—but she felt an unaccustomed springiness to her step, and a tension in her leg muscles that wasn't at all unpleasant. She wanted to dance about, she wanted to sing as loudly as she could. Her scalp, her head, tingled with life from the hard brushing she'd given her hair. Her eyes shone flirtatiously. Ah, is *that* Marya! Marya who lives out the Canal Road! And her hair, that lovely hair which even Wilma conceded was beautiful: it fell in thick glossy rippling waves across her tanned shoulders and back, down to her waist, Indian-black in this light, shot with chestnut glints. . . .

So she assessed herself, the hairbrush raised. And thought, I will make him notice me: I will *make* him like me.

From the lake they drove in several cars to the Whitefish Tavern north of the reservoir, and Marya, pushy Marya, managed to sit beside Emmett Schroeder, no matter that he'd made no effort to sit beside *her*. (You didn't care for me at first, did you, she asked afterward, that night at Wolf's Head Lake, for instance; but Emmett didn't remember, or pretended not to. You wouldn't even *look* at me, at first, she said, exulting now in her triumph.) In the car she noted covertly the darkly tanned skin that stretched tight across his wide, flat cheekbones; she stared in fascination at his muscular arms, thickly haired, tanned almost black. (Emmett worked as a laborer for his father all summer long. He would be going into the construction business with him but his father was determined to make him earn every penny he was paid.) Emmett was physically large, yet graceful—more graceful, she thought, than she was herself—but his largeness, his expansiveness, had more to do with an attitude: his sense of himself as superior: superior to his environment, superior to most of his friends. Quickly Marya saw that he saw himself as superior to *her*; and fell in love with him that night.

A few months later, when they were seeing each other fairly steadily, sometimes alone and sometimes in the company of others, Emmett told her one evening that she didn't have to —well, *try* so hard.

Marya was stunned, wounded. "What do you mean," she said, faltering, "try so hard?"

"You don't have to entertain people all the time," Emmett said awkwardly, stroking her hair. "You know—say smart things, funny things. Make them laugh."

"I don't *try,*" Marya said quickly and falsely.

Emmett must have seen that he'd hurt her so he changed the subject. He stopped talking altogether—burrowed his face in her hair, ran his hard deft fingers up and down her sides, tickling her, making her laugh wildly, squirm. She could be reduced to a squealing gasping infant, Marya could, if you knew how to go about it. If you didn't go too far.

Sometimes they lay together in Emmett's car, kissing drowsily, talking of Emmett's concerns—he wanted more money from his father or he was going to leave home, get a job somewhere else; he was beginning to find his friends boring, and a waste of time, but he hadn't any others—How do you make friends, he wondered, after high school? At such times Marya exulted in her very anonymity; her invisibility. She murmured replies, gave advice, consoled him, agreed with him, sympathized with him. At such times he didn't see her—he wasn't judging her, assessing her. She needn't be bright and quick and ruthless, performing as if she were in a movie, she need only relax against him, and allow him to kiss her, and caress her, and explain himself to her, and continue his repetitious arguments with others—his father, his friends—by way of her. Would marriage be much different, she wondered, much more of a task? It was so easy, after all, to be accommodating. It almost felt natural.

She tried not to mind that he was seeing another girl, or girls, at this time; she told herself—so cold, so calculating was she, even at the age of seventeen—that it took pressure off *her,* if he was able to sleep with *them.*

One night he said something terrible, something casual and terrible, which Marya was never to forget: he told her he wouldn't have asked her out if he had known her age, how much younger she was than he. After all, he might get into trouble, there was her uncle Everard, her brother—cousin?—Lee; he didn't want to get mixed up with *them.*

But Marya looked, he said, older than seventeen. Nineteen, he would have guessed, at least. Maybe twenty. She *looked,* he said, half smiling, not sensing how he was insulting her, she *looked,* well, as if she'd been around.

She rummaged anxiously through Wilma's things, through the boxes in her closet, discovered a packet of snapshots—old, yellowed, curling—exactly what she was searching for. Joe and Vera. Joe and Vera and Wilma and Everard and their friends. Taken long ago. A lifetime ago. Old and yellow and curling and so painful Marya began to cry, spreading them out on the top of Wilma's bureau.

Why, they were all *kids!*—as young as Marya and Emmett —photographed in their bathing suits on the dock at Wolf's Head Lake, photographed clowning about on the old rattle-trap bridge by the Waterside Inn, the women hardly more than girls, the men so astonishingly young. . . . So this is "Vera," Marya thought, holding one of the snapshots to the light, examining it closely—a thin dark woman with long windblown hair, smiling cautiously into the camera, shading her eyes against the harsh sun with a raised hand: pretty enough, very pretty in fact, though the nose is a little long, the eyes rather suspicious. (She must have been about twenty at the time. Dressed in a holiday costume—checked blouse with a wide scalloped collar, flaring skirt, high-heeled shoes. The background was blurred, unfamiliar.) And here is "Joe"—in fact there are a half-dozen pictures of him—Joe with Vera, his arm around her shoulders; Joe with his brother and two other men whom Marya can't recognize; Joe holding a baby aloft, grinning in triumph: *Joe & Marya, 1947.* He too is very young, very lean, his hair dark and springy, his expression cheerful and belligerent.

Marya felt her heart wrenched, she couldn't stop herself from crying: her dead father, her lost mother, and Everard and Wilma as well—weren't they lost, too, those smiling people in the snapshots? Cavorting at picnics, sitting on the hood of someone's car, posed in their bathing suits with their hands on their hips. . . . It always seemed to be summer, the sun always struck so perpendicularly, so harshly.

Marya hid the snapshots away, terrified of being discovered. No one was home at the time but her nerves jumped at every sound. It isn't fair, she thought, still crying bitterly; "It isn't fair," she said aloud, though she hadn't any idea what she meant; what wasn't fair.

Because Marya was leaving for Port Oriskany just after Labor Day, and Clarence Michalak was leaving for boot camp in North Carolina the following week, they scheduled the going-away party for September 7.

Bonnie Michalak stopped by at the office to tell Marya about it. And though Marya was surprised—in fact she was rather astonished, and deeply moved, that anyone should care enough to have a going-away party for *her*—she couldn't help but notice how Bonnie glanced around the trim little office with its chocolate-brown venetian blinds and its Formica-topped furniture, as if picturing herself in it, in Marya's place. (Marya had been gently pressured into recommending Bonnie as her replacement. The job as second secretary to Morris Fowler paid more than waitressing or clerking at Wool-worth's; there was a great deal of local distinction in being able to say that you were working in a "law office," however small and inconsequential the office was.) "Do you really mean it," Marya said, "a going-away party for *me*?" And Bonnie said, "For you and Clarence: we thought that might be a good idea."

Marya could see why her friends might want to give a party for Clarence—he was amiable, funny, well-liked—but it quite puzzled her that they should include her. She fussed about looking for a tissue, she couldn't think what to say to Bonnie; it would sound ridiculous to confess that she'd never had a party in her life, a party for *her*. Wilma would have snorted in derision at the very idea . . . and of course there hadn't ever been enough money. "Is Emmett coming," Marya asked, "did you invite Emmett?"

Bonnie said that Kyle Roemischer was going to ask him, they didn't know yet whether he'd come. They thought— well, if he *wanted* to come, even though he and Marya had broken up, it might be all right. Unless Marya objected—

"Why should I object?" Marya asked, blowing her nose.

"It's maybe the last time we'll all see you," Bonnie said almost shyly.

Marya stared at her. "That's . . . that's a strange thing to say," she murmured, "what do you mean by it?"

"Oh well I don't know," Bonnie laughed. "Somebody was saying the other day—somebody's mother, I guess—Once Marya leaves Innisfail she probably won't come back— whyever *should* she?"

"What do you mean by that?" Marya asked.

"Oh you know, your scholarship and all," Bonnie said carelessly, "and the kind of things you're always saying about people around here—"

"But it's my home," Marya said, crumpling the tissue in her fist, "I don't have any other place. . . ."

"A going-away party? For you?" Wilma said.

"For Clarence Michalak and me, not just *me*," Marya said, slightly embarrassed. "He's going into the army."

(119)

"It's the night before you leave?"

"Well—I can have everything packed and ready. I won't really be taking much," Marya said.

"Is Emmett going to be there?"

"How do I know if Emmett is going to be there! You're asking too many questions."

"I thought the two of you weren't speaking."

"I'm not *not* speaking to him."

"I didn't think you ran around with Lester and Kyle and Bonnie and that gang any more," Wilma said. "That bunch of smart alecks. I *thought* you told me—"

"Anyway," Marya interrupted, "they're giving a party out at the lake. So I'll be going out that night."

"And you expect to get up early the next morning?"

"Of course I'll get up early the next morning," Marya said impatiently. "I'll take the nine-thirty bus, I'll get there by one o'clock, the first meeting, or whatever it is, isn't until four that afternoon. . . ."

"Don't you talk smart to me, you."

"I'm not *talking smart,* I'm just telling you."

"Running around with that gang, drinking beer and getting in trouble, that loud-mouth Lester Hughey—"

"It isn't just Lester, it's Erma and Ron too, and Annie, and probably Eulalie Steadman, and Jinny Dietz, and I asked them to invite Warren Maccabee and Robbie Ducharme, you know they're going away too—"

"You needn't talk so loud, Marya. I can hear you perfectly well."

"I'm not talking loud," Marya said, feeling her face go hot. "But you just don't *listen.*"

"You're all excited because they're giving a party for you, and so you can't help sticking your nose up around here. And it's all you can do, isn't it, to stay home one night of the week," Wilma said. She turned away from Marya, fixing her hair at the back of her head—she'd gathered it up in a limp ponytail, secured by a rubber band. Her nails had been polished a few days ago and the bright pink polish had begun to chip. "Why don't you move out right now, move to Port Oriskany? I know you'd like to—you and your high-class scholarship! As if anybody's begging you to stay!"

Ordinarily Marya would have answered her back, her blood leaped at the prospect of a fight, but for some reason she didn't have the heart, this afternoon: she stifled a sob, pressed her hands over her ears, ran out of the kitchen, and let the screen door slam behind her. She might have been a small child again—it might have been years ago.

"As if anybody's begging you to stay!" Wilma shouted after her.

The day of the party Marya shampooed her hair and let it dry in the afternoon sun, spread out about her on a blanket in the side yard. She observed with satisfaction her long smooth tanned legs and arms, she'd examined her image in the mirror a dozen times: How will she reply to Emmett if he greets her? How will she raise her eyes to his?

She and Wilma were barely speaking. Tomorrow morning Marya would be leaving for college, this morning Wilma avoided her at breakfast, was it all coming to an end?—a decade of living in Wilma and Everard's house, of being their "second daughter" (for so, to her surprise, Marya had once heard Everard call her), coming to an end, like this? Sleepy in the sun yet not entirely relaxed, Marya closed her eyes and saw confused patchy shapes, heard someone—it must have been Wilma—shouting *You little savage! You little savage, you!*

She woke up but of course it wasn't Wilma, it wasn't anyone at all.

She could hear Wilma talking on the telephone, probably to one of her women friends. They complained of their children who were living at home and their children who *weren't* living at home. . . . Lee was on a naval carrier right now, somewhere in the Pacific, and all he ever sent home was postcards, a few scribbles, as Wilma said, never telling them anything much, always in a hurry, or so it seemed—just listing places, islands, naval bases no one had ever heard of. And as soon as he was shipped back home, as soon as he got discharged, he'd marry that Metcalf girl, Wilma just knew it.

Wilma's voice was high, whining, but capable of sudden startling modulations. Sometimes when you thought she was complaining she was only being funny; carrying on, exaggerating, stretching her face in a comical moping way. She was still a good-looking woman with all that streaked-bleached hair, that smooth slightly flushed skin . . . but getting rather thick-waisted and heavy in the thighs . . . even the skin of her upper arms was getting flaccid. Marya saw her so constantly she'd long since stopped noticing her. She shuddered to think how pathetic, how *old,* her aunt was getting: in her early forties at least: was that possible?

As if anybody's begging you to stay! came the mocking voice.

As if I want to stay a day longer than I have to! Marya shouted in reply.

Marya told herself that she wasn't going to be embarrassed in front of Emmett; she wouldn't give him that much power over her.

But as it turned out Emmett spent only an hour or so at the party, and he was in the company of a young woman Marya didn't know—high-piled blond hair bleached bone-white, a black halter top that barely restrained her large pale breasts, a sweetly shrill drunken giggle. She splashed about the shore, her skirt tucked up around her thighs, calling to Bob and Kyle out on the float, while Emmett stood a few yards away smoking a cigarette, looking bored. He hadn't brought along a swimming suit—wore jeans and a pullover shirt, an old stretched shirt Marya remembered well. His skin looked as if it had been dyed a rich mahogany color; his hair was growing long, curling over his collar. When he smiled at Marya—his smile quick as a snake's tongue—she felt her heart trip absurdly; but she managed to greet him in the very same way. No display of embarrassment, chagrin, regret.

We love each other, we should get married. . . .

Sure, thought Marya.

Shit, thought Marya.

Marya rode out to the lake with Bonnie and her fiancé, Fred, and for a while she stayed in their company, saying very little, drinking beer and trying to listen—pretending to listen —to the conversations about her. She must have looked distinctly unhappy because Bonnie muttered in her ear that *she* thought it was rude of Emmett to bring that girl—nobody knew who she was and nobody cared.

Marya turned uneasily away. "*I* don't care," she said, almost inaudibly.

"Emmett never said he was going to bring anybody at all," Bonnie complained. She was watching Marya closely.

So this was the going-away party!—Marya saw almost with satisfaction that it was a mistake; a blunder; beyond even disappointment. *These* people—what did she care for them, what did they care for her? did they even know her? The gathering was only another end-of-summer picnic, another drunken beer-bash as Wilma would say, loud music blaring from a plastic radio, loud oafish voices, laughter. . . . Marya recalled a biology class of two or three years before when she'd been moved almost to tears as their teacher explained the principle of human reproduction: the miracle (for it *was* a miracle, an authentic miracle) by which a single egg and a single sperm fused; and formed a single cell; and the cell divided itself in two . . . and then in four . . . and then in eight . . . and so on to infinity. At a certain stage cells emerged for certain parts of the human body so that the living protoplasm became *human*: now it would have a human brain, for instance. Where does that come from, Marya asked their teacher. I mean *that, that* cell, how does it know to be a brain? how does it know ahead of time to be a brain? Her classmates were yawning, or doodling, or pretending to listen; or, like Kyle Roemischer at the rear of the room, whispering smutty jokes. (You want to know where it comes from, Marya, they laughed afterward in the hall, y'want to see?) Their teacher acknowledged the fact that no one knew; no one had the faintest idea. Marya was struck dumb by the idea that out of nowhere, suddenly, the human essence appeared . . . the brain, the soul . . . the personality. Why does that cell form when it does, Marya wanted to know, but knew that she wouldn't ever know: it was one of those things.

And at the rear of the room the boys telling their dirty stories, scarcely listening. "It's just one of those things, Marya," their teacher told her after class. He seemed half-way embarrassed at her sudden intense interest—as if he'd started something, provoked a response, he hadn't at all intended. "All we know is *what* it does, we don't know exactly *how* . . . and we certainly don't know *why*," he said.

"Yes," said Marya, frowning, her nose twitching, "but *why?*"

Here is Marya Knauer, valedictorian of the class, Marya in her red-checked cotton dress with the low back, showing her long smooth tanned back and shoulders, her tanned arms. Marya drinking beer out of a can like the boys, throwing her head back to laugh helplessly at one of Lester Hughey's crude jokes; feeling with spiteful satisfaction the heavy warm weight of her hair down her back. The boys are crowding around her, she's really quite popular despite the fact that *she's* going away and *they're* staying (at least for the time being, they explain: eventually they'll all follow Clarence into the army, or Lee Knauer into the navy, or, if they're men enough, they'll try for the marines like Emmett Schroeder), despite the fact that they've always been a little wary of her razorish wit. Marya is leaving for Port Oriskany in the morning, Kyle is going to drive her to the Greyhound bus station, they're joking about maybe Marya won't have to go home at all . . . just go directly from the lake to the bus station. . . .

Aren't her friends going to miss her! Marya thinks. Oh yes aren't they!

She is watching Emmett and the blond girl (she's a beautician in Yewville, only early twenties but already divorced), watching them walk away, Emmett's hand lightly resting at the nape of her neck, the two of them talking (about what?), leaving the party without saying goodbye to Marya, but that isn't important—Marya thinks: It isn't important at all, we've already said goodbye.

Hell, says Marya under her breath, turning brightly away, it *isn't* important.

Afterward, she won't remember clearly all that happened.

Static-y rock music from Kyle's transistor radio. Mosquitoes biting, big soft amazing swellings on the back of Marya's thighs, her upper arms. Scratching until the blood comes: God *damn* it, what does she care, the bites are itching like crazy and anyway her dress is red, blood spots won't show. Beer and ale; potato chips; cold greasy chicken parts devoured by hand, and the unwanted parts—wings, necks—thrown at anyone who isn't on guard. The boys are rowdy, crashing about in a game of touch football gone slightly askew (they *are* touching, they're even shoving and bumping), shouting words meant to be funny, friendly—ugly words: cocksucker, bullshit, fuck-face, jerk-off, cunt—until Kyle runs into Bob Bannerman deliberately, crouched low so that his shoulder rams Bob's stomach, and the game is over. Lester Hughey dumps a Styrofoam container of potato salad on the ground. I'm not going to eat this shit, he says, it doesn't taste like anything, it tastes like *shit*. So Erma Dietz is angry because she made the potato salad: Erma Jelinski, that is: and now she and Ron are leaving and she takes Marya aside, pinching her arm, saying, *You,* you'd better come with us, Marya, half chiding, as if she was Marya's big sister or something, as if she was Wilma in fact, and Marya says no, *she's* having too good a time.

Anyway—she's supposed to ride back with Bonnie and Fred. Unless they've already left.

Next, some confusion about a watermelon—some craziness—smashing it and scooping up handfuls of the watery pulpy flesh and throwing it at one another. The hilarity of seeds stuck in Bob Bannerman's spiky hair.

Eulalie's boyfriend, a tall skeletal silent boy from Kincardine who drives a Harley-Davidson and is very much envied by the Innisfail crowd, takes offense for some reason: shoves Lester Hughey backward: and when Eulalie tries to calm him down (pulling at his arm, giggling, acting as if somehow *she* might be to blame) he strikes her across the chest with a sweep of his arm, hard. Then suddenly it is over and Eulalie and the boy are driving away. An earsplitting roar as the motorcycle revs up, tires churning in the gravel. . . .

What time is it? Marya is hiding behind a tree, trying desperately to vomit. She gags and gags—feels her very eyeballs straining with the pressure—but nothing comes up.

Then finally it does. Splashing on the gnarled roots of the old tree, splashing onto her feet and ankles.

Marya, Marya! they are calling.

Raindrops strike the lake hard, like pebbles. It's queer, the rippling and swaying rhythm. A wall of raindrops rushes upon the mild waves of the lake, peppering the waves, so that it looks like machine-gun bullets. Marya runs barefoot along the beach and seems not to mind that a splinter of glass has cut her toe. It's her big toe, she reasons, hilarious as always, it has lots of blood to lose.

"That liar Bonnie," Marya complains to the boys, "she said she wasn't in any hurry to leave, now she and what's-his-name are gone."

"Oh that fuck-face, don't give a shit about *him,* honey," Lester says.

"I *don't.* Or Bonnie either. But she promised me a ride home and—"

"It isn't time yet for anybody to go home," Bob Bannerman says.

Someone has opened the trunk of Lester's car, and now the boys are fooling around with the tools: a hammer, a monkey wrench, a clipping shears, a coil of wire, a box of spikes. "What the hell are you doing!" Lester screams. "That stuff's my brother's! That stuff's my fucking brother's, he'll knock the shit out of me!"

"Nobody's hurting *anything,* for Christ's sake," Kyle says laughing, "don't piss your pants or anything—"

One of the boys is trying to hammer a spike into the top of a picnic table but the blows are so hard the tabletop splits.

Marya, they are calling, where's Marya? She has run into the girls' bathhouse to be sick. Vomiting into one of the toilets, leaning against the wooden seat. Oh dear God the stench is almost unbearable.

"Where's fuck-face Marya?"

"Ain't-I-hot-shit Marya! Where's she hiding?"

Suddenly lights shine through the trees—red lights, revolving swiftly, the state troopers, it must be—so they scramble off in a panic, running to the cars, but Lester has to gather up his brother's tools and in the commotion Kyle's transistor radio is knocked to the ground (or is it thrown down?—it's so badly damaged, Kyle discovers afterward)—and a tall leggy beery-breathed boy named Jerry, from Mt. Horne, is dragging Marya along saying, C'mon, c'mon honey! c'mon! no matter that the gravel in the parking lot hurts her bare feet and she's whimpering in pain.

Then the lights are gone. Maybe they hadn't ever been there—maybe somebody was playing a trick on them—

Hey you guys listen, the fucking po-lice, y'know what they do: turn their lights off! turn their siren off! Lester whispers. Then they wait for you and get you!

They wait, crouched and panting. Marya's breath comes in desperate gasps, her head is ringing, swaying. If it wasn't for someone holding her up she'd fall forward into the weeds. And the mosquitoes, the mosquitoes . . . she feels them biting at a distance . . . at a great distance . . . but can't stop them. Dear God one side of her face is swollen, how will she look tomorrow morning . . . ?

There's *nobody* there, Bob Bannerman says angrily.

The stand of pine is perfectly silent except for the wind, and the raindrops falling heavily.

What time is it, someone asks, the park closes at twelve.

The hell it does! This is a free country!

This is a fucking free country!

What happened to the police? Kyle asks wonderingly.
You think it was a helicopter or something?

I didn't see any lights.

They were right there, *I* saw them.

Well—are we going or not? Is there any beer left?

A flying saucer, maybe it was a flying saucer: Kyle's such
an asshole he wouldn't know a flying saucer if he saw one!

There *wasn't* anything there, you cocksucker.

Them lights—them red lights that go around—

You saw them, Marya, didn't you?

Marya shakes her head to get it clear. But she isn't quick
enough, she can't manage to speak.

Marya wants to go home, one of the boys says.

Marya's sick, she smells like puke.

Has to get up early, don't you?

Going to Port Oriskany, huh? To college?

Got a scholarship!

I-got-a-scholarship!

Ain't-I-hot-shit!

Hey Marya where're you going—

Marya is running across the empty parking lot, whimpering. One of the straps of her red dress has broken, she doesn't
remember when.

Marya nobody's going to hurt you—

Hey Marya, one of the boys laughed, there's nothing
down *that* way.

She's looking for Emmett! big-deal hot-shit Schroeder!

Schroeder and his fancy Buick prick!

Lester Hughey, or is it Kyle Roemischer—or the boy
from Mt. Horne—jumps whooping upon her. Bob Bannerman—she knows it is Bob, she can smell him—comes running
up, panting, his shirt flapping open, his chest gleaming pale
behind curly kinky black hairs. He's rubbing his hands together in imitation of the principal on assembly days. Well
now what have we here, let's just see what we have *here*, boys
and girls quiet down let's just *see*—

Marya fights them but she doesn't scream.

She doesn't scream, she knows enough not to waste her breath; not to tire herself out. On the basketball court, playing girls' softball—keep your mouth shut, don't breathe through your mouth—

Marya fights them, scrambling at the edge of the parking lot, half naked, sobbing, panting, striking at them with her fists, trying to kick them in the groin. She knows, Marya does, how to fight. But they're whooping and laughing and shouting, Easy does it! Hey, easy does it!

Nobody's going to hurt you, Marya—

For Christ's fucking sake—

She strikes one of them in the throat. Kicks and kicks, wild, frantic, still not screaming, not screaming aloud, until one of them catches her by the ankle, yanks her off her feet. Hooting with laughter: but is it Stan's voice rising, furious? She's crazy! You better let her go! The fuck-face ugly bitch!

Grappling in the mud. The harsh raindrops still falling, pelting. Her breasts, terribly bare: exposed: helpless. Her hair in her eyes, in her mouth. She's choking. Someone sits on her stomach, holding her chin in his hand, shaking her head from side to side. Who the hell do you think you're kicking, fuck-face! Who the hell do you think you *are*!

She remembers, afterward, one of them prying her legs apart—she remembers him prodding and jabbing at her— trying to enter her—trying to force his penis in her—but she might have squirmed free, arching her back, or one of the others hauled him away—and then Lester Hughey—it *was* Lester—scrambled over her with the shears chortling Clippe-ty-clippety-clip!—take care not to hurt yourself, sweetheart! He gripped her in an embrace, his forearm around her neck, and still she threw herself from side to side, and the shears' blades stabbed at her cheek, narrowly missed an eye, and the boys were all shouting That's it, that's it, you got her, that's it, and panting and grunting Lester brought the blades of the shears up against the nape of her neck, as close to her skull as he could manage, and began cutting.

6

The semester Marya became acquainted with Imogene Skillman, thefts began to occur in Maynard House, where Marya
was rooming in her sophomore year at Port Oriskany: at odd,
inspired, daring hours, sometimes in the early morning when
a girl was out of her room and showering in the bathroom just
down the corridor, sometimes late at night when some of the
girls sat in the kitchen, drinking coffee, their voices kept low
so that the resident adviser would not hear. (The kitchen was
supposed to close officially at midnight. Maynard House itself
"closed" at midnight—there were curfews in those days, in
the women's residences.) A wristwatch stolen from one room,
seven dollars from another, a physics textbook from yet another . . . the thief was clearly one of the residents, one of the
twenty-six girls who roomed in the house, but no one knew
who it was; no one wanted to speculate too freely. Naturally
there were wild rumors, cruel rumors. Marya once heard the
tail end of a conversation in which her own name—"Knauer"

—was mentioned. She had brushed by, her expression neutral, stony. She wanted the girls to know she had heard—she scorned even confronting them.

One Saturday morning in November Marya returned to her room after having been gone less than five minutes—she'd run downstairs to check the mail, though she rarely received letters—to see, with a sickening pang, that the door was ajar.

Her wallet had been taken from her leather bag, which she'd left carelessly in sight, tossed on top of her bed.

Her lips shaped empty, angry prayers—Oh God please *no*—but of course it was too late. She felt faint, sickened. She had just cashed a check for forty-five dollars—a week's part-time wages from the university library—and she'd had time to spend only a few dollars; she needed the money badly. "No," she said aloud, baffled, chagrined. "God damn it, *no.*"

Someone stood in the opened doorway behind her saying, Marya? Is something wrong? but Marya paid her no notice. She was opening the drawers of her bureau one by one; she saw, disgusted, frightened, that the thief had been there too—rooting around in Marya's woolen socks and sweaters and frayed underwear. And her fountain pen was gone. She kept it in the top drawer of the bureau, a prize of her own, a handsome black Parker pen with a thick nub . . . now it was gone.

She had to resist the impulse to yank the drawer out and throw it to the floor—to yank all the drawers out—to give herself up to rage. A flame seemed to pass through her, white-hot, scalding. It was so unfair: she needed that money, every penny of that money, she'd worked in the library in that flickering fluorescent light until she staggered with exhaustion, and even then she'd been forced to beg her supervisor to allow her a few more hours. Her scholarships were only for tuition; she needed that money. And the pen—she could never replace the pen.

It was too much: something in her chest gave way: she burst into tears like an overgrown child. She had never heard such great gulping ugly sobs. And the girl in the doorway—

Phyllis, whose room was across the hall: shy, timid, sweet-faced Phyllis—actually tried to hold her in her arms and comfort her. It's so unfair, it's so unfair, Marya wept, what am I going to *do.* . . .

Eventually the wallet was returned to Marya, having been found in a trash can up the street. Nothing was missing but the money, as it turned out. Nothing but the money! Marya thought savagely. The wallet itself—simulated crocodile, black, with a fancy brass snap—now looked despoiled, worn, contemptible. It had been a present from Emmett two years before and she supposed she'd had it long enough.

She examined it critically inside and out. She wondered what the thief had thought. Marya Knauer's things, Marya Knauer's "personal" possessions: were they worth stealing, really?

For weeks afterward Marya dreaded returning to her room. Though she was careful to lock the door all the time now it always seemed, when she stepped inside, that someone had been there . . . that something was out of place. Sometimes when she was halfway up the long steep hill to Stafford Hall she turned impulsively and ran back to her dormitory seven blocks away, to see if she'd remembered to lock the door. You're breaking down, aren't you, she mocked herself as she ran, her heart pumping, perspiration itching beneath her arms, this is how it begins, isn't it: cracking up.

In the early years of the century Maynard House must have been impressive: a small Victorian mansion with high handsome windows, a wide veranda rimmed with elaborate fretwork, a cupola, a half-dozen fireplaces, walnut paneling in several of the downstairs rooms. But now it had become dim and shabby. The outside needed painting; the wallpaper in most of the rooms was discolored. Because it was so far from the main campus, and because its rooms were so cramped (Marya could stand at her full height on only one side of her room, the ceiling on the other slanted so steeply), it was one of the lowest-priced residences for women. The girls who roomed there were all scholarship students like Marya and, like Marya, uneasily preoccupied with studies, grades, part-time employment, finances of a minute and degrading nature. They were perhaps not so humorless and unattractive as Maynard House's reputation would have it, but they did share a superficial family resemblance—they might have been cousins, grimly energetic, easily distracted, a little vain (for they *were* scholarship winners after all, competition for these scholarships was intense throughout the state), badly frightened at the prospect of failure. They were susceptible to tears at odd unprovoked moments, to eating binges, to outbursts of temper; several, including Marya, were capable of keeping their doors closed for days on end and speaking to no one when they did appear.

Before the theft Marya had rather liked Maynard House; she prized her cubbyhole of a room because it was *hers*; because in fact she could lock the door for days on end. The standard university furniture didn't displease her—the same minimal bed, desk, chair, bureau, bedside table, lamp in each room—and the sloped ceiling gave the room a cavelike, warmly intimate air, especially at night when only her desk lamp was burning. Though she couldn't really afford it Marya had bought a woven rug for the floor—Aztec colors, even more fierce than those in her and Alice's rug at home—and a new lampshade edged with a festive gold braid; she had bought a Chagall print for ninety-eight cents (marked down because it was slightly shopworn) at the University Store. The walls were decorated with unframed charcoal drawings she had done, sketches of imaginary people, a few glowering self-portraits: when she was too tense or excited to sleep after hours of studying, or after having taken an exam, she took up a stick of charcoal and did whatever it seemed to wish to do —her fingers empowered with a curious sort of energy, twitchy, sporadic, often quite surprising. From the room's walls smudged and shadowy variants of her own sober face contemplated her. Strong cheekbones, dark eyes, thick dark censorious brows. . . . She had made the portraits uglier than she supposed she really was; that provided some comfort, it might be said to have been a reverse vanity. Who is *that*? one of the girls on the floor once asked, staring at Marya's own image. Is it a man? a woman?

Marya prized her aloneness, her monastic isolation at the top of the house, tucked away in a corner. She could stay up all night if she wished, she could skip breakfast if she wished, she could fall into bed after her morning classes and sleep a heavy drugged sleep for much of the afternoon; and no one knew or cared. It seemed extraordinary to her now that for so many years she had had to submit to the routine schedule of Wilma's household: going to bed when she wasn't sleepy, getting up when the others did, eating meals with them, living her life as if it were nothing more than an extension of theirs. She loved to read for pleasure once her own assignments were completed: the reading she did late at night acquired an aura, a value, a mysterious sort of enchantment, that did not usually belong to daylight. It was illicit, precious beyond estimation. It seemed to her at such times that she was capable of slipping out of her own consciousness and into that of the writer's . . . into the very rhythms of another's prose. Bodiless, weightless, utterly absorbed, she traversed the landscape of another's mind and found it like her own yet totally unlike—surprising and jarring her, enticing her, leading her on. It was a secret process yet it was not criminal or forbidden—she made her way with the stealth of the thief, elated, subdued, through another's imagination, risking no harm, no punishment. The later the hour and the more exhausted she was, the greater, oddly, her powers of concentration; nothing in her resisted, nothing stood aside to doubt or ridicule; the books she read greedily seemed to take life through her, by way of her, with virtually no exertion of her own. It scarcely seemed to matter what she read, or whom—Nietzsche, William James, the Brontës, Wallace Stevens, Virginia Woolf, Stendhal, the early Greek philosophers—the experience of reading was electrifying, utterly mesmerizing, beyond anything she could recall from the past. She'd been, she thought severely, a superficial person in the past—how could anything that belonged to Innisfail, to those years, matter?

A writer's authentic self, she thought, lay in his writing and not in his life; it was the landscape of the imagination that endured, that was really real. Mere life was the husk, the actor's performance, negligible in the long run. . . . How could it be anything more than the vehicle by which certain works of art were transcribed . . . ? The thought frightened her, exhilarated her. She climbed out of her bed and leaned out her window as far as she could, her hair whipping in the wind. For long vacant minutes she stared at the sky; her vision absorbed without recording the illuminated water tower two miles north of the campus, the flickering red lights of a radio station, the passage of clouds blown livid across the moon. Standing in her bare feet, shivering, her head fairly ringing with fatigue and her eyes filling with tears, she thought her happiness almost too exquisite to be borne.

The first time Imogene Skillman climbed, uninvited, to Marya's room at the top of the old mansion, she stood in the doorway and exclaimed in her low throaty amused voice, "So *this* is where you hide out . . . this depressing little hole!"

Imogene was standing with her hands on her hips, her cheeks flushed, her eyes moving restlessly about. Why, Marya's room was a former maid's room, wasn't it, partitioned off from the others on the floor; and it had only that one window—no wonder the air was stale and close; and that insufferable Chagall print!—wasn't Marya aware that everyone on campus had one? And it was a poor reproduction at that. Then Imogene noticed the charcoal sketches; she came closer to investigate; she said, after a long moment, "At least these are interesting, I wouldn't mind owning one or two of them myself."

Marya had been taken by surprise, sitting at her desk, a book opened before her; she hadn't the presence of mind to invite Imogene in, or to tell her to go away.

"So this is where Marya Knauer lives," Imogene said slowly. Her eyes were a pellucid blue, blank and innocent as china. "All alone, of course. Who would *you* have roomed with?"

The loss of the money and the Parker fountain pen was so upsetting to Marya, and so bitterly ironic, partly because Marya herself had become a casual thief.

She thought, I deserve this.

She thought, I will never steal anything again.

Alice had led her on silly little shoplifting expeditions in Woolworth's: plastic combs, spools of thread, lipsticks, useless items (hairnets, thumbtacks) pilfered for the sheer fun of it. Once, years ago, when she was visiting Bonnie Michalak, she made her way stealthily into Mrs. Michalak's bedroom and took—what had it been? a button, a thimble, two or three pennies?—from the top of her dresser. A tube of much-used scarlet lipstick from the locker of a high school friend; a card-sized plastic calendar (an advertisement from a stationer's in town) from Mr. Schwilk's desk; stray nickels and dimes, quarters, fifty-cent pieces. . . . One of her prizes, acquired with great daring and trepidation, was a (fake) ruby ring belonging to someone's older sister, which Marya had found beneath carelessly folded clothing in a stall in the women's bathhouse at Wolf's Head Lake; but had never dared to wear. The thefts were always impulsive and rather pointless. Marya saw her trembling hand dart out, saw the fingers close . . . and in that instant, wasn't the object hers?

There was a moment when an item passed over from belonging to another person to belonging to Marya; that moment interested her greatly. She felt excitement, near-panic, elation. A sense of having triumphed, in however petty a fashion.

(It had come to seem to her in retrospect that she'd stolen Father Shearing's wristwatch. She seemed to recall . . . unless it was a particularly vivid dream . . . she seemed to recall slipping the watch from his table into her bookbag, that old worn soiled bookbag she'd had for years. Father Shearing was asleep in his cranked-up bed. Though perhaps not . . . perhaps he was watching her all along through his eyelashes. Marya? Dear Marya? A common thief?

(No, she had only thought of stealing it.)

Since coming to Port Oriskany she felt the impulse more frequently but she knew enough to resist. It was a childish habit, she thought, disgusted, it wasn't even genuine theft, intelligently committed. Presumably she wanted to transgress; even to be punished; she *wanted* to be sinful.

Odd, Marya thought uneasily, that no one has ever caught me. When I haven't seemed to care. When I haven't seemed to have *tried.*

It happened that, in her classes, she found herself gazing at certain individuals, and at their belongings, day after day, week after week. What began as simple curiosity gradually shaded into intense interest. She might find herself, for instance, staring at a boy's spiral notebook in a lecture class . . . plotting a way of getting it for herself, leafing through it, seeing what he'd written. (For this boy, like Marya, was a daydreamer; an elaborate and tireless doodler, not without talent.) There was an antique opal ring belonging to a girl in her English literature class: the girl herself had waist-long brown hair, straight and coarse, and Marya couldn't judge whether she was striking, and very good-looking, or really quite repulsive. (Marya's own hair was growing long again— long and wavy and unruly—but it would never be that length again; the ends simply broke off.) Many of the students at Port Oriskany were from well-to-do families, evidently, judging from their clothes and belongings: Marya's eye moved upon hand-tooled leather bags, and boots, and wristwatches, and earrings, and coats (suede, leather, fur-trimmed, camel's hair) half in scorn and half in envy. She did not want to steal these items, she did not *want* these items, yet, still, her gaze drifted onto them time and again, helplessly. . . .

She studied faces too, when she could. Profiles. That

blond girl in her political science class, for instance: smooth clear creamy skin, china-blue mocking eyes, a flawless nose, mouth: long hair falling in a braid over one shoulder. Knee-high leather boots, kid gloves, a handsome camel's-hair coat, a blue cashmere muffler that hadn't been cleaned in some time. An engagement ring with a large square-cut diamond.... But it was the girl's other pieces of jewelry that drew Marya's interest. Sometimes she wore a big silver ring with a turquoise stone; and a long sporty necklace made of copper coins; and a succession of earrings in her pierced ears—gold loops that swung and caught the light, tiny iridescent black stones, ceramic disks in which gold-burnished reds and blues flashed. Marya stared and stared, her heart quickening with—was it envy?—but envy of precisely what? It could not have been these expensive trinkets she coveted.

Imogene Skillman was a theater arts major; she belonged to one of the sororities on Masefield Avenue; Marya had even been able to discover that she was from Laurel Park, Long Island, and that she was engaged to a law student who had graduated from Port Oriskany several years ago. After she became acquainted with Imogene she would have been deeply humiliated if Imogene had known how much Marya knew of her beforehand. Not only her background, and her interest in acting, but that big leather bag, those boots, the silver ring, the ceramic earrings. . . .

It might have been Imogene's presence in class that inspired Marya to speak as she frequently did; answering their professor's questions in such detail, in such self-consciously structured sentences. (Marya thought of herself as shy, but, as it turned out, she could often speak at length if required—she became, suddenly, articulate and emphatic—even somewhat combative. The tenor of her voice caused people to turn around in their seats and often surprised, when it did not disconcert, her professors.) It wasn't that she spoke her mind —she rarely offered opinions—it seemed to her necessary to consider as many sides of an issue as possible, as many relevant points, presenting her case slowly and clearly and forcefully, showing no sign of the nervousness she felt. It was not simply that most of her professors solicited serious discussion—gave evidence, in fact, of being greatly dependent upon it to fill up fifty minutes of class time—or even that (so Marya reasoned, calculated) her precious grade might depend upon such contributions; she really became caught up in the subjects themselves. Conflicting theories of representative democracy, property rights, civil disobedience . . . the ethics of propaganda . . . revolution and counterrevolution . . . whether in fact terrorism might ever be justified. . . . Even when it seemed, as it sometimes did, that Marya's concern for these issues went beyond that of the professor's, she made her point; she felt a grudging approval throughout the room; and Imogene Skillman turned languidly in her seat to stare at her.

One afternoon Imogene left behind a little handwoven purse that must have slipped out of her leather bag. Marya snatched it up as if it were a prize. She followed after Imogene —followed her out of the building—that tall blond girl in the camel's-hair coat, striding along, laughing, in a high-spirited conversation with her friends. Marya approached her and handed her the purse, saying only, "You dropped this," in a neutral voice; she turned away without waiting for Imogene's startled thanks.

Afterward she felt both elated and unaccountably fatigued. As if she had experienced some powerful drain on her energy. As if, having returned Imogene's little purse to her, she now regretted having done so; and wondered if she had been a fool.

Marya's friendship with Imogene Skillman began, as it was to end, with a puzzling abruptness.

One day Imogene simply appeared beside Marya on one of the campus paths, asking if she was walking this way? and falling comfortably in step with her. It was done as easily and as effortlessly as if they were old friends; as if Imogene had been reading Marya's most secret thoughts.

She began by flattering her, telling her she said "interesting" things in class; that she seemed to be the only person their professor really listened to. Then, almost coyly: "I should confess that it's your voice that really intrigues me. What if— so I ask myself, I'm always trying things on other people!— what if *she* was playing Hedda—Hedda Gabler—with that remarkable voice—and not mine—*mine* is so reedy—I've heard myself on tape and can barely stop from gagging. And there's something about your manner too—also your chin— when you speak—it looks as if you're gritting your teeth but you *are* making yourself perfectly audible, don't be offended! The thing is, I'm doing Hedda myself, I can't help but be jealous of how you might do her in my place though it's all *my* imagination of course. Are you free for lunch? No? Yes? We could have it at my sorority—no, better out—it's not so claustrophobic, out. We'll have to hurry, though, Marya, is it? —Marya?—I have a class at one I don't *dare* cut again."

It gave Marya a feeling of distinct uneasiness, afterward, to think that Imogene had pursued *her.* Or, rather, that Imogene must have imagined herself the pursuer; and kept up for weeks the more active, the more charitably outgoing and inquisitive, of their two roles. (During their first conversation, for instance, Marya found herself stammering and blushing as she tried to answer Imogene's questions—Where are you from, what are you studying, where do you live on campus, what do you *think* of this place, isn't it disappointing?—put in so candid and ingenuous a manner, with that wide blue-eyed stare, Marya felt compelled to reply. She also felt vaguely criminal, guilty—as if she'd somehow drawn Imogene to her by the very intensity of her own interest, without Imogene's conscious knowledge.)

If Imogene reached out in friendship, at the beginning, Marya naturally drew back. She shared the Knauers' peasant shrewdness, or was it mean-spiritedness: what does this person want from *me,* why on earth would this person seek out *me?* It was mysterious, puzzling, disconcerting. Imogene was so pretty, so popular and self-assured, a dominant campus personality; Marya had only a scattering of friends—friendly acquaintances, really. She hadn't, as she rather coolly explained to Imogene, time for "wasting" on people.

She also disapproved of Imogene's public manner, her air of flippancy, carelessness. In fact Imogene was quite intelligent—her swiftness of thought, her skill at repartee, made that clear—but she played at seeming otherwise, to Marya's surprise and annoyance. Imogene was always *Imogene,* always *on.* She was a master of sudden dramatic reversals: sunny warmth that shaded into chilling mockery; low-voiced serious conversations, on religion, perhaps (Imogene was an agnostic who feared, she said, lapsing into Anglicanism—it ran in her family) that deteriorated into wisecracks and bawdy jokes simply because one of her theater friends appeared. While Marya was too reserved to ask Imogene about herself, Imogene was pitiless in her interrogation of Marya, once the formality of their first meeting was out of the way. Has your family *always* lived in that part of the state, do you mean your father was really a *miner,* how old were you when he died, how old were you when your mother died, do you keep in touch with your high school friends, are you happy here, are you in love with anyone, have you ever been in love, are you a virgin, do you have any plans for this summer, what will you do after graduation? what do you think your *life* will be? Marya was dazed, disoriented. She answered as succinctly and curtly as she dared, never really telling the truth, yet not precisely lying; she had the idea that Imogene could detect a lie; she'd heard her challenge others when she doubted the sincerity of what they said. Half-truths went down very well, however. Half-truths, Marya had begun to think, were so much more reasonable—so much more convincing—than whole truths.

For surely brazen golden-haired Imogene Skillman didn't really want to know the truth about Marya's family—her father's death (of a heart attack, aged thirty-nine, wasn't that a possibility?—having had rheumatic fever, let's say, as a boy); her mother's disappearance that was, at least poetically, a kind of death too (automobile accident, Marya ten at the time, no one to blame). Marya was flattered, as who would not be, by

Imogene's intense *interest* and *sympathy* ("You seem to have had such a hard life . . .") but she was shrewd enough to know she must not push her friend's generosity of spirit too far: it was one thing to be moved, another thing to be repulsed.

So she was sparing with the truth. A little truth goes a long way, she thought, not knowing if the remark was an old folk saying or something she'd coined herself.

She told herself that she resented Imogene's manner, her assumption of an easygoing informality that was all one-sided, or nearly; at the same time it couldn't be denied that Marya Knauer visibly brightened in Imogene Skillman's presence. She saw with satisfaction how Imogene's friends—meeting them in the student union, in the pub, in the restaurants and coffee shops along Fairfield Street—watched them with curiosity and must have wondered who Imogene's new friend was.

Marya Knauer: but who is *she?* where did Imogene pick up *her?*

Marya smiled cynically to herself, thinking that she understood at last the gratification a man must feel, in public, in the company of a beautiful woman. Better, really, than being the beautiful woman yourself.

They would have quarreled, everything would have gone abrasive and sour immediately, if Marya hadn't chosen (consciously, deliberately) to admire Imogene's boldness, rather than to be insulted by it. (*Are you happy, are you lonely, have you ever been in love, are you a virgin?*—no one had ever dared ask Marya such questions. The Knauers were reticent, prudish, about such things as personal feelings: Wilma might haul off and slap her, and call her a little shit, but she'd have been convulsed with embarrassment to ask Marya if she was happy or unhappy, if she loved anyone, if, maybe, she knew how Wilma loved *her.* Just as Lee and Everard might quarrel, and Lee might dare to tell his brawny hot-tempered father to go to hell, but he'd never have asked him—he'd never have even imagined asking him—how much money he made in a year, how much he had in the bank, what the property was worth, did he have a will, did he guess that, well, Lee sort of looked up to *him,* loved *him,* despite all these fights?)

Marya speculated that she'd come a great distance from Innisfail and the Canal Road—light-years, really, not two hundred miles—and she had to be careful, cautious, about speaking in the local idiom.

Imogene was nearly as tall as Marya, and her gold-gleaming hair and ebullient manner made her seem taller. Beside her, Marya knew herself shabby, undramatic, unattractive; it was not *her* prerogative to take offense, to recoil from her friend's extreme interest. After all—were so very many people interested in her, here in Port Oriskany? Did anyone really care if she lied, or told the truth, or invented ingenious half-truths . . . ? In any case, despite Imogene's high spirits, there was usually something harried about her. She hadn't studied enough for an exam, play rehearsals were going badly, she'd had an upsetting telephone call from home the night before, what in Christ's name was she to *do?* . . . Marya noted that beautiful white-toothed smile marred by tiny tics of vexation. Imogene was always turning the diamond ring round and round her finger, impatiently; she fussed with her earrings and hair; she was always late, always running—her coat unbuttoned and flapping about her, her tread heavy. Her eyes sometimes filled with tears that were, or were not, genuine.

Even her agitation, Marya saw, was enviable. There are certain modes of unhappiness with far more style than happiness.

Imogene insisted that Marya accompany her to a coffee shop on Fairfield—pretentiously called a coffee "house"—where all her friends gathered. These were her *real* friends, apart from her sorority sisters and her fraternity admirers. Marya steeled herself against their critical amused eyes; she didn't want to be one of their subjects for mimicry. (They did devastating imitations of their professors and even of one another —Marya had to admit, laughing, that they were really quite good. If only she'd known such people back in Innisfail!—in high school!—she might have been less singled out for disapproval; she might have been less lonely.)

Marya made certain that she gave her opinions in a quick flat unhesitating voice, since opinions tenuously offered were usually rejected. If she chose to talk with these people at all she made sure that she talked fast, so that she wouldn't be interrupted. (They were always interrupting one another, Imogene included.) With her excellent memory Marya could, if required, quote passages from the most difficult texts; her vocabulary blossomed wonderfully in the presence of a critical, slightly hostile audience she knew she *must* impress. (For Imogene prided herself on Marya Knauer's brilliance, Marya Knauer's knowledge and wit. Yes, that's right, she would murmur, laughing, nudging Marya in the ribs, go on, go *on*, you're absolutely right—you've got them now!) And Marya smoked cigarettes with the others, and drank endless cups of bitter black coffee, and flushed with pleasure when things went well . . . though she was wasting a great deal of time these days, wasn't she? . . . and wasn't time the precious element that would carry her along to her salvation?

The coffee shop was several blocks from the university's great stone archway, a tunnel-like place devoid of obvious charm, where tables were crowded together and framed photographs of old, vanished athletes lined the walls. Everyone—Imogene's "everyone"—drifted there to escape from their living residences and to sit for hours, talking loudly and importantly, about Strindberg, or Whitman, or Yeats, or the surrealists, or Prufrock, or Artaud, or *Ulysses,* or the Grand Inquisitor; or campus politics (who was in, who was out); or the theater department (comprised half of geniuses and saints, half of losers). Marya soon saw that several of the boys were in love with Imogene, however roughly they sometimes treated her. She didn't care to learn their names but of course she did anyway—Scott, and Andy, and Matthew (who took a nettlesome sort of dislike to Marya); there was a dark ferret-faced mathematics student named Brian whose manner was broadly theatrical and whose eyeglasses flashed with witty malice. The other girls in the group were attractive enough, in fact quite striking, but they were no match for Imogene when she was most herself.

Of course the love, even the puppyish affection, went unrequited. Imogene was engaged—the diamond ring was always in sight, glittering and winking; Imogene occasionally made reference to someone named Richard, whose opinion she seemed to value highly. (What is Imogene's fiancé like, Marya asked one of the girls, and was told he was "quiet"— "watchful"—that Imogene behaved a little differently around him; she was quieter herself.)

One wintry day when Marya should have been elsewhere she sat with Imogene's friends in a booth at the smoky rear of the coffee shop, half listening to their animated talk, wondering why Imogene cared so much for them. Her mind drifted loose; she found herself examining one of the photographs on the wall close by. It was sepia-tinted, and very old: the 1899 university rowing team. Beside it was a photograph of the 1902 football team. How young those smiling athletes must have felt, as the century turned, Marya thought. It must have seemed to them . . . *theirs.*

She was too lazy to excuse herself and leave. She was too jealous of Imogene. No, it was simply that her head ached; she hadn't slept well the night before and wouldn't sleep well tonight. . . . Another rowing team. Hopeful young men, standing so straight and tall; their costumes slightly comical; their haircuts bizarre. An air of team spirit, hearty optimism, doom. Marya swallowed hard, feeling suddenly strange. She really should leave. . . . She really shouldn't be here. . . .

Time had been a nourishing stream, a veritable sea, for those young men. Like fish they'd swum in it without questioning it—without knowing it was the element that sustained them and gave them life. And then it had unaccountably withdrawn and left them exposed. . . . Forever youthful in those old photographs, in their outdated costumes; long since aged, dead, disposed of.

Marya thought in a panic that she must leave; she must return to her room and lock the door.

But when she rose Imogene laid a hand on her arm and asked irritably what was wrong, why was she always jumping up and down: couldn't she for Christ's sake sit *still*?

The vehemence of Imogene's response struck them all, it was in such disproportion to Marya's behavior. Marya herself was too rushed, too frightened, to take offense. She murmured, "Goodbye, Imogene," without looking at her; and escaped.

It was that night, not long before curfew, that Imogene dropped by for the first time at Maynard House. She rapped on Marya's door, poked her head in, seemed to fill the doorway, chattering brightly as if nothing were wrong; as if they'd parted amiably. Of course she *was* rather rude about the room —Marya hadn't realized it must have been a maid's room, in the house's earliest incarnation—but Imogene's rudeness as always passed by rather casually, in a sort of golden blur.

Tell me about these drawings, she said, I didn't know you were an artist. These are *good*.

But Marya wasn't in a mood for idle conversation. She said indifferently that she *wasn't* an artist; she was a student.

But Imogene insisted she was an artist. Because the sketches were so rough, unfinished, yet they caught the eye, there was something unnerving about them. "Do you see yourself like this, though? Marya?" Imogene asked almost wistfully. "So stern and ugly? it *isn't* you, is it?"

"It isn't anyone," Marya said. "It's a few charcoal strokes on old paper."

She was highly excited that Imogene Skillman had come to her room: had anyone on the floor noticed? had the girl downstairs at the desk, on telephone duty, noticed? At the same time she wished her gone, it was an intrusion into her privacy, insufferable. She had never invited Imogene to visit her—she never would.

"So this is where you live," Imogene said, drawing a

(146)

deep breath. Her eyes darted mercilessly about; she would miss nothing, forget nothing. "You're alone and you don't mind, that's *just* like you. You have a whole other life, a sort of secret life, don't you," she said, with a queer pouting downward turn of her lips.

Friendship, Marya speculated in her journal, the most enigmatic of all relationships.

In a sense it flourished unbidden; in another, it had to be cultivated, nurtured, sometimes even forced into existence. Though she was tirelessly active in most aspects of her life she'd always been quite passive when it came to friendship. She hadn't time, she told herself; she hadn't energy for something so . . . ephemeral.

Nothing was worthwhile, really worthwhile, except studying; getting high grades; and her own reading, her own work. Sometimes Marya found herself idly contemplating a young man—in one of her classes, in the library; sometimes, like most of her female classmates, she contemplated one or another of her male professors. But she didn't want a lover, not even a romance. To cultivate romance, Marya thought, you had to give over a great deal of time for daydreaming: she hadn't time to waste on *that.*

Since the first month of her freshman year Marya had acquired a reputation for being brilliant—the word wasn't hers but Imogene's: "Do you know everyone thinks you're brilliant, everyone is afraid of you?"—and it struck Marya as felicitous, a sort of glass barrier that would keep other people at a distance. And then again she sometimes looked up from her reading and noted that hours had passed; where was she and what was she doing to herself? (Had someone called her? Whispered her name? Marya, Marya. . . . You little savage, Marya. . . .) Suddenly she ached with the desire to see Wilma, and Everard; and her brothers; even Lee. She felt as if she must leave this airless little cubbyhole of a room—take a Greyhound bus to Innisfail—see that house on the Canal Road— sit at the kitchen table with the others—tell them she loved them, she loved them and couldn't help herself: what was happening?

Great handfuls of her life were being stolen from her and she would never be able to retrieve them.

To counteract Imogene Skillman's importance in her life, Marya made it a point to be friendly—if not, precisely, to *become friends*—with a number of Maynard House girls. She frequently ate meals with them in the dining hall a few blocks away, though she was inclined (yes, it was rude) to bring along a book or two just in case. And if the conversation went nowhere Marya would murmur, Do you mind? I have so much reading to do.

Of course they didn't mind. Catherine or Phyllis or Sally or Diane. They too were scholarship students; they too were frightened, driven.

(Though Marya knew they discussed her behind her back. She was the only girl in the house with a straight-A average and they were waiting . . . were they perhaps hoping? . . . for her to slip down a notch or two. They were afraid of her sarcasm, her cutting wit. Then again, wasn't she sometimes very funny? If you liked that sort of humor. As for the sorority girl Imogene Skillman: what did Marya see in *her*? what did *she* see in Marya? It was also likely, wasn't it, that Marya was the house thief? For the thief still walked off with things sporadically. These were mean, pointless thefts—a letter from a mailbox, another textbook, a single angora glove, an inexpensive locket on a tarnished silver chain. Pack-rat sorts of thievery, unworthy, in fact, of any girl who roomed in Maynard.)

When Marya told Imogene about the thief and the money she'd lost, Imogene said indifferently that there was a great deal of stealing on campus, and worse things too (this, with a sly twist of her lips), but no one wanted to talk about it; the student newspaper (the editors were all friends of hers, she knew such things) was forever being censored. For instance, last year a girl committed suicide by slashing her wrists in one of the off-campus senior houses and the paper wasn't allowed to publish the news, not even to *hint* at it, and the local newspaper didn't run anything either, it was all a sort of totalitarian kindergarten state, the university. As for theft: "*I've* never stolen anything in my life," Imogene said, smiling, brooding, "because why would I want anything that somebody else has already had? something secondhand, used?"

Your friend Imogene, people began to say.

Your friend Imogene: she dropped by at noon, left this note for you.

Marya's pulses rang with pleasure, simple gratitude. She was flattered but—well, rather doubtful. Did she even *like* Imogene? Were they really friends? In a sense she liked one or two of the girls in Maynard better than she liked Imogene. Phyllis, for instance, a mathematics major, very sharp, very bright, though almost painfully shy; and a chunky farm girl named Diane from a tiny settlement north of Shaheen Falls, precociously matronly, with thick glasses and a heavy tread on the stairs and a perpetual odor of unwashed flesh, ill-laundered clothes. . . . But Diane was bright, very bright; Marya thought privately that here was her real competition at Port Oriskany, encased in baby fat, blinking through those thick lenses. (The residence buzzed with the rumor, however, that Diane was doing mysteriously poorly in her courses, had she a secret grief? an unstated terror?) Marya certainly liked Phyllis and Diane, she recognized them as superior individuals, really much nicer, much kinder, than Imogene. Yet she had to admit it would not have deeply troubled her if she never saw them again. And the loss of Imogene would have been a powerful blow.

She went twice to see the production of *Hedda Gabler* in which Imogene starred. For she really did star, it was a one-woman show. That hard slightly drawling slightly nasal voice, the mercurial manner (cruel, seductive, mock-sweet, languid, genuinely anguished by turns), certain odd tricks and mannerisms (the way she held her jaw, for instance: had she pilfered that from Marya?)—Imogene was *really* quite good; really a success. And they'd made her up to look even more beautiful on stage than she looked in life: her golden hair in a heavy Victorian twist, her cheeks subtly rouged, her eyes enormous. Only in the tense sparring scene with Judge Brack, when Hedda was forced to confront a personality as strong as her own, did Imogene's acting falter: her voice went strident, her manner became too broadly erotic.

Marya thought, slightly dazed, Is she really talented? Is there some basis for her reputation, after all?

Backstage, Marya didn't care to compete for Imogene's attention; let the others hug and kiss her and shriek congratulations if they wished. It was all exaggerated, florid, embarrassing . . . so much emotion, such a *display*. . . . And Imogene looked wild, frenzied, her elaborate makeup now rather clownish, seen at close quarters. "Here's Marya," she announced, "Marya will tell the truth—here's Marya—shut up, you idiots!—she'll tell the truth—*was* I any good, Marya?— *was* I really Hedda?" She pushed past her friends and gripped Marya's hands, staring at her with great shining painted eyes. She smelled of greasepaint and powder and perspiration; it seemed to Marya that Imogene towered over her.

"Of course you were good," Marya said flatly. "You know you were good."

Imogene gripped her hands tighter, her manner was feverish, outsized. "What are you saying? You didn't care for the performance? It wasn't right? I failed?"

"Don't be ridiculous," Marya said, embarrassed, trying to pull away. "You don't need me to assess you, in any case. You *know* you were—"

"You didn't like it! Did you!"

"—you were perfect."

"*Perfect!*" Imogene said in a hoarse stage voice. "But that doesn't sound like one of your words, Marya—you don't *mean* it."

It was some seconds before Marya, her face burning with embarrassment and resentment, could extricate her hands from Imogene's desperate grip. No, she couldn't come to the cast party; she had to get back to work. And yes, yes, for Christ's sake, *yes*—Imogene had been "perfect": or nearly.

Friendship, Marya wrote in her journal, her heart pounding with rage—play-acting of an amateur type.

Friendship, she wrote—a puzzle that demands too much of the imagination.

So she withdrew from Imogene, tried even to stop thinking about her, looking for her on campus. (That blue muffler, that camel's-hair coat. And she had a new coat too: Icelandic shearling, with a black fur collar.) She threw herself into her work with more passion than before. Exams were upon her, papers were due, she felt the challenge with a sort of eager dread, an actual greed, knowing she could do well even if she didn't work hard; and she intended to work very, very hard. Even if she got sick, even if her eyes went bad.

Hour upon hour of reading, taking notes, writing, rewriting. In her room, the lamp burning through the night; in one or another of her secret places in the library; in a corner of an old brick mansion a quarter mile away that had been converted into the music school, where she might read and scribble notes and daydream, her heartbeat underscored by the muffled sounds of pianos, horns, violins, cellos, flutes, from the rows of practice rooms. The sounds—the various musics —were all rather harmonious, heard like this, in secret. Marya thought, closing her eyes: If you could only *be* music.

At the same time she had her job in the library, her ill-paid job, a drain on her time and spirit, a terrible necessity. She explained that she'd lost her entire paycheck—the money had been stolen out of her wallet—she *must* be allowed to work a little longer, to clock a few more hours each week. She intended (so she explained to her supervisor) to make up the loss she'd suffered by disciplining herself severely, spending no extra money if she could avoid it. (The Parker pen could never be replaced, of course. As for the money: Marya washed her hair now once a week, and reasoned that she did not really need toothpaste, why did anyone *need* toothpaste?—she was sparing with her toiletries in general, and, if she could, used other girls', left in the third floor bathroom. She was always coming upon lost ballpoint pens, lost notebooks, even loose change; she could appropriate—lovely word, "appropriate" —cheap mimeograph paper from a supply room in the library; sometimes she even found half-empty packs of cigarettes—though her newest resolution was to stop smoking, since she resented every penny spent on so foolish a habit. Her puritan spirit blazed; she thought it an emblem of her purity that the waistbands of her skirts were now too loose, her underwear was a size too large.)

After an evening of working in the library—her pay was approximately $1 an hour—she hurried home to Maynard, exhausted, yet exhilarated, eager to get to her schoolwork. Once she nearly fainted running up the stairs and Diane, who happened to be nearby, insisted that she come into her room for a few minutes. You look terrible, she said in awe—almost as bad as I do. But Marya brushed her aside, Marya hadn't time. She was lightheaded from the stairs, that was all.

One night Imogene telephoned just before the switchboard was to close. What the hell was wrong, Imogene demanded, was Marya angry at her? She hurried out of class before Imogene could say two words to her—she never came down to Fairfield Street any longer—was she secretly in love? —was she working longer hours at the library?—would she like to come to dinner sometime this week, at the sorority?— or next week, before Christmas break?

Yes, thought Marya, bathed in gratitude, in golden splendor, "No," she said aloud, quietly, chastely, "but thank you very much."

Schopenhauer, Dickens, Marx, Euripides. Oscar Wilde. Henry Adams. Sir Thomas More. Thomas Hobbes. And Shakespeare—of course. She read, she took notes, she daydreamed. It sometimes disturbed her that virtually nothing of what she read had been written by women (except Jane Austen, dear perennial Jane, *so* feminine!) but in her arrogance she told herself *she* would change all that.

Is this how it begins, she wondered, half amused. Breaking down. Cracking up.

Why breaking *down* . . . but cracking *up* . . . ?

Her long periods of intense concentration began to be punctuated by bouts of directionless daydreaming, sudden explosions of *feeling.* At such times Shakespeare was too dangerous to be read closely—Hamlet whispered truths too cruel to be borne, every word in *Lear* hooked in flesh and could not be dislodged. As for Wilde, Hobbes, Schopenhauer . . . even cynicism, Marya saw, can't save you.

At such times she went for walks along Masefield Avenue, past the enormous sorority and fraternity houses. They too were converted mansions but had retained much of their original glamour and stateliness. Imogene's, for instance, boasted pretentious white columns, four of them, in mock–Southern Colonial style. The cryptic Greek letters on the portico struck an especially garish and irrelevant note. What did such symbols mean, what did it mean (so Marya wondered, not quite bitterly) to be *clubbable*? In the winter twilight, in the cold, these outsized houses appeared especially warm and secretive; every window of their several stories blazed. Marya thought, Why don't I feel anything, can't I envy, even feel envy . . . ? But the sororities were crudely discriminatory (one was exclusively for Catholic girls, another exclusively for Jewish girls, the sixteen others had quotas for Catholics and blackballed all Jews who dared cross their threshold: the procedure was that blunt, that childish). Dues and fees were absurdly high, beyond the inflated price for room and board; the meetings involved pseudo-religious "Greek" rituals (handshakes, secret passwords, special prayers). Imogene complained constantly, was always cutting activities and being fined ($10 fine for missing a singing rehearsal!—the very thought made Marya shiver in disbelief), always mocking the alums, those well-to-do matrons with too much time on their hands. Such assholes, all of them, Imogene said loftily, such *pretentious* assholes. It was part of Imogene's charm that she could be both contemptuous of pretension and marvelously—shamelessly— pretentious herself.

Time is the element in which we exist, Marya noted solemnly in her journal. We are either borne along by it or drowned in it.

It occurred to her with a chilling certitude that *every moment not consciously devoted to her work* was an error, a blunder. As if you can kill time, Thoreau said, without injuring Eternity.

Lying drowsily and luxuriously in bed after she'd wakened . . . conversations with most people, or, indeed, *all* people . . . spending too long in the shower, or cleaning her room, or staring out the window, or eating three meals a day (unless of course she brought along a book to read) . . . daydreaming and brooding about Innisfail, or the Canal Road, or that wretched little tarpaper-roofed shanty near Shaheen Falls that had been her parents' house . . . crying over the past (though in fact she rarely cried these days) as if the past were somehow present. In high school she had been quite an athlete, especially at basketball; in college she hadn't time, hadn't the slightest interest. It pleased her that she always received grades of A but at the same time she wondered, Are these *really* significant grades, do I *really* know anything? Or is Port Oriskany one of the backwaters of the world, where nothing, even "excellence," greatly matters? She needed high grades in order to get into graduate school, however; beyond that she didn't allow herself to think. Though perhaps she wouldn't go to graduate school at all . . . perhaps she would try to write . . . her great problem being not that she hadn't anything to write about but that she had too much.

Unwisely, once, she confided in Imogene that she halfway feared to write anything that wasn't academic or scholarly or firmly rooted in the real world: once she began she wouldn't be able to stop: she was afraid of sinking too deep into her own head, cracking up, becoming lost.

Imogene said at once that Marya was just the type to be excessive, she needed reining in. "I know the symptoms," she said severely. Anyway, what good would academic success— or any kind of success—do her, if she destroyed her health?

"You're concerned about my health?" Marya asked incredulously.

"Of course. Yes. I *am.* Why shouldn't I be," Imogene said, "aren't I a friend of yours?"

Marya stared at her, unable to reply. It struck her as wildly incongruous that Imogene Skillman, with her own penchant for abusing her health (she drank too much at fraternity parties, she stayed up all night doing hectic last-minute work), should be worrying about Marya.

"Aren't I a friend of yours?" Imogene asked less certainly. "Don't I have the right . . . ?"

Marya turned away with an indifferent murmur, perhaps because she was so touched.

"My health isn't of any use to me," she said, "if I don't get anything accomplished. If I fail."

Of course it was possible, Marya saw, to ruin one's health and fail anyway.

Several of her fellow residents in Maynard House were doing poorly in their courses, despite their high intelligence and the goading terror that energized them. One of them was Phyllis, who was failing an advanced calculus class; another, a chronically withdrawn and depressed girl named Mary, a physics major, whose deeply shadowed eyes and pale grainy skin, as well as her very name, struck a superstitious chord of dread in Marya—she avoided her as much as possible, and had the idea that Mary avoided *her.*

The university piously preached an ethic of knowledge for its own sake—knowledge and beauty being identical—the "entire person" was to be educated, not simply the mind; but of course it acted swiftly and pragmatically upon another ethic entirely. Performance was all, the grade-point average *was* everything. Marya, no idealist, saw that this was sound and just; but she felt an impatient sort of pity for those who fell by the wayside or who, like the scholarship girls, in not being *best,* were to be judged *worthless* and sent back home. (Anything below a B was failing for them.) She wanted only to be best, to be outstanding, to be . . . defined to herself as extraordinary . . . for, apart from being extraordinary, had she any essence at all?

The second semester of her freshman year she had come close to losing her perfect grade-point average. Unwisely, she signed up for a course in religion, having been attracted to the books on the syllabus and the supplementary reading list (the Upanishads; the Bhagavad-Gita; the Bible; the Koran; *Hymns of the Rig-Veda*; books on Gnosticism, and Taoism, and medieval Christianity, and the Christian heresies, and animism, magic, witchcraft, Renaissance ideas of Platonic love). It was all very promising, very heady stuff; quite the antidote to the catechismal Catholicism in which Marya no longer believed, and for which she had increasingly less tolerance. The professor, however, turned out to be an ebullient balding popinjay who lectured from old notes in a florid and self-dramatizing style, presenting ideas in a mélange clearly thrown together from others' books and articles. He wanted nothing more than these ideas (which were fairly simple, not at all metaphysical or troubling) given back to him on papers and examinations; and he did not encourage questions from the class. Marya would surely have done well—she transcribed notes faultlessly, even when contemptuous of their content—but she could not resist sitting in stony silence and refusing to laugh when the professor embarked upon one or another of his jocular anecdotes. It was a classroom mannerism of his, almost a sort of tic, that each time he alluded to something female he lowered his voice and added, as if off the cuff, a wry observation, meant not so much to be insulting as to be mildly teasing. He was a popular lecturer, well-liked by most, not taken seriously by the better students; even the girls laughed at his jokes, being grateful, as students are, for something—anything—to laugh at. Marya alone sat with her arms folded, her brow furrowed, staring. It was not until some years later that she realized, uncomfortably, how she must have appeared to that silly perspiring man—a sort of gorgon in the midst of his amiable little sea of admirers.

So it happened that, though Marya's grades for the course were all A's, the grade posted for her final examination was C; and the final grade for the course—a humiliating B+.

Marya was stunned, Marya was sickened—she would have had to reach back to her childhood—or to the night of that going-away party—for an episode of equal mortification. That it was petty made it all the more mortifying.

I can forget this insult and forget him, Marya instructed herself, or I can go to him and protest. To forget it seemed in a way noble, even Christian; to go to the man's office and humble herself in trying to get the grade raised (for she knew very well she hadn't written a C exam) somehow childish, degrading.

Of course she ran up to his office; made an appointment to see him; and, after a few minutes' clucking and fretting (he pretended she had failed to answer the last question, she hadn't handed in both examination booklets, but there the second booklet was, at the bottom of a heap of papers—ah, what a surprise!), he consented to raise the grade to A. And smiled roguishly at her, as if she had been caught out in mischief, or some sort of deception; for which he was forgiving her. "You seem like a rather grim young woman," he said, "you never smile—you look so *preoccupied.*" Marya stared at his swinging foot. He was a satyrish middle-aged man, red-brown tufts of hair in his ears, a paunch straining against his shirtfront, a strangely vulnerable smile; a totally mediocre personality in every way—vain, uncertain, vindictive—yet Marya could see why others liked him; he was predictable, safe, probably decent enough. But she hated him. She simply wanted him dead.

He continued as if not wanting to release her, waiting for her smile of blushing gratitude and her meek *thank you*— which assuredly was not going to come; he said again, teasing, "Are you *always* such an ungiving young woman, Miss Knauer?"—and Marya swallowed hard, and fixed her dark loathing stare on him, and said: "My mother is sick. She's been sick all semester. I know I shouldn't think about it much . . . I shouldn't depress other people . . . but sometimes I can't help it. She isn't expected to live much longer, the cancer has metastasized to the brain. . . . I'm sorry if I offended you."

He stared at her; then began to stammer his apologies, rising from his desk, flushing deeply—the very image of chagrin and repentance. In an instant the entire atmosphere between them changed. He was sorry, he murmured, so very sorry . . . of course he couldn't have known. . . .

A minute later Marya was striding down the corridor, her pulses beating hot, in triumph. In her coat pocket was the black fountain pen she had lifted from the man's cluttered desk.

An expensive pen, as it turned out. A Parker, with a squarish blunt nub, and the engraved initials E.W.S.

Marya used the pen to take notes in her journal, signing her name repeatedly, hypnotically: *Marya, Marya Knauer, Marya Marya Marya, Marya Knauer,* a name that eventually seemed to have been signed by someone else, a stranger.

The shame of having humbled herself before that ignorant man had been erased by the shame—what should have been shame—of theft.

So Marya speculated, thinking of that curious episode in her life. Eventually the pen ran out of ink and she put it in the top drawer of her bureau.

Phyllis began staying out late, violating curfew, returning to the residence drunk, disheveled, tearful, angry—she couldn't stand the four walls of her room any longer, she told Marya; she couldn't stand shutting the door upon herself.

One night she didn't return at all. It was said afterward that she had been picked up by Port Oriskany police, wandering downtown, miles away, dazed and only partly clothed in the bitter cold—the temperature had gone as low as −5 degrees F. She was taken at once to the emergency room of the city hospital; her parents, who lived upstate, were called; they came immediately the next morning to take her back home. No one at Maynard House was ever to see her again.

All the girls in the residence talked of Phyllis, somewhat dazed themselves, frightened. How quickly it had happened —how quickly Phyllis had disappeared. Marya was plied with questions about Phyllis (how many subjects was she failing, who were the boys she'd gone out with) but Marya didn't know; Marya grew vague, sullen.

And then the waters close over your head. This phrase ran through Marya's mind repeatedly.

They talked about Phyllis for two or three days, then forgot her.

The following Saturday, however, Phyllis' mother and older sister arrived to pack up her things, clean out her room, fill out a half-dozen university forms. The resident adviser accompanied them; they looked confused, nervous, rather lost. Both women had Phyllis' pale blond limp hair, her rather small, narrow face. How is Phyllis? some of the girls asked, smiling, cautious, and Mrs. Myer said without looking at anyone, Oh, Phyllis is fine, resting and eating and sleeping right again, sleeping good hours, she said, half reproachfully, as if sleeping right hadn't been possible in Maynard House; and they were all to blame. Marya asked whether she might be returning second semester. No, not that soon, Mrs. Myer said quickly. She and the silent older sister were emptying drawers, packing suitcases briskly. Marya helped with Phyllis' books and papers, which lay in an untidy heap on her desk and on the floor surrounding the desk. There were dust balls everywhere. A great cobweb in which the desiccated corpses of insects hung, including that of the spider itself. Stiffened crumpled Kleenex wadded into balls, everywhere underfoot. An odor of grime and despair. . . . Marya discovered a calculus bluebook slashed heavily in red with a grade of D; a five-page paper on a subject that made no sense to her—Ring theory?—with a blunt red grade of F. It seemed to Marya that Phyllis was far more real now, more present, than she had been in the past . . . even when she'd tried to comfort Marya by taking her in her arms.

Marya supposed she had been as close a friend as Phyllis had had at Port Oriskany. Yet Phyllis' mother and sister hadn't known her name, had no message for her . . . clearly Phyllis had never mentioned her to them at all. It was disappointing, sobering.

And the waters close over your head, Marya thought.

Then something remarkable happened: Marya had risen from Phyllis' closet, a pile of books in her arms, her hair in her face, when she happened to see Mrs. Myer dumping loose items out of a drawer into a suitcase: a comb, ballpoint pens, coins, loose pieces of jewelry—and her black fountain pen. *The* pen, unmistakable.

My God, Marya whispered.

No one heard. Marya stood rooted to the spot, staring, watching as her prize disappeared into Phyllis' suitcase, hidden now by a miscellany of socks and underwear. *The* pen— the emblem of her humiliation and triumph—disappearing forever.

It wasn't until months later that someone in Maynard made the observation that the thefts seemed to have stopped . . . since Phyllis moved out. And the rest of the girls (they were at breakfast, eight or ten of them at a table) took it up, amazed, reluctant, wondering. Was it possible . . . *Phyllis* . . . ?

Marya said quietly that they shouldn't say such things since it couldn't be proved; that constituted slander.

Wednesday dinner, a "formal" dinner, in Imogene's sorority house, and Marya is seated beside Imogene, self-conscious, unnaturally shy, eating her food without tasting it. She *can* appreciate the thick slabs of roast beef, the small perfectly cooked parsley potatoes, the handsome gilt-edged china, the white linen tablecloth ("Oh it's Portuguese—from Portugal"), the crystal water goblets, the numerous tall candles, the silvery-green silk wallpaper, the housemother's poised social chatter at the head table . . . and the girls' stylized animation, their collective stylized beauty. For they *are* beautiful, without exception; as unlike the girls of Maynard House as one species is unlike another.

Imogene Skillman, in this dazzling context, isn't Marya's friend; she is clearly a sorority girl; even wearing her pin with its tiny diamonds and rubies just above her left breast. Her high delicate laughter echoes that of the others . . . she isn't going to laugh coarsely here, or say anything witty and obscene . . . she can be a little mischievous, just a little cutting, at best. Marya notes how refined her table manners have become for the occasion; how practiced she is at passing things about, summoning one of the houseboys for assistance without quite looking at him. (The houseboy in his white uniform!— one of a subdued and faintly embarrassed little squadron of four or five boys, he turns out to be an acquaintance of Marya's from her Shakespeare class, who resolutely avoids her eye throughout the prolonged meal.)

Marya makes little effort to take part in the table's conversation, which swings from campus topics to vacation plans —Miami Beach, Sarasota, Bermuda, Barbados, Trinidad, Switzerland ("for skiing"). Where are you going? Imogene asks Marya brightly, and Marya, with a pinched little smile, says she will spend a few days at home, then return to school; she has work to do that must be done here. And Imogene's friends gaze upon her with faint neutral smiles. Is this the one Imogene boasted of, who is so intelligent and so well-spoken . . . ? So *witty* . . . ?

For days Marya has been anticipating this dinner, half in dread and half in simple childish excitement. She feared being ravenous with hunger and eating too much out of anxiety; she feared having no appetite at all. But everything is remote, detached, impersonal. Everything is taking place at a little distance from her. A mistake, my coming here, she thinks, my being invited. But she doesn't feel any great nervousness or discomfort. Like the uniformed houseboys who stand with such unnatural stiffness near the doorway to the kitchen, Marya is simply waiting for the meal to end.

She finds herself thinking of friendship, in the past tense. Phyllis, and Diane, and one or two others at Maynard; and, back in Innisfail, Bonnie Michalak, Erma Dietz. She *might* have been a close friend to any of these girls but of course she wasn't, isn't. As for Imogene—she knows she is disappointing Imogene but she can't seem to force herself to care. She half-way resents Imogene for having invited her—for having made a fool out of *herself,* in bringing Marya Knauer to dinner.

"How pretty you look," Imogene said, very nearly puzzled, when Marya arrived at six-thirty, "what have you *done* to yourself?"

Marya flushed with annoyance; then laughed; with such exuberance that Imogene laughed with her. For it *was* amusing, wasn't it?—Marya Knauer with her hair attractively up in a sort of French twist; Marya Knauer with her lips reddened and her eyebrows plucked ("pruned," she might have said); Marya Knauer in a green-striped jersey dress that fitted her almost perfectly. A formal dinner meant high heels and stockings, which Marya detested; but she was wearing them nonetheless. And all for Imogene.

Yet now, seated beside Imogene, she pays very little attention to her friend's chatter; she feels subdued, saddened; thinking instead of old friendships, old half friendships, that year or so during which she'd imagined herself extraordinary, because it had seemed that Emmett Schroeder loved her. She had not loved him—she wasn't capable, she supposed, of loving anyone—but she had certainly basked in the sunny intensity of *his* love: she'd lapped it up eagerly, thirstily (so she very nearly saw herself, a dog lapping water), as if convinced that it had something to do with her. And now Imogene's friendship, which she knows she cannot keep for very long . . .

Imogene who has a reputation for being as recklessly improvident with her female friends as with her male friends. . . . Why make the effort, Marya reasons, when all that matters in life is one's personal accomplishment? Work, success, that numbing grade-point average . . . that promise of a future, any future. . . .

While Imogene and several of the others are discussing (animatedly, severely) a sorority sister not present, Marya studies her face covertly; recalls an odd remark Imogene made some weeks ago. The measure of a person's love for you is the depth of his hurt at your betrayal: *that's* the only way you can know how much, or how little, you matter.

Imogene's face had fairly glowed in excited triumph, as she told Marya this bit of wisdom. Marya thought, She knows from experience, the bitch. She knows her own value.

Imogene is telling a silly convoluted story about a dear friend of hers (it turns out to be Matthew, devoted Matthew) who "helped" her with her term paper on Chekhov: she'd given him a messy batch of notes, he was kind enough to "arrange" them and "expand upon them" and "shape them into an 'A' paper." He's a saint, Imogene says sighing, laughing, so sweet and so patient; so pathetic, really. But now Imogene is worried ("terrified") that their professor will call her into his office and interrogate her on her own paper, which she hadn't had time to read in its entirety; it was thirty pages long and heavy with footnotes. The girls assure her that if he marked it "A" it *is* an "A"; he'd never ask to see it again. Yes, says Imogene, opening her eyes wide, but wait until he reads my final exam, and I say these ridiculous things about Chekhov!

Part of this is play-acting, Marya knows, because Imogene is quite intelligent enough, on the subject of Chekhov or anything else connected with drama; so Marya says, though not loudly enough for the entire table to hear: "That wasn't a very kind thing for *you* to do, was it? and not very honest either."

Imogene chooses not to hear the tone of Marya's remark;

she says gaily: "Oh, you mean leading poor Matt on? Making him think—? But otherwise he wouldn't have written so *well,* there wouldn't have been so many impressive *footnotes.*"

Marya doesn't reply. Marya draws her thumbnail hard against the linen tablecloth, making a secret indentation.

Imogene says, making a joke of it, "Marya's such a puritan—I know better than to ask help of *her.*"

Marya doesn't rise to the bait; the conversation shifts onto other topics; in another fifteen minutes the lengthy dinner is over.

"You aren't going home immediately, are you?" Imogene says, surprised. She is smiling but there are strain lines around her mouth. "Come upstairs to my room for a while. Come *on,* we haven't had a chance to talk."

"Thank you for everything," says Marya. "But I really have to leave. I'm pressed for time these days. . . ."

"You *are* angry? about that silly Matthew?" Imogene says.

Marya shrugs her shoulders, turns indifferently away.

"Well—are *you* so honest?" Imogene cries.

Marya gets her coat from the closet, her face burning. (Are *you* so honest! *You!*) Imogene is apologizing, talking of other things, laughing, while Marya thinks calmly that she will never see Imogene Skillman again.

"There's no reason why you shouldn't take this coat, it's a perfectly good coat," Imogene said in her "serious" voice—frank, level, unemphatic. "I don't want it any longer because I have so many coats, I never get to wear it and it *is* perfectly lovely, it shouldn't just hang in the closet. . . . Anyway here it is; I think it would look wonderful on you."

Marya stared at the coat. It was the camel's-hair she had long admired. Pleasantly scratchy beneath her fingers, belted in back, with a beautiful silky-beige lining: she estimated it would have cost $250 or more, new. And it was almost new.

(Marya's coat, bought two or three years before in Innisfail, had cost $45 on sale.)

Imogene insisted, and Marya tried on the coat, flicking her hair out from inside the collar, studying herself critically in Imogene's full-length mirror. Imogene was saying, "If you're worrying that people will know it's my coat—it *was* my coat—don't: camel's-hair coats all look alike. Except they don't look like wool imitations."

Marya met Imogene's frank blue gaze in the mirror. "What about your parents, your mother? won't someone wonder where the coat has gone?"

Imogene puckered her forehead quizzically. "What business is it of theirs?" she asked. "It's *my* coat. My things are mine, I do what I want with them."

Marya muttered that she just couldn't *take* the coat, and Imogene scolded her for talking with her jaw clenched, and Marya protested in a louder voice, yet still faintly, weakly. . . . "It's a beautiful coat," she said. She was thinking: It's too good for me. I can't accept and I can't refuse and I hate Imogene for this humiliation.

Imogene brought the episode to an end by saying rather coldly, "You'll hurt my feelings, Knauer, if you refuse it. If you're weighing your pride against mine, don't bother—mine is far, far more of a burden."

"So you are—Marya," Mrs. Skillman said in an ambiguous voice (warm? amused? doubtful?) in the drab front parlor of Maynard House, as Marya approached. She and Mr. Skillman and Imogene were taking Marya out to dinner, downtown at the Statler Chop House, one of the area's good restaurants. "We've heard so much about you from Imogene," Mrs. Skillman said, "I think we were expecting someone more . . ."

"Oh, Mother, what on earth!" Imogene laughed sharply.

". . . I was going to say *taller,* perhaps *older,*" Mrs. Skillman said, clearly annoyed by her daughter's interruption.

Marya shook hands with both the Skillmans and saw to her relief that they appeared to be friendly well-intentioned people, attractive enough, surely, and very well-dressed, but nothing like their striking daughter. *She* might have been their daughter, brunette and subdued. (Except she hadn't dared wear the camel's-hair coat, as Imogene had wanted. She was wearing her old plaid wool and her serviceable rubberized boots.)

In their presence Imogene was a subtly different person. Rather more ingenuous, childlike, sweet. Now and then at dinner Marya heard a certain self-mocking tone in her friend's voice ("Am I playing this scene correctly? How is it going down?") but neither of the Skillmans took notice; and perhaps it was Marya's imagination anyway.

Then, near the end of the meal, Imogene got suddenly high on white wine and said of her father's business, "It's a sophisticated form of theft."

She giggled; no one else laughed; Marya kept her expression carefully blank.

". . . I mean it *is,* you know . . . it's indirect . . . 'Savings and Loans' . . . and half the clients blacks who want their big Dee-troit cars financed," Imogene said.

"Imogene, you aren't funny," Mrs. Skillman said.

"She's just teasing," Mr. Skillman said. "My little girl likes to tease."

"I do like to tease, don't I? Marya knows," Imogene said, nudging her. Then, as if returning to her earlier sobriety, she said, "*I never mean a word of what I say and everybody knows it.*"

The subject leaped to Imogene's negligence about writing letters, or even telephoning home. "If we try to call," Mrs. Skillman said, "the line at the house is busy for hours; and when we finally get through you aren't in; you're *never* in. And you never return our calls. . . ."

Imogene said carelessly that her sorority sisters were bad at taking down messages. Most of them were assholes, actually—

"Imogene!" Mrs. Skillman said.

"Oh, Mother, you know they *are,*" Imogene said in a childlike voice.

After an awkward pause Mr. Skillman asked about Richard: Richard had evidently telephoned *them,* asking if something was wrong with Imogene because he couldn't get through to her either. "Your mother and I were hoping there wasn't some sort of . . . misunderstanding between you."

Imogene murmured that there weren't any misunderstandings at all between them.

"He seemed to think . . . to wonder . . ." Mrs. Skillman said. "That is, as long as we were driving up to visit. . . ."

Imogene finished off her glass of white wine and closed her eyes ecstatically. She said, "I really don't care to discuss my private matters in a restaurant. Anyway, Marya is here: why don't we talk about something lofty and intellectual? *She's* taking a philosophy course—if she can't tell us the meaning of life no one can."

"You and Richard haven't quarreled, have you?" Mrs. Skillman said.

Imogene raised her left hand and showed the diamond ring to her mother, saying, "*Please* don't worry, I haven't given it back, it's safe." To Marya she said lightly, "Mother would be mortified if Dickie demanded it back. It's somebody's old dead socialite *grandmother's.*"

"Imogene," Mr. Skillman said, his voice edged with impatience, "you really shouldn't tease so much. I've just read that teasing is a form of aggression . . . did you know that?"

"Not that I'd give it back if Dickie *did* demand it." Imogene laughed. "It's mine, I've earned it, let him *sue* to get it back—right, Marya?—he's going to be a hotshot lawyer, after all. Let him *practice.*"

Everyone, including Marya, laughed as if Imogene had said something unusually witty; and Imogene, in the cool voice she used to summon the houseboys at her sorority, asked a passing waiter for more wine.

Richard.
"Dickie."
Am I jealous of someone called "Dickie"? Marya wondered, lying sprawled and slovenly across her bed. She was

doing rough, impatient charcoal sketches of imaginary faces—
beetle-browed, glowering, defiantly ugly—that inevitably
turned out to be forms of her own.

In Imogene's cluttered room on the second floor of the
baronial sorority house Marya had come upon, to her astonishment, copies of *Bride* magazine. She leafed through them,
jeering, while Imogene hid her face in laughing protestation.
Wedding gowns! Satin and pearls! Veils made of antique lace!
Orange blossoms! Shoes covered in white silk! And what is
this, Marya said, flapping the pages in Imogene's direction, a
wedding-cake bridegroom to go with it all?—standing a little
out of the range of the camera's focus, amiable and blurred.

"Ah, but you'll have to be a bridesmaid," Imogene said
dryly. "Or a maid of honor."

Imogene showed her snapshots of the legendary Richard,
flicking them like playing cards. Marya saw that, yes, Richard
was a handsome young man—dark strong features, a slightly
heavy chin, intelligent eyes. He was demanding, perhaps; an
excellent match for Imogene. But it was difficult, Marya
thought, to believe that the person in the snapshots—*this* person, standing with his hands on his hips, his hair lifting in the
wind—would be capable of loving Imogene as much as she
required being loved.

Imogene threw herself across her bed, lay on her back,
let her long hair dangle to the floor. Her belly was stretched
flat; her pelvic bones protruded. She smoothed her shirt across
her abdomen with long nervous fingers. "The first time I came
with him," she said hesitantly, but with a breathy laugh, "it
wasn't . . . you know . . . it wasn't with him inside me, the way
you're supposed to . . . I was afraid of that then, I thought I
might get pregnant. And he was so big, I thought he'd hurt
me, they're *very* big compared to . . . compared to us. The first
time it worked for me he was, well, you know, kissing me
there . . . he'd gotten all crazy and wild and I couldn't stop
him, and I never thought I would let anyone do that . . . I'd
heard about that . . . because . . . oh Marya, am I embarrassing

you? . . . because afterward," she said, laughing shrilly, "they only want to kiss you: and it's disgusting."

She rolled over amid the tumble of things strewn on her bed and hid her face from Marya.

After a long time she said, her breath labored, her face still turned away, "Am I embarrassing you?"

Marya's throat and chest were so constricted she couldn't reply.

A Marya Knauer anecdote, told by Imogene with peals of cruel ribald laughter.

Imogene insisted that Marya accompany her on a date, yes a "date," an actual "date" (though it was generally thought that Marya shunned men because she imagined they weren't *serious* enough). Her escort was Matthew Pine, of all people—Matthew who had seemed to dislike Marya but who in fact (so Imogene revealed) had simply been afraid of her.

"Afraid of me? you're being ridiculous," Marya said. She hardly knew whether to be hurt or flattered.

"Of course he's afraid of you, or was," Imogene said. "And my poor sorority sisters!—they told me afterward they'd never seen such eyes as yours—taking them all in and condemning them! *Those* assholes!"

It would be an ordinary evening, Imogene promised, no need to dress up, no *need* for the high-heels-stockings routine, though it was perfectly all right (so Imogene said innocently) if Marya wanted to comb her hair. Imogene's date for the evening was a senior in business administration and advertising whose name Marya never caught, or purposefully declined to hear. They drove out to a suburban mall to see a movie— in fact it was a pretentious French "film"—and then they went to a local Italian restaurant where everyone, excepting of course Marya, drank too much; and then they drove to the water-tower hill where numerous other cars were parked, their headlights off. Marya stiffened. Matthew had not yet touched her but she knew that he would be kissing her in

another minute; and she had no idea of how to escape grace-
fully.

"... few minutes?" Imogene murmured from the front
seat.

She was sending them away! Marya saw with disbelief
that, by the time she and Matthew climbed out of the car,
Imogene and her date were locked in a ravenous embrace.
One would have thought the two of them lovers; one would
have thought them at least fond of each other. Marya's heart
was beating frantically. That bitch! That bitch! Marya worried
that she might suffocate—she couldn't seem to catch her
breath.

Matthew took her cold unresisting hand. He slipped his
arm around her shoulders.

They were meant to stroll for a few minutes along the
darkened path, to contemplate, perhaps, the view of Port
Oriskany below, all sparkling winking lights. A romantic
sight, no doubt. Beautiful in its way. Matthew was saying
something rather forced, making a joke of some kind—about
the French movie?—about Imogene's reckless behavior?—but
Marya interrupted. "Isn't she supposed to be engaged?" she
asked. "Yes, I suppose so," Matthew said in resignation, "but
she does this all the time. It's just Imogene." "She does this
all the *time?*" Marya said, "but why?" Matthew laughed uncomfortably. He was not quite Marya's height and his dark
eyes shied away from hers. "I don't know," he said defensively. "As I said, it's just Imogene, it's her business. Why
shouldn't she do what she wants to do? Don't be angry with
me."

He was nervous yet keenly excited; Marya sensed his
sexual agitation. Behind them, parked along the graveled
drive, were lovers' cars, one after another; from this distance,
the car in which Imogene and her "date" were pawing at each
other was undistinguishable from the others.

"You might not approve," Matthew said, his voice edged
now with an air of authority, "but Imogene is a free soul, she
does what she wants, I don't suppose she actually *lies* to her

fiancé. He'd have to allow her some freedom, you know, or she'd break off the engagement."

"You know a lot about her," Marya said.

"Imogene is a close friend of mine, we've worked together . . . I was stage manager for *Hedda Gabler,* don't you remember?"

"It's all so . . . trivial," Marya said slowly. "So degrading."

"What do you mean?"

"Oh—this."

"This?"

Marya indicated the cars parked along the drive. Her expression was contemptuous.

"You take an awfully superior attitude, don't you," Matthew said, with an attempt at jocular irony. He tightened his arm around her shoulders; he drew nearer. Marya could hear his quickened breathing.

Is this idiot really going to kiss me? Marya wondered. Her heart was still beating heavily; she could see Imogene's profile, the cameo-clear outline of her face, illuminated for an instant as the headlights were extinguished. Then she moved into the young man's embrace, she kissed him, slid her arms around his neck. . . .

"Does she make love with them?" Marya asked.

"Them?"

"Different boys. Men. One week after another."

"I don't know," Matthew said resentfully. "I suppose so —if she wants to."

"I thought *you* were in love with her," Marya said mockingly.

"We're just friends," Matthew said, offended.

"Oh no," said Marya, "everyone knows you're in *love* with her."

Matthew drew away from Marya and walked beside her without speaking. There was nothing for them to do, suddenly; not a thing left to say. It was still March and quite cold. Their footsteps sounded dully on the crusted snow. Marya thought, The various ways we seek out our humiliations. . . .

After a few minutes Matthew said something conciliatory about the night, the stars, the city lights, "infinity," certain remarks of Pascal's; but Marya made no effort to listen. She kept seeing Imogene kissing that near-stranger, Imogene locking her arms about his neck *as if he mattered. As if they were lovers.*

She was going to observe aloud, cynically, that making love was as good a way as any of passing the time, if you hadn't anything better to do, when Matthew, brave Matthew, turned her and took hold of her shoulders and tried to kiss her. It was a desperate gesture—his breath smelled of sweet red wine— but Marya would have none of it. She shoved him roughly in the chest.

"Marya, for Christ's sake grow up," Matthew said angrily. "You're a big girl now—"

"Why should you *kiss* me?" Marya said, equally angry, "when you don't even *like* me? When you know I don't like you in the slightest, when we haven't anything to say to each other, when we're just waiting for the evening to get finished! in fact we've been made fools of, both of us. And now you want to kiss me," she said, jeering, "just for something to do."

He began to protest but Marya dismissed him with a derisory wave of her hand. She was going to walk back, she said; she was through with them all. Especially Imogene.

Matthew followed along behind her for a few minutes, trying to talk her into coming back to the car. It was almost midnight, he said; the campus was two miles away; what if something happened to her . . . ? Marya ignored him and walked faster, descending the hill past a slow stream of cars that were ascending it, their headlights blinding her eyes. She lowered her head, tried to hide her face, her hands thrust deep in the pockets of her camel's-hair coat. At first she was furious —almost sick with fury—her head rang with accusations against Imogene—but the cold still night air was so invigorating, so wonderfully cleansing, she felt quite good by the time she got to Maynard House, not very long after midnight. She felt *very* good.

Next day, Sunday, Imogene stood at the downstairs desk ringing Marya's buzzer repeatedly, one two three four, one two three four, and then one long rude ring, until Marya appeared at the top of the stairs, her hair in a towel. "Who the hell—?" she called down. She and Imogene stared at each other. Then Imogene said contemptuously, "Here's your purse, you left your purse in the car, Knauer. D'you know, Knauer, your behavior is getting eccentric, it isn't even amusing, just what if something had happened to you last night— walking back here all alone—a college girl, in some of those neighborhoods!—don't you think Lyle and Matt and I would feel responsible? But *you,*" she said, her voice rising, *"you* haven't the slightest sense of—of responsibility to other people—"

"Just leave the purse," Marya said, leaning over the banister. "Leave it and go back to screwing what's-his-name— that's *your* responsibility—"

"Go screw yourself!" Imogene shouted. "Go fuck yourself!"

"Go fuck *yourself!*" Marya shouted.

As the stories sifted back to Marya, over a period of a week or ten days, they became increasingly disturbing, ugly.

In one version Marya Knauer had been almost attacked —that is, raped—in a black neighborhood near the foot of Tower Hill; and had run back to her residence hall, hysterical and sobbing. It was an even graver insult that her purse had been taken from her—her purse and all her money.

In another version, Marya was so panicked at being simply touched by her date (she was a virgin, she was frigid, she'd never been kissed before) that she ran from the car, hysterical and panting . . . ran all the way back to campus. The boy was a blind date, someone in drama, or maybe business administration, it was all a total surprise to him that Marya Knauer was so . . . crazy.

In a third improbable version it was Imogene Skillman's fiancé who offered to take Marya back to the residence, because she was so upset—having a breakdown of some kind—and when they were halfway there she threw herself on him in the car *while he was actually driving.* And then, ashamed, she opened the car door and jumped out *while the car was still in motion.*

"It's Imogene," Marya said, licking her numbed lips. "She's making these things up. . . . Why is she *doing* this to me . . . !"

There were vague rumors too that Marya had borrowed small sums of money from Imogene. And items of clothing as well—the camel's-hair coat, for instance. (Because she hadn't a coat of her own. Because her coat had literally gone to shreds. Because she was so *poor,* a scholarship student from the hills, practically a *hillbilly.* . . .) As far as she was concerned, Imogene was reported saying, Marya Knauer could keep the coat if she was that desperate. Imogene no longer wanted it back.

Marya telephoned Imogene and accused her of telling lies, of telling slanderous tales. "Do you think I don't know who's behind this?" Marya cried. But Imogene hung up at once: Imogene was too wise to reply.

Marya began to see how people watched her . . . smiling covertly as she passed. They were pitying, yet merciless. They knew. Marya Knauer with all her pretensions, Marya Knauer who had made a fool of herself with another girl's fiancé, Marya Knauer who was cracking up. . . .

In the fluorescent-lit dining hall she sat alone in an alcove, eating quickly, her head bowed; it was too much trouble to remove her plates and glass of water from the tray. Two boys passed near and she heard them laugh softly. . . . *That* the one? There? one of them whispered. She turned back to her book *(the thought of suicide is a strong consolation, one can get through many a bad night with it)* but the print danced in her eyes.

At about this time Marya was notified that a short story she had submitted to a national competition had placed first; and, not long afterward—within a week or ten days, in fact—she learned that another story, sent out blindly and naively to a distinguished literary magazine, was accepted for publication.

She thought of telephoning Wilma and Everard . . . she thought of telephoning Imogene . . . of running along the corridors of Maynard House, knocking on doors, sharing her good news. But her elation was tempered almost at once by a kind of sickened dread—she was going to be unequal to the task of whatever it was (so her panicked thoughts raced, veered) she might be expected to do.

Lately her "serious" writing frightened her. Not just the content itself—though the content was often wild, disturbing, unanticipated—but the emotional and psychological strain it involved. She could write all night long, sprawled across her bed, taking notes, drafting out sketches and scenes, narrating a story she seemed to be hearing in a kind of trance; she could write until her hand ached and her eyes filled with tears and she felt that another pulse beat would push her over the brink —into despair, into madness, into sheer extinction. Nothing is worth this, she told herself very early one morning, nothing can be worth this, she thought, staring at herself in the mirror of the third floor bathroom—a ghastly hollow-eyed death's head of a face, hardly recognizable as Marya, as a girl of nineteen.

Give up. Don't risk it. *Don't* risk it.

So she cautioned herself, so she gave and took warning. There was another kind of writing—highly conscious, cerebral, critical, discursive—which she found far easier; far less dangerous. She was praised for it lavishly, given the highest grades, the most splendid sort of encouragement. She should plan, her professors said, to go on to graduate school . . . they would advise her, help her get placed, help her make her way. . . . Don't risk this, she told herself, the waters will suck you down and close over your head: I know the symptoms.

And she did, she did. As if she had lived a previous life and could recall vividly the anguish of . . . whatever it was that might happen.

One windy morning at the end of March she saw Imogene Skillman walking with several of her friends. Imogene in sunglasses, her hair blowing wild, her laughter shrill and childish. Imogene in tight-fitting jeans and a bulky white ski sweater, overlong in the sleeves. That slatternly waifish affect. . . . Marya stood watching. Staring. Poor Marya Knauer, staring. Why did you lie about me! she wanted to cry. Why did you betray me! But she stood silent, paralyzed, watching. No doubt a figure of pathos—or of comedy—her snarled black hair blowing wild as Imogene's, her skin grainy and sallow.

Of course Imogene saw her; but Imogene's eyes were discreetly hidden by the dark-tinted glasses. No need for her to give any sign of recognition. No need.

Marya wrote Imogene a muddled little note, the first week in April.

> *Things aren't going well for me, I missed a philosophy exam &*
> *have no excuse & can't make myself lie. I don't know . . . am I unhappy*
> *(is it that simple?) or am I coming down with some sort of exotic illness*
> *(is it that simple?) Why don't you drop by & see me sometime . . . or*
> *I could come over there & see you. . . .*

Yet she felt a revulsion for Imogene; she *really* disliked her. That lazy drunken dip of her head, her lipstick smeared across her face, sliding her arms around the neck of . . . whoever it had been: kissing open-mouthed, simulating passion. Would you two let us alone for a few minutes, Imogene drawled. Would you two like to go for a stroll, for a few minutes?

I'll come over there, Marya wrote, *and strangle you with that pretentious braid of yours.*

In all she wrote a dozen notes, some by hand and some on the typewriter. But she sent only the first (*"why don't you drop by & see me sometime . . . or I could come over there & see you"*), not expecting, and not receiving, an answer.

What is fictitious in a friendship, Marya pondered, and what is "real": the world outside the head, the world *inside*: but whose world? from whose point of view?

If Imogene died . . .

If Imogene were dying . . .

She wouldn't lift a hand to prevent that death!—so she thought.

At the same time she quizzed herself about how to respond, should Imogene really ask her to be a bridesmaid. (She had declined being a bridesmaid at Alice's wedding; but then she had the excuse of schoolwork, distance.) Imogene's wedding was going to be a costly affair held in New York sometime the following year. The bridesmaid's dress, the shoes . . . the shoes alone . . . would be staggeringly expensive.

I can't afford it, Marya would say.

I can't afford *you*.

Though they hadn't any classes together this semester Marya learned that Imogene had been absent from one of her lectures for three days running. So she simply went, one rainy April afternoon, to Imogene's residence—to that absurd white-columned "house" on Masefield Avenue—and rapped hard on Imogene's door; and let herself in before Imogene could call out sleepily, Who is it . . . ?

The shades were crookedly drawn. Clothes and towels and books were strewn about. Imogene lay half undressed on the bed with the quilted spread pulled over her; the room smelled of something acrid and medicinal.

"Oh Marya," Imogene said guiltily.

"Are you sick?" Marya asked.

They had both spoken at the same time.

"A headache, cramps, nothing worth mentioning," Imogene said hoarsely. "The tail-end of this shitty flu that's been going around."

Marya stood with her hands on her hips, regarding Imogene in bed. Imogene's skin looked oddly coarse, her hair lay in spent greasy tangles on the pillow, spilling off the edge of the bed; her body was flat, curiously immobile. Without makeup she looked both young and rather ravaged. "If you're really sick, if you need a doctor, your sorority sisters will see to it," Marya said half mockingly.

"I'm not really sick," said Imogene at once. "I'm resting."

After a long pause Marya said, as if incidentally: "You told so many lies about me."

Imogene coughed feebly. "They weren't exactly *lies,* there was an essence. . . ."

"They were lies," Marya said. "I wanted to strangle you."

Imogene lay without moving, her hands flat on her stomach. She said in a childish vague voice: "Oh, nobody believed anything, it was just . . . talk . . . spinning tales. . . . You know, thinking 'What if' . . . that sort of thing. Anyway there was an *essence* that was true."

Marya was pacing about the room, the balls of her feet springy, the tendons of her calves strained. "I don't intend to let you destroy me," she said softly. "I don't even intend to do poorly in my courses." She brushed her hair out of her face and half smiled at Imogene—a flash of hatred. "You won't make me lose my perfect record," she said.

"Won't I," said Imogene.

Marya laughed. She said, "But why did you concoct a story about your fiancé and me? you know I've never even met him; I don't have any interest in meeting him."

"Yes you do," Imogene said, a little sharply. "You're jealous of him—of him and me."

"You're angry that I'm not jealous *enough*," Marya said. "Do you think I'd want to sleep with your precious 'Dickie'?"

"You think so goddam fucking highly of yourself, don't you," Imogene said, sitting up, adjusting a pillow impatiently behind her. "*You* can't be cracked open, can you? a nut that can't be cracked," she said, laughing, yawning. "A tight little virgin, I suppose. And Catholic too! what a joke! Very very proud of yourself."

"Why didn't you talk to me on the phone, why didn't you answer my note?" Marya asked quietly.

"Why did you avoid me on campus?"

"Avoid you when?"

"Why do you always look the other way?"

"Look the other way *when*?"

"*All the time.*"

Marya was striking her hands, her fists, lightly together. She drew a deep shaky breath. "As for the coat—you *gave* me the coat. Your precious Salvation Army gesture. You *gave* me the coat, you *forced* it on me."

"Oh Knauer, nobody forces anything on *you*," Imogene said, sneering. "What bullshit!"

"I want to know why you've been spreading lies about me and ridiculing me behind my back," Marya said levelly.

Imogene pulled at her hair in a lazy, mawkishly theatrical gesture. "Hey. Did I tell you? I'm transferring out of here next year," she said. "I'm going to school somewhere in New York, N.Y.U. probably. The drama courses are too *restrained* here, there's too much crap about *tradition....*"

"I said I want to know *why*."

"Oh for Christ's sweet sake what are you talking about!" Imogene cried. "I'm sick, my head is spinning, if you don't leave me alone I'm going to puke all over everything. I haven't been to a class in two weeks and I don't give a damn but I refuse to give *you* the satisfaction.... Transfer to New York, Marya, why don't you: you know you think you're too good for us *here*."

Marya stared at her, trembling. She had a vision of running at her friend and pummeling her with her fists—the two of them fighting, clawing, grunting in silence.

"Your jealousy, your morbid possessiveness. . . ." Imogene was saying wildly, her eyes wide, ". . . the way you sat in judgment on my parents . . . my poor father trying so hard to be *nice* to you, to be *kind,* because he felt *sorry* for you . . . and my mother too. . . . 'Is she one of your strays and misfits,' Mother said, 'another one of that gang that will turn on you?' . . . As for my sorority sisters. . . ."

Marya said slowly, groping, "And what about you? You're spoiled, you're vicious. . . . And you don't even act that well: people here baby you, lie to you, tell you the kind of crap you want to hear."

At this Imogene threw herself back against the flattened pillows, laughing, half sobbing. "Yes," she said. "Good. Now leave me alone."

"Do you think they tell you anything else? anything else but crap?" Marya said carelessly. "People who are in love with you? People who don't even know who you *are?*"

Imogene pawed at the bedspread and pulled it roughly over herself. She lay very still but Marya could hear her labored breath. "I took some aspirin before you came in, I want to sleep, maybe you'd better let me alone. I think you'd better let me alone."

She closed her eyes, she waved Marya away with a languid gesture.

"Goodbye, Marya!" she whispered.

On the sidewalk outside the house Marya took out the earrings boldly to examine them.

The Aztec ones, the barbarian-princess ones, bronze and red and blue, burnished, gleaming. . . . Marya had seen her hand reach out to them but she did not remember *taking* them from the room.

She tossed them in the palm of her hand as she strode along Masefield Avenue, smiling, grinning. No one, she thought in triumph, can keep me from my perfect record.

She went that day to an earring shop down on Fairfield Street; asked to have her ears pierced and Imogene's splendid earrings inserted. But the proprietor told her that wasn't the procedure; first, gold studs are inserted . . . then, after a few weeks, when the wounds are healed. . . .

No, Marya insisted, put in *these.* I don't have time to waste.

But there was the danger of infection, she was told. Everything has to be germ-free, antiseptic. . . .

"I don't give a damn about that," Marya said fiercely. "These earrings *are* gold. Put antiseptic on *them. . . .* Just pierce my ears and put them in and I'll pay you and that's all."

"Do you have five dollars?" the young man said curtly.

Crossing the quadrangle between Stafford Hall and the chapel one cold May afternoon, Marya caught sight of Imogene approaching her. It had been approximately two weeks since the theft of the earrings—two weeks during which Marya had worn the earrings everywhere, for everyone to see, to comment upon, to admire. She and Imogene had frequently noticed each other, usually at a distance, though once in rather close quarters on a crowded stairway; and Marya had been amused at Imogene's shocked expression: and the clumsy way she'd turned aside, pretending she hadn't seen Marya and Marya's new earrings.

Not a very good actress after all, Marya thought.

Now, however, Imogene was approaching head-on, though her movements were rather forced, wooden. Marya didn't slacken her pace; she was headed for the library. She wore her raincoat half unbuttoned, her head was bare, her hair loose, the earrings swung heavily as she walked, tugged at her earlobes. (Yes, her earlobes *were* sore. Probably infected, Marya thought indifferently, waking in the night to small stabs of pain.)

Imogene's face was dead white, and not very attractive. Something horsy about that face, after all, Marya thought. Her mouth was strained, and the tendons in her neck were clearly visible as, suddenly, she ran at Marya. She was screaming something about "hillbilly bitch"—"thief"— She grabbed at Marya's left ear, she would have ripped the earring out of Marya's flesh, but Marya was too quick for her: she knew instinctively what Imogene would try to do.

She struck Imogene's hand aside and gave her a violent shove; Imogene slapped her hard across the face; Marya slapped *her.* "You bitch!" Imogene cried. "You won't get away with this! *I know you!*"

All their books had fallen to the sidewalk, Imogene's leather bag was tripping her up, passersby stopped to stare, incredulous. What a sight, Imogene Skillman and Marya Knauer fighting, in front of the chapel, both in blue jeans, both livid with rage. Marya was shouting, "Don't you touch me, you! What do you mean, touching *me*!" She was the better fighter, crouching with her knees bent, like a man, swinging at Imogene, striking her on the jaw. Not a slap but an actual punch: Marya's fist was unerring.

The blow was a powerful one, for Marya struck from the shoulder. Imogene's head snapped back—blood appeared on her mouth—she staggered backward and swayed, almost lost her balance. "Oh Marya," she said.

Marya snatched up her things and turned away. Her long fast stride and the set of her shoulders, the set of her head, must have indicated confidence; angry assurance; but in fact she was badly shaken . . . it was some time before she could catch her breath. When she turned to look back Imogene was sitting on the ground and a small crowd had gathered around her. You'll be all right, Marya thought, someone will always take care of *you*.

After that, very little happened.

Marya kept the earrings, though her ears *were* infected and she had to give up wearing them; Imogene Skillman never approached her again, never pressed charges; nor did anyone dare bring the subject up to either of the girls.

Marya's record remained perfect but Imogene did poorly at the end of the semester, failing two subjects; and in place of transferring to another university she quit college altogether.

That fall, Marya learned that Imogene was living in New York City. She had broken off her engagement over the summer; she had joined a troupe of semiprofessional actors and lived in an apartment off St. Mark's Square. It was said that she had a small role in an off-Broadway play scheduled to open sometime that winter but Marya never learned the title of the play, or when, precisely, it opened; or how successful it was.

7

Marya's career prospered, Marya was doing very well for herself, all sorts of things were cautiously promised for her. She rarely returned to Innisfail, though in weak moods she thought a great deal about it. She thought a great deal about the past—the profitless past—in her weak moods.

When she telephoned home—she still called Everard and Wilma's place "home" though it hadn't been her address in years—she heard her voice shift into another register, become bright and shadowless, hearty. She sounded like the university instructor and graduate scholar she was. Marya Knauer with all her fellowships and prizes, Marya Knauer with her *somewhat precocious* (as one of her professors called them) publications. . . . But if her voice wasn't strengthened at such times she knew it would go faint and reedy; she knew it would fail her.

Telephoning home, she was certain to ask about everyone, including neighbors, in detail. And Wilma, echoing

Marya's bright manner, answered her in detail; though interrupting herself now and then, to say with a nervous little laugh
that this conversation was long distance, wasn't it, and must be
costing a small fortune, and did Marya *really* want to know all
these things . . . ? "Oh, hardly a small fortune," Marya protested, though in truth she didn't always exactly follow all that
Wilma reported. Joey had a part-time job working for . . . and
Davy was on the first-string football team . . . and Lee's wife
Brenda had another little girl, the sweetest thing . . . or had
Wilma told her that last time? Everard's blood pressure was
high and the fool was *supposed* to be off salt but Marya knew
how he was: stubborn as an ox: still twenty pounds too heavy.
But business was all right, Wilma said almost reluctantly. She
supposed they couldn't complain.

The telephone line was beset with static when Marya, in
turn, spoke rapidly and half in embarrassment of herself. She
had the idea that Wilma followed very little of what she said,
that her questions and approving murmurs were only courte-
sies (an article accepted where?—what kind of journal?—will
it be on the newsstand in town, will people see it?); but at the
same time it was Marya's obligation to supply Wilma with
something—virtually anything—about which she might casually boast to her women friends. (Oh, Marya called last night,
she keeps in close contact though her life is very busy, yes she's
planning to come visit next time she has a chance. . . .)

Afterward Marya's ear invariably ached from pressing the
receiver so hard against it. She rubbed it, caressed it, gently,
for some time.

It was true that her career prospered; she was doing very well
for herself indeed. For instance, Maximilian Fein so clearly
favored her that the others in his circle were jealous and even
a little offended. She was one of the newer students in the
program, after all; she was a woman of a certain sort . . .
attractive, outspoken, possibly rather contentious; she certainly wasn't self-effacing. (Maximilian Fein preferred his

women—and his young men too, for that matter—to be self-effacing; or so it had always been thought.)

If Marya had been awarded a certain coveted grant for next summer, it was clearly Fein's doing; if one of her seminar papers was scheduled to appear in *Speculum*, that most distinguished of journals, it could only be by way of intercession by Fein . . . after all, he was an advisory editor, wasn't he? . . . and known to force his protégés on others.

One of Marya's colleagues, a perpetually melancholy young man named Ernest who had been an assistant of Fein's for several years, asked her pointedly one day what Fein was really like—the implication being, of course, that Marya was on some sort of intimate basis with him. She felt her face go hot; she chose her words carefully. "If I were in a position to know," she said, "anything I said would be a betrayal. And I'm not that sort of person."

She hadn't intended to fall in love with Fein, or even to fall under his spell, as so many people, male and female, evidently did. That wasn't Marya Knauer's style, that wasn't quite the way she saw herself in this phase of her career. (Adulatory, calculating, subservient, "feminine." She had learned to think of herself as genderless, just as knowledge itself was genderless; just as the scholarly life was genderless. In truth she had learned in graduate school to think of *herself* scarcely at all—she was too absorbed in her work.)

But of all her professors Fein was the one who most insisted upon a personal relationship. At their first meeting—when Marya sought him out to ask, to insist, that she be allowed into his seminar—he interrogated her for some minutes, keeping her standing awkwardly in a doorway; neglecting, or not wishing, to invite her inside to have a seat. He wanted to see how serious she was. How substantial her background was. Frankly (so he said, adjusting his blue-tinted glasses and regarding her critically)—frankly, he and her adviser didn't get along very well; the man's notions of the medieval period were asinine. His single published book in

the field was a disaster of misguided energies. . . . Not knowing what she did, Marya found herself nodding, smiling
vaguely, seeming to agree.

Fein stared at her. "But why are you *agreeing?*" he asked
sharply. "Are you really in an intellectual position, Miss
Knauer, to know enough to *agree?*"

So she was shamed, exposed. But she went away buoyant
enough since Fein had—reluctantly, magnanimously—allowed her into his seminar.

Some months afterward Marya was singled out for the awkward honor of looking after the Fein household for ten days
while the Feins were in Europe. Maximilian was scheduled to
speak at a medieval conference in Munich (his paper was on
a newly discovered manuscript attributed to Agrippa von Net-
tesheim); following which the Feins were flying to Madrid to
visit the Prado. (Every few years, Fein explained, the need
came over him to see Bosch again, to stand in his extraordinary presence. It was more than need—it was hunger, sheer
desire.)

Marya, embarrassed at being chosen, and more excited
than she cared to know, consented at once. It would be no
trouble to bicycle over from the graduate college a mile
away . . . she would be delighted to tend to the Fein's several cats. . . . She didn't ask Fein if he trusted her alone in his
house because of course he must have trusted her.

(Someone had broken into the house a few years ago, he
told Marya, when he and Else were at a similar conference.
But the poor man went away with little because of course the
books meant nothing to him—not even the treasured *Chymical
Wedding,* or the volumes of Picinelli. He might have intended
to steal the Sung funerary urn but something about it—its
weight, its smell, the little rattle of the bones inside—dis-
couraged him. So he took only a few dollars' worth of stamps,
a portable typewriter, some of Else's grandmother's gold-
plated spoons. . . . Fein hadn't troubled to report the theft to

the police, he said, because he didn't want any more strangers in his house.)

When Marya let herself into the gloomy front hall she felt intimidated at once; even a little apprehensive, as if she might be stepping into a trap of some kind. She might be Maximilian Fein's favored student at the moment but she didn't really know him—she certainly wasn't on intimate terms with him. "Hello," she called out cautiously, though she knew no one would answer, "hello, it's just Marya—Marya Knauer—" She reasoned that an intruder, hearing her, would flee.

The Feins had taken possession, twenty years before, of one of the splendid eighteenth-century houses on the river, owned and to some extent serviced by the university. Though they had one child—a daughter, Marya gathered—they had never cared to buy property, evidently; Maximilian was not the sort to wish to be encumbered by such things. (Didn't he make contemptuous reference now and then, in his seminar, to the property-holding bourgeoisie; to the contamination of the human spirit by such things as the "burden of excessive ownership"?) A scholar in the classic European tradition, he owned books; his treasure was all in books, old manuscripts, *objets d'art.*

Marya had visited the Fein residence when Fein's graduate seminar—his "circle"—was invited over, but of course she had never been there alone; she had never been free, as she was now, to explore the downstairs rooms . . . with their high shadowy beamed ceilings, their slightly warped parquet flooring, their narrow leaded windows that appeared to glow with, rather than to transmit, sunshine . . . and, of course, the rows and rows of books. Even in the dining room books were shelved nearly to the ceiling; even in the narrow hallways. Ah, what a feast of books! Marya had begun to assemble a library of her own, she could appreciate Fein's collection of some forty-odd years. (He owned a first edition of Hegel's *Logic,* for instance. A first edition of Goethe's completed *Faust.* Volumes by Nietzsche, Schiller, Mallarmé, Hölderlin, Locke, Kant. Medieval manuscripts in German, French, English. Inscribed copies of Mann's *Dr. Faustus,* Broch's *The Sleepwalkers,* volumes by Georg Lukacs, Erich Kahler, Hannah Arendt, Lévi-Strauss . . . and many others, which privileged members of the circle were allowed to examine and even to consult if their work required.)

Marya entered the living room—two steps down—a narrow cavernous room with its shades partly drawn. Her eye darted nervously about but there was nothing to see, nothing out of place. The Romanesque bas-relief (a mirthless grinning angel) on the mantel above the fireplace, the tilted old mirrors in their heavy frames, the overstuffed furniture, the discolored lampshades, the slightly frayed carpets. . . . There was a smell of dust, mildew, pipe tobacco, old books which she found highly agreeable.

What might it be, Marya dared wonder, to live here by rights, to be Maximilian Fein's wife.

One by one the Feins' cats appeared, blinking mistrustfully. There was Deuteronomy, there was Cagliostro, and now Twill. . . . Marya coaxed them to come closer but they kept their distance. She thought them exceptionally beautiful creatures but it rather annoyed her that she had to court them anew each time she came to the Feins'. And now she was their custodian for more than a week. Empowered to change their cat litter, freshen their bowls of water and food, squat before them and make the effort of scratching their ears: an ignoble sort of task, Marya supposed, but so long as no one observed, she did not greatly mind. In fact she did not mind at all.

She tried to pet Cagliostro—silky, gray, suspicious, with widened greeny eyes—but the cat stepped haughtily away and Marya was left squatting off balance, groping at the air.

Occasionally, in a charitable gesture toward putting the members of the circle at their ease, Fein drew one of his elegant pets onto his lap and stroked and petted it as he continued his informal remarks; he was the sort of professor whom Marya most admired—capable in an instant of making adroit and witty references to whatever suddenly presented itself, as if he had prepared the digression beforehand. (Cats as heraldic figures in art; cats as bearers of "occult" messages; cats in medieval texts, Renaissance lyrics, crudely pictured in *A Discourse of Witchcraft,* of 1621—a facsimile of which Fein happened to own, and delighted in showing them. *Witchcraft,* warned the Discourse, *is a practice of deluded minds, / Where Grace is wanting soon admission finds.*) But it was an eccentricity of the circle and of Fein's students generally—wrongly ascribed as an eccentricity of *his*—that they did not particularly want to be put at their ease. They resisted, they smiled stiffly, shyly. As Marya's friend Ernest dryly observed, You don't come this far, and humble yourself in so many small ways, only to be reassured by Maximilian Fein that he is after all *ordinary.*

In any case, Marya thought, he wasn't ordinary; no one could ever be deceived in that direction.

So Marya changed the malodorous cat litter, flushing it down the toilet (there was a windowless little toilet just beside the door to the cellar) and spreading in fresh litter; she changed the cats' bowls, wiped them with paper towels, continued to speak cajolingly to the wary animals; but with little success. As she emptied a packet of cat food into one of the bowls the mottled black-and-white Persian, Twill, condescended to brush his silky tail against Marya's leg; and that was all.

Marya thought of that enigmatic sonnet of Shakespeare's with which, oddly, quirkily, she had in a way identified, years before:

> *They that have power to hurt and will do none,*
> *That do not do the thing they most do show,*
> *Who, moving others, are themselves as stone,*
> *Unmoved, cold, and to temptation slow. . . .*
> *They are the lords and owners of their faces,*
> *Others but stewards of their excellence.*

She liked to think of Marya Knauer as unmoved, cold, and to temptation slow.

In fact she had hardened her heart beforehand, that she might not succumb to the romance of this university—its fame, tradition, wealth—the singular beauty of its Gothic architecture—its atmosphere of privilege and academic rigor; she was an alien here, she felt her presence in a way subversive, a tactical error on the part of others. For this part of the world (its geographical as well as its intellectual location) was as different from the State University at Port Oriskany as Port Oriskany itself was as different from Innisfail. Yet it was romance, and she had partway succumbed; she simply could not resist. For this was an environment that sheltered persons like herself: brilliant, she might have boasted, and genderless: it was an environment in which genius and near-genius were honored. In such disciplines as mathematics, physics, and certain branches of philosophy, "genius" was unmistakable, and usually declared itself at a very early age (there was a world-famous logician in the Philosophy Department who had come to the university at the age of twenty-eight, given the highest rank and any number of academic privileges); in other disciplines—Comparative Literature and Languages, for instance, which Maximilian Fein taught—"genius" was rather more a matter of speculation, debate, prejudice. Fein's many admirers took it for granted that he was a man of genius—consider, for instance, the quality of the offers he received from other universities in North America and abroad—but his detractors granted him only a flamboyant, rather precious sort of talent, a talent of *style,* awkwardly wedded to an obsessive scholarly methodology. Fein was inimitable, they claimed: so very *sui generis,* of what value was his work ultimately? At the age of twenty-five he had published a brilliant and controversial study of the "therapeutic" function of the perverse, in sixteenth-, seventeenth-, and eighteenth-century Western Europe; at the age of fifty-five—for so Marya knew him to be, having looked up his birth date in a biographical encyclopedia —he was hardly less controversial, provocative.

It was known that Fein had been working on a definitive examination of the medieval mind for the past fifteen years, and, judging from a few chapters he had allowed to be published, his revisionist study would alter forever all scholarship in the field. Hence Fein's circle at the university, and the various "circles" that had formed about him over the years— passionately faithful to their master, chronically ill at ease in his actual presence, hopeful of being included in however peripheral a way in what promised to be his grand sweeping conquest of his branch of the profession.

(Marya was grateful for the fact that Fein's study, at the ground floor rear of the house, was kept locked; she didn't want to be responsible in any way for that gathering of books, manuscripts, notes, drafts. It was even said that the study was off-limits to Else Fein herself; but Marya indulged herself in a fantasy, a harmless sort of schoolgirl fantasy, of being one day invited in. "Should you like to assist me . . ." Maximilian Fein would begin, fixing Marya with his impenetrable blue-tinted gaze—for he wore his tinted glasses at all times, even at night; "Should you feel you have the time to spare from your own work. . . .")

Marya went boldly into the kitchen: she would celebrate by making herself a cup of tea.

This was her year, this was her time. Or so it seemed. For wasn't she at this very moment in Maximilian Fein's kitchen, moving unhesitatingly about as if she belonged here? . . . opening cupboard doors, peering into drawers, daring to examine the contents (very few, actually) of the old refrigerator. She was so close to euphoria that the teacup she'd chosen for herself nearly slipped through her fingers.

Marya, calm down. Marya, for Christ's sake. *He* isn't even on this continent at the present time; nothing *you* do matters.

She was too restless to sit at the cramped kitchen table so she prowled about, sipping tea, looking out the rear windows to the steep rocky lawn that dropped to the river some seventy feet below. Evidently neither of the Feins tended the yard, which was hardly more than a patch of weeds amid the remains of a rock garden. Marya noted an old swing, a child's swing, painted red but now badly flecked with rust. Straggly climbing roses on a rotted trellis; a stone wall, perhaps twelve feet high, that had begun to crumble. The Feins' house at 37 Azazel

Drive belonged to the university but neither of them must have reported the condition of the wall; nor, Marya gathered, the somewhat shabby condition of the house generally, outside and in. There were water stains around the windows, the linoleum floor in the kitchen was badly warped, most of the kitchen and bathroom fixtures were old, even antiquated; the sink in particular was shocking, deeply stained, even rutted. It could never be scoured clean, Marya thought. Not even if *she* were to try her hand at it.

She half closed her eyes and saw Else Fein enter the kitchen. For it was her kitchen, after all—she couldn't really have wished one of her husband's young women students to have made herself so much at home. Else Fein with her stolid ungiving handsome face, the gray eyes watchful rather than animated, the features sharp as chiseled stone; Else Fein with her rather thin streaked hair pulled back into an old lady's bun; Else Fein, *his* wife, of whom it was whispered that she was a disappointed scholar herself . . . a former student of classical languages who only did, now, occasional translations for the university press. Everyone in the circle had a theory about Mrs. Fein, who had never troubled to learn their names or sort them out from one another. (Perhaps because there were so many? because the composition of the circle was always changing as older students moved on and newer students joined?) It was thought that, like many transplanted Germans, she believed herself superior to her American environment; then again it was thought, even argued, that she was a desperately lonely and isolated woman who believed herself inferior . . . for, after all, she hadn't many acquaintances, and virtually no friends, among the foreign-born faculty members and their wives. Ernest Slater, who could boast self-mockingly of being Fein's "oldest" student at the present time, claimed that Fein had simply exercised an Old World prerogative in keeping his wife to himself, a true *Hausfrau.* She stayed away from the living room when the seminar met, except to serve coffee and tea; she was rarely heard speaking above a murmur, and then in German, with her husband, rather than English. Ernest joked of her famous coldness, her stubbornness in refusing (for so it seemed) to learn his name after four years. She hates us all, he said genially, her very gaze is thistles in the heart, an elbow in the ribs, surely you've noticed?

Marya flinched at the woman's imagined presence. Yes, that steely-gray stare was unyielding and resolutely unfriendly; perhaps it was even a warning of sorts. Marya wanted to protest that she had not wronged her—how had she wronged her?

Marya rinsed her cup at the sink and was careful to replace it exactly where she had found it. With a stiffened old sponge she even made a few spirited swipes at the rust stains in the drain, as if she were back on the Canal Road with Wilma hovering over her. *Leave things neat as you found them* was one of Wilma's pet admonitions. Then again: *Clean hands, clean heart.* (Both remarks were meant to be funny, even witty. Wilma always joked about matters she took perfectly seriously.)

Since she had fed the cats and checked the downstairs windows and doors, Marya supposed she should leave; there really wasn't any purpose in staying longer. Suppose a neighbor noticed her bicycle outside. . . . Or one of Fein's circle, nosing about on Azazel Drive. . . . She had work to do waiting for her in her room at the graduate college; this little excursion had been an interlude, a reward of sorts, since she'd been reading and transcribing notes all morning.

But she knew she wasn't ready yet to leave.

When she returned to the living room one or two of the cats scurried before her. She paced about, her hands on her hips, still excited, apprehensive, on the verge of a mysterious euphoria. Usually, by this time of day, she felt fairly exhausted; today she was suffused with a childlike sort of energy. If only *he* were present! . . . surprising her with his brusque greeting . . . striding forward to shake her hand, and to inquire how she was. He was wonderfully lean, lithe, sharp-featured, striking rather than handsome: with a somewhat pocked skin, and thin lips, and a long angular nose. Or was he in fact ugly,

Marya wondered, as if it mattered in the slightest. (To dispel Fein's immediate influence upon her, Marya had tried to speak casually of him, months ago. She told Ernest Slater that their professor was certainly articulate, perhaps a little glib at times, didn't he think? and Ernest responded quite coldly. Fein was incapable of glibness, he said. Marya saw then that she must say nothing about Maximilian Fein to his other students unless she was prepared to love him as much as they did.)

She examined the bas-relief above the mantel, a dour grinning angel with close-set eyes: rather like a gargoyle, impish and malicious, at this distance. Next, a row of funerary urns, all in graceless black stone that exuded damp. Then the large reproduction of Hieronymus Bosch's early allegory "The Cure for Folly" that hung above a horsehair settee, overpowering that corner of the room. The painting was an oval "miniature," a frame within a frame, filled in with calligraphic ornamentation that seemed to mock the burlesque scene depicted, and the victim's prayer—*Master, cut the stone out quickly—my name is Lubbert Das.* It was one of Bosch's engagingly ugly works; Marya tried to see it through Fein's admiring eyes, tried to find it engaging rather than repulsive. She had read Fein's excellent little book on Bosch so she knew what she was supposed to be seeing: the medical "master" wore a funnel on his head, and a pitcher (the sign of Satan) at his waist; the anxious patient in red tights begged to have folly (an actual stone) cut out of his skull—like any frightened sinner begging for deliverance. Close by, a monk with a tankard in his hand offered a sort of bland encouragement; and a nun looked on, bemused, with a large red book—a book of wisdom?—or fallacious knowledge?—balanced foolishly on her head. The colors were dark and earthen; the sky a faint watery blue. Church and steeple in the distance. A queer dreamlike slant to the earth. Fein had concluded his discussion of the allegory by saying that one could analyze it at great length without ever quite grasping it—its iconographic surface yielded superficial meanings, like most of Bosch's work; its depth, its mysterious *essence,* remained elusive.

Marya shaped the words aloud, softly and wonderingly: " 'Master, cut the stone out quickly—my name is—' "

One of the cats brushed against her bare ankle, startling her. She stooped to pick it up—it was Twill, the snub-nosed Persian—but it shrank away.

Marya half closed her eyes, rocked on her heels, tried to summon back the last meeting of the circle in this very room. It had been at the very end of April, a Thursday evening. Marya had delivered a paper on the role of the madman as prophet in several sixteenth-century texts, and Fein had praised it—had praised it moderately—but then his most lavish praise *was* never more than moderate. He had startled the group, and Marya as well, by concluding that "Miss Knauer has a future awaiting her . . . if she is equal to its rigors."

Afterward, when the academic focus of the evening ended and something approaching a social hour began, Maximilian Fein appeared to be in an excellent mood. He drifted among his student guests like any responsible host; he laughed more frequently and with more warmth than usual; Marya was gratified that he paid so much attention, however obliquely and circumspectly, to *her.* He was witty, entertaining. A master of the wayward and revealing detail—the detail that suddenly sets an entire relationship into perspective. Did they know, for instance, that Freud's wife Martha was a compulsive housekeeper and husbandkeeper, so attentive to her genius that she even put toothpaste on his toothbrush daily? And the motherly wife of one of the local geniuses (a youngish mathematician: no names supplied) not only brought his food to him on a tray three times a day, but bathed him, shampooed his hair, helped him dress every morning . . . while his brain spun its incalculable fancies and his eyeballs rolled inward. "The privilege of genius appears to be a curse to others," Fein observed. "But in fact it provides a sacred obligation, a religious 'path,' to the close-at-hand—the adoring spouse; and, by way of the spouse, the larger world is served. Thus genius is a phenomenon of symbiosis; it can only be a relationship, not a condition in itself."

Marya could hear his voice distinctly. The Germanic—southern Germanic—accent; the erratic rhythm of the sentences—slow and almost drawling, rapid at the close. She could see the gleam of his metal-framed glasses but of course she could not see his eyes.

Before meeting Fein, Marya would not have thought that one might have a sacred obligation to another person; she had long given up—in fact she had rejected with distaste—the very notion of the convent, the cloistered life, decades spent in selfless adoration of Christ. It had not occurred to her that there might exist mortal versions of Christ . . . human and secular saviors. But then she had lived her life until now in what she saw as a remote and irrelevant corner of the world.

She meant to leave; she saw with surprise that a half-hour had passed rapidly by. But some books on a nearby shelf drew her attention—old editions of the *Bardo Thödol* with numerous commentaries by English, German, French, Italian scholars. And here, close at hand, *Theologie und Glaube, A History of Satan in the Netherlands, Finnische und Estnische Volksmärchen.* In an old mahogany cabinet, untidy copies of *The Journal of Modern Gnostic Studies* dating back to 1946; a yellowed stack of offprints of an article by Fein himself ("The *Coniunctio* of Male and Female in the Drawings of Opicinus de Canistris") published in the Winter 1958 issue. Squatting, her leg muscles beginning to ache, Marya read excitedly through the essay. It dealt with issues Fein was to explore some years later, in more detailed form, in his masterful study of the medieval, *Quête du Saint Graal.* She wondered: Would anyone ever notice, if she took a copy of the essay away with her? . . . for it *was* an offprint, after all, printed up to be given away to colleagues and students; surely, if Fein knew of her interest, he would happily give it to her, perhaps even with an inscription.

She folded the offprint over twice—rather awkwardly, since it was more than twenty pages long—and slipped it into one of her pockets. No, no one would ever notice; it was absurd even to hesitate.

Following this, however, Marya began to behave oddly. Or so it seemed to her in retrospect.

She wanted to leave and return to her room, to her work; yet she found herself prowling about the house, checking windows she knew were locked, checking the rear door a second time, even turning the handle doorknob of Fein's study on the ground floor . . . and pressing her ear to the door. What did she hear, what could she expect to hear, except the agitated murmur of her own blood? . . . a dull distant heartbeat.

The thought that *no one was in the house except Marya* ran though her head, struck her as a new discovery. The thought that she was free, unobserved, a kind of bride. . . . She had a future awaiting her, Fein had casually prophesized, if she was equal to its rigors.

She examined the contents of a singularly messy closet, breathed in a rather agreeable odor of wool, boots, damp, tobacco, dust, dirt. She believed she could detect *his* smell. . . . She found herself on the stairs (but she did not *want* to go upstairs, she was disapproving, mildly incredulous), innocent and reckless as an overgrown child. Even the cats had caught on to this alteration of mood—Cagliostro ran past her, pretending to be frightened, his plume of a tail bristling.

She poked her head into the bathroom at the top of the stairs, ventured inside. Why not? Who could prevent her? A fly was buzzing at the window, feebly. The shower curtain over the tub was new, bright yellow-and-black striped plastic, but the rest of the room was old, shabby, badly in need of renovation. An outsized tub, rust-stained; a shower nozzle flecked with rust; a stained sink and toilet bowl; worn linoleum tile, once black. In the medicine cabinet mirror Marya's face looked flushed but she did not care to examine it too closely. And what was inside the cabinet? . . . nothing very interesting apart from six or seven bottles of prescription pills, two for "Dr. Fein" and the rest for "Mrs. E. Fein." But Marya reasoned that anything crucial to their well-being would have been taken along with them to Europe.

She left, she hurried along the corridor. A linen closet . . . another clothes closet . . . a former child's room, now used (evidently) for storage . . . and now the master bedroom itself: furnished with a surprising formality, and rather somber, shadowy: with wine-dark velvet draperies at the windows, and wallpaper in an austere fleur-de-lis pattern, and a brass chandelier, and a high old-fashioned bed covered in an elegant white crocheted quilt.

On the dresser beside the bed, in an oval frame, was the photograph of a dark-haired child: sullen, pretty, with a small fierce chin and shadowed eyes: perhaps ten years of age. There was something both infantile and malicious about her expression. Marya held the photograph to the light and examined it for several seconds, intently. She could see—she believed—Maximilian Fein's features in the child, about the mouth especially.

(Disconcerting, to think of the Feins as parents. Else Fein giving birth, Maximilian Fein an excited father. Both of them young—Marya's age perhaps. And then what had happened? The girl had died of rheumatic fever—or was it a respiratory disease—they had grieved, mourned, had no further children. Marya was greatly moved though she could not have said why. Someday, she thought, she might ask Fein about his daughter —if she dared. If they were ever that close.)

Now the child eyed her with a faint mysterious smile. Her deep-set gaze gave an old-world, legendary quality, a look of fate, as if she knew very well that she was destined to die young; and wanted no sentimental pity.

For some reason Marya thought of an incidental remark Fein had made during one of their early seminars. The subject was asceticism and the mortification of the flesh in the ancient world, the so-called pagan world; Fein spoke of the voluntary self-castration of priests in the service of the Magna Mater. Evidently self-castration and the inducing of impotence by way of herbal medicines were not at all uncommon in the ancient world: but now (so Fein mused, with his thin-lipped smile), if a man merely speculated about such practices, what might society call him!

The members of his circle shifted uneasily in their seats, one or two made an attempt to laugh—for perhaps Fein meant to be funny? Marya, frowning, had been making little nervous zigzag marks in the margin of her notebook. . . . In the service of the voracious Magna Mater, men were driven to strange forms of worship, Fein concluded.

By this time Marya was damp with perspiration and her heart seemed to be swinging from side to side. Elation, euphoria, on the verge of—might it be panic? The terror of mortals as they approached the great god Pan, in the chartless depths of the ancient forest?

One of the cats (it was snow-white Deuteronomy) leaped onto the bed; circled several times and lay down in the indentation between the pillows. He seemed to know the spot well but Marya wondered if she had better haul him away. Had the door to the Feins' bedroom been ajar, or had she opened it herself? . . . She couldn't remember.

She opened the door to the enormous clothes closet, which smelled of mothballs, stale warm air, that rich tobacco scent. Fein's clothes—coats, trousers, shirts, sweaters, neckties —were to one side; his wife's to the other. His shoes to one side and his wife's to the other. But the division of the closet was distinctly uneven—Fein had far more clothes than his wife. And Fein's side of the closet was more neatly arranged.

Marya, not knowing what she did, pressed her face against the sleeve of one of Fein's tweed coats. She gripped it tight, the scratchy wool, the small leather-covered buttons.

She closed the door carefully; paused to take in her tall slender reflection in a bureau mirror; wondered how she would ever be able to sleep that night. In her cell of a room. In her narrow bed.

And now she could not resist the dresser, opening the first of the drawers, the second, the bulky third . . . her heart still swinging, her pulse beating hard. You little savage, someone chided, aren't you a little savage! Don't we know you through and through! The bottom drawer of the dresser was crammed with Fein's things, somewhat haphazardly. Stray cuff links, single socks, linen handkerchiefs, tie clips and stickpins, loose papers, rubber bands, buttons. A worn leather portfolio which, naturally, Marya could not resist taking out and opening. . . .

The handwritten note seemed to leap out at her, to strike her between the eyes.

My dear brazen Marya—

She stared; blinked; felt a wave of faintness rise in her; a knowledge that yes, yes, she had halfway expected something like this. To be caught like a trespassing child, a thief, to be exposed as the low-minded criminal she was. . . .

At this point she might have closed Fein's portfolio and slipped it carefully back into the drawer (had it been on the right side, or the left?); she might have retreated, fled; but of course she did not. She read the note. She even went to the window to hold it to the light.

> My dear brazen Marya—
> If you hold this in your hand, if you have ventured so far, I think it futile for us to keep up certain pretenses. I know you—I seem to have recognized you from the first—do not be frightened, my dear (do not be less brazen) if I shortly make my claim upon you.
> —Maximilian Fein

Fein was forced to descend periodically, he later told Marya, into the Underworld, the Night World; but not by choice.

It was a species of hell contained within the perimeters of his skull—or, if you like, his soul.

Nor could it be shared. Even by a lover or a disciple. Even by a wife.

What had happened was simply that, as a young man of twenty-two, traveling alone in Egypt, he had picked up an infection of the inner ear. Within forty-eight hours he experienced terrifying symptoms—dizziness, vertigo, nausea, a sense that the world was disintegrating, and he himself with it; he had never been, he said, so entirely *alone* before—nor had he been so convinced of the individual's metaphysical isolation in the universe. ("Is this the 'benign indifference' of which the existentialists so blandly spoke? I wonder!" Fein said.) He had collapsed in his hotel room; was taken to a hospital in Cairo—a noisy, unsanitary, wretched place; too sick to be moved, he had had to stay there for weeks, with the consequences that his eyes were infected as well—he was actually blind for more than a month. It was simply hell; he had prayed to die. Consciousness *was* hell. As his vision returned by degrees he suffered terrifying hallucinations which he still saw, three decades later, in his dreams; he was convinced he'd experienced the "hell" of the Tibetan "twilight following death"—which he later recognized when he studied the tradition of the *Bardo Thödol—The Tibetan Book of the Dead.*

It was his belief too that one must not reject such visions: they were fragments of a whole: an *entire* vision, shattered into innumerable pieces. Did Marya understand? No? Yes? Well, perhaps she was too young and too innocent at the present time to understand.

After Fein's discharge from the hospital in Cairo he spent a convalescence in Munich, during which time his vision partly returned. For the remainder of his life, however, he would have to wear tinted glasses; and it was inadvisable for him, even with these glasses, to venture out into bright sunshine. His head would ache ferociously, the terrible vertigo might return. He felt the need—it was spiritual as well as physiological—to retreat from the world periodically, to "descend" once again into the depths of his own consciousness: he would remain in his study for days at a stretch, sleeping on a couch there, reading very little, eating virtually nothing, the room darkened, silent, his thoughts turned inward—absolutely inward. His study was ideally suited for such meditation since it had only one window, facing the river; it was at the rear of the house; of course it had no telephone. At such times Else protected him from all interruptions though he also locked the door against *her*.

For it was true, Fein said passionately, that Hell is ourselves, nor are we out of it; but most people shrink from acknowledging the fact. They prefer to think that Hell is *other, alien*. They prefer to think that this twilight of the soul—this inevitable fact of the soul—can be successfully eluded.

Marya, who loved him, believed anything he said—anything *he* said. But for all her intelligent sympathy she could not make her belief quite credible to him.

No, Fein concluded, with a fatherly sort of patience, she was too young, too innocent, she struck him as supremely American; a creature of health and daylight.

"I'm not young," Marya protested, "not really."

Her voice was so soft, so hesitant, Fein had to ask her to repeat what she'd said.

Why do you drive yourself so hard? Ernest asked.

I want to be perfect, Marya said, showing her teeth in a semblance of a smile. To indicate that of course she was being ironic, self-mocking.

To *be,* or to *seem?*

Marya was puzzled, not understanding. To *be,* or to *seem?*

To *be* perfect will get you nowhere, Ernest said, if you don't also *seem* perfect. In this part of the world reality counts for very little apart from its appropriate appearances. As Wilde so sharply observed. . . .

Ernest Slater spoke with the fastidious melancholy of one who has seen, if not experienced, a great deal. He was all of twenty-six years old; married; he'd *almost* been a father, once —but he and his wife had done the pragmatic thing, the necessary thing, and had an abortion. He had been in the graduate school for five years—"enclosed in its stony womb"—studying Old High German, Middle High German, Old Norse, Anglo-Saxon, Medieval French, linguistic theory. And all in preparation for what promised to be a massive dissertation under Maximilian Fein's guidance. He was slender, tall, prematurely balding; his shyness could be mistaken for severity; his playful and gently ironic tone could be mistaken—as it frequently was, even by his friends—for cynicism. He had recently discovered, he told Marya, inexcusable gaps in his background: he would have to study Romance linguistics and semantics before beginning his dissertation with Fein—which meant a delay of another year, at least. He hoped, he told Marya half-seriously, that his wife wouldn't leave him in the interim.

Marya, not knowing what sort of response Ernest wanted, could neither concur nor protest.

"But there are no shortcuts in *this* life, after all," Ernest said. "Unless it's to failure. Or death."

The Feins returned from Europe on schedule, Marya handed the key over to them, she and Professor Fein exchanged a long neutral look as they stood together in the shadowy front foyer of the house . . . Marya flushed and a little breathless from her bicycle ride, Fein rather severe, edgy. He was, he said, suffering a mild sort of reaction to the transatlantic flight. His wife was really a better traveler than he—her health, her nerves, were sounder. And what of Marya, did she like to travel? Had she been to Europe?

No, Marya said. Not yet.

At the next Thursday evening meeting of the seminar Fein surprised them all with a little banquet.

They were served stuffed cabbage loaf; potato griddle cakes; fried pork sausage; egg noodles; and an elaborate brioche filled with candied apricots. Mrs. Fein had prepared the food but an undergraduate student served it—Mrs. Fein made no appearance downstairs at all, though Marya and the others would have liked to thank her for her kindness, and tell her how superb the food was. ("Well—Else does not need to be *told* such things, perhaps," Fein said. "It is enough for her to nourish us all and then to absent herself . . . it is her *Kaiser-slauten* temperament.")

Fein himself was in an excellent mood. He found things to praise in the several papers that were presented in the seminar; his critical remarks were less acerbic than usual; he smiled a great deal; he was even wearing a somewhat informal outfit—a black turtleneck sweater with a lightweight beige coat. Though he remarked that the conference had drained him of a great deal of energy they gathered that it had been a considerable success, so far as his presentation was concerned; and the visit to the Prado had been immensely invigorating. Bosch's ecclesiastical *diableries* filled him with a curious sort of atavistic rapture, as if he were in his temperament—though assuredly not in his intelligence—a fifteenth-century man. A late cousin to Philip II of Spain.

For most of the evening he and Marya behaved toward each other with impeccable discretion; they were formal, courteous, grave; perhaps too grave—Marya generally questioned some of Fein's remarks during the course of an evening, it was her habit to draw him out in her odd shyly aggressive way. But tonight she was quiet, rather contemplative. She was watching him, hearing *My dear brazen Marya, my dear brazen Marya, I know you, I seem to have recognized you from the first, I know you, know you* . . . and so it was difficult for her to attend to what he and the others were pursuing so energetically.

(Warring and mutually exclusive theories of human behavior: Might belief in free will be said to be the product of an evolved consciousness, or was it a symptom of arrested development—of simply knowing too little, from the cosmic to the microscopic; might there be an unexpected freedom in determinism, after all? It was Fein's playful position that if one's fate was decided beforehand, one was then free to do whatever one wished: for how was a "mistake" possible? How could "sin" exist?)

The seminar usually ended by eleven o'clock but tonight everyone stayed longer, tonight was clearly a festive occasion, perhaps Fein was welcoming himself home; celebrating a secret success. They were treated to brandy and bitter chocolates given to Fein in Munich by a Russian delegate to the conference: which is to say (so Fein corrected himself) a *Soviet* delegate. For some reason the Soviets were courting him—inviting him to spend a year at Moscow University, or in Leningrad—as if he, Maximilian Fein, would wish to spend even a few weeks in that unspeakable country. All that *he* believed in they really branded "decadent"; they had not the crudest notion of academic or scholarly freedom; they wanted to use his name and reputation—as they used those of all foreign visitors—to give an imprimatur to their totalitarian madness.

He spoke with unusual passion. Marya found herself quite moved. It was false to charge Maximilian Fein with being indifferent to politics, as certain of his colleagues did, when it was clearly his work—*his* unique work—that might be designated as indifferent, disinterested, impersonal.

For he was primarily a scholar, as he said, and his allegiance was to the objectivity of Truth; he was a scholar before he was a citizen of any political state.

Marya was staring at him, no longer caring if he noticed. She did love him—she was greedy and exultant with love of him—it was absurd to pretend otherwise; as he himself had said, it was futile.

Do not be frightened . . . if I shortly make my claim. . . .

The highly potent brandy went to Marya's head. She knew herself beautiful—indeed, she *was* beautiful—she believed herself absolutely free for the first time in her life, and absolutely in control of her future. It might be rigorous but she would be equal to it.

Since she did not care to outwait the others she excused herself not long after eleven-thirty, and Fein graciously saw her to the door. He was a tall man, Marya saw with satisfaction; he carried himself with a certain languid assurance. So very charming, so very European . . . telling Marya that it was a pleasure to have seen her this evening and to have known, while he was abroad, that she, and no one else, occasionally entered his house. Marya laughed, saying that it *had* been a pleasure—an unexpected sort of pleasure.

She made an attempt to be playful, reckless, as at ease as he. But when he took hold of her hands, when she breathed in that warm intimate scent of tobacco and ashes—so familiar, so harshly fragrant—she experienced a moment of absolute fright. She might have been a young girl who had never been kissed—who had never been touched by a man.

Fein was saying half chidingly that her hands were cold; then, as if the question was related, "Are you angry?"

Marya hadn't the strength to draw away.

"*Are* you angry?" he asked.

She wanted to say lightly, Why should I be angry? but she heard herself say instead, in a quavering voice, "What do you want from me?"

"Oh—everything!" Fein laughed.

Marya had never deeply loved anyone; Marya had never been attracted to anyone—except briefly perhaps to Emmett Schroeder. Since the day after the going-away party, Marya had declared herself inviolable—autonomous—entirely self-sufficient.

As for the cravings of others, of men—why should she honor them? why even take them seriously?

Her attitude was rarely articulated because, being shrewd as well as naturally puritanical, she avoided such occasions: she avoided being alone with men, being approached as a woman and not as a colleague. Perhaps she was a nun in her own way —she felt that Clifford Shearing might have approved. An uncloistered nun, a self-determined virgin.

(One of the young women with whom she had become friendly here complained wistfully to Marya that, despite her numerous academic honors and prizes, despite the fact that she would be moving on, with her Ph.D., to Stanford—her family, her mother in particular, seemed only to be waiting for news that she would be married. Nothing else mattered, evidently; nothing else struck them as ultimately significant. She asked if

Marya's family was like that, or were they more enlightened? "Enlightened!" Marya laughed. Then it occurred to her that Wilma never said anything—never asked anything—about her plans for the future. Nor did anyone else back home. Davy, now seventeen years old, and Joey, fifteen, gave the impression of being uneasy in her presence—vaguely embarrassed, strained—and would never have broached any personal subject whatsoever. None of them thinks of me as a woman, Marya realized.)

She supposed she had remained a virgin so long because she hadn't exactly believed in other people—in men. In what they might bring to her that she didn't already possess, in the most secret inchoate depths of her being.

One afternoon in June, when Marya had been Maximilian Fein's lover for less than a week, she happened to encounter Ernest Slater on the steps of the graduate college. She saw how his eyes moved swiftly over her, how his mouth shaped itself into its usual ironic pose. She noted for the first time his disconcerting youth—his air of being somehow unfledged, not yet entirely formed, despite his high intelligence. She noted too the narrow wedding band on his left hand.

He had a sharp eye, did Ernest. What was that remarkable old book she was carrying? could he see it?

"*Musaeum hermeticum*—in an 1820 edition? How did you get hold of *this*?" he marveled. He leafed through it, examined it closely, taking his time while Marya stood close by, her cheeks smarting. He said, "You must be researching medieval alchemy: it *is* a fascinating subject. Making gold out of base metals . . . making something precious out of something quite worthless." When Marya said nothing he went on, rapidly, "I've never known it to be his custom to lend out books, any books at all, let alone something of such rarity—Fein, I mean. This *is* his book, I assume?"

Marya had no choice but to say yes. She said it quietly,

almost inaudibly. Without either the sense of triumph or the frightened guilt she felt.

It was Maximilian Fein, of all persons, who told Marya she must try to locate her mother before too much more time elapsed. Fein, with his reputation for being cold, self-absorbed, resolutely unsentimental.

But I have no idea how to locate her, Marya said at once.

Of course you have some *idea,* Fein said. Don't be childish.

Marya was deeply shocked, offended, rather angry. She did feel like a child caught out in deceit. She had thought—in fact she had been quite confident—that her lover would assure her she was better off without such a mother; that things had certainly worked out for the best, with a creature like Vera Sanjek absent from her life.

Marya repeated, less certainly, that she wouldn't know how even to begin any kind of search. Her mother had been missing for so many years . . . she *had* made inquiries about her, now and then . . . it really didn't seem to be her responsibility, did it, and not her mother's . . . ?

And in any case, Marya said, her aunt and uncle would be insulted.

She loved them, she said. She didn't want to hurt them.

Fein was putting his glasses back on, adjusting them in his slow, rather distracted way. He seemed suddenly indifferent to their conversation, as if the subject had been dropped.

I don't want to hurt people who have been good to me, Marya whispered, when . . . when *she* abandoned me . . . my brothers and me . . . when she's worthless . . . she doesn't deserve. . . . I've been told even that she was probably sent to prison for a while, she may even have died there for all I know, she's really nothing to me now.

Fein was bored with her, Marya saw; his mood had changed in a matter of seconds. He said, She's nothing to you now, *really*—as if it were more a statement than a question;

and Marya, blinking angry tears from her eyes, said Yes, yes, yes. Oh God *yes*.

To her relief (and to her disappointment?) Fein never brought the subject up again, during all the months of their relationship. Perhaps he simply forgot. Perhaps he *was* bored. And Marya, who intended to do nothing about locating Vera Sanjek, nothing whatsoever, pushed the issue out of her mind entirely.

She had enough to absorb her at the present time. She was in fact pushing herself a little too far, at the present time.

Can there be love, Marya wonders, if the word itself is never uttered; if it seems to stick in the throat . . . ?

Still, there are the manifestations of love; the long rapturous moments; the sobbing exclamations. Marya's lover caresses her with slow reverent fingers, speaks constantly of her beauty—the beauty that resides in her flesh—charts an iconography altogether new to Marya herself. She reminds him, he says, of certain baroque madonnas—there is a powerful *mater dolorosa* by the Spaniard Murillo—has Marya ever seen it? Fein will show her; Fein has all the books in his library, the costly full-color reproductions.

Marya, brushing her hair out of her eyes, still short of breath, finds herself laughing in delight—being confronted with a Marya not herself, a fictitious Marya, worshiped if not precisely loved.

Marya loses herself deliberately in long aimless daydreams. To recollect, to anticipate, to brood, to puzzle over—these are wholly absorbing activities, complete in themselves. When she is actually with Maximilian (in one or another of the anonymous hotel rooms to which he takes her, or in his very study on Azazel Drive) the experience is blurred, her sense of things confused. She hears herself speaking—she seems to see herself behaving in certain prescribed ways—but it is not altogether real to her: not so real as the anticipation was, or the languorous memory will be.

In her daydreams she is invariably challenging Maximilian with *her* love; declaring it, confessing it; exacting from him a confession in turn. Yes I love you, Marya, of course I love you, Marya, how can you doubt me?

For a while Marya's passion for Maximilian Fein inspires her in her work. He cannot see her very often, not even every day: he has warned her that they must leave each other a considerable measure of privacy. So she does her meticulous research —she studies her languages—she writes her essays—with Fein as her ideal audience, her admiring listener. She is, in fact, always speaking to him in her imagination; sometimes, locked away in her room, very late at night, she murmurs aloud—to him, always to him, in reference to him. If she spends some time gazing at herself in a mirror it isn't Marya-seeing-Marya but her-lover-seeing-Marya. And the young woman he sees *is* invariably beautiful—with the pale suffering features of a Latin *mater dolorosa*.

If anyone should inquire, Marya's official relationship to Maximilian Fein is that of his research assistant. But no one inquires—not even Else Fein who, in midsummer, suddenly goes away for several weeks. Her absence is a surprise to Marya; but Fein insists that the trip had been planned all along. For most of the time Else will be staying with a friend in Cape May, New Jersey, the widow of a professor of German, German-born herself, like Else. Has she left because of us, Marya would like to inquire, but of course she does not. The very word *us,* uttered in Fein's presence, would have a proprietary ring her lover might find disturbing.

Marya waits, Marya waits . . . for Fein to suggest that she move temporarily into the house with him; after all, he isn't really equipped to live alone and unattended, wifeless. But Fein never brings up the subject, Fein can manage with a cleaning woman once or twice a week, and of course, with Else gone, he is invited out to dinner far more frequently: there's something attractive, even rakish, about Maximilian Fein as a scholarly otherworldly bachelor, alone for six weeks during the summer.

He does speak vaguely of their going to a seashore of their own, perhaps in Maine—then again the mountains, the Adirondacks, might be even more secluded—but of course there is the problem of his work, his innumerable books, papers—there is the problem of his "capricious" health.

Marya is alarmed, apprehensive: for several days during his wife's absence Maximilian goes into seclusion, tells Marya not to come by. He is going to steep himself in that other world, that Night World: he'll spend most of the time in his study with the blinds drawn, sleeping there, eating very little, descending into . . . well, he supposes it is only himself. But by way of that self he enters a dimension of psychic experience otherwise inaccessible.

What about me? is Marya's immediate childish rejoinder.

Then, more prudently: I wish I were capable of accompanying you.

Fein laughs, strokes her hair, smooths it away from her brow. She can see that he loves her, in fact he adores her; why has she ever thought otherwise? Marya the beautiful one, Marya the adored. . . . He says in a tone she can only interpret as fatherly, "No, Marya, you really *don't* wish that."

Gradually it happens that there are two "times" in Marya's experience, two aspects of time. One is vivid and pulsing with life (the hours she spends with Maximilian), the other is bleak, drab, achromatic (the hours apart from him—which in fact constitute most of her experience). A familiar story, Marya instructs herself—a woman yearning to be completed in a man, by way of a man. As if she hadn't a soul of her own.

It is a story, a fiction, in which Marya Knauer does not truly believe, and one she would never have condescended to write, herself. She might take up the challenge of seeking out romantic and antiromantic structural patterns in medieval French narratives—the *Chanson de Roland,* for instance, *Tristan et Yseult, Le Roman de la Rose*—but she does not wish to "believe" in such extravagant fates as possibilities in life.

Still, she consoles herself with fantasies of Maximilian Fein as her husband; *her* husband; for hasn't he made oblique references to . . . hasn't he indicated that one day they might . . . and of course his relationship with Else is dead, burnt out, that goes without saying. He has spoken of certain parts of Vienna, Rome, Florence, even Cairo, with such enthusiasm, surely he means to take Marya there one day soon; perhaps it is simply a matter of her professional coming-of-age. (She will have her Ph.D. in two years, she calculates. If her work with Fein goes well. If there are no setbacks.)

Tell me about yourself, Fein says.

And Marya's imagination goes blank—for what is there to tell, apart from *this*?

You have been in love before, surely? You have been *loved*?

Marya shakes her head mutely, wonders if she might alter the mood of the moment by being (for instance) ironic, witty, droll? The Marya of her high school days, the Marya who "cracked up" her friends and sometimes even her teachers.

But in Maximilian Fein's presence, especially in his embrace, she is not that Marya at all. She finds herself inordinately quiet for long periods of time; aware of her lover regarding, and admiring, *her*; she is suffused with a sense of her own precarious beauty, and the power (for surely it is power?) that resides in that beauty. *We love each other, we should get married* is a sudden vulgar refrain that runs through her head but she would not dream of uttering it aloud; such a sentiment belongs, after all, to another level of being . . . country-and-western music, perhaps.

Tell me about yourself, Marya. Why are you so secretive?

There is nothing to tell.

Oh—surely *not*!

Nothing, nothing significant. . . .

You're a hard young woman, aren't you? hard on yourself.

Apart from you, Marya whispers, close to tears, there is
nothing.

The summer ends and Else Fein returns, the house on Azazel
Drive is hers by rights, Marya finds herself banished for days
at a time, fired to work, *work,* to keep from despair. She is
convinced that the fierce sexual excitement she sometimes
displays in her lover's presence disgusts him; she wonders if
his occasional bouts of impotency are related to that disgust,
or to his waning interest in her, or, as he himself has ruefully
said, simply to his age—his health.

Marya would like to assure him that making love is not
that significant to her. She has always experienced sexual sensation as something that happens to her, not that she initiates
or wills; a sudden explosion of the senses that overcomes her
as if imposed from without. In any case it only accompanies
her love for him, it is only related to her intense feeling for
him.

But perhaps her feeling is too intense. Perhaps he has
come to dread it.

Once he said half seriously that young women require
young lovers; and Marya, stung, replied that he shouldn't
think of her as *young*—she never thought of herself in those
terms.

"Are you ageless, then? A creature out of mythology?"
Fein asked, bemused. "You sometimes behave as if you were.
As if your own self, your human self, were temporarily in
abeyance."

Marya laughed, as if he had said something witty.

So the weeks pass. The months. *He* has no soul, Marya finds
herself thinking, with a pang of envy.

She is working with no less concentration than ever. Or
so it seems. It is the Marya of Port Oriskany, celibate, fierce,

(214)

determined. When she isn't with her lover, after all, she finds the remainder of life so slow, so dull, so purposeless—what choice has she but to sink herself into work, as deeply and as obsessively as she can? It is a way of commending herself to him, proving herself, hour after hour. For Marya Knauer's writing, her thinking, her very being, take value now solely in reference to Maximilian Fein.

Odd physical symptoms have begun to plague her. Jagged headaches, stinging eyes, dizziness when she climbs a flight of stairs, frightened dreams. . . . On the very edge of sleep she hears someone call her. But she can't respond. She sees shadowy shapes in the room but she can't respond. Her face is caressed by groping invisible fingers—her breasts, her belly. A flamelike sensation rises between her legs. One night she is paralyzed with terror by the spectacle of a man—a pink husk of a man—only a torso and part of an abdomen, broken open like an eggshell!—a creature that turns to her with a malevolent impish grin, opens his great dark mouth slowly, and sticks out an immense tongue.

Marya, dear Marya. Dear brazen Marya.

In the autumn Marya began to sabotage her love for Fein, though she seemed not to know it at the time; she would have thought she was behaving commendably.

She spent several days working on an essay analyzing the relationship between the "perverse" and the "normal" in contemporary American society, applying some aspects of Fein's methodology to the subject, if not precisely Fein's ideas. Though the piece was broad in conception and not at all academic, it was forcefully argued; and very carefully composed. To Marya's surprise it was accepted for publication at *The Meridian*, a New York biweekly of some distinction. The editor, in accepting it, invited Marya to submit more work and, if she was so inclined, to do some reviews for them.

When she showed the published piece to Fein, however, he wasn't at all impressed. His expression showed disdain, immediate boredom. Though Marya had meant for him to keep the copy of *The Meridian,* he leafed through it in her presence and handed it back, saying that he hadn't time for journalism and he was surprised that she had time. "Even journalism with the lugubrious moral tone of *The Meridian,*" he said.

Marya was hurt, puzzled; her blood pulsed with a childish resentment. She had thought his theory would lend itself to a political application, she said. She'd given him credit throughout, hadn't he noticed? . . . Wasn't he interested?

No, Fein said politely. He was afraid he wasn't interested. "Politics is invariably journalism," he said, "and journalism has simply never had any appeal for me. Even when it's intelligently and cleverly done. Even when it's under the byline— that *is* the term, isn't it?—of Marya Knauer."

So she took back *The Meridian* and filed away her copies without troubling to read through the issue. She was sickened, ashamed. She wrote a note to the editor, Eric Nichols, declining his offer. She hadn't time, she said. She hadn't time.

"You mustn't expend your spirit in the pursuit of phantasms," Fein said afterward, forgiving her. "A phantasm of your own *self,* caught up in imbecilic habits of mind."

"Yes," said Marya dully. "I mean no. No."

Suddenly she really was Maximilian Fein's research assistant. He had arranged for her to receive a generous stipend from the graduate school in addition to her fellowship; he was already citing her as having provided him with "invaluable help" in an article to appear in *The Journal of Philological Studies* —Marya Knauer in a footnote, but acknowledged, praised, nonetheless. Sanctified, one might have said, in print.

(Marya worried that the other students would be upset, that they might complain of her preferential treatment. Ernest Slater, for one: he was so distant with her these days, so abrasive. But Fein was almost defiantly unconcerned. "People gossip in any community," he said, "and this happens to be a highly claustrophobic community. Where's the harm? Whose folly is it?'')

So Marya visited Fein's study at his bidding, several times a week, always in the late afternoon. There were two entrances to the cavernous room, one by way of the cellar (which of course Marya never took), the other by way of the rear of the house. It always seemed a miracle to Marya that her timid knock would be honored, that Maximilian Fein would really open his door to her. Her breath caught as she stepped inside, out of the sunshine . . . stepping into the very earth, it seemed, by way of an opening hewed in rock.

He blinked at her, gravely pleased to see her; he kissed her forehead in greeting. His manner was often abstract, vague, as if she had interrupted him at his work.

The low beamed ceiling, the stone walls, and the subdued lamplight gave the room a cozy sequestered air. Fein kept the blinds drawn against the sunlight because of his eyes; he joked that he would have liked very much to work in the dark. "Yes," Marya whispered, laughing, "you really are a nocturnal creature."

She was exhilarated, slightly on edge, here in Fein's study. This room of secrets which (as the legend held) Else Fein herself was never allowed to enter. Yet it was in most respects a perfectly ordinary room—furnished with leftover items from the rest of the house, including a badly worn carpet of indeterminate color, an ancient battered rolltop desk, a brown velvet chaise longue that smelled of mildew and tobacco.

Sometimes they set to work at once (Fein despaired of having so much work to do, and his eyes ached almost daily with strain), sometimes they made love on the couch, only partly undressed, panting and clutching desperately at each other. *Making love*—so it seemed to Marya, every muscle and nerve in her body strained to the utmost, that their love had to be consciously made, fashioned, even forced: she shut her eyes against the sudden penetration of her body, imagining that her heart too was being pierced. The tension was almost too powerful to be borne—there was no pleasure in it, only sheer sensation. I love you, please forgive me, I love, love you . . . *you* . . . Marya heard herself whisper in a kind of delirium. Could such things be happening, to her? Here, in this place, to her? But Fein, kissing and mauling her, burying his damp face against her, did not seem to hear.

Sometimes he couldn't make love to her. Not in that way. He tried, he tried, half sobbing and clutching at her, pummeling her flesh, he tried and failed: she knew he despised her for his failure, she knew her breasts and belly and the insides of her thighs would carry the bruises for days. It doesn't matter, Marya consoled him, it *doesn't* matter. . . . But of course it did, to her aging lover it mattered greatly.

Afterward, exhausted, drained of spirit, they lay in each other's arms like guilty children, drifting into a light dazed sleep. In fact sleep seemed to drift over them—Marya felt it as a thin sheet of some semitranslucent material edging toward her, closer, yet closer, finally covering her, emptying her of all resistance. Fein twitched in his sleep, shivered, murmured unintelligible words. He gripped her hard, his weight was considerable for so thin a man, Marya held her breath, held her breath so as not to be hurt any more.

Overhead footsteps sounded. In one direction, and in another. A pause. Was she listening? Did she know? . . . And then the ceiling overhead creaked again. (Mrs. Fein was in her kitchen, Marya thought. Now going to the cupboard . . . now going to the sink. Marya pictured herself in the kitchen with her. They were going to have tea together. Mrs. Fein had asked Marya to sit at the table, and she was sitting. She was flushed with self-consciousness but pleased nonetheless. The kitchen was old-fashioned, homey, not at all what one might expect judging from the rest of the downstairs. But then of course Maximilian never came into this part of the house if he could avoid it. Mrs. Fein was going to tell Marya about the loss of her little girl as soon as the teakettle began to boil, as soon as the tea was prepared. There were two cups, white, fluted at their edges, their gilt long since worn off, set side by side on the cupboard counter.)

Fein roused himself from sleep, groggy, dazed, struck by something he had dreamed. *"Das blaue Schiff*—the blue ship —I see us in it together, Marya," he said. His voice quivered with an unusual excitement.

Marya was always thinking, These days, these weeks, I am in control of the situation. I am in control, in control, of the situation.

On his bad days Fein lay by himself on the sagging chaise longue with a cold cloth over his eyes. If she would be so kind —but he would *not* make demands upon her—Marya might change the cloth from time to time, dip it into ice water, return it gently to his face. His weak watering throbbing eyes. His finely creased forehead—the bone so prominent, so defined. (Had Marya the right to kiss his eyes?—the right, and then the left—so gently!—gently! And he smiled in surprise at her. In surprise he said, "Your lips are so cool, dear Marya. . . . My *mater dolorosa*. . . .")

He lay very still so as not to provoke the pain in his head and eyes. Marya held his hand, stroked the long thin fingers. In a slow cautious voice Fein told her of his visions . . . the splits, he called them, the cracks in consciousness . . . so that he was both awake and asleep, awake and alert and articulate ("Am I not doomed to being such?") and at the same time asleep, floating in a kind of trance. He saw figures, spirits shaped in flesh. He knew them, and they knew him. Master, they called him. But they were demons, it was only mockery. Master, we are come, oh Master!—come to do your bidding! —but it was mockery, *he* knew better. A dwarf with a gigantic head and popping eyes: a lewd expression: saliva-wet lips drooping, sly little tongue. Master, cut the stone out quickly! Oh I am in pain—in agony! And close by a tall, tall child with a saintly face and—can it be?—hermaphrodite features: the tender pink genitals of the female, the blood-engorged sprouting genitals of the male, crowded close together; a great bush of red pubic hair. Oh Master, Master! We are all yours—we come at your bidding—*we* will tend to you in your infirmity!

It was Marya's intention to transcribe whatever Fein said at these times, but she found herself only listening, not writing. All that her lover felt, all that he so powerfully experienced, could never be successfully translated into mere words. Only stark visual images, perhaps. . . .

Sometimes he spoke of his daughter too. His dead daughter. (How had she died, precisely? By drowning? An accident? An accident that was no one's fault?) But at such times his voice was clear and wondering, his words so slowly shaped that Marya had to listen closely to fit them together. And of course there was nothing to transcribe—nothing she dared transcribe.

At such times Marya was obliged to stay with Fein for hours. From late afternoon to nine or ten in the evening. She entered the house in sunshine, left in night, reeling with fatigue. Often the first floor of the house was all but darkened ("She has given up waiting for him," Marya reasoned), only one or two rooms on the second floor were lit ("She has gone to bed by herself").

Afterward Marya was too restless, too distraught, to return to her room. That cell of a room. That cave of her own, piled high with books, steeped in dreaming, plotting, romantic calculations. Instead she walked, walked—fled with relief the residential drives and lanes of the university area—found herself passing shops, gas stations, diners, taverns—not thinking of Maximilian Fein—not thinking of Marya Knauer who was mad with love of him—mad, mad, with love—Marya who was mad—Marya who was in love—not thinking of anything at all but looking closely at what was in front of her eyes: a street, slow-moving traffic, parked cars, the winking neon lights of a bowling alley, the darkened marquee of a movie house (closed down, out of business, the glass covering old posters cracked), Hardee's Tavern & Chop House, which was doing very good business indeed.

Sometimes, hearing the maudlin twang of country-and-western music, Marya went inside one or another of these taverns—dared to order a beer at the bar and to drink it there —her pulses alert, alive, with the risk of the situation—the possibility of danger—Marya alone in a tavern in the "wrong" part of town—Marya Knauer who belongs elsewhere but who is defiantly *not* elsewhere—ordering a second glass of beer, savoring the cold acrid taste, thinking, He doesn't know where I am: I'm free.

Dear Else Fein, Marya composes, You must know by now that your husband no longer loves you, you must know that . . . he loves . . .

Marya begins again: Dear Mrs. Fein, you must know. . . .

Her breath catches in her throat, she turns her head, tries to force herself awake. Dear Mrs. Fein, Don't you know how he loves me . . . adores *me* . . . don't you know me, Marya . . . am I not beautiful to you too . . . am I not your Marya, your Marya. . . .

She wakes suddenly, sticky with perspiration. Her eyes burn as if she has been using them all night. It is very early yet, only a few minutes past six . . . and the day, the long day, all before her.

Professor Maximilian Fein flies to Toronto to lecture at the Medieval Institute, in early December, and his assistant Marya Knauer accompanies him. (Is there talk, gossip, speculation? Perhaps. Very likely. But whom does it harm, whose folly is it . . . ?) Miss Knauer is a tall dark-haired young woman, gravely handsome, inconspicuously dressed, very quiet; it is clear to all that she takes her role, her function, quite seriously.

Fein appears uncharacteristically nervous at first, but then he settles in, he presents his lecture superbly, it is the unfailing Fein manner: mandarin, graceful, just slightly rhetorical, bracingly provocative (he offers a revisionist perspective on Boguet's *Discours des sorciers* of 1602 and one or two similar documents of the time), knowing how to pace his lecture and how to end at the necessary moment. He is only slightly impatient with a few foolish questions put to him afterward by young faculty members who (evidently) don't respect his reputation as much as one might expect.

Afterward, in the high-rise hotel room overlooking the smoggy city, Fein suffers one of his eye attacks, thinks it wisest to retire early, to retreat, as he says, from the contest of words. Though he urges Marya to go out—there is a dinner planned for him, a cocktail reception—she remains with him, sleepless through much of the night, nursing him, stroking his forehead, urging him into sleep.

Toward morning he tells her of the way his little Ursula died: pulled away from shore by an undertow off Cape Hull, along a stretch of beach presumed to be safe. But the sea floor had recently eroded away and there was an abrupt falling-off no one knew about . . . until that morning.

She died in my arms, Fein says, vomit and blood and then nothing, nothing.

That sudden weight, Fein says, squeezing Marya's hand hard, do you know *that* weight, Marya? have you ever held it?

Vomit, blood—nothing.

(The child would be thirty-two years old now, Marya calculated. That pretty little face, that sullen droop of the lips, those sly knowing eyes. . . .)

Marya thought, through the winter, One day Else Fein will come to me and make her own claim.

She rehearsed her faltering little speech beforehand. Choosing words carefully, fearfully. As if with tweezers. *The fact is that he and I love each other . . . he no longer loves you . . . in quite that way. The fact is, Mrs. Fein. . . .* Her eyes watered violently, her head throbbed with pain. *The fact, the fact is. . . . The fact. . . .*

So she prepared unassailable strips of language, she steeled herself against those gray eyes, that accusing mouth. Because Maximilian had become so strangely dependent upon her now. Because she was increasingly in demand at 37 Azazel Drive. (And even elsewhere, suddenly: it began to be remarked that Fein was seen in public with one of his young woman graduate students—on the streets, on campus, even in the dining room of the faculty club. And who was it? Which one? The tall dark somber girl with the reputation for being brilliant, if contentious; the one who had already begun to publish . . . no doubt with her lover's strong-armed assistance.) *Mrs. Fein it's painful to tell you this but your husband no longer loves you I'm sorry sorry to inform you sorry to be upsetting you but the fact is. . . .*

Still, when Else Fein did come one morning in early February, Marya wasn't at all prepared for her. She wasn't at all prepared.

These weeks and months, Marya continued to perform beautifully, as she had always done. She thought of herself as a figure skater, executing extraordinary spins and leaps and patterns on the ice, in a very circumscribed space.

She went through the motions of a daylight life. She was still the good girl, the A-plus student, fired by competition and virtually inexhaustible. Or so it seemed. Attending all her seminars and lectures, acquitting herself admirably. Sometimes she observed herself from a little distance, quite impressed. The baroque figures—the ingenious tricks!—of the seasoned ice skater.

On her free evenings she began to go out, alone. To concerts mainly. Losing herself in . . . it scarcely mattered what: a Bach cantata performed by the university chorus, a Brahms string quartet, that powerful second piano sonata of Chopin's.

Her skin grew chapped and rather sallow, her eyes watered frequently, went bloodshot. It was a familiar consequence of winter—she seemed to have no defenses. On her really bad days she learned to apply a little dime-store makeup to her face, smeared on a little lipstick, why not? She had to admit it was remarkable, the difference so commonplace a trick made.

Fein held his seminar in his home on Thursday evenings, it was an old custom of his, it allowed people to say of him that, yes, he really *was* friendly and accessible, he wasn't at all like his reputation. But now it began to be somewhat awkward, at times it was frankly embarrassing . . . because quite clearly there was something between him and Marya Knauer; and the more pointedly the two of them behaved otherwise, the more evident it became. (Fein ignored Marya for an entire evening. Or glanced frequently in her direction. Or spoke her name with just the wrong inflection—too harshly, too gently. As for Marya, earlier in the year you couldn't shut her up, now she sat silent, mute, staring at the carpet; holding one of those enormous cats in her lap. She no longer questioned Fein's enigmatic remarks and she only laughed at his jokes—breathlessly, a little hysterically—when she saw that the others were already laughing.)

Else Fein no longer made even a token appearance on those nights. It was thought that she'd left the country—perhaps she was visiting relatives in Germany—but one or another of Fein's students would often remark after a meeting of the seminar that he was certain he'd heard footsteps upstairs. A faint, almost imperceptible creaking of the floorboards. . . .

Marya really did go through the motions of another sort of life, though it struck her as improbable, afterward. She must have been improvising clumsily since she forgot the substance of most of these experiences almost as soon as they occurred.

For instance, she had a few romances in embryo. Mere ideas, wisps, of romance.

There was a young Englishman studying physics who seemed quite taken with her, perhaps because her manner with him was so unforced, so casual, and he was accustomed to far more determined American women. There was a young assistant professor of history who approached her at the Bach cantata, and afterward took her out for dinner several times—though in fact Marya always insisted upon paying her bill. A youngish man squired her about the computer center under his guidance (he was in "computer science"), took her to an on-campus showing of a Fellini film, and afterward—deeply offended, it seemed, by her insistence that she had to go to bed early, she couldn't invite him to stay in her room—came close to raping her. (The struggle took place in silence. Though they each grunted, panted, swore. He tried to lock Marya in an armhold and force her down onto her bed, Marya resisted strenuously, Marya managed to knee him in the groin. . . . Only then did he cry out: "God damn you! Cockteaser! *Cunt*!")

Ernest Slater too dropped by but his approach was oblique and circumspect. He chatted for a while about the books they were reading and the books they hoped to write. Finally he said, "You *are* an attractive woman, Marya," as if the issue had been hotly debated; Marya stared at him with no idea of how to reply. She had seen him once or twice with a young woman she assumed to be his wife: limp fair hair, glasses, a narrow pretty face, features rather like Ernest's. He had not troubled to introduce them, nor had Marya sought an introduction.

Can it be, Marya thought, mesmerized, stiffening, in another minute he's going to touch me? In another minute something will happen?

But the minute passed. Nothing happened.

Ernest roused himself to his feet, yawned nervously, ran a hand through his hair. On the way out of Marya's room he said suddenly, in a rush of words, "Does he ever mention me?

I mean, you know, now and then—just in passing—incidentally? Does he ever allude to me at all?"

Marya noted a chilling aphorism of Nietzsche's. *Terrible experiences give one cause to speculate whether the one who experiences them may not be something terrible.*

She would have liked to hear Maximilian say these words in his native German, with that special Bavarian inflection.

Marya and her lover began to quarrel frequently but it was never entirely clear what they quarreled about.

In Fein's car—a 1959 Mercedes-Benz, deep blue exterior, pale and slightly soiled beige interior—parked at the edge of an anonymous woods, in a damp snowfall; in room 14-C of the Shamrock Motor Inn some ten or twelve miles from the university; in the stately old dining room of the university's faculty club; in Fein's dim-lit study, where damp and cold exuded from the floorboards, and his antiquated space heater clicked noisily on and off, radiating a singularly dry heat. Sometimes the quarrel seemed to be about the fact that Fein wanted her with him ("at his side," "close by his side") more and more frequently, at *his* convenience; sometimes it was about the fact that Marya was lonely, Marya was ill-treated, Marya was feeling distinctly unloved and unwanted. ("You derive pleasure from pushing me closer and closer to the edge, don't you," Marya accused him. She made fists, dug her nails into her flesh, heard the childish whine in her voice and hated him the more for it. "You want me to be like yourself, a form of yourself, don't you!" she whispered fiercely. She had no idea what she was saying, the words simply tumbled out. It was sheer passion, sheer despair. And of course Fein comforted her. He was enough of a gentleman, yet enough of a lover, to know how to comfort her.)

Marya's quarrel with Fein in the faculty club was low-pitched but hardly less passionate. Fein had invited her to have lunch with him and a colleague of his in Comparative Literature—a well-known critic of contemporary French literature and culture with whom Marya had not yet studied but one day would. The man was Fein's age but portly, ruddy-faced, resolutely cheery, provocative. He and Fein discussed the possibility of a uniquely structural analysis of narratives, independent of meaning. For was not the very concept of meaning now outmoded, stale? the language of art being entirely self-referential, a language *sui generis,* linked to nothing beyond itself. Literature is comprised of such units as words and sentences —Flaubert, for instance, recognized the anguish of the situation and lamented ecstatically of having spent his life *making sentences*: separate, finite objects. As for the old notion of character as revealed by narrative, the naive prejudice that fiction is "about" real persons—even Aristotle had questioned it, saying that character is subordinate to action; there may be actions without "characters" in a narrative, but never characters without an action. Narrative is a matter of units—words, sentences—possessing weight in themselves in proportion as they are cleansed of meaning.

Fein appeared to be entertaining his colleague's ideas as if he took them seriously—as if, for Marya's sake perhaps, or for the benefit of whoever happened to be listening, he, Maximilian Fein, he too, though a medievalist and something of a conservative, could be as fashionable as the newest "radical" theories. Fein even said, with a glance at Marya, that there was something to the reductivist notion that art *is* only playful and provisional; he couldn't bear those earnest-minded citizens who drone about politics, society, moral content . . . the effluvia of meaning.

Marya had been sitting in silence for a half-hour or more; she knew that, if she spoke, she had better perform well—for certainly Fein had not brought her here, to display her to his male colleagues, merely to enjoy herself. But when she spoke her manner wasn't at all conciliatory, her words were rushed, disjointed. She said they were each talking of *meaning* without *meaning* what they said; there was no "moral content" to their remarks; why should they be taken seriously?

The ruddy-faced gentleman regarded Marya with per-

plexity and amusement; Fein, with an ambiguous expression
—he disapproved, of course, of such an outburst, but he *was*
amused: Marya Knauer was his creature, after all.

Fein goaded her by saying that scholarship as well as art
was very likely, at bottom, only play and improvisation and
illusion; it *played* at meaning in order to justify its extraordinary demands of time, spirit; when one has spent his adult life
in the service of certain projects one wants the world to believe, after all, that they have some relevance to the world.
And Marya replied, stammering, that he surely didn't mean
that; wasn't his own work a testament to—? He knew very
well that his own work, his own ideas, were— And Fein
interrupted her by saying with a trace of impatience that she
was too young ("too young and too ferocious") to even know
what he meant: to know that there was a position—intellectual, moral, perhaps even physiological—from which all
points of view are equally valid, or invalid. And Marya, stammering yet more angrily, said that he was simply pretending
to be cynical—it was only a pose—she *knew*—she *knew* he
didn't mean what he was saying; and Fein interrupted her
again, to say in a low rapid furious voice that she was displaying the mentality of an *average* citizen of the fifteenth century
—or perhaps it was that of the *average* citizen of twentieth-
century America—

So he lectured Marya, and she sat humiliated and
shaken, until, laughing to cover his embarrassment, Fein's
colleague observed that they were each wonderfully persua-
sive; listening to them, he felt like the animals in Orwell's
parable who agreed with whatever was being said while it
was being said. . . . But he excused himself soon afterward
and left Marya and Fein alone together, no longer speaking,
each flush-faced and resentful, staring at each other.

Fein brought a bottle of whiskey to the motel room, and they
drank out of plastic cups, and said very little, and Marya
thought, eyeing her lover's pale pocked face and those blue-
tinted glasses, In this man there's the answer to the very riddle

of my life, but I can't find it. And Fein, regarding her somberly, unsmilingly, may well have had the same thought.

Still, they made love successfully that afternoon. Maximilian Fein, slightly intoxicated, was hilarious—an almost boyish lover—inventive, improvisational, willing to be silly. And Marya, greatly aroused, dared pummel and wrestle him in their ludicrous king-sized bed, even snatching at his penis, jabbing, tickling—as if, in this neutral territory, nothing she did or said mattered.

Then of course the reaction came. There was always a reaction—a recoiling—on Fein's part. And he didn't telephone her for days, forced her to telephone him, told her vaguely that he was caught up in his work, that Else wasn't feeling well. . . .

"Yes. Oh yes. I see. I understand," Marya said quietly. Since she really did see, she really did understand.

Marya was lying in the dark, alone, in her bed. Though perhaps she wasn't entirely alone.

Something crouched in one of the corners. A frail, shadowy, hunched shape. Something was scuttling crabwise across the ceiling. *Marya, dear Marya, we have come to make our claim.* . . . Suddenly a hot little demon did a jig on her belly, digging in his heels. *Hey nonny nonny hey nonny nonny d'you love me Marya will you kiss me Marya* . . . !

She shook herself frantically awake. The creatures were still in the room with her but they had become invisible. A terrible pressure grew in her head—she had never experienced such a sensation before. Tighter and tighter it grew: ever tighter: now tighter still: a pain beyond pain, stretched to the breaking point. Marya knew suddenly that this was madness, this was death. This was extinction.

Now the pressure, the pain, became a bubble—pink-streaked, translucent—growing larger and larger, about to burst—

But now she did manage to shake herself into consciousness. And the telephone was ringing.

Else Fein came by in the Mercedes to pick Marya up, to drive her to the hospital where Fein lay in a coma, dying. (Though at that time it wasn't known that he was dying, only that he was in very critical condition in intensive care.)

Mrs. Fein began to speak as soon as they were in the car together, though she hadn't looked Marya full in the face, and her manner was both distracted and oddly calm, methodical. She told Marya that Fein had collapsed in his study. Sometime during the previous evening. Sometime between the hours of six and ten o'clock. She told Marya in her quick, accented, slightly admonitory voice that Maximilian had deliberately locked himself away in his study; that he had gone into one of his states, his stubborn sick spells, and had not eaten for almost three days. When she knocked at the door he shouted for her to leave him alone, he couldn't be interrupted, he would come out when it was time. Even though she pleaded with him, begged him. . . . ("Did he tell you he would be doing this?" Mrs. Fein asked Marya in an aside that took her by surprise, and Marya, numb, frightened, her head still aching from that terrible pressure, said at once, "No, no, he never told me such things.")

Yesterday evening, Mrs. Fein said, she began to grow frantic. Maximilian had never behaved quite like this—to such an extreme. When she rapped at the door there was no response: nothing. She had halfway considered telephoning Marya then, to inform her of the situation, to ask would she come to the house and make *her* appeal. . . . Her reasoning was, she said with a glance at Marya, and a mirthless little laugh, her reasoning was, he would have opened the door to Marya if he would have opened it to anyone at all.

Marya, who did not believe this to be true, nonetheless sat in silence, her gloveless hands clasped tight together. She could not have said what seemed to her at that moment more frightening, unthinkable—the fact that her lover was gravely ill or the fact that her lover's wife knew about her, seemed to know a great deal about her, had probably known all along.

She noted with what rough nervous skill the older woman drove the Mercedes along the narrow winding residential streets close by the university; how unhesitatingly she pushed into traffic on a larger street, even sounding her horn. She gripped the steering wheel hard; she was wearing smart black kidskin gloves. Marya's own hands were chapped, her fingernails bitten and raw, but she made no effort to hide them. Her teeth were chattering from the cold.

Shortly before midnight, Else Fein continued, she had telephoned the hospital and the police. And an ambulance was sent at once, it arrived within minutes, and the door was forced open, and Maximilian was discovered lying on the floor . . . he'd had a cerebral hemorrhage, as it turned out.

Hearing these words, knowing now that all this would have a name, Marya began to cry.

Else Fein reached out to give both her hands a hard little squeeze, chiding, reproachful. She told Marya that she would have to be brave, wouldn't she. She must not give in, she must not think the worst. For what if Maximilian had regained consciousness when they arrived, what if he wanted to see her. . . . Else Fein's sudden intimacy, even the pressure of her strong fingers, struck Marya as unsurprising, familiar, though the woman had never touched Marya before. Though the two of them had never been alone together before.

Marya had no idea how far away the hospital was. She sat stiff, numbed, her cheeks wet with tears, listening to Else Fein's accented voice (she spoke now disjointedly of interns, the emergency room, the remarkable quick service, she had counted at one time eleven persons, doctors and nurses both, attending her husband: she had faith that they would save him); watching the slushy street, the damp falling snow, the windshield wipers. None of this could be happening, yet it was happening with the effortlessness of a dream. Or was it in fact far less strenuous than a dream. . . . The two of them making their way through the twilight of a winter morning, in a sleigh of some kind, or was it a boat, a little blue boat, pushing its way bravely forward. She didn't know their destination. She had not been told. She shut her eyes and made her secret wish: that their journey would never end.

8

Sylvester was black. That was the first—but was it the most significant?—of the problems.

Heavyset middle-aged Sylvester with his bloodshot eyes and his plump pouting lips, the color of mashed grapes; Sylvester with his jaunty railroadman's cap pulled low over his forehead, and a cigarette (the ash grown long, precarious) slanted in his mouth; Sylvester swinging past with his noisy wheeled contraption—pail, wringer, cloth mop—mumbling in a low graveled voice, "G'morning, Professor Knauer." Though the man gave the impression of being harassed, overworked—he panted, sweated, his skin exuded a rich oily moisture even on cold mornings—he usually had time to contemplate Marya, to stare very hard at Marya, and to give the innocent words "Professor Knauer" an exquisite sort of spin.

She dreamed of him. Though she had never looked him fully in the face. Though she didn't know him at all. . . . Yet her anxious dreaming mind picked up details that turned out to be authentic: a thin wavering scar on his left cheek, a gold filling in one of his canine teeth that gave him a rakish appearance. He limped just perceptibly. The muscles of his shoulders and arms had gone fatty. He wasn't good-looking now but he had certainly been good-looking years ago, with that fussy little mustache riding his upper lip, those wide-set shrewd eyes. "G'morning, Professor Knauer," he said, his gaze dropping to her feet and rising, slowly, defiantly, to her face. "G'afternoon, Professor," he said, a little catch in his throat as if he could hardly keep from laughing, "real nice day ain't it?"

In the beginning, at the high-flying euphoric start of the academic year, Marya had said hello to Sylvester frequently, and warmly. She had taken him at face value—noting no irony in his greeting, or mockery in his heavy-lidded gaze or in that twitch about the lips meant to signal a smile. Perhaps unconsciously she had assumed that irony was a prerogative of the learned segment of the white race. In any case, she was mistaken. It was a year, generally, of mistaken assumptions.

Marya was now twenty-five years old. She had the rank of assistant professor of English in a prestigious but rather small old New Hampshire college that had never, in its two-hundred-thirty-year history, awarded any woman tenure or promoted her to a higher rank; until three or four years ago no woman had been hired at all. The implications of such facts had not exactly escaped Marya but she seemed to be, at this time, in one of her zealous optimistic phases. After Fein's death she had completed her Ph.D. work with another scholar and in another field entirely; her five-hundred-page study of mid-nineteenth-century American prose was scheduled for publication at Yale; she had discovered in herself an almost too ecstatic passion for teaching; and, exhausted as she often was, she nonetheless felt, for the first time in her life, young . . . or at any rate youthful. Surely the world wished her well; how could it not?

"G'morning, Professor Knauer," the black custodian

said as they passed in the corridor of the Humanities Building. "G'*day*, Professor," he might say, bunching one plump cheek as he smiled with half his face, the jeering inflection in his voice so very subtle Marya hadn't picked it up for weeks, months. Later she heard it all the time. But by then Sylvester had begun other strategies of harassment as well, none quite so subtle.

She finally sought him out one morning in late January.

As soon as she unlocked the door to her office she knew immediately that he had been in there again—the smell of cigarette smoke assailed her, and the way the venetian blind had been yanked to the very top of the high window. Even the metal wastebasket was defiantly out of place. Sylvester has been here, Sylvester has made his mark, left his calling card. . . . It might be a cigarette butt mashed out in one of Marya's potted ivy plants on the windowsill, it might be a Kleenex stiffened with a yellow stain, crumpled and left on the very seat of her chair, it might be a cigarette dropped in the toilet bowl in her lavatory, sodden, unraveling, striking the eye, for an instant, like a tiny piece of feces. Marya knew herself upset out of all proportion to what was happening, what was actually being done, she knew it was absurd to have so immediate a reaction (her heart pounded, her blood seemed to go cold—the old hackneyed symptoms, dear Christ!), but it was impossible to remain calm.

Why, she thought, like any victim, swallowing her anger, her sickening fury—why me, why *me*?—why *me* at this time in my life?

It took her a very long time to enter the room and close the door behind her and make her way to the desk, walking carefully, her head held as if she were balancing something precariously on it. Yes, the black custodian had been here, of course he had been here, it was his responsibility to keep the offices in his building clean, he had every right to enter her office. . . . And if he felt the need to smoke, to make his wretched job a little more agreeable, Marya needn't take it as a personal affront. . . .

She saw that the middle drawer of the desk had been left an inch or two open, as Sylvester always left it when he wanted her to know he'd been rifling through her things, examining them, rearranging them according to an eccentric pattern of his own. Perhaps it would be wisest for Marya not to investigate at the moment; she had a class to teach in twenty minutes, a lecture on Emily Dickinson, two hundred students to face in an old amphitheater with rising tiers of seats. . . . It might be prudent not to check the little lavatory either.

Yes, the swivel chair behind the desk was out of place. Sylvester had been sitting in it not long ago, his heavy thighs straining at his khaki work pants, his expression earnest, somber, the cigarette drooping between his lips. His big beefy fingers poked about in the drawer, but what was there lately, now that Marya had taken away her personal letters? Rubber bands, pencils, ballpoint pens, paper clips, departmental memos, loose change. (Of course Sylvester never touched money. He wasn't a thief, not Sylvester; you couldn't accuse him of that.)

At the beginning of the school year the departmental secretary had apologized to Marya, for the fact that her office —along with the offices of several other new appointees—was in the old Humanities Building, and not in the new; and for the fact that it was rather old, shabby, ill-lit, furnished with odds and ends—that battered old desk, for instance, all scratches and stains and scorch marks, a half century old, with drawers that couldn't be locked. Marya hadn't at all minded, however—she would have been embarrassed to say how grateful she was for the office, for any office at all; for a place, a salary, a tangible slot in the world. She was vain enough to love it that her name, on a tiny white card, was affixed to the front of the door; she loved it that she had an entire office, and a rather spacious one, to herself; there was even a tiny lavatory at the rear. In the past the room had been used for seminar meetings: so it was furnished haphazardly with mismatched items of furniture—chairs in various derelict stages, a floor lamp with a dusty shade, a narrow table measuring some six feet in length. The ceiling of hammered tin must have been fifteen feet high, the window faced south, sunshine flooded the room on clear winter mornings. It warmed Marya's back when she sat at the desk, it cheered her up when she needed cheering.

Marya had begun to fill in the office with things of her own. A Dürer woodcut, a framed lithograph by an artist friend who lived now in New York, a print of a Cézanne landscape that reminded her, obliquely, of the countryside near Shaheen Falls. (All three items had been moved at one time or another by Sylvester, presumably because he wanted to clean the cobwebs off the wall; but there were always cobwebs, unless Marya brushed them off herself. The Dürer in particular took his fancy, he was always making it crooked by an inch or two.) Marya had brought in a few plants from the five-and-dime, some ceramic mugs, a fair number of books. She wondered at the protocol of filling up those floor-to-ceiling bookcases when her appointment at the college wasn't necessarily permanent. Did it bespeak simple optimism and enthusiasm, or presumption, defiance?

When Marya first realized that the black janitor for the building had been deliberately leaving traces of himself in her office, and that his manner with her wasn't quite so ingenuous as she had thought, her first response was simple disbelief. It could not be happening, *this* could not be happening! Had she come so far (from Innisfail, from the Canal Road, from the tarpaper shanty of a house near Shaheen Falls) to be persecuted by a stranger . . . ? She was incredulous, baffled. Then she was angry. Then frightened. One day she casually brought up the subject of Sylvester (whose name she hadn't known at the time) to a departmental secretary; not precisely complaining but indicating, hinting, that there were some problems with him. The woman was sympathetic at once. She knew, she knew, everyone knew—Sylvester could be difficult. He was sometimes rude to students, even to faculty members; he called in sick at least once a week; he drank beer down in the basement, and frequently got drunk; he did a poor job of cleaning, was generally lazy, unreliable. Unfortunately he belonged to the union and couldn't be fired. He could only be shifted about the college from one building to another, working his way down, so to speak, to the old Humanities Building, where the plaster was falling in many of the rooms and the furnaces were so old. She didn't know what the next stop for Sylvester might be—perhaps there wasn't any. Marya might find it easier, she said, to look after her office herself, except of course for the heavy cleaning.

Yes, Marya murmured, subdued, in a way chastened, I will.

Today there was the drawer left open; and she couldn't resist (though it was foolish to upset herself, to get her nerves racing) glancing into the lavatory, where the toilet had been used and not flushed. She flushed it herself. She thought, This could all be accidental. She thought, The filthy pig.

The class went well, her lecture was a success, Marya's spirits were high, brash. So she sought out Sylvester on the stairs leading down to the basement. He was lounging in a doorway, smoking a cigarette, half dozing, inert. All bulk, gone shapeless and sullen, with that soiled railroadman's cap perched cockily on his head. When he saw Marya he blinked in surprise; his eyes actually flashed yellow.

She told him that she didn't want him "interfering" with her things any longer. It wasn't necessary for him to clean her office at all—she could do it herself. It wasn't necessary for him to ever go into it again.

By now he had regained his composure. His blood-threaded gaze took her in with mock sobriety. He mumbled words she couldn't hear, shrugged his shoulders, stared grinning at her feet. (Marya was wearing black leather knee-high boots with a knobby little heel in a style she believed quite chic; they had in any case cost her a fair amount of money.) He cleared his throat and said it was his *job* to clean all the offices, he didn't "have no right not to," that was why he was being paid. . . .

"Then I'll have to report you," Marya said angrily, "if there's any more trouble."

"Trouble?"

"You know what I mean. Trouble."

He stared at her, his teeth still bared. The gold filling gleamed like a witticism. He was in his forties, perhaps, very dark, burnished-dark, his skin oily, his nose slightly flattened. He belched and Marya smelled beer. "Doan know what in hell you *do* mean, Professor," he said, with that little catch in his throat that signaled mirth.

As Marya walked away (she was losing her nerve, she couldn't keep it up, another minute and she'd be shouting), he spoke more loudly, laughing, angry himself, as if addressing an audience, "Doan know what the hell *that's* all about, what kind of shit she handing me! Ain't no trouble I ever heard of!"

Marya could hear him all the way up the stairs. Even his accent, his black dialect, Marya thought, was in mockery.

Racial prejudice was so much a fact of life back home, the separation of the races (economic, social, demographic) so taken for granted, Marya had long ago vowed to stand apart from it; which is to say, above it. So she made the effort now to think of Sylvester not as a black man, but simply as a man; a workingman with a very poor job; hostile toward others because he despised his own condition in life.

(In fact Marya uneasily suspected that Sylvester wasn't all that badly paid. The custodians' local had gone on strike the year before, their contract was reputed to be impressive, Marya's colleagues often joked about it in reference to their own salaries.)

She tried to separate the man from his skin; Sylvester from his blackness. She tried not to *see* him—only to envision his nettling little pranks in her office, the pictures hanging crooked, the stiffened Kleenex, the unflushed toilet. There was the thin scar on his cheek . . . there was the gold filling . . . the slight limp . . . the slump of the fatty rounded shoulders. Sylvester. Sylvester and his "G'morning, *Professor!*"

Did she imagine it, did he one day call after her softly, "—Marya!"

Months before, in October, Marya was walking on a downtown street with several of her colleagues when she happened to see Sylvester approaching: a tall big-bodied black man in checked trousers, a pinkish-orange shirt, a maroon cloth cap set atop his wiry hair. He was walking with a black woman of his own approximate age, lighter-skinned, chunky, with an attractive face that had gone puffy and sullen. Marya, caught up in an autumnal mood of gaiety and camaraderie, called out hello; but Sylvester, his chin uplifted, passed by without so much as glancing at her. (His companion, however, had stared at Marya. Who do you think *you* are, she seemed to be asking.)

Marya's friends asked her who the black man was. Marya, flushed with embarrassment, said he was the janitor—the custodian—in their building; didn't they recognize him? She was also rather angry at having been so resolutely and so publicly snubbed.

No, Marya's friends said, they hadn't recognized him, they didn't know him, and, anyway, weren't there several black custodians in the building?

Not long afterward the window in Marya's office was left open at the top over a weekend; rain soaked into the carpet, damaged papers and books on Marya's desk, gathered in a little puddle on the floor. Marya was puzzled at the time because she never opened the window from the top and found it highly difficult to manipulate the window at that angle at all. But it wasn't until a while afterward—she was slow, very slow, in coming to certain conclusions—that she realized the janitor had done it. Even then it was a while before she realized he had done it deliberately, to punish her for calling out to him on the street, for making a pretense of their sociability.

After that the persecution became more evident. Though it was still sporadic and unpredictable. Though, with so many other urgent things to consider, she rarely had time to consider *that*. (Wasn't it petty and demeaning, Marya asked herself. Purposeless. Childish. And here she was on the faculty of one of the most distinguished colleges in the Northeast, twenty-five years old, well respected by her students and colleagues, passionately caught up in teaching, teaching, teaching . . . which she wanted to make her life's work.) Still, it was difficult to ignore Sylvester's taunts when he made it a point of passing her in the corridor, on the stairs, dipping his head in her direction in a parody of gallantry, twisting his mouth around the word "Professor" until it had never sounded so forlornly pretentious. And then she discovered one afternoon (how long had it been there? had any of her students noticed?) a bloodstained sanitary napkin placed innocently on the bottommost shelf of one of the bookcases. The thing had dried and stiffened into a peculiar arched shape.

Weeks passed, nothing further happened, nothing that impressed itself upon Marya's feverish brain. She was so caught up in the present tense, hurrying from place to place, spending much of her free time in the library, taking notes, preparing lectures, assembling ideas for articles, essays, for her second book. (She wanted to study "magical" narratives in nineteenth-century fiction . . . apocalyptic romances of a sort. . . . She wanted to pay a good deal of attention to neglected writers, to unknown women writers, in whose work radical and even revolutionary themes might be discovered, beneath, or behind, the formal conventions of a genre. And at the same time she had begun to be interested in writing pieces of a more immediate general interest: why no one in this part of the state had ever explored in print the significance of the Rhinelander Air Force Base thirty miles to the north where the Pentagon stored cruise missiles, and B-52's—two, three, five, seven, as many as a dozen at a time—incessantly combed the sky. It should be a matter of great local interest, Marya thought, that, if or when the "enemy" struck, Rhinelander would be one of their first targets. An enormous nuclear blast—firestorms of incalculable ferocity—invisible radiation borne on the wind! Professors in the humanities spent their lives rigorously analyzing texts, classical and otherwise, but displayed a curious reluctance to examine the "text" in which they played out their own lives. Perhaps the irony of the situation might be explored, Marya thought.

So she thought only occasionally of Sylvester; and was able to forget him for days at a time. She worked very hard and thrived on it, was invigorated by it, uncomplaining, zealous, filled with ideas about how to organize her classes, how to draw out her quieter students, how to . . . make her way in this extraordinary phase of her life. Because she was new on the staff she hadn't the immediate pressures of promotion and tenure to deal with; she even thought it rather petty, rather *vulgar,* of certain of her colleagues to spend so much time in careerist speculation. They were a few years older than Marya, extremely bright, competitive, hard-working; slightly fanatic on the subject of their futures; their youth a bit tarnished by habits of drollery and self-mocking irony. Impatient with the tone of an entire evening's sociability, Marya made the point that teaching and scholarship really ought to be their primary concerns, and that this dwelling upon competing with one another, always competing, competing, made anything approaching friendship extremely difficult. And the group turned laughing on her, their good humor a little tinged with contempt: Why, how very extraordinary of Marya to have made this discovery! And had she come to such conclusions by herself? And was she planning not to "compete" but to leave the field to . . . her friends?

One winter afternoon, late, Marya returned to her office from the library, to discover Sylvester seated boldly at her desk.

Big plump kingly Sylvester. Seated there at Marya Knauer's desk, in her swivel chair. His face burnished and gleaming, his eyes hooded, the usual cigarette slanted in his lips. He must have heard her key in the lock and made the quick decision not to jump to his feet, not to betray any surprise or confusion or guilt. Instead it was Marya who was surprised, Marya who recoiled in alarm. The building had emptied out, they were alone on the floor together, it was past five-thirty and quite dark. . . .

Marya asked him what he was doing, what did he want, and though she was really quite frightened her voice sounded steady enough. Sylvester rose sighing and grunting from the chair, hitching his trousers. He made a last perfunctory swipe at the desk with one of his rags. "Just makin' things neat," he muttered, not looking at her.

Marya drew a deep breath and said, "I don't want you going through my things. You know that. I asked you not to. I asked you. . . ."

Sylvester repeated that he was just making things neat, polishing things up, "just doin' my job, Professor, how come you always *at* me?" She caught the little hiccup of merriment in his voice, saw the flash of his wicked gold tooth. When he brushed past her she smelled beer, sweat, tobacco smoke, Sylvester's special dark odor of ammonia and disinfectant.

It *was* true, he had been polishing the desk. At least the top. But a pile of her things lay on the carpet where he'd dumped them—memos, papers, pens, a personal letter from a friend in Boston, a two-page letter from the editor of *The Meridian* saying that he would like to publish her essay but would she consider making certain deletions and adding a few more paragraphs on the subject of . . . Marya's face burned with shame, that Sylvester could see *this*; that he should have the opportunity to guess how she might be measured elsewhere, judged, found deficient. (If Sylvester took the time to read. If indeed he could read at all.)

You black bastard, she whispered.

She rehearsed future confrontations with Sylvester. ("You must stop harassing me or I will be forced to report you to . . . ") She rehearsed an interview with the department's executive secretary, even with the chairman of the department himself. ("This is a very minor matter but I suppose it might become more serious and so I thought . . . I don't want to really file a complaint of any official kind but . . .")

Sometimes, alone in her apartment or, working late, alone in her office, she rehearsed a ghostly exchange: Why do you hate me, Sylvester, what have I done to provoke you? . . . Pro-fessor I doan know what in hell you talkin' about. . . . But Sylvester why do you *hate* me when I'm nice to you haven't I always been nice to you how have I provoked you? . . . Professor I'm tellin' you I doan know what kind of shit you handin' me, ain't I paid to do my job . . . ain't I paid to do my job . . . ?

Marya, for years so absorbed in her work that she had never had much time for colleagues, fell quickly into the habit of speaking with them—talking, laughing, gossiping, even dawdling—whenever she had the opportunity. If Sylvester observed he would understand that she had companions, friends. She had people to protect her should she require protection.

Their names were Ian, and Florence, and Ralph, and Gregory, and a visiting professor named John from Trinity College, Dublin, whose laughter was gratifyingly loud and warming. On lightless winter days Marya readily consented to invitations for lunch at the faculty club, or a cup of coffee, even a drink . . . even dinner, if she wasn't too pressed for time. She imagined Sylvester watching her from a darkened doorway or a basement window, taking note, revising his plans.

To Gregory Hemstock, whose office was a few doors down from hers, she complained lightly, laughingly, of their "not always very competent" janitor. And Gregory laughed in turn, admitting that he now emptied his own wastepaper basket and did some dusting and sweeping once in a while, when things got too disgraceful. Should we really be doing such things, Marya wondered, when after all the man was being paid and it was *his* job; and Gregory said no, of course they shouldn't, but none of them was in a position to complain ("to appear to be less than perfectly happy here—if you understand my point"), and in his own case he didn't *really* mind a little housekeeping now and then. In fact, Gregory said suddenly, would Marya like him to clean her office too?—once a week or so, nothing systematic.

One midwinter afternoon when Marya was working late in her office, two of her colleagues—Florence and Ralph—dropped by to ask if she'd like to join them for dinner in town. (They gave every appearance of being a couple these days, inclined to outbursts of laughter and unexpected little kindnesses. Like asking Marya Knauer to dinner.)

But Marya said she couldn't accept, she had too much work to do . . . she was swamped, she said, with work. Her hair was in her eyes and her skin was pale and slightly clammy.

Was she going to stay there much longer, in the building, alone? Florence asked. It was going on seven.

Marya hadn't noticed the time. She often worked late, she said.

So they went away; and she forgot them within a few minutes. She liked the building at this time of day, evening—students never interrupted her, the telephone never rang. If she turned to look out the window she saw only, reflected against the darkness, her own tremulous reflection. But she did not feel at all tremulous: she felt stolid, resolute. This was her office; her name was even on the door.

Farther down the corridor came the sound of vacuuming. The thump of the heavy-duty machine, the muffled companionable roar, Sylvester working late. He often worked late these days because (so Marya had heard) he came in late. Someone had mentioned that his drinking was getting serious and he would really have to be disciplined by the union soon, if not fired. And where would he go? Marya asked.

She immersed herself in her work—sketching out the first draft of an article, writing pages of commentary on her students' term papers, preparing the next day's classes—and when she was next aware of the time it was already past eight o'clock. The minutes had passed so swiftly, she'd forgotten even to be hungry. She had forgotten the circumstances of her situation, here in the old Humanities Building.

Most of the lights in the building had been extinguished. Sylvester had gone home, everyone had gone home, only Marya Knauer remained behind . . . groping her way along the pitch-black corridor until she came to the stairway, where there was a light switch she could turn on. If she could find it.

Marya's night thoughts had to do with the wonderland of junked cars belonging to her uncle Everard . . . and with B-52 jets threading the sky, all skies, with trails of filmy white vapor. . . . Though she didn't sleep she found herself rising suddenly from sleep, waking, thinking calmly, Is our secret that we want to die? —we want to die together, in a nuclear explosion?—making an end of things that otherwise will never end.

She thought of Sylvester. It would give *him* angry comfort, she knew, if everyone died at once. If he could have a hand in it, himself.

Five dollars disappeared from Marya's desk—the bill had been carefully hidden beneath the pen groove in the center drawer —but she knew better than to confront Sylvester: he wasn't a thief, after all. (I doan know what in hell you gettin' at, Professor. I only doin' my job, Pro-fessor.)

Then it turned out that Sylvester had taken two weeks off, that another man was taking his place temporarily. . . . Marya didn't ask, Is he black? She did ask what was wrong with Sylvester.

No one knew. He often took sudden sick leaves. He went on binges, it was thought; he had woman trouble; spent a night or two in jail, D & D, drunk and disorderly, quite a character . . . if you cared for characters. ("He used to talk my ear off if I let him," one of the older members of the department said.

"He was really sort of appealing if you had the time to draw him out. . . .")

Of course Sylvester returned, reappeared. On the stairs, in Marya's corridor. Hauling his wheeled wringer mop along with the greatest possible noise. Big-bellied, limping, trailing ashes. In his wake the air quivered with powerful rank odors that could not be ignored: Marya smiled to see two young women undergraduates wrinkle their noses in surprised disgust but make the effort *not* to glance at each other or to comment—they weren't racists, after all. They were very pretty very bright liberal-minded young women, uncontaminated by the prejudices of another generation. Marya Knauer was a few years their senior but she was assuredly one of them.

Of course Sylvester returned, this was his job, his livelihood. G'morning, Pro-fessor Knauer, how're *you* Pro-fessor Knauer. . . . Marya's office stank of cigarette smoke and Sylvester's sweat; her window was shut tight and locked; the radiator had been turned up full blast; it was late March now and almost warm. . . . When Marya walked into the room, into that blast of dry heat, she felt the very pores of her skin contract in a panic that was sheerly physiological. Oh Sylvester, she thought, oh dear Christ *why* . . . ?

The chairman of the department liked Marya, he declared himself impressed by Marya, but had his doubts—as he frankly, forthrightly told her—about the areas of scholarship in which she was interested. Of course he couldn't presume to dictate, or even to suggest, but since she was new in the profession and new at the college. . . .

All that week rumors had been flying about, ignoble rumors, shameful rumors: whose contract would not be renewed, who would be given a final one-year contract, who would be granted tenure, even promoted: it was a new experience for Marya, and not a very pleasant one, suddenly caring about matters she'd resolutely promised herself to ignore.

Sink yourself in work, Marya; or, if you're too nervous suddenly (*are* you nervous? or only excited, apprehensive?) then sink yourself in the work of others, in great thoughts, elevated souls, Walt Whitman and William James and Emily Dickinson and Henry David Thoreau. . . .

An old ploy, learned from poor Mr. Schwilk, so very long ago.

Still, such practices gave her solace. They gave her, these edgy days, a certain measure of dignity.

Now her thick dark hair was worn almost short, fashionably short, shaped like a helmet with the ends turned smoothly under, against their natural wave. She rubbed in a very light makeup beneath her eyes to disguise the faint shadows; and the disguise was wonderfully successful. She was no madonna now, no somber *mater dolorosa* waiting inside a gilt frame to be adored; she was an Amazon of a sort, a warrior woman, making her own way, confident and assured . . . or so it seemed.

She regarded herself in the mirror with critical satisfaction. Yes. Good. That was her *self*—the way she was turning out—the way in which her fleshly destiny led. (Such extravagant metaphors should have embarrassed her, but did not; in this phase of her life—rather brief, rather overwrought, but in any case "successful"—she felt that each hour, each minute, was in some way the mystical consummation of all that had gone before. She intended to be equal to it.)

Staring at herself, she wondered if Maximilian Fein would approve of her now. Seeing that he had helped shape her—*this*. And what of Emmett, Emmett Schroeder, what might he think; would he be impressed, would he (did he know enough to be) envious, jealous? (All she knew of Emmett these days, these years, was that he'd married a girl not known to Wilma, lived in Innisfail, was a partner in his father's construction business.)

Would Vera Sanjek know her, Marya wondered, eyeing

herself, raising her forehead into a pattern of light creases, would they even recognize each other, face to face?

The departmental chairman called Marya into his office to tell her good news, the kind of news (he said, clearing his throat nervously) he dearly wished he might tell everyone. . . . Her contract was being renewed for three years; the salary increment she would be receiving was higher than the average—in fact, for her rank, considerably higher; the committee on promotion and tenure had received a number of very strong letters of evaluation from her students, though, evidently, she had been grading rather conservatively. ("New teachers sometimes make the error of inflating grades," he told Marya, "hoping to flatter their students into liking them, admiring them. But it doesn't work here—it earns their disrespect. It might work very well at other colleges where standards aren't quite so high but it doesn't work here.")

The tension between them was almost palpable because of course Marya hadn't known until now whether . . . whether, crudely put, it was thumbs-up or thumbs-down: one more year and then termination, or three more years with a possibility (for there was always the *possibility*) of a future. So it was a relief, wasn't it, to be told good news. To be chatting companionably with the chairman of the department, talking for a while of general matters, as if they were equals. It was all right. She was all right. She hadn't failed this time, she hadn't been stopped.

By degrees the strain lessened; when Marya rose to leave she had quite enjoyed their talk, she could see why her chairman was so well-liked, even by persons whose careers he had (always reluctantly, with a pose of helplessness) destroyed. He asked her whether she had any requests, any complaints, and Marya said, as they shook hands, "No, of course not."

Marya unlocks the door to her office, senses at once Sylvester's presence—the ghostly contour, that is, of his absence—the stale stink of cigarette smoke, the sour tinge to the air. Again the window has been shut tight though it is a mild morning in late April and Marya had the window open, propped up with a book, just the evening before.

And what else? The brass floor lamp is in an odd corner of the room, unplugged. The Cézanne print is just perceptibly crooked. As for the things on her desk—they've been shuffled about but so far as she can see nothing is missing. He isn't a thief, after all; he's careful about that.

Marya shuts the door behind her and locks it. She doesn't want to be interrupted.

Sylvester with his blood-threaded gaze, his puckered smile, the caressing lilt to his voice. Marya's colleagues, Marya's many students. She feels how they are watching her, observing closely, waiting. For she was a woman, she *must* weaken under the strain. . . .

She goes to the little lavatory. As soon as she opens the door she is assaulted by the commingled smell of cigarette smoke and urine.

She sees, in the unflushed toilet bowl, a cigarette butt floating, the tobacco unraveling, the paper nearly dissolved, turning slowly—quivering—vibrating—trembling—in response to a celestial tide too subtle for her to sense—riding the deep amber of Sylvester's urine.

9

It might be said that their lives—their professional futures—
were being decided for them *that very day*: so weren't they
free? blameless? innocent as children?

They might go for a thirty-mile bicycle ride on an impulse, Gregory said. Or hire a Piper Cub and be flown to the
ocean. Or a balloon, one of those gorgeous striped hot-air
balloons, did Marya know what they were?—the fee was $50
an hour per person. Not so much, really, when you considered
that the sport was dangerous, the balloon *could* collapse.

When Marya didn't immediately respond he gripped her
head between his hands and pretended to be erasing frown
lines from her forehead with his long lanky thumbs. "You
look like a mourner, Marya," he said, chiding, teasing, on the
very edge of bullying, "aren't you being premature?"

She drew away, laughing. She hated his hands when he
was being willfully playful, when his mood was forced, a pretense of gaiety, stoical high spirits. They were not precisely

lovers, after all—it couldn't have been said *what* they were—
so Marya was spared the necessity of falling in with his moods,
placating and pleasing. She said that the bicycle ride might be
just the solution. To dispel anxiety, nerves, animal terror—she
was smiling, saying this—to take them *away*.

A man she once knew, Marya continued, feeling now
rather playful herself, used to say that if the future is as strictly
determined as the past, aren't we really free to do what we
wish?—and all without being blamed.

Who was that, Gregory asked immediately, one of your
lovers?

Marya stiffened. She felt the frown lines reassert themselves.

No, she said. Not really.

So they set out early the following morning, Marya and Gregory, on their ambitious bicycle ride. They even told a few
friends about it—boasted of it, warily, self-mockingly—anything to get them *away* while the Dean and the Provost and
one or two others decided their fates for them. ("Odd, how
we use words like 'fate,' " Gregory observed, "when we mean
only good or bad luck.") Gregory's bicycle was a handsome
ten-speed English racing bike with smart blue reflectors that
spun about, affixed to the spokes of the wheels; Marya's was
a fairly shameful old thing—a mere three-speed with a worn
seat, slightly rusted pedals, a frayed wicker basket into which
she usually stuffed books and papers. She didn't yet own a car:
if she lost her job here, she'd buy one at once, she'd need it
to move away in, maybe rent one of those U-Haul trailers and
pile in her things. . . .

"Are you thinking about *it*?" Gregory said reproachfully.
"If you are, stop."

They had vowed not to think about *it* for the duration of
the bicycle trip. For, after all, *it* was out of their hands. They
would bicycle all the way to a town called Nelson's Mills—
Gregory knew a place there, an old stone inn, they could stay
the night—they would return to the college by late afternoon

of the following day; and by then the decisions would have been made, Marya Knauer's and Gregory Hemstock's letters prepared for them, everything properly official and irrevocable. *It is my pleasure to inform you. . . . It is with deep regret that I inform you. . . .* Form letters; formula congratulations or condolences; as resolutely impersonal as if printed out by a machine.

Except of course these were human decisions, Marya thought. Decisions made by men. Not a woman among them.

Tall lean long-boned Gregory with a red headband around his forehead; Gregory in a white T-shirt and shorts and runner's shoes, without socks, looking young and antic as any of his students. Or nearly. (For Gregory was nearly thirty now, two years older than Marya.) His legs were thin but strong, tight with muscle; his thighs flat and hard. Marya admired the curve of his long narrow back as he hunched over the racing bike's handlebars, she admired the contrast between the sporty red headband and his fine white-blond hair. He had fastened amber plastic lenses over his glasses, had secured his glasses in place with a strip of black elastic, gave every impression of being a serious rider with a serious destination. He and Marya had gone out bicycling a few times on winding country roads in the area but the rides had been easy, companionable, not at all competitive; they'd mostly ridden abreast, talking. Gregory had never been able to talk her into accompanying him on a long trip before—she hadn't the time, she said, she wasn't really that confident a bicyclist, and in any case didn't your mind simply drift onto other things, to the usual worries and problems, on long monotonous rides?

The sport isn't monotonous, Gregory said. There are only monotonous-minded people.

Marya laughed, chastened. She quite liked Gregory when he put her in her place, deflated her pretensions. She was less comfortable with his mercurial moods—his frequent self-reproach, his melancholy, his outbursts of sentiment, piety, possessiveness. (A year ago he suggested suddenly that they move Marya's things into his apartment, that they "experiment along those lines" for six weeks or so. Marya hadn't been inclined to take the proposal seriously.)

Bicycling, Marya felt herself propelled by an indefinable energy—now anxiety, now elation, now a muscular sort of rage, concentrated in her legs and thighs. Was she angry? But at whom? She felt good, despite her circumstances. She felt strong. It was her fantasy that even if she were promoted, awarded tenure, even if everything worked out well . . . she would only teach for another year or two; then resign; move to New York City; begin another sort of life. More spacious, more idiosyncratic. It was a fantasy she suspected might be commonplace, among people in her situation.

As for Gregory—he disliked speculation, the fabrication of "plans" that were hardly more than wishes in disguise.

As for Gregory—he kept himself to himself, as the old expression went.

So long as they were bicycling along residental streets Marya had no trouble keeping pace with him. It was a sunny autumn day, just perceptibly chilly, bracing. She did feel good, invigorated. But once they were in the open country Marya began to fall behind by degrees. "Gregory, wait," she called out, laughing, trying to laugh, and if he heard her he obligingly slackened his pace; if not, he pedaled on ahead for some minutes before he became aware of outdistancing her.

Finally he told her to ride ahead—that way he could keep his eye on her.

"Why can't we ride side by side?" Marya asked, irritated.

"It isn't done," Gregory said, "on roads like these."

The slight edge of reproof in his voice was Marya's first intimation that the bicycle ride, for all its romantic promise, might be an error.

Suddenly there were surprises, unanticipated discomforts. The wind was far stronger than it had been in town—blowing across open corn and wheat fields, sweeping along the highway itself. Marya's hair whipped frantically about her head, she regretted not having brought along a scarf. When the sun disappeared for long minutes at a time she was cold and shivering; when it reappeared she was hot within seconds —dressed too warmly, evidently, in jeans and a long-sleeved shirt. Gregory appeared to be dressed sensibly; the very equanimity of his temper shamed her.

Sunshine . . . wind . . . the smell of dried grasses . . . the smell of cultivated fields . . . the hypnotic movement of the pavement . . . the potholes, creases, ruts, rivulets . . . the ceaseless alterations in the road's shoulders, now muddy, now sandy, now alarmingly eroded. . . . Marya's shoulders and knees had begun to ache by late morning and she found herself wondering (childishly, nervously) how long they had to go before the first stop. Gregory had told her the mileage, he'd told her the name of the little town, but she couldn't remember and didn't want to ask. She was conscious of him watching her from behind, noting the arhythmic movement of her feet on the pedals, the occasional swerve in her steering. Her initial rush of energy and confidence had gradually drained away; she wondered if Gregory had known this would happen, if he had suggested the excursion merely to humiliate her.

But that was absurd. He was her closest friend, after all.

Still, this meant that Marya was straining herself, pushing herself. By noon she'd already pushed far beyond the perimeters of their other rides—she was reminded of the long bicycle rides into Innisfail, years ago—on her American-style bicycle with the balloon tires and the rusted wire basket. If her knees and shoulders ached that was a good thing; if the calves of her legs pulled, throbbed, that simply meant—didn't it?—that the muscles were being exercised. And if her mind wandered along unproductive lines, if she felt now and then little jabs of panicked apprehension, it was simply the case, as Gregory had said, that she was to blame—the sport wasn't monotonous, surely.

She wondered with a thrill of anticipation how many miles she *was* capable of covering, how many hours she could keep it up. Gregory complained that his own years of serious bicycling were past—he smoked too much, his wind was short. (He was nearly thirty, and rapidly aging, as he liked to joke, running his hand through his pale filmy thinning hair.)

Marya began to hope for, to *will,* hills going down; gentle sloping banks in the pavement that allowed her to hug the shoulder of the road, to keep as much distance as possible between her and passing cars. (She reasoned that Gregory would shout a warning to her if a car or truck came too close, but what if her wheel struck a pothole at the wrong moment, what if a stone or pebble were flung up and struck her . . . ?) Pedaling uphill, gamely, stoically, she felt the tendons in her legs and knees go livid with pain; her breath came shorter and shorter, her vision swam, Gregory pumped effortlessly past her, saying, "Get off, Marya, and walk, for Christ's sake conserve your strength: you're going to need it."

But she kept on, now panting, near-despairing, furious. She could always count on a rush of sudden strength, she thought—she wasn't going to give in.

Gregory waited for her, straddling his bicycle, at the top of the long, long hill. She disliked him, suddenly; she resented it that he was taking advantage of her exhaustion, her pain, by *resting,* now, and waiting for her . . . watching her wobbly progress with an expression of infinite patience.

"Now stop for a minute, Marya," he said, when Marya pulled up beside him. "Don't keep going. *Please* don't be stubborn."

"I'm not stubborn," Marya said, her breath ragged. "I'm really not tired."

"And when you take this next hill, use your brakes," he said. "Don't let your speed get too high."

"I know how to ride a bicycle," Marya said.

"Yes, but you haven't been on hills quite like these and you've probably never been quite so tired. If you had—"

"I bicycled all the time as a child," Marya said. "I bicycled to *work.*"

He stared at her; his eyes looked pale, colorless, behind the tinted lenses; his own face was flushed and his hair disheveled. Despite the jaunty headband his face was damp with perspiration. He doesn't love me, Marya thought in a surge of self-pity, he wants me to fail, she thought, turning away unsmiling, brushing her hair out of her eyes.

Gregory broke the mood by leaning over to squeeze her shoulder and kiss her cheek. "Hey," he said, "I'm proud of us, aren't you?—getting this far without fighting."

They were headed west and south, curving gradually downward toward the river, now approximately fifteen miles away. Marya took heart from the fact that the ride was *half over*: one could endure anything, she thought, with the knowledge that it was *half over*. A dull ache between her shoulder blades, numbness in her knees, head faintly throbbing. . . . Sunshine, pavement (broken and patchy, tarry, coarse), wind, that damned incessant wind making her eyes water. . . . Once Gregory shouted for her to get over just as she heard a car rushing up behind, and she reacted too quickly, desperately, running her front wheel off the road, nearly falling, stumbling . . . knocking her ankle against the pedal. . . . She had to stop and wait for a minute, two minutes, three, until the pain subsided. "You're doing very well," Gregory said cautiously. "We could turn back, you know, any time you like."

Marya said, teasing, that the two halves of his remark didn't scan: either she *was* doing well (was she? oh yes?) or he was thinking they could turn back for a good reason (since he never said or thought anything without a good reason).

"I wouldn't want to think you were humoring me," Marya said.

"Certainly it's the last thing on my mind," Gregory said, stooping to examine her ankle.

The previous spring Marya had met a man named Eric Nichols at a conference in New York City. She told Gregory about him—as much as she knew of him—in a slow, careful voice. "Well, it can't be said that you were unfaithful to me." Gregory laughed. "There's that in our favor."

His laughter was abrupt and jarring. "I haven't been unfaithful to anyone," Marya said.

She was angry but her voice sounded weak. She began to cry.

"Oh no. No. Is all this for *me*?" Gregory said, spreading his fingers in mock amazement. "Tears? for *me*?"

"I haven't been unfaithful to anyone," Marya said.

The conference had been on the general subject of Latin American culture, held in the Americana Hotel, as it was then called, on Seventh Avenue. Though the subject had nothing to do with Marya's academic field of specialization—though in fact it constituted a serious divergence from her specialization —Marya had lately found herself intensely interested in Latin America; she was studying Spanish and Portuguese, rather unwisely at the same time. Eric Nichols, the editor of *The Meridian*, was on a large and combative panel that addressed itself to the question of whether Latin American culture had a future, or only a highly interesting past. It was the first panel Marya had ever attended at which people spoke loudly, passionately, even furiously; she was accustomed to conferences on English and American literature at which no one ever raised a voice.

Of course Marya was acquainted with Eric Nichols, indirectly: he had published several articles of hers in his journal, he'd assigned her a dozen books to review, but they had never met before. Nichols was younger than Marya might have thought, in his early forties, perhaps, with a quizzical lined face, heavy graying eyebrows, an attractive dark-skinned pallor. Nichols' voice was the quietest but the most persistent voice on the panel; he couldn't be goaded into losing his temper. Marya thought, watching him, Oh yes. Yes. Him.

Afterward she introduced herself to him and they shook hands rather shyly, staring, smiling. Marya murmured a foolish little observation—that he didn't look at all the way she expected. Nichols, laughing, delighted, said that Marya looked exactly as he had expected "Marya Knauer" might look.

If Marya lost her job, if, after her qualifications had been sifted through for the third or fourth time, weighed, judged, found not *quite* right for this particular college—which was, after all, a highly prestigious college, known for its academic excellence and the general wealth of its alumni—the blame might well be lodged against Eric Nichols, who had encouraged her, inspired her, published her in his journal. Such publications did not count for very much in academic and scholarly terms; in fact they often counted against a candidate. (In addition to *The Meridian,* Marya now published essays and essay reviews in *The Nation, The New Republic,* and *The New York Review.* Gregory joked that if she began to publish in the *Times Literary Supplement* and *The New York Times Book Review* her senior colleagues in the English Department would be fearful of letting her go; her enmity might prove dangerous.)

Of course Marya had other qualifications, other strengths. She had published a well-received scholarly book, she continued to publish articles and reviews in her field, she had acquired the reputation for being a dedicated and exacting teacher; she was a woman whose womanliness was neither an issue nor a distraction. She had become shrewd enough to say nothing at all about her nonacademic writing, or to allude to it in the slightly disparaging way in which such writing is generally alluded to, in her profession. (She remembered Maximilian Fein's dismissal of politics and journalism; she felt at times a stab of guilt—or was it guilty satisfaction?—that she had betrayed him.) Only Marya's early piece in *The Meridian,* on the awkward subject of the college community's relationship with the Rhinelander Air Force Base, had aroused a fair amount of local controversy. Marya had not been prepared for quite such a response: coverage in two regional papers, as well as the student paper; requests for interviews; remarkable letters "pro" and "con"—some angry, some ignorant, but a number supportive and intelligent and encouraging. She had come off rather well in the dispute but she knew enough not to risk anything quite so provoking in the near future. There were now only five full-time women among the tenured staff at the college, and none at all in Marya's own department; a situation that inspired a great deal of amused contempt on the part of women instructors in private, but virtually no comment at all in public. "Public" generally meant within earshot of a man.

As for Gregory Hemstock—his academic qualifications were probably stronger than Marya's, in Marya's opinion; in any case they were more solidly professional. He had published a book at Oxford University Press on Yeats's visionary poetry and plays; he was completing a study of Pound's *Cantos*; he had served admirably—stoically—on several key committees outside the department; his students liked him immensely—his great fear, an entirely justified one, was that he might be judged by his older colleagues as too popular with undergraduates. (Marya Knauer, whose severe grading, and whose penchant now and then for the quick, ironic, brittle remark, earned her at best a middling popularity with the masses of students, hadn't at least *that* to worry about; she joked that she could relax and make friends with her students only after her career had settled in.)

Eight assistant professors competing for a single position, eleven assistant professors competing for two positions. . . . Interviews by the departmental committee and the Dean's committee and the Provost's committee. . . . Endless bibliographic lists, and excerpts from work-in-progress, and embarrassed requests for letters of recommendation from scholars at other colleges. . . . Isn't it all degrading, Marya and Gregory and the others in their position were always saying to one another, isn't it humiliating, numbing, banal and tedious and as real as, what?—death?—or merely a protracted debilitating illness? Difficult not to resent and eventually despise those who are sitting in judgment on you, Marya thought. She wondered if the bitterness was primarily because all her judges were men; or simply because the situation was intolerable.

(Gregory said dryly that *he* was a man, wasn't he; and he had come to loathe the whole bunch of them by this time— even those who meant well, who were really very nice men. Perhaps his situation was more intolerable than Marya's because he *was* a man. "Consider our raging insatiable egos, our famous need to fight," he said. "All my brute's adrenaline rushing about to no purpose.")

From time to time Marya noted the irony, even the humor, of her situation; tried to view it in mature perspective. After all, even if she failed at this crucial point in her career (which is to say, her life) she had in any case come a remarkable distance from the Canal Road.

At lunch in the sunny walled garden of a pre-Revolutionary inn, Marya and Gregory were each ravenous with hunger. They ate heartily, greedily, unapologetically. Marya saw that eating was a serious business—food was a great deal more than an idea or a metaphor. "Isn't this black bread delicious? Maybe we could steal some of it to take with us," Marya said, taking yet another piece and tearing it in two; and Gregory, chewing, his mouth full, said, "At this point everything is delicious, my love—don't distract us."

Marya forgot her strained back, her throbbing leg muscles, even her swollen ankle. She squeezed Gregory's thigh beneath the table and congratulated him on leading them so unfalteringly to this inn, and for having had the brilliant idea of the bicycle ride itself. "It's carried us a considerable distance from that other couple," she said, lifting her glass of red wine, "cowering with worry, sick with apprehension, playing at being stoical and mature . . . or whatever it is we've been playing at. I feel so sorry for them, and so contemptuous. . . ."

"Yes," said Gregory, reaching for another slice of bread, "they *are* contemptible. Let's not allow them at the table. Let's not even take the time to pity them. *Please.*"

"Do you think the committee is at lunch right now?" Marya said, looking at her watch. "Yes, probably, they've been meeting six, eight hours a day, trying to clear the books—"

"Stop," Gregory said. "We promised to give each other a respite."

"*I* couldn't do the sort of things they're doing," Marya said with a thrill of self-righteousness. Her face was sunburnt from the morning's ride; her cheeks blazed. "I really don't think I could."

"Marya. Please."

Gregory laughed, and shuddered, and poured the last of the wine ceremoniously into their glasses. He said, after a thoughtful minute, "Yes—you probably could," in a voice so subdued Marya almost didn't hear.

Long ago Gregory told Marya an anecdote about his father, who had died when Gregory was nineteen and a sophomore at Brown.

His father had been a highly successful insurance executive with Prudential; he loved to work and he was happy only when he was working. Life was that simple, that clear. One afternoon in his office he felt pains in his chest . . . a constriction, a sense of suffocation . . . but he ignored them for a while; then informed his secretary irritably that he wasn't to be interrupted; and got down on the floor and began to do push-ups. . . . He was going to overcome the problem, whatever it was. He was going to triumph.

What happened, Marya asked, though she wasn't certain she wanted to know.

He did thirty-seven push-ups before he fainted, Gregory said.

But he didn't *die,* said Marya.

Not that time, said Gregory.

Several of Marya and Gregory's colleagues had cultivated an air of cynicism, to deal with their anxiety; several were annoy-ingly and rather maniacally idealistic; a few had taken on a melancholy philosophical tone, as if the crisis were over and, yes, the worst had occurred. Yet even the doomed were frequently overtaken by cruel flashes of hope; and the optimistic, by bouts of despair. After all, there were virtually no jobs in their rarefied profession any longer. There were *these* jobs, which they now held, but which, despite their industry and good intentions, they were very likely going to lose.

Gregory swung extravagantly from mood to mood. Since, as everyone said, he fully deserved good fortune (wasn't he the best of the lot?), he suspected he would never receive it; then again, how could he *not* receive it, since in fact he was deserving?

It was like trying to conceive of mortality, he said. Trying to envision the world on the morning after your death.

Marya had tried each of the strategies in turn though none really suited her. She vowed not to be bitter if the decision went against her, then again, why shouldn't she be bitter? bitter and angry and resentful? By the morning of the bicycle ride she no longer knew how she felt at all; even if she felt anything. Perhaps she was burnt out already, at the age of twenty-eight. Perhaps the initiation into her profession was in fact a powerful emetic.

Marya thought, observing Gregory whom she loved, Do we have a future, or only futures?

Sometimes she thought one way, sometimes another. She had no idea what Gregory thought.

After lunch the day deteriorated rapidly.

The pain between Marya's shoulder blades returned. Her kneecaps seemed to have calcified during the long luxurious rest. As Gregory bicycled ahead, leading them through traffic, Marya found it increasingly difficult to match her pace with his. The red headband leaped and swam in her vision.

Suddenly the river road widened, leading inland. It was now a four-lane highway dangerous with trucks; Marya felt nauseated by the diesel fumes. Perspiration ran down her striving sides, her hair whipped fiercely in the wind. She was struck by a childish sort of panic: what if Gregory abandoned her, what if he simply forgot her. . . . She had been an idiot to put herself in so vulnerable a position, pitting her inadequate strength against his. . . .

Patiently, sweetly, without a word of adverse comment, he waited for her atop hills; his face too was rather luridly sunburnt, and slick with perspiration. Now he couldn't ask her if she would like to turn back because it was too late to turn back. Now he didn't dare ask how she felt because he could see the exhaustion in her face.

Poor Marya. Poor luckless Marya.

On a long steep hill just above Nelson's Mills, one of the longest and steepest and most luxurious downhill stretches of the entire day, Marya began to pull away from Gregory; she supposed it was dangerous but she couldn't resist. Coasting so freely and effortlessly, she was able for once to sit up straight and ease the ache in her spine . . . she was able to grip the handlebar with one hand. . . .

Semitrailers roared by, kicking up pebbles. The pavement was broken and uneven. Her hair whipped madly, her eyes watered, sometimes she couldn't see precisely where she was headed . . . nor could she hear Gregory shouting behind her. . . . She wasn't certain if he was shouting or if she only imagined it. She couldn't turn to look. With a thrill of satisfaction she knew she was speeding faster than she'd ever sped before; and accelerating every second. Certain childhood presences observed her, forced to marvel. Her cousin Lee. The boys at the country school. Lester Hughey, and Kyle Roemischer, and Bob Bannerman, and . . . who were the others? . . . she'd been so frightened of them at one time, and now. . . .

Now you can all go to hell, she thought.

How wild this ride, this long downhill plunge! Marya had never experienced anything quite like it.

She supposed that Gregory would want her to use the brakes, that was probably why he'd been shouting, but when

Marya began to apply them—cautiously, lightly—they seemed to make no difference at all. She was still accelerating. She couldn't be stopped.

TRUCKS USE LOW GEAR—the sign whipped past.

Just as she thought herself fortunate that the pavement along this stretch was smooth, the asphalt gave way abruptly to concrete. Now there came potholes, creases, ruts, small ravines that made the bicycle bounce wildly. Her breasts had begun to ache with the strain, her teeth rattled in her head. I'm going to be killed, Marya thought.

Behind her Gregory's shouts had grown faint. She was pulling away from him—speeding faster at every second—now hunched low over the handlebars like a racer, her hair whipping back and her eyes flooded with tears. Panic numbed her. Her bowels constricted. She tried the hand brakes in desperation: the left, the right, tentatively, then a little harder, both together, perhaps too hard—her tires skidded on the pavement—and when she released the brakes she was going as fast as before.

I can't stop, Marya thought. This speed. This flight. I can't stop except to die.

Then she was off the road, hurtling along the rutted shoulder, screaming for help, sobbing—

She fell—was dragged along for several yards—panting, whimpering with pain—

Then it was over. The flight was over. Marya crawled away from the overturned bicycle amid old beer cans, broken glass, tall oil-stained grasses. Her right knee, her entire leg . . . there was a bleeding gash in her leg. . . . She sobbed helplessly, pressing her knuckles into her mouth. Oh God the pain, the incredible pain, had she broken her leg, and her right wrist? . . . What was she going to do? . . .

Gregory crouched over her, comforting and scolding. Marya Marya Marya *Marya*. God damn it, Marya. You might have killed yourself, Marya. He had his little first aid kit in hand; he knew what to do. Marya saw that his skin had gone dead white—she'd frightened him as badly as she had frightened herself.

Gregory spat hurriedly into a tissue and tried to get the worst of the grit out of her lacerated knee. There was a six-inch tear in her jeans; he ripped it a little farther. Marya lay helplessly back on the gravel and watched his fingers, her head still spinning and her eyeballs loose and seared as if they had nearly flown out of her head. The wound was bleeding freely. Both her wrists ached; and several of her ribs; her right elbow had gone numb. . . . No less than you deserve, Marya thought calmly.

She saw that Gregory would be promoted, and not she: she would remain in town as a wife: if she was very fortunate.

"I should have broken my neck," Marya said angrily. "It would have solved all my problems."

"Our problems?" Gregory said lightly.

He was winding a long strip of gauze around her knee to soak up the blood. His fingers moved deftly, a little roughly. He tried to joke with her. To tease. It looked as if she had been trying to race the traffic. Forty-five miles an hour, maybe fifty, he'd never seen a bicyclist going *quite* so fast. . . .

At least the bicycle wasn't seriously damaged; Marya insisted upon walking it down the remainder of the hill. Her heart was still pounding and she couldn't seem to get her breath but she didn't want any more of Gregory's assistance; she didn't need it.

Gregory led them to a Holiday Inn where Marya could use the women's room. She didn't want to think how she must look —an adult woman with her jeans torn and bloody at the knee, her hair wild, her face dirty, a glassy sheen to her eye. Marya Knauer, humbled and brought low as she deserved. She wondered that people did not stare at her in pity.

Gregory chided her for being so angry, so stubborn. She ought to be grateful, he said, she wasn't in an emergency room stretched out on a table.

Yes, said Marya sullenly. She knew.

He told her to wash the cuts thoroughly, and to dab on some antiseptic; to bandage them up carefully; then to lie down and rest, even if it was only for five minutes. She'd had a considerable shock after all, she *might* have died. . . . He would be waiting for her in the coffee shop.

Yes, said Marya, limping away.

At the fleshy-pink door of the ladies' room Marya turned to look back but Gregory had already left the lobby.

Inside, Marya tore off the bandages with trembling fingers, grateful to be alone. She washed her numerous wounds with soapy water, mercilessly, gritting her teeth against the pain. She might have thought that pain itself had antiseptic virtues.

She stripped off her shirt and washed hurriedly. Her sweaty chest, her breasts, her underarms. . . . There were dozens of tiny pimples, invisible to the eye but hard as grit beneath her fingertips, scattered on her shoulders and chest. Prickly heat, or the aftermath of panic, nerves. . . . How ugly I am after all, she thought, eyeing that pale reproachful face in the mirror.

She bandaged up her wounds again but her fingers lacked Gregory's deftness; she was still shaking. While trying to comb her snarled hair she thought suddenly that it was past four o'clock and by now the committee would surely have made its decision . . . by now there was no margin for hope. She and Gregory had gone on their desperate little outing while their lives were being decided for them; they were helpless as children; ah, how contemptible! She remembered a telephone booth just outside the door. She could call the college, demand to speak with the Dean himself, or perhaps with her departmental chairman; he would be far more kindly, sympathetic. Oh yes Marya, yes, I'm afraid I have disappointing news for you. . . .

No, Marya thought, frightened, it would be far more dignified to wait for the letter. *Dear Miss Knauer, We regret to inform you. . . . Dear Mr. Hemstock, We regret to inform you. . . .* But they can't possibly dismiss us both, she thought.

She was very tired. She lay down on a vinyl-covered couch and pressed her hands over her eyes. Her fingers were rather cold, her face warm. Every part of her body seemed to be aching. Her right knee, her right ankle, her wrists, her elbow . . . maybe she had fractured a rib or two . . . maybe she had a concussion, a hairline crack in the skull.

"It would solve my problems," she said aloud, though she knew in fact it would not.

In the air-conditioned, drafty Buccaneer's Lounge Gregory was sitting at a window booth, waiting for her. He'd taken off the rakish red headband; he looked subdued, chastened, exhausted. Marya noted how unevenly his face was sunburnt—pale at the forehead, an alarming pink at the end of his nose. He gripped a bottle of beer in one hand and a glass in the other, and when she slid into the booth across from him his smile was rather forced.

"The bleeding seems to have stopped," Marya said in an undertone.

"Yes. Good. I thought it would."

"Only one of the cuts is very deep. . . ."

"Yes, that's good."

His manner was vague, distracted.

After a moment he roused himself to ask if she would like something, a beer, maybe, a soft drink, a cup of coffee? Marya signaled for a waitress herself and ordered a cup of coffee and a glass of ice water. When the ice water came she pressed the glass against her forehead. She began circumlocutiously to apologize for the accident, for having ridden so recklessly, the wine at lunch must have gone to her head, of course Gregory was right and she should have been more careful.

He nodded vaguely. He smiled in her direction, without quite seeing her. He was sitting with his shoulders slumped, leaning forward on his elbows, his pale hair in his eyes, his sunglasses crooked. He looked, Marya thought, like a man who has absorbed without flinching a sudden terrible blow.

"I'm sorry if I frightened you," Marya said slowly, "I suppose it must have looked as if— I'm sorry to have been so—"

"Yes. Well. Well, it's over now," Gregory said politely.

"What should we do now? How will we get back home? Or should we continue with what we'd planned?" Marya asked. "I'm not sure whether I can—"

Gregory was signaling for the waitress, he wanted another bottle of beer. When the waitress was slow in coming he slid out of the booth and went to the bar himself; Marya heard his voice raised, curt and impatient. His charm had an edge to it, he was accustomed to giving instructions, to being taken seriously. His mild manner could be quite misleading. His anger lay deep, potent. . . . They can't have dismissed him, Marya thought suddenly.

She waited until he returned to the booth with his beer, which he was already pouring carelessly into a glass. "You called the college, didn't you!" Marya said. "You broke our promise!"

Her voice was shriller than she had intended. Gregory lifted one shoulder in a shrug, slid into the booth, didn't meet her eye.

"You called them, didn't you? and what did they say?" Marya asked.

Gregory made that negligent gesture with his shoulder a second time. His voice was steady, subtly ironic. "About my position, Marya, or about yours?" he said.

10

She was learning of torture in Uruguay, torture in Brazil. Secret police, unmarked uniforms, wraparound mirrored sunglasses, American-built jeeps and vans. . . . Headquarters in the midst of capital cities with stone walls six feet thick. . . . There was an invisible army, Marya learned, of hundreds, thousands, of routine killers; killers-for-hire in the pay of their governments in the pay (not very indirectly) of the United States Government. She had heard much of this before and had read even more of it in recent years but she listened, holding her headphones steady with one hand while she took rapid notes with the other. Her expression was one of pained concentration but her manner as always was professional.

A catalog, a litany, beginning nowhere and ending nowhere, names begging to be remembered, honored. Journalists . . . students . . . a fifty-four-year-old Uruguayan poet imprisoned without charges and not yet brought to trial, suffering from emphysema, no medical care, unspeakable prison conditions; a nineteen-year-old university student, his body covered with first-degree burns, weighing less than one hundred pounds at the time of his death; a twenty-seven-year-old Frenchwoman, a free-lance journalist, "disappeared" in Rio. Of course the authorities knew nothing. It was one of the privileges of authority to know nothing.

And now the first-hand reports of torture by electric shock, starvation, near-drowning, mutilation, routine beatings, stompings: this too Marya had heard before in slightly different accents and tones. Delegates spoke rapidly, passionately, often interrupting one another. Sometimes several persons spoke at the same time. Marya, taking notes, converting pain and the recollection of pain into notes, observed (not for the first time: she was thirty-four years old) that the human voice is a frail vehicle. It requires breath, amplification, tonality. As soon as it falls silent the surrounding air will remain as before, unaltered. The surrounding walls will remain as before. A ventilator will be heard humming, finely vibrating; perhaps a plane far overhead; someone—perhaps even Marya Knauer—will be observed coughing into a tissue.

She knew Spanish well enough not to require the headphones most of the time but her Portuguese was poor, useless. So she was dependent upon the simultaneous translator, a young man from the United Nations, olive-skinned, handsome, very much in control, rather beautifully in control. He made every effort to communicate, even to mimic, the outrage of the Brazilian delegates: their despair at the conditions in their own country and their despair at the indifference of Americans, even knowledgeable Americans. Marya watched him as he spoke, translated, rapidly and unhesitatingly, his voice beneath its Latin rhythms level and mellifluous, commanding. Unlike the South Americans he never paused; he never swallowed in the midst of a lengthy tangled remark; he never faltered, gave up, hid his face in his hands. *Help* was the universal human plea, *please help me* was the demand, but the simultaneous translator dealt with it in a thoroughly professional manner.

Marya was not to collapse until the third day of the conference but her strength began to drain from her on the morning of the second day, when she found herself observing the translator more and more, and the delegates less.

The delegates had to be taken head-on, directly; the translator inhabited another degree of consciousness. He was protected by his glass booth and his electrical equipment. Nothing was so unspeakable (the mashing of testicles, the forcing of live rats into vaginas) that the translator could not deal expertly with it, choosing always the perfect words and phrases. If he was alarmed, or disgusted, or sickened, or humanly terrified, he gave no indication; that was not his role; he simply converted cascades of words from one language into another language, like a sleight-of-hand artist. Marya imagined a waterfall of living words, incomprehensible at its source, rendered into a stream of fluent English which flowed over the American delegates, forcing them to hear, to attend. When English was spoken they could not not attend: that was the translator's power. Yet he himself was untouched.

Or was he untouched, Marya wondered, staring into the glass booth from the far end of the table, some twenty feet away. Did he perhaps soften some of the very cruelest details, did he censor the obscenities now and then, even as his voice moved skillfully on . . . ? She would ask him. She would draw him aside, before lunch perhaps, and ask him. He was about her age though his mustache was tinged with gray, his sideburns graying, he would be flattered by her attention, he would probably have heard of her and be flattered, that was a card Marya could always deal if she chose.

(Marya Knauer, the author of . . . Marya Knauer the "controversial" cultural critic . . . and wasn't she also the lover of, who was it, Eric Nichols? . . . Yes, Nichols, the editor of *The Meridian*. Though Nichols has been married for twenty years. Though Knauer and Nichols are rarely seen in public together.)

Marya wanted to learn the simultaneous translator's sleight-of-hand before it was too late. She wanted to convert human pain into human words, she wanted to convert the memory of intense emotion in the past into intense emotion in the present, and to be herself unmoved. But she had begun to doubt her ability. She had certainly begun to doubt her strength. Already, since the impassioned opening sessions of the conference, her handwriting had altered several times and was not always intelligible. Even on a single page it varied— slanted to the right, slanted archly to the left, overlarge, coyly small, now script and now block print, peppered with dots that signaled dismay, despair, and exclamation points that signaled approximately the same responses. For long minutes at a time her mind went blank, and though she appeared to be listening to the delegates' speeches in Portuguese and the translator's English equivalent she really wasn't hearing anything at all. The words riddled her like bullets but did not lodge in her flesh.

Death from without & death from within, she discovered scrawled in the margin of one notebook page. On another, where her notes trailed off, *Death from without vs. death from within: which?* She remembered having written it only vaguely, dimly, the way she remembered having done equally almost-plausible things in dreams.

When they broke at one o'clock she would telephone Eric in New York to report to him the substance of the morning's reports. To amuse him she would dwell (perhaps) on the predictable handwringing response of the chairman of the American delegation, an old Yale classmate and genial enemy of Eric's; she would single out two or three atrocity stories, fresh statistics that were shocking, or improbable, unverifiable in any case; she would abbreviate the accusations of American intervention, with which Eric was already too familiar. (*The Meridian* had printed the first exposés of CIA-financed "anti-Communist" activity in Latin America years ago, in a series of articles on the Guatemalan White Hand; Eric Nichols had campaigned vigorously, and to little purpose, against Nixon and Kissinger's "diplomacy" in Allende's doomed Chile.)

She would not tell him about her interest in the translator

from the United Nations, which he might misinterpret. She would tell him about the curious words, *Death from without, death from within,* which, she discovered, she had written out several times.

Then she remembered that Eric himself was dead. This was October, it was not last April, when she had telephoned him from a similar conference in Mexico City and they had talked for nearly two hours. Time pleats oddly, cruelly, Marya thought, times rush together, when you are wearing the same headphones, taking notes you've already taken in a hand you can't always recognize. She thought it might be the headphones, mainly. The weight, the uncomfortable warmth, the close intimate stream of words in the ear, from a stranger in a glass booth.

Death from without, death from within. Marya admired the balance, the restraint. She did wonder what Eric would have made of it.

These days, when Marya's mind drifted, she sometimes fancied that something was growing in her womb.

She had never been pregnant, nor had she so much as imagined herself pregnant. She had once observed with her customary irony that, by having failed to have an abortion, let alone several, she had cut herself off irrevocably from the common experience of many of her female contemporaries. (This was the sort of lightly self-deprecatory remark Marya Knauer often heard herself making to friends, or caught herself writing in letters. Eric disapproved in theory—if he loved her it hurt him to think she didn't love herself—but he always laughed, in practice. With other people, women especially, Marya was often harder on herself, pitiless. She knew it was a form of vanity but she couldn't resist: if she was hard on others, she was obliged to be harder on herself.)

She fancied that something was taking shape in her womb, in that innermost, most secret part of her body, in which nothing had ever lodged, let alone grown. At first it was the size of a melon seed. Then the size of a currant. Then the size of a grape, a plum. . . . But why the agreeable imagery of fruits? Why not the imagery of, say, marbles, golf balls, tennis balls? Marya forgot about it for days at a time (it was, after all, illusory), then remembered it at inexplicable times, walking along the street, settling back in a taxi, strapping herself into an airline seat and preparing (psychologically, physiologically) for takeoff: those few crucial seconds during which a plane might nose-dive and crash, but probably would not.

Dear Eric, Do you think you are responsible . . . ?
Dear Eric, Do you think your death is responsible . . . ?

Marya knew about hysterical pregnancies because she had read about them. She had read about most things by now, at least in a cursory manner. She even knew about the alleged pregnancies of women in the sixteenth and seventeenth centuries, in England and Europe, who were charged with consorting with the Fiend, and hanged (in England) or burned alive (on the Continent) as witches. In fact she had once spent some weeks researching Henri Boguet's *Discours des sorciers,* a document of the early seventeenth century whose pious author wished that all witches might be united in one single body that they be "consumed in one single blessed conflagration." She knew of, had actually studied the floor plans of, the infamous Witch House at Bamberg, where the holy Bishop Johann George II tortured numberless witches, male and female, and put them to death. . . . Marya might have observed that the instinct for extreme cruelty in mankind was not appreciably different in late medieval Europe or in twentieth-century Europe, in uncivilized Latin America or in "civilized" Latin America. But it was the sort of clever observation Eric disliked in her, or had disliked. It suggested resignation, an unearned cynicism, despair. In Eric's puritanical cosmology one had to earn such sad luxuries of the spirit.

Marya knew that the tight elasticity of her womb was inviolate but if she made the conscious effort—lying in a warm fragrant bath, for instance, or waking in the morning in a strange hotel room—she could sometimes summon forth the thing's shape, envision (as she embodied?) its shadowy contours. It was a whim, a nervous fancy, an indulgence, one of those romantic obsessions she supposed she'd outgrown. If obliged to translate it into anecdotal and therefore amusing form she would have said that she was pregnant with her lover's death. She would have said that it had begun on the very day of his death: the first intimation of something lodged in her that would suck her strength, her spirit, her famous vitality, the first intimation of pain to come.

Except that would have been a lie, strictly speaking. Because Marya's obsession had not begun on the day of Eric Nichols' death but on the day—no, the morning after the evening—of her discovery of his death, twelve days after the fact. She had been out of the country at the time. Inaccessible. Incognito. No telegram could reach her and indeed no telegram did: she hadn't been his wife, after all.

(Perhaps, Marya thought, she *would* translate this quirky obsession into an anecdote. She was good at anecdotes. All her friends and acquaintances were. It was a meager art form they despised in print but quite reveled in, in life. *I, Marya Knauer, the very embodiment of rationality and female enlightenment. . . . I, Marya Knauer, whose sanity is so tediously steadfast. . . .* Over the years many of Marya's acquaintances had slipped over the border into lunacy at various times and to various degrees, and they had invariably been humored, and sympathized with, even, upon occasion, nursed back to sanity; now it was Marya's turn.)

Death without, death within. . . .

By the third morning of the conference Marya realized that she was not going to make it.

Though she had slept a full seven hours the night before, in a veritable stupor of unconsciousness (yes she had been mildly intoxicated, no it would not become a habit), her mind wasn't tuned to its usual sharpness; she felt light-headed, even dizzy; she began to think she was recognizing not only stereotyped words and phrases but entire speeches. A lengthy embittered denunciation of American liberals ("that pampered self-righteous class") by a fierce young Nigerian playwright who now lived in London; a passionate monologue on the ideals of freedom, world peace, and brotherhood, by an East German writer and translator now living in West Berlin; a bright, sardonic, fast-paced denunciation of Americans, liberals, and the "pieties of brotherhood" by an English literary journalist of some renown. (The journalist, gauged more or less as Marya's opposite number, appeared to be addressing her in particular as he spoke. He quoted Orwell, Waugh, Jonathan Swift. Marya could not determine whether he saw in her a fellow skeptic or whether he was deftly attacking her and what, in his imagination, she represented. She would have liked to ask him. She would have liked to ask what Marya Knauer's beliefs were, since he knew them well enough to be attacking them.)

This too would have made an anecdote of sorts to tell Eric. That she had begun to imagine she'd heard all the speeches—the denunciations—the spontaneous outbursts—beforehand.

Another anecdote for Eric or even, in modified form, for *The Meridian*: the night before, in the jazzy twilit Orchid Lounge of the hotel, several delegates in Marya's company had fallen into a confused but heated discussion of Jews. Of their ideas of Jews. One was a Peruvian novelist who now lived in Paris, another was the secretary of the Moscow Writers' Union, the third was the fierce black Nigerian playwright. Marya was asked courteously if she was Jewish (she had that "look," did she?) and when she said no the men began to speak freely. Both the Russian and the Nigerian claimed that Jews were always a "separate and distinct nation within a nation," and that their literature was "Jewish literature," religious and political. The Peruvian, drunk on martinis, claimed that all Jews were Zionists overtly or secretly and that Zionism was the fascism of the second half of the twentieth century. Marya laughed as she challenged these remarks, she felt rather fierce herself, combative, until suddenly the strength drained from her. And she fell silent. And didn't care.

Also she'd begun to realize that the men interpreted her willingness to debate with them as a provocative and very American species of coquetry. As chic as Marya's stylishly cut hair, her white linen blazer and trousers. . . .

A second anecdote for Eric, though this would be calculated to upset rather than amuse: 2:05 A.M. in Marya's sumptuous eleventh-floor hotel room and there was Marya naked and shivering (Marya always slept naked even in unfamiliar beds between sheets that were slightly abrasive against her skin: that too was chic) talking rapidly through her partly opened chain-locked door to a man whose name she didn't know from—was it Costa Rica? Honduras?—claiming at first she'd promised to have a nightcap with him downstairs then berating her for having teased him, then drunkenly pleading, *"Tengo la información que puede interesarti mucho—no puede esperar hasta mas tarde—"* and Marya said, *"Gracias, hablamos mañana, no, gracias,"* over and over like an incantation. With the door judiciously chained as it was, the young man (he did sound young, insulted, and in pain) could not see Marya, nor could she see him, for which, she thought, God be praised. He pleaded, threatened, whispered words she couldn't understand, then suddenly began pounding on the door as if he meant to force the chain off. But Marya was too strong for him, too desperate: she got the door shut and locked it.

(Though the faceless young suitor had his revenge that night. In Marya's troubled fleeting dreams. Blurred and fleeting and persistent he was, *No puede esperar hasta mas tarde,* naked as Marya herself, eel-like, brutal. He smelled of a mixture of cocoa, mint, liqueur. He called her *señorita* and promised not to hurt her any more than she deserved, his voice shading into Eric's as the dream died.)

It was a measure of Marya's lack of interest in the young man that, in the morning, she didn't trouble to determine which of the delegates he was. She understood he'd never approach her again—his manhood had been diminished, insulted. *No puede esperar hasta mas tarde.*

The tone of the conference had shifted subtly. Now the reports appeared to be set pieces, rehearsed and carefully delivered. Hour followed hour followed hour. A frightening sense of familiarity, *déjà vu,* and none of this could be converted into anecdotes for Eric Nichols or deft little three-page articles for his magazine. . . . A Soviet novelist (of whom no one in the West had heard) rose to speak; began with the usual humility of the Soviet delegates ("I am of peasant stock, a practical man, as the great Mayakovsky said, 'I look at things simply' "), went on to attack the "vainglorious and lying" speeches given by several of the delegates the day before—the "marketplace ideology" of American literary politics—the "hypocrisy" of certain Latin American delegates who had betrayed the Revolution—the fact that American capitalist publishers favored Soviet dissidents ("those who trade in the politics of spite") rather than "authentic" Soviet voices. . . . Marya held the earphones steady, listening. She was certain she had heard this speech before. Since quitting her academic position five years before, she had attended a number of international conferences—sometimes in Eric's company, sometimes alone —and she thought it might have been in Yugoslavia, in 1982, that she had first heard this particular speech. Certain of the details had been altered but the substance was the same. Surely it was the same. Mayakovsky was often quoted, those very words, handy in refuting (so the Soviets believed) Western poses of needless obfuscation and decadence.

The Russian's remarks provoked considerable anger, as he had intended. A Mexican novelist—gold-rimmed glasses, handsome Indian features—demanded the floor to reply; but it soon became evident that his speech—delivered in near-faultless English—had very little to do with the Russian's. He spoke of the inadequacy of existing translations from the Spanish and Portuguese into English; the betrayals of American publishers who were obsessed with the marketplace; the "literary imperialism of the West." His manner was fiery, peppery, and his speech was interrupted several times by spontaneous applause. At least it had the air of spontaneity. . . . Following him a white-haired and -bearded American delegate rose to speak. His theme was the need for a "world community of writers," "defenders of the flame of human freedom." The man was a minor poet who had in recent years acquired a major reputation, primarily by way of such public addresses and appeals. Any mention of "freedom" at these conferences was a code for anti-Soviet sentiment, certain to provoke discomfort if not open rancor, but the poet spoke in a passionate rambling voice, gripping his microphone in both hands. He was speaking past the delegates, Marya supposed, into posterity.

She half closed her eyes and saw the balloon speeches rising to the ceiling far above. Slowly they rose, slowly, glancing off one another, bobbing about the ceiling, striking lightly and harmlessly against the chandeliers. (The meeting was being held in a rather comically splendid old room, called simply Ballroom A—faded velvet draperies and cornices, arabesques of gilt, ebony, jade, ancient moldings, heavy crystal chandeliers. If Marya wrote about the conference she would surely make ironic reference to its setting, but she knew now that she would probably not write about the conference. She would probably not be writing anything for some time.)

Death from without contended with death from within but sometimes they were in logical conjunction. Whether one could immediately discern the logic or not.

In Eric Nichols' case for instance.

In Marya Knauer's case for instance.

He had been dead, Marya thought, a remarkably long time by now. It could no longer be measured in terms of weeks, let alone days. Already it had become months. Four months . . . five months . . . was it going to be six . . . ? Though the man had been dead for so long (constantly dead, one might say), Marya still dreamed up anecdotes and amusing or touching or outrageous or edifying tales to tell him. After all, what was the purpose of her sensibility, her singular way with words, if she could not present them in some form to Eric Nichols? It was difficult to imagine her life without reference to him. It was difficult to imagine that her life had a point, without reference to him.

Which meant, Marya supposed, that she had loved him very much. That she loved him at the present time.

Eric's funeral had been a private one. Some observers noted that it was a selfish one, arranged by a spiteful wife, a vindictive family. Last rites in the First Episcopal Church of Duluth, Minnesota; the body interred in the adjoining cemetery; only wife, children, family, relatives in attendance. That was how they had solved the problem of Eric's New York City friends and acquaintances, but primarily it was how they solved the problem of Marya Knauer.

No doubt they had half expected her to appear in Duluth, to make her presence known at the funeral. Austere and unsmiling, accusing, perhaps even weeping, as if she had a legitimate reason for grief. As if she had been Eric Nichols' wife and not simply . . . whatever they might call her: mistress? whore? friend? Or did they relent in private, when Eric's wife was nowhere near, and allude to Marya as Eric's lover . . . ?

Marya rather suspected they never referred to her at all. She didn't exist to them, she was at most a face, a photograph, examined on the back of a book's dust jacket, scrutinized closely, critically, and discarded.

In any case she had been out of the country at the time of the funeral. She had not had to contend with the temptation to fly to Duluth, to risk the contempt of strangers.

Marya passed a twice-folded note to the chairman of the American delegation, requesting a few minutes' time to speak. She was going to denounce them all. She was going to speak in Eric Nichols' calm outraged voice, denouncing them all as frauds, traitors.

Eric had always said that it was an honorable role, a

necessary role, to be a witness. Throughout the long—incredibly long—duration of the Vietnam War. In the time of the "unrest" in Latin America. There is blood on our hands, Eric said, if we don't do all we can to help others, to be witnesses to their suffering . . . to absorb and register and preserve and communicate the pain of their experience. During his lifetime he had often been misinterpreted, but immediately following his death he had been widely honored. A front-page obituary in *The New York Times,* flattering portraits and columns elsewhere, testimonials, editorials, even by those who defined themselves as "ideologically opposed" to Eric Nichols. *The Meridian: A Weekly Journal of Politics & the Arts,* whose peak circulation of 100,000 subscribers (acquired in the late sixties) had gradually declined to 75,000 and whose debts were considerable, was now being lauded as one of the finest publications of its kind in recent history. None of this greatly surprised Marya, who took it as a simple confirmation of her cynicism.

Marya pulled off her earphones, awaited her turn to speak. An exiled Colombian novelist was denouncing his government and the government of the United States. The Nigerian playwright rose to speak out of turn, excitedly, angrily, and his fury—so passionate, so seemingly spontaneous—had to be honored. Marya was losing a sense of continuity even within speeches. Perhaps it was necessary to concentrate on the flow of words, the music of words—their rhythm?—and meaning would follow. Significance would follow. She waited.

The hovering perspiring faces, the balloons of words, bobbing, drifting, glancing harmlessly off one another. And in her womb something was growing if indeed she had a womb.

Early in the conference, when everyone was gregarious, cheery with drink and rich foods, the secretary of the Moscow Writers' Union ("a vicious party hack, a murderer"—so he had been identified in the American delegation's debriefing session) presented Marya with a copy of one of his novels, in Russian. He was courtly, anxious to charm and to please, eyes like frost, boyish persistent smile. The inscription inside read *For Marya Knauer the favorite American authorless of the living.* Marya had stared at the inscription for some seconds before laughing and thanking her Soviet colleague for his kindness. Unfortunately, she said, she hadn't with her a copy of either of her books to give him.

This too was a small nugget of treasure to hoard for Eric. She could hear his hearty laughter, feel his fingers clutching at her forearm in mirth.

Marya waited nervously for her turn to speak. She had already given one ten-minute report on the first day which had been well received—assuming it had been understood. One could never tell with translations. With translators. Subtleties were lost, irony was a risk. . . . Of course Marya would not denounce her fellow delegates, who was she to denounce any of them? She would speak of other things, urgent things. She would speak in Eric Nichols' place since he could not be present.

Many people had commiserated with her, offered her condolences. Though she had no legitimate cause for grief—they hadn't even lived together, after all. Their liaison might be said to have been an informal one.

A delegate from Uruguay was speaking in rapid, heavily accented English. Marya's gaze drifted about the long brightly lit room. Velvet draperies and gilt-edged cornices and the immense curved table at which they were all sitting, hooked up to headphones, microphones before them, yellow note pads, glasses of tepid water, ashtrays, attaché cases. . . . A bald mustached gentleman from Mexico to Marya's left, a chain-smoking Frenchwoman (a "radical feminist semiologist-Marxist") to her right, leaning far forward, her thin shoulders hunched, her leathery face creased in concentration. . . . Torture was the subject again, instruments of torture, pliers and electric grids and again rats, rats struck an almost classic note, had a familiar ring, provoked atavistic visceral responses: there must always be rats, Marya thought. In the twentieth century as in the fifteenth.

She was beginning to feel ill. It was futile to think otherwise. Her skin felt clammy, her heart beat erratically, waves of dizziness rose and fell and rose again. . . . I can't break down, Marya thought, knowing she was breaking down, I must be a witness.

A young woman photographer in a leather jumpsuit, hair spilling down her back, was taking flash photographs of the delegates for one of the national newsmagazines. She was deft, professional, patient, shrewd. Squatting to one side, crouched in another, easing forward on her haunches, willing to annoy some of her subjects in return for a good close-up; she will take a photograph of me, Marya thought, if I faint.

The blood drained swiftly from Marya's head. Her skin must have gone dead white. Even as she signaled weakly for help to one of the young woman organizers of the conference she saw, or felt, all the lights of Ballroom A explode in a single noiseless ecstasy, before going out.

Eric Nichols had died the previous May at the age of fifty-one, in an automobile accident on the New York State Thruway just south of Albany. He was on his way to visit his youngest son, Kenny, who went to a private school near Lake Champlain; this was the son from whom, as he told Marya, he had long felt estranged. But now that the boy was sixteen years old, and going to school outside the city, things were less strained between them. ("He doesn't accuse me of having abandoned his mother," Eric said. "He doesn't walk out of a room when I walk in.")

Eric's car had gone out of control and sideswiped a retaining wall; he'd died in the emergency room of the Albany General Hospital, in the early evening of May 18. Since the death was caused by an automobile accident that had in turn been caused by a sudden heart attack it might be said that the death came both from without and within. The mystery, which Marya never tired of speculating upon, lay in the conjunction, the timing.

Suppose I had been with him, Marya thought. I might even have been driving.

Marya had been away at the time on one of her periodic retreats. She might have been in a borrowed villa in the Mexican Sierra Madres or in a borrowed apartment on the Croulebarbe in Paris; it happened that she was in a borrowed cabin in the Laurentian Mountains, west of Quebec City, where, in the late spring, a light snowfall could be expected almost daily. The only way she could accomplish a fair amount of work was to retreat entirely from New York City, to go where there were no telephones, no connections of any kind. She cut herself off from the world of distractions and obligations and sentiment. She required spiritual solace as well—the healing quiet, the emptiness—the luxury of never being required to answer to her name or to regard her troubling image in a mirror. In isolation she quickly forgot her name, she quickly became invisible to herself.

She was gone, that time, for three remarkable weeks. Even her occasional bouts of loneliness were exciting, instructive; she knew whom she missed, with whom she ached to speak, to laugh. . . . One night she broke her resolution and telephoned Eric's apartment from a pay phone in a motel but there had been no answer, nor was his answering service in operation, and she thought no more of it. Eric was a supremely busy man, the quintessence of the intellectual who believes himself debilitated by social life when in fact he is energized by it, forced to perform feats of accomplishment in small isolated blocks of time; prodigies of accomplishment, in fact. Marya understood his need to keep in motion. She felt it herself. Energy is life, after all; energy is sheer delight. Death would never grow inside them so long as they stayed in motion, swift and happy as a ray of light—a phrase of Nietzsche's Marya had always liked. Swift and happy as a ray of light.

Eric had once accused Marya of being selfish, in going away on her retreats. That was at the height of their love, perhaps—two years, three—when he had been susceptible to mysterious periods of jealousy. He wasn't in a position to marry her but he wanted her always in the same city with him, accessible by taxi, telephone. He wasn't even in a position to live with her but he wanted her nearby. In turn Marya told him that he was being selfish. "I don't demand that you divorce your wife, after all," she said.

She waited for a reply to that observation, made over the telephone very late one night. She waited for a long time.

Marya, who had turned sentimental in her early thirties, gave Eric a wristwatch—the wristwatch willed to her by Clifford Shearing—for his forty-seventh birthday. Eric claimed not to believe in presents except for children but he was greatly moved by Marya's gesture nonetheless.

For weeks, months, after his death Marya waited to hear whether the watch had been willed back to her again. She hadn't quite realized that she was waiting for such an absurdity but evidently she was; that was the degree to which her judgment had become corroded.

Eric's will was a standard will, made out years ago. Public announcements of his death were standard, each obituary concluded with the same words, *Mr. Nichols is survived by his wife, Barbara, his children . . . two brothers, a sister, a mother. . . .* Sometimes a photograph of Eric ran with the obituary, sometimes not. The photograph in *The New York Times* showed a shadowed face, smiling, earnest, apprehensive. It had been taken before Marya had known him and she might not have recognized him if not for the caption, the headline, ERIC NICHOLS DIES IN AUTO ACCIDENT UPSTATE. His life crowded into two columns of newsprint continued on an interior page, ending with the predictable damning words, *Mr. Nichols is survived by his wife, Barbara, his children, David, Laura, and Kenneth . . .* and the rest.

Only after his death did Marya become jealous of his wife who was now his widow and would be "his" widow for life. Whereas Marya Knauer had nothing and was nothing and could make no claim, legitimate or sentimental. And Clifford Shearing's watch, of course, never made its way back to her.

Not long after Marya quit her teaching position and moved to New York City, and began to travel with Eric Nichols (who was always traveling, always in motion), the two of them found themselves walking hand in hand along a narrow London street, somewhere in Chelsea; slightly intoxicated from a long, late lunch; uneasy and brash at being, in public, so unmistakably lovers—should anyone care to observe. (No one did.) The day was warm, overcast, oppressive, delicious. Marya could not remember whose suggestion it was that they investigate a curious little basement gallery, all stark white brick, indirect lighting, chic chrome fixtures, but she always supposed in retrospect that it had been she.

The exhibit turned out to be "Torture Through the Ages"—a selection of torture instruments from the "renowned" collection of one T. Tyndall-Cross. Only a few of the instruments were for sale and they were priced extremely high.

An iron mask, badly rusted, from the time of the Spanish Inquisition.

A spike collar, large, with four dull spikes pointing inward, from the same period. Forged in Barcelona.

A "fighting slave collar." Very much like a dog collar except that it was made of heavy iron, now rusted. Early 1800s, America.

A chastity belt, hardly a "belt" but a sort of girdle made of iron, to be locked in place. Two keys and two keys alone were made for the lock: one to be in the husband's safekeeping, the other in the safekeeping of a trusted friend. Twelfth- or thirteenth-century France.

An iron rack, approximately six feet high. Finger racks, smaller. Branding irons. An odd device called a cloverleaf . . . all from the twelfth or thirteenth century, southern Europe.

Against the white brick walls these objects showed to

great advantage, were perhaps works of art of a sort. So the gallery owner seemed to think. And the receptionist with her frosted blond hair, her half-moon glasses, her low melodious voice, welcoming Eric and Marya to browse.

They walked slowly, rather numbly, through the exhibit. Staring. Examining. Reading the captions alongside the instruments. The iron mask, for instance, had an interesting history. It was used to punish heretics and subversives, enemies of the Roman Catholic Church. The victim was locked in the mask and chained in the sun so that gradually, by degrees, the metal heated and, by degrees, his brains began literally to boil. Marya would have liked to know how long it took before death occurred, or the merciful loss of consciousness, but the caption did not provide this information.

The spike collar was used for the same general purpose but it allowed onlookers the opportunity to bet on how long the victim could remain standing. So long as he was on his feet, evidently, the spikes touched his throat only lightly; when he grew weak—staggered—fell—the spikes penetrated his skin.

As for the "fighting slave collar"—it was made of iron, with a small ring through which the slave owner's chain might be secured; the slave was therefore on a leash and could be prevented from escaping. Marya had not known that American slave owners pitted their strongest slaves against one another, following the principle of the dog- or cock-fight. But she supposed, if the stakes were high enough, the fights were worthwhile.

The chastity belt, or girdle, drew Marya's particular attention. It resembled armor, which of course it was, except for the absurd little spikes pointing outward. There was a narrow, a very narrow, slot for urination; defecation must have been a more serious problem—Marya could not see how it was possible. And what if the hapless woman were pregnant without anyone knowing, before the contraption was fitted in place; what if both husband and "trusted friend" disappeared with the keys. . . . She wondered too whether it had been simply a point of honor for a wife to submit to the chastity belt:

did a woman do so graciously and willingly? did she concur in her imprisonment? The thing was not only rather comically grotesque, it was highly unsanitary.

Eric was examining the cloverleaf, a device of which he had never heard. It was fairly simple, a matter of mechanics: the victim's arms and legs were clamped into the rings so that he was bent double and forced to die within a few hours, depending (according to the gallery note) on his degree of obesity.

Marya and Eric looked at each other, distracted, rather pale, shaky. There might have been a way of dealing with the exhibit, of nullifying its effect upon their spirits, but neither could think of anything. Nervous clever remarks, a brief discussion of the long history of "man's inhumanity to man," that sort of thing, but Marya could not hope to strike the right tone and Eric, poor Eric, was beginning to look positively ill. They had had two bottles of wine at lunch, they had been up very late the night before.

The Chelsea adventure ended abruptly. They took a cab back to their hotel in Bloomsbury, closed the windows and blinds against the clatter of the street, lay down, tried to make love, tried to comfort each other, wound up crying in each other's arms. They were weakened, fearful, demoralized as children. The torture exhibit could not have been the cause of their sudden grief but they had no idea what the cause might be. It would be the first, but by no means the last, time they would cry in each other's arms.

Depending on who told the anecdote, and the degree to which Marya Knauer was admired, envied, resented by the speaker, she was said to have "collapsed" at the conference during a graphic account of torture in Argentina; or that she had been suddenly "taken ill" as a consequence of overwork and exhaustion; or that she had grown bored with the proceedings and had feigned illness in order to escape.

Marya had no theory. She put the humiliating episode behind her, she thought it best not to dwell upon causes or consequences. Back in New York City she made an appointment with a gynecologist for a routine examination and a Pap smear test and learned, not entirely to her surprise, that there was nothing wrong with her. The results of the Pap smear were negative—which is to say, positive. There was nothing wrong with her and nothing, grape-sized or otherwise, growing in her womb.

The assistant editor of *The Meridian* became the editor-in-chief.

Marya Knauer, who had had an informal connection with the journal for several years, was invited to be one of six associate editors; but she declined the honor.

It was too sentimental and self-pitying a position to say that *The Meridian* "wouldn't be the same without Eric" but that was precisely what Marya felt, what Marya knew. So she said nothing. Except that she was declining the honor.

Next year *The Meridian* was to celebrate its thirty-fifth anniversary but it still seemed young, precarious, even in a way provisionary. Eric had started it in the (cramped, inadequate) kitchen of his Morningside Heights apartment when he was taking classes at Columbia and teaching part-time at Cooper Union. He had a wife, a small baby, friends dropping by who stayed for hours, occasionally for days. But he borrowed money from his family to start a journal of "politics and the arts." At the time he'd had no exceptional ambitions or sense of destiny but he certainly had strong opinions; he was known for his strong opinions. It became his passion to see if he could marshal the evidence to substantiate his opinions. He thought of himself in those days as a soldier in an undefined and undeclared war within the territorial boundary of the United States.

His wife, he told Marya, had dissociated herself from the magazine long before the two of them were legally separated. ("She stopped loving it," he said. "I think I see her point.") Eric's family continued even now to think of the magazine as a youthful gesture of Eric's, an ongoing irritant and embarrassment. (Eric's father had been a prominent Duluth business-man and philanthropist, a registered Republican all his life; one of Eric's uncles had been a congressman for twenty-odd years, among the most faithful of the Joe McCarthy men.)

Shortly after Eric's death a rumor made the rounds that *The Meridian* would be discontinued. It had been a one-man journal, after all. Another rumor was that Eric's wife had inherited it and would sell it to pay off its creditors. She was a vindictive woman, Barbara Nichols, wasn't she?—so Marya was asked. But Marya said truthfully that she didn't know. She had never met the woman and never would.

Marya, in her borrowed cabin in Quebec, had never felt more independent and triumphant than on the day of her thirty-fourth birthday, which she spent entirely alone.

She dared think that if Eric did not divorce his wife within the year without a word from Marya (it was important that it be "without a word"), she would break off the affair. She could live alone without great hardship; she had her own work, her friends and acquaintances, her travel. She had her *life.* Surely these periodic retreats were proof of her own strength and independence. . . . She recalled her friend Imogene's belief that you only know how much someone loves you (you only know how much you love him) when the relationship is over, fractured past mending.

It happened quite by chance that Marya and Imogene Skillman were friendly acquaintances again, if not precisely friends. Shortly after Marya's second book was published and she had moved to New York City, to a sublet apartment in the West 70's (the apartment belonged to a friend of Eric Nichols), she was overtaken in the street one day by a lanky blond woman in jeans and a chic Italian sweater and sunglasses who pummeled her in the ribs and introduced herself as Imogene: "For Christ's sake, Marya, don't you know me? I'd recognize *you* any-where." Imogene had not only seen Marya's book reviewed and on display in one or another bookstore in the city, she had actually bought a copy and read it and claimed to be "quite impressed" with it. And had Marya kept up *her* career...? No, Marya wouldn't have; that was just like Marya.

"You were always so totally self-absorbed, I envied you your concentration," Imogene said.

She laughed so gaily, she was so breathless and charming, naturally Marya could not take offense.

Imogene Skillman acted now and then in "unusual" or "superior" off-Broadway productions; she had been associated for a while with the Circle Repertory; now she made a fair amount of money—kept the household going, in fact— from daytime television. Though she wasn't particularly proud of the fact. Yes she was married, no they weren't currently living together, no it wasn't to the man—Richard— whom Marya had met in Port Oriskany (but Marya had *not* met him), yes she had children, two little girls, a seven-year-old and a three-year-old, beautiful and spoiled ("you must come and see them soon, Marya—they truly *are* beautiful"), yes her life was going well though it had become rather complicated recently with the prospect of a new play and a new lover. . . .

So Marya and Imogene were reacquainted. They saw each other occasionally for lunch or dinner. Imogene sent Marya tickets to openings of plays of hers, Marya introduced Imogene to people she believed Imogene might like and who might like her, including Eric Nichols, whom Imogene professed to admire. (Eric was less certain of Imogene. In her presence, he said, he was always quite enchanted; afterward he felt puzzled and cheated, as if he hadn't met a woman at all, only admired a performance.) When Eric died Imogene telephoned several times, even sent Marya a terse, formal little note of condolence. Marya thought, If Imogene is a friend then I will see her, I will talk to her about what I'm going through. But she never got around to arranging a meeting.

Even before Eric's death, even before Marya had experimented carelessly with the idea of giving him up—of renouncing, rejecting, triumphing over *him*—she found herself thinking frequently about her mother.

Poor Vera Sanjek.

Poor Vera Knauer.

Was she alive or dead; was she living anywhere in the state; had there ever been any truth to the rumor (if what Wilma had said could constitute "rumor") that she'd spent some time in prison . . . ? Perhaps she was in prison still. Or in a mental hospital.

The mental hospital was altogether likely, Marya thought. She recalled the alcoholic stupors, the drunken rages, the weeping, something mad and terrifying about a wildflower growing alongside the road (Queen Anne's lace? the very look of it made Marya sick with apprehension to this day). Yes, the mental hospital was likely. Vera Sanjek disheveled and fat, toothless, incontinent, chattering away at the walls or mute, mute as stone: which would it be? She was in her early fifties by now. Not old. Not at all old. But in the mental hospital she would have aged grotesquely. Marya saw her dumpy crouched figure, the breasts straining against her blouse (plain hospital issue? something of her own, missing one or two buttons?), Marya saw the narrow suspicious eyes, the lips bright with spittle. This is your daughter Marya, Mrs. Knauer, one of the attendants would say, and Marya, foolish smiling trembling Marya, would step forward and extend her hand and . . .

But the absurd vision faded. Marya banished it, forgot it. She only thought of her mother (even the expression "mother" was forced) in weak moods, when she clearly wasn't herself.

These days, Marya thought, she often wasn't herself. The very question of "self" intrigued her. (For if she could raise her emotional confusion to a philosophical plane, might she not be redeemed? It was an old, old tradition.)

In classic habits of thinking, essence preceded existence:

what one *does* follows from what one *is*. In America, however, the reverse seemed more likely, and more rewarding: what one *is* follows directly from what one *does* ("Doing determines being," as William James succinctly observed). So Marya immersed herself in activities. She moved to another apartment not unlike her previous apartment but in a quieter neighborhood, along a leafy stretch of West 11th Street; she took on an assignment for *The New York Times Magazine,* to do an article ("analytical but with a popular slant") on radical French feminism; she agreed to give six evening lectures at the New School, on contemporary feminist thought in general, though she knew beforehand that the experience would be exhausting. In any case Eric Nichols would have approved.

She collected anecdotes to tell him, droll little tales, some of them bitter and amusing, some merely bitter; she wanted him to know that she felt no rancor against him—for abandoning her, for leaving her so totally bereft that she wasn't even (legally) his widow. From time to time, in weak despondent moods, she could feel the tiny thing growing in her womb. But she ignored it. She ignored all notions that did not correspond to her knowledge of herself. She believed she was tough and shallow and unreliable, capable of total self-absorption (didn't people say that of her?—complaining, chiding, admiring?), and consequently incapable of serious grief.

She was never in her apartment. The "radical" French feminists bored her with their slovenly logic and silly polemics. The lectures at the New School attracted a motley assortment of people, few of them serious students, so far as Marya could judge, but all of them with strong opinions on feminism. (She was angrily denounced by the radical lesbians. But insulted, very nearly assaulted, by charges of "lesbianism" from other quarters.)

Eric would have urged her to laugh at the situation.

You think *you* have troubles? was his standard comic retort, delivered in a heavy Yiddish accent.

Use your troubles, write about them, expose them, make them serve you. . . . This was an old, old tradition.

The eternal hourglass of existence is turned over and over, and you with it, a grain of dust. She reread Nietzsche less for consolation than for confirmation of her sorrow.

If the tiny seed in her womb would only grow, and not be washed away in a messy flow of blood (erratic, never predictable, attended now by severe cramps and nausea), she believed she might be saved; her body if not precisely her soul.

Her sleep was light and filmy, insubstantial. Slipping into it she often observed something liquid and phosphorescent swirling down a drain.

She was invited out to Montauk, to visit friends for a few days. On the second day she was bitten by a wasp, or what she believed to be a wasp; the delicate inside of her forearm swelled, and throbbed with pain, and then with itching— Marya had never felt such itching. The wasp's venom accounted for a mound of flesh the size of a peach, pinkish-red except for a perfect circle of dead-white inside it, and, inside that circle, the almost-invisible red dot made by the wasp's stinger. Marya applied ointment, Marya suffered, everyone commiserated with Marya. In truth the wasp's sting fascinated her. The frantic itching, the throbbing pain, the swollen hot flesh. In private she scratched and scratched the swelling, abandoning herself to the angry luxury, the intensified pain, until her nails raised welts even on the swelling.

Back in the city, asked how her little vacation on the ocean had gone, Marya mentioned the wasp's bite: by far the most intriguing thing that had happened to her, physically, in some time.

An old friend of Eric's, lately divorced from *his* wife, telephoned Marya frequently, took her to lunch, dinner, invited himself over to her apartment. In his presence she was rather cool, even formal; away from him she contemplated becoming his lover, experimentally . . . they could talk a great deal about Eric, they could indulge themselves in mourning Eric while yet enjoying him, laughing over him (there must be a cornucopia of Eric Nichols anecdotes and tales, Marya thought greedily, she hadn't yet heard). Also, if she had a lover again, the ghostly thing in her womb might disappear. It might be pounded forcibly into extinction.

One day Eric's friend telephoned Marya to propose that they go together to a literary conference to be held in Budapest the following spring. One of those prestigious gatherings, all expenses paid, "distinguished" writers from fifteen nations East and West, many familiar faces no doubt, and Budapest was supposed to be exotic, the very best of the Communist capitals: had Marya ever been there?—wouldn't she like to go?—he could easily arrange for her to be invited. "They seem to be desperate for women and I'm sure your name is already known to them," he said.

Marya told him she had already been to this conference.

She had already met the "distinguished" writers.

She had heard their prepared speeches and she had heard their spontaneous outbursts.

She had shaken all the delegates' hands and received their courtly compliments. She had been toasted in Hungarian; her hand had been kissed.

She had seen Budapest, she said, though she'd never been there. She had seen the lavish interior of the Budapest Hilton though she'd never been there.

Her response had begun calmly, quietly enough, meant only to be ironic, to amuse, but as she continued her voice rose hysterically, her words came faster and faster, she found herself gripping the telephone receiver so hard that her fingers ached.

"I've heard all the speeches, do you know what that means?" she said, laughing, angry. But when she finally paused to catch her breath she discovered that the line had gone dead, her friend had hung up.

"Do you know what that means . . . ?"

He sent her a postcard a few days later with the message *I don't think you've necessarily heard ALL the speeches, Marya,* but she didn't trouble to reply to it, she tossed it carelessly aside.

She and Eric were walking along the narrow Chelsea street, hand in hand, defiant, silly, imagining themselves very daring indeed, immortal. They had consumed two bottles of red wine at lunch, they had devoured the contents of a little wicker bread basket and had had the Yankee temerity to request more. Eric was telling Marya one of his hilarious family anecdotes—something about an alleged ghost, a great-great-great-grandmother, from Sweden—who was famous for haunting the Nicholses' cottage on Lake Superior. The telling was all, inimitable. It was sheerly Eric. It could never be told again.

II

What commonly happens, Marya was told by an acquaintance who had been an adopted child ("we're never *not* 'adopted children' no matter our age"), is that the lost child, grown, locates the lost mother; and the mother pretends not to know who he or she is. Usually the first direct approach is by telephone—"they're not good at answering letters," Marya's acquaintance said. Sometimes the mother will say you've called the wrong number: there isn't any woman by that name at that address. Or she isn't home right now. Or she isn't living any longer.

You have to persist, Marya was told. Because any woman who has abandoned her children is a guilty woman and probably a very sick woman—or at least she was, at one time. You have to have faith that it's worth pursuing—the "lost" mother, any mother at all—because it will change your life more than you can calculate.

"Yes," said Marya. "That's the point."

Marya had not thought of her mother for years, or so she believed. Now, for no reason, for no logical reason, she thought of her constantly.

The woman would be fifty-three or fifty-four years old now. If she was still living.

They would not have seen each other for twenty-eight years.

Was it possible?—and each of them still alive?

Marya forgot, for long periods of time, that she had two younger brothers; she did have blood relations whom she knew, though they were hardly intimate friends. (Davy, long known as Dave, was thirty-one years old now, with three children, an informal partnership in Everard's thriving service station; Joey, or Joe, was twenty-nine, engaged to be married, a worker at the new Innisfail division of Allis-Chalmers. Marya and her brothers kept in touch, in a manner of speaking. Sometimes Marya felt a pang of childish envy, that Dave and Joe had remained so close while she had been excluded; she recalled only vaguely that she had been the one to edge away, to declare her superiority.)

Once, years ago, back home for a brief midwinter visit, Marya had asked Dave whether he ever heard news of, or rumors of, or anything at all of—and he'd interrupted her and said, No, no he hadn't, and he didn't want to. Marya had followed him into the kitchen so that they could speak in private but after this awkward exchange there was nothing more to say.

It wasn't at all uncommon, Marya learned, for the "siblings" of a "rejecting mother" to go for years—for lifetimes, in fact—without alluding to the mother; without alluding to their shared circumstances. It wasn't uncommon for them to grow away from one another, even to dislike one another. And of course they secretly nursed a lifelong resentment of "normal" people. "Existence for some of us," said a friend of Marya's who was himself adopted, "is fundamentally embarrassing."

Casually, betraying no emotion, as if she were merely assembling ideas and theories and "interesting" stories, Marya made inquiries about adoption—about having been abandoned, lost, given away, *left,* and then adopted—among people she knew. She discovered only a few men and women who admitted to having been adopted. Some were obsessed and bitter; some were merely obsessed.

What had rarely troubled them as children and even as teenagers now troubled them a great deal. Yes they thought about having been first abandoned; and then adopted, virtually all the time; no they weren't in the habit of talking about it with anyone, certainly not with their adoptive families. Very few had located their "birth" mothers and no one at all with whom Marya spoke had located his father. The subject was painful, disagreeable, why was Marya so curious . . . ?

"I suppose because time is running out," Marya said.

She told herself that her circumstances were entirely different. She had *seen* her mother, after all—she hadn't been abandoned in a church doorway, or at the entrance of an orphanage. The great consuming mystery for all of the "abandoned children" to whom she'd spoken was: what did the mother look like? who *was* she? If the father was mentioned less frequently, in fact quite rarely, it was simply the case that one enormous heartbreak preceded another. It was also the case that the mother seemed more blameworthy, more unnatural.

Marya knew that her mother resembled her; which is to say, she resembled her mother. Consequently there should have been no inordinate mystery. . . . If she wanted to speculate on what her father might be now, in middle age, she had only to contemplate her uncle Everard: tall, ruddy-faced, with heavy shoulders, beefy forearms, hair receding from the crown of his head, an attractive silvery-brown. He had been a good-looking man in his youth and he was still good-looking now, in his late fifties. Marya thought, I don't hate him any longer, do I?—for outliving my father.

She had always half believed that Everard *knew*. And one day he would tell her. (Not Davy or Joey. Marya. Because there was a special feeling between them, wasn't there: he *had* to love her more than he loved his daughter Alice because Marya was so much sharper, smarter, so much her father's daughter.) But in the end, and quite casually, it was Wilma who would give Marya all the information she required.

Marya had begun to make official inquiries after her mother, Marya even placed personal classified ads, without success. No one named Vera Sanjek Knauer had ever been imprisoned in the state, or even arrested for any crime; nor had she been admitted as a mental patient to any state facility. The only public records pertaining to her were a record of birth and a marriage certificate. (Studying the photostatted documents Marya made the simple calculation that her mother had been seventeen at the time of her marriage to Joseph Knauer, seventeen and five months at the time of Marya's birth, and twenty-five when she abandoned Marya and her brothers.)

She was stunned to discover, not long afterward, that Vera had never even been reported missing from Shaheen Falls. No one in the sprawling Sanjek family had cared enough, or had wanted to get involved with the authorities; and Everard and Wilma evidently hadn't wanted her back. (Marya seemed to remember one or the other of them saying good riddance—"good riddance to bad rubbish" was the expression. Though that may have been Marya herself, Marya as a slightly older child, who said it.)

So long as a missing person is above the age of eighteen and isn't wanted for any crime, being "missing" isn't in itself criminal; it isn't in fact all that uncommon in the United States. So Marya learned.

The personal ads were run for weeks in a dozen local

newspapers across the state. She labored over their wording but the results were painful, meager, embarrassing.

> Mrs. Vera Knauer urgently sought by daughter. Please contact M.K., Box ____, at once.

And:

> Information concerning Mrs. Vera Sanjek Knauer, widow of Joseph Knauer, urgently requested. Reward. Please contact M.K., Box ____, at once.

For the first time in her life Marya scanned the personal columns. She began to notice here and there ads that resembled hers, that were as patently futile—information sought concerning people not seen in decades, lost fathers, husbands, mothers, wives, runaway children, the lot. In three of the papers in which her ad ran she happened to notice:

> HELP. URGENT. Information sought concerning a baby boy (Caucasian, no birth defects) left at the intersection of Prospect & Ninth, Yewville, NY, Sept. 5, 1941. REWARD. Contact W.H., Box ____.

The ads ran for their prescribed time and then disappeared. Marya heard nothing. She realized from the several days of sharp depression that followed that she had actually expected a response. Perhaps she was only eight years old after all—perhaps not that much time had elapsed.

Then, the following spring, she went back to Innisfail for her brother Joey's wedding.

The Knauers had entered a period of prosperity. The Canal Road had long been paved, the Innisfail Pike was a four-lane highway, Everard's service station had been moved to a larger garage, the old car lot—that graveyard of derelict rusting hulks—was hidden from the road by a trim ten-foot redwood fence. The old house was unrecognizable behind white aluminum siding and smart red shutters. There was a glassed-in porch, there was a carefully tended lawn, there were trellises with yellow climbing roses. Everard and Wilma lived alone here now: Wilma had her own car and worked part-time at the Innisfail hospital as a receptionist.

Over the years Everard had been buying up land along the Canal Road, most of it scrubland, wild and marshy, worthless for farming. But now people were buying in the area; building houses; there was even talk of a subdivision—"Pinewood Acres"—on the Innisfail Pike. And at the intersection with the pike Everard owned twelve acres of flat, cleared land, "prime" land he called it, leased at the present to an Innisfail entrepreneur who organized farmers' open-air markets, flea markets, auctions, and the like, held on summer weekends. On the Friday Marya drove up for her brother's wedding she was astonished to see a carnival of some kind being held on the lot: a children's Ferris wheel, a merry-go-round, perhaps a dozen booths, several tents; she heard the amplified twang of country-and-western music. Here, where in the old days there had been nothing but scrub willow, oak, grass!—a small wilderness no one had noticed.

She sat in her car for a while watching the activity at the carnival. Listening to the whine of the country music—slapdash and melancholy at once, rather romantic, hokey. These are others' memories, she thought calmly. Other children, young girls. The world filling up with memories.

Marya's aunt and uncle were in high spirits though Everard was heavier than Marya recalled: his torso fatty, belly straining at his belt. The look of prosperity? self-assurance at last? And Wilma was almost aggressively trim—her hair curled, frizzed, tinted; nails manicured. She even wore white linen slacks. And white sandals, Italian-looking, with a small stylish knobby heel. "Here you are at *last!*" she said, hugging Marya hard as if she'd been waiting for her for a long time.

The old flash of grief, half-angry affection, remorse:

Wilma wasn't the right person. Wilma stood in her place but she wasn't the right person.

Marya was slightly dazed at first, greeted with Everard's conspicuous white smile (which must mean he had false teeth now: and they suited him), and Wilma's breezy new social manner, nervous and coquettish (which must mean she had women friends in town, women who knew how things were done). She was taken proudly about the house, told of Wilma's new car (a secondhand Honda), told of the expanded service station (Everard had taken out a loan at one of the banks in town). She was shown color snapshots of her nieces and nephews—Lee's, Alice's, Dave's grinning children mingled together.

Wilma was chatting excitably about the upcoming wedding and about being a grandmother. A grandmother—her! "You just don't think it can happen," she said, fixing Marya with a quizzical little smile, "then it does, and it seems so easy, like it was there all along. I mean—it was there all along, waiting."

Marya's cheeks felt flushed. She heard herself exchanging news, talking, chatting, as if she belonged here. She told herself that nothing had greatly changed. And she did belong here, as much as she belonged anywhere.

Marya stayed on after the wedding, to Wilma's pleased surprise.

It was the first time she hadn't hurried away, Wilma said.

Yes, said Marya. I haven't anywhere to hurry to.

But that was the wrong tone to take with Wilma: she admired strength, not weakness. She had admired Marya's stubbornness, even her selfishness, in the old days.

At breakfast one morning when they were alone Marya asked, over coffee, why they had fought so much, the two of them. She remembered running out of the house and crying, hiding back in the car lot. She remembered wishing she was dead. And Wilma herself in tears; shouting at her; slapping her hard. ("And I know I deserved it," Marya said.) Why so much quarreling, so many tears . . . ?

Well, said Wilma, startled, blushing—being unaccustomed, as they all were, to such direct personal questions—she supposed people mainly fought with whoever was close at hand. That was all they had, after all, wasn't it?

Marya visited her father's grave in the hilly Shaheen Falls cemetery, Marya drove slowly and cautiously along the old Mill Road, which had never been paved, looking for the shanty, or cabin—or might it have been called a house?—in which they had lived. The Mill Road, as it was still called, ran parallel to a larger road and appeared to be nearly untraveled. No one lived on it any longer, so far as she could judge. No telephone wires. No mailboxes. The sawmill had long disappeared, collapsed and overtaken by underbrush. Farmland on one side, uncultivated fields and woods on the other. Enormous black birds (crows, sparrow hawks?) much in evidence. Marya had become enough of a city person to stop the car and watch when a herd of eleven white-tailed deer fled across a field.

Near the junction with a larger road, set back behind a hilly cow pasture, was the old Kurelik farm. It looked saddened, diminished. A weatherworn gray house, several sagging barns, a windmill no longer in operation. The name on the dented tin mailbox was faded to illegibility. Only a half-dozen dairy cows grazed in the enormous pasture. Marya felt a brief childish impulse to drive back the rutted lane, knock on the farmhouse door, introduce herself, and ask . . . but what would she ask? What did she want to know, that the people in that old house might tell her?

She had driven the full length of the Mill Road, and had come through to the highway, without having seen a sign of her parents' house; it was pointless to turn her car around and go back. She thought of the terrified white-tailed deer, the noisy black birds with their flapping wings, the dust billowing up behind the car.

Once you start crying, Marya's mother had warned them, you won't be able to stop. Marya couldn't test the truth of this blunt prophecy because she had never allowed herself to start.

You won't recognize downtown Innisfail!—so Wilma kept telling Marya, as if she had a surprise in reserve.

On the final morning of Marya's four-day visit Wilma drove her to town along the busy pike, keeping up a rapid bemused commentary on local progress. Stretches of new ranch-style houses . . . a McDonald's and a Burger King and a Friendly's . . . a glassware and china outlet ("They have really good bargains in Corningware if you know how to find them") . . . a discount clothing store ("Even better than Norban's used to be") . . . even, on the outskirts of the city, a small shopping mall ("Now all they need is an A & P"). Marya would not have wanted to confess that her eye took in very little of all this newness; it sought out the older houses, the old farms, a stretch of woods here and a marshy expanse there, untouched, which she recalled with a curious biting nostalgia. She had bicycled along the pike so many times as a girl; she'd taken the Greyhound bus; ridden in cars. She had memorized the landscape without knowing. But now everything was so jumbled, so comically rearranged, how could she locate herself in it . . . ? The enormous Maccabee property had been sold and subdivided: acres of farmland given over now to "ranch" and "colonial" houses with treeless lawns and smart black asphalt driveways. The cider mill owned by the Jelinskis had been demolished long ago, when Marya was still an undergraduate at Port Oriskany; its site above the Shaheen Creek was overgrown in scrub willow and oak. And there was the Dubnovs' tavern, to which Emmett had once taken her, spruced up now with aluminum siding and a paved parking lot, and a new name (The Pike Inn & Bar-B-Que). And the old foursquare Methodist church, a battered veteran from another time . . .

Marya felt herself a time traveler, being driven along Innisfail's almost unrecognizable Main Street. The downtown, Wilma kept saying with satisfaction, was getting a facelift: junky old buildings razed and smart new buildings erected in their place—there was even a pedestrian mall, on lower Ash Street—and most of the streets were one-way. Marya's eye darted almost frantically about. Why did Ash Street look so strange? had the cobblestones been taken up and replaced with nice smooth featureless paving? Where were the old Grant's, the old Woolworth's, the Royalton Theatre . . . ? She noted the Royalton Café, finally, in a block that had been partly modernized: its broad glassy front tricked out in "Gothic" gilt letters. But the movie house was gone.

She saw a sign, Schroeder Bros., attached to a construction site fence.

She found herself wondering how one would catch the Riverside bus, with Genesee Street now one-way.

Wilma's talk was all of new stores, new restaurants, a crafts exhibit out at the mall ("they have some really beautiful things, Marya, you'd be impressed") . . . friends she was making by way of the Women's Auxiliary of the Innisfail General Hospital ("I showed them some clippings about you, they're dying to meet you"). . . . Marya seemed to be listening, but she was very distracted. She didn't know whether to be alarmed or amused by her own confusion.

She thought, Already the past is lost territory, it can't be entered.

While Wilma waited for a traffic light Marya noticed a teenaged girl standing at the curb, black hair spilling down her back, jeans, and ill-fitting sweater, an unsmiling face. *She* takes herself very seriously, Marya thought. The girl's gaze moved restlessly onto hers, moved restlessly away. . . . Was this someone she knew? Marya thought for an instant, her heart rising. But the moment passed. She knew no one in Innisfail, after all. And the girl, glancing in Marya's direction, probably couldn't have seen her that clearly—the windshield would have distorted her features.

In the Royalton Café, where they stopped for coffee and croissants—"croissants" in Innisfail!—Wilma talked for a while of the wedding, and her new in-laws, and of how well Joey had turned out: "He's a really nice guy, you know—the best-natured of the three boys, I always thought." She asked Marya her opinion of Lee's wife, who had put on weight since her last baby, and hadn't ever been—in Wilma's opinion—"really warm" toward the Knauers; but Marya, deciding to be prudent, said only that she seemed pleasant enough . . . still quite pretty. Wilma hesitated, then said, squinting in her old conspiratorial way, that she hoped Lee wasn't "cheating" on Brenda; but she'd heard some disturbing rumors. She'd heard. . . .

After this it seemed a natural step for her to bring up, suddenly, the subject of Marya's "advertisement" in the newspaper, which someone had pointed out to her. And before Marya could reply—she was prepared for this, she'd resolved not to betray embarrassment or guilt—Wilma went on to say, quickly, still in a lowered voice, that she knew where Marya's mother lived. More or less. "Up in the northern part of the state, New Canaan County," she said. "But not under any name you'd know—not Knauer or Sanjek. It's Murchison."

Marya was staring in disbelief. "Murchison?" she repeated blankly.

"Her second husband. Or maybe her third," Wilma said. She paused, carefully avoiding Marya's eye. The moment was oddly light, blurred; not so strained as one might imagine; served up as it was in the tacky old Royalton Café, at eleven in the morning, amid chatter from other tables—women shoppers, mainly, some with small children. (Marya realized belatedly that her aunt must have been humoring her, in agreeing to come here for coffee. She would have preferred one of the newer places, surely—the bustling coffee shop of the Ramada Inn, or that place up the street with the hanging plants and macramé and bare parquet floors.) "I think he was her third but I'm not certain of the details," Wilma said defensively. "Word gets around, you know. Especially after that ad of yours ran. But you know Innisfail—you can't always believe all you hear."

Marya was staring at Wilma, who was busily buttering a croissant. She wanted to ask how long Wilma had known but she decided against it, the words might have struck the wrong note. Instead she said, laughing, weak, breathless, "My mother is alive, and she's . . . living up in New Canaan County? And her last name is *Murchison* . . . ?"

Marya's laughter was louder and sharper than she might have wished. But no one at the other tables seemed to hear —no one glanced around.

"Well," Wilma said, slightly flushed, frowning, not yet meeting Marya's eye, "you know I can't vouch for any of this. It's just something I heard. There was this girl in the hospital for kidney stones, hardly more than a girl, and somebody came to visit her that's a cousin of your mother's, and we got to talking one day, and she knew who *I* was, and it sort of came out. . . . As I say, though," she repeated, her voice taking on an admonitory note, the half-chiding tone of the Wilma of long ago, "you can't always believe all you hear. Especially from the Sanjeks."

But Marya didn't drive up to New Canaan County the next morning.

She went home, back to her apartment in New York City, and waited a few days . . . and composed a letter . . . in truth, numberless versions of a letter. She thought about telephoning. (But hadn't someone warned her about telephoning?) She thought, Now that I know the woman is alive, does anything else matter? Do I really care about seeing her?

She discovered that she was badly frightened.

She discovered that she didn't know what she wanted; she hadn't the faintest idea.

She felt, a dozen times a day, the need to telephone Eric —to ask him what to do.

Apart from Eric there was no one she could ask for advice, no one whose advice she valued. She imagined Wilma fixing her with a quizzical frown and saying, For Christ's sake, Marya, why have you always taken yourself so seriously . . . ?

She waited a week, ten days. Then, as she was preparing to write a second time, a letter from Vera Murchison arrived.

Her agitation was such that she couldn't open the envelope immediately. As if a dream secret and prized in her soul had blossomed outward, taking its place, asserting its integrity, in the world. . . . She placed the envelope carefully on a table and sat in front of it staring, smiling, a pulse beating in her forehead. How odd to see her name—Marya Knauer—*her* name—in a handwriting that belonged to her mother, a handwriting she did not recognize.

Marya, this is going to change your life, she thought, half in dread.

Marya, this is going to cut your life in two.

Finally she opened the envelope. She took out a sheet of white stationery with trembling fingers, and there was a color snapshot as well, she dropped it clumsily to the floor, stooped to pick it up, suddenly frightened, her heartbeat quick and suffocating. The snapshot showed a middle-aged woman with stiff gray hair, shadowed eyes, a taut suspicious expression, strong facial bones. Marya's own cheekbones and nose. Her eyes. The woman's mouth was tense but she might have been about to smile, summoning the strength to smile. She wore a dark dress with white trim, her shoulders were sloping and her bust rather heavy, her head defiant, erect. The print was just perceptibly blurred as if whoever had taken the picture had moved the camera at precisely the wrong moment.

Marya went to the window, holding the snapshot to the light, and stared and stared, waiting for the face to shift into perfect focus.